SEDUCED BY INNOCENCE

"Desire," said Garrett, "is one thing. Good sense is quite another. Should you give in to this . . . impulse, you'd regret it."

"My heart flutters when you're near. My knees feel weak, my fingers tingle. I didn't know before, but that's desire, isn't it?"

"It is."

"You desire me, too."

"God help me, I do."

"I want to lie with you, Garrett Knox." Verity looked up at him. "I want you because everyone I loved is gone, and you are so alive. If we lie together, I think I will be alive, too."

"Society would frown." Garrett couldn't repress a smile.

She smiled, too. "We'll keep it to ourselves, shall we?"

Garrett hesitated, then scooped her up into his arms. "I never did care much for the constraints of society!"

DANGEROUS GAMES   (0-7860-0270-0, $4.99)
by Amanda Scott

When Nicholas Barrington, eldest son of the Earl of Ulcombe, first met Melissa Seacort, the desperation he sensed beneath her well-bred beauty haunted him. He didn't realize how desperate Melissa really was . . . until he found her again at a Newmarket gambling club—being auctioned off by her father to the highest bidder. So, Nick bought himself a wife. With a villain hot on their heels, and a fortune and their lives at stake, they would gamble everything on the most dangerous game of all: love.

A TOUCH OF PARADISE   (0-7860-0271-9, $4.99)
by Alexa Smart

As a confidence man and scam runner in 1880s America, Malcolm Northrup has amassed a fortune. Now, posing as the eminent Sir John Abbot—scholar, and possible discoverer of the lost continent of Atlantis—he's taking his act on the road with a lecture tour, seeking funds for a scientific experiment he has no intention of making. But scholar Halia Davenport is determined to accompany Malcolm on his "expedition" . . . even if she must kidnap him!

A
BRIGHTER
DAWN

Stobie Piel

Pinnacle Books
Kensington Publishing Corp.

http://www.pinnaclebooks.com

PINNACLE BOOKS are published by

Kensington Publishing Corp.
850 Third Avenue
New York, NY 10022

First Printing: June, 1997
10 9 8 7 6 5 4 3 2 1

Printed in the United States of America

"Where is the love, beauty, and truth we seek
But in our mind? and if we were not weak
Should we be less in deed than in desire?"

—*Julian and Maddalo*, P. B. Shelley

Part One

The Army of
the Potomac

"So, purposing each moment to retire,
    She lingered still."
        —*The Eve of St. Agnes,* John Keats

Chapter One

Falmouth, Virginia
March, 1863

A fine, cold rain drizzled relentlessly on the Union campsite at Stoneman's Switch. Soldiers in blue marched in file, their boots kicking up mud, splattering through the icy mist. Mounted officers shouted commands obeyed with precision.

A tall, slender woman watched the orderly parade for a moment, then tapped a sergeant's shoulder. "Can you direct me to the Twentieth Massachusetts?"

The young soldiers of the 1st Vermont spotted the girl. Distracted, they lost the train of command. "Back in line!" shouted a major. The sergeant nodded toward an uneven row of tents, and the girl started away, oblivious to the soldiers who craned their necks for a better look.

A Minnesota regiment collided with the small company from Vermont, but the girl took no notice.

"Who was that?" questioned a young Vermonter.

"Don't know," said the sergeant. "Fine looking girl. Boston type."

"Oh," sighed the soldier. "One of those."

"Aye. One of those."

Verity Talmadge surveyed the vast encampment, struggling to see through the fine sheet of icy rain. A harsh wind drove the rain in gusts now, and she pulled her felt cloak tighter around her body. A woman dragging a large sack walked by, and Verity called to her.

"Excuse me. I'm looking for the Twentieth Massachusetts—"

"Garrett Knox, eh?" guessed the woman. A wily grin spread across her face. She dropped her sack into the mud and approached Verity.

"How do you know?" asked Verity. Despite the cold and the rain, the woman wore an exceptionally revealing dress. Large, fleshy breasts struggled against her low bodice.

"Why else would a pretty girl be out and about today? Hell, now. He's worth it, ain't he?"

The woman slapped Verity's shoulder in a friendly manner. Verity drew up indignantly, but the woman didn't notice.

"You may have to wait a bit, Honey. Girls buzzing around his tent all day, 'til they get driven off."

"I'm not buzzing."

"Well, now," chuckled the woman. "You may right enough consider yourself proper." She blithely pulled back Verity's hood to study her face. Verity felt tempted to slap the woman's hand, but she restrained herself.

"Pretty little thing, ain't ye? Don't think it'll get you far, though. The Major, he puts off fine ladies right on as fast as us charity girls. Good luck to you, though. A face like yours is bound to get itself noticed."

Verity drew a calm breath, then tugged her hood back in place. "I'm here on business," she informed the woman, assuming the ice in her voice was understood.

"Sure you're on business, Sweet Pea. Ain't we all?"

"If you'll be so good as to direct me." Verity wished she'd never spoken to this woman in the first place.

"There you'll find the Twentieth." The woman turned and pointed at a collection of tents and huts. "Maybe you'll get luckier than the rest, eh?"

Dirty laundry bulged from the sack, and the woman bent down and stuffed a sock back in place. "Got to do something to keep up appearances. Keep busy doing the laundry, and then at night . . ." Her eyes widened suggestively, and Verity grimaced.

"Thank you, you've been most helpful."

A lady of the night. That explains the exposed cleavage. Verity felt tempted to question the woman on her dubious career. Despite her curiosity, Verity restrained herself. Her few concessions to propriety existed because she suspected her parents watched her from the Otherworld. Unseen, but felt.

The Webster's Unitarian minister in Boston had told her this was impossible, that her parents dwelt in Heaven's eternal peace. Verity considered eternal peace a boring hell in itself. Saying so had caused a lecture from the minister that revealed the true meaning of hell.

"Can I help you, Miss?" A large, burly sergeant spoke to Verity, a broad smile on his bearded face. He seemed much less forbidding than the prostitute.

"Perhaps you can, Sergeant. Thank you. I am looking for Major Garrett Knox. He serves with the Twentieth Massachusetts."

"Indeed he does!" said the sergeant. "He commands my division. Fine man, that. I'll take you right to him."

"Thank you." Verity needed the man's assistance, not his conversation.

The sergeant studied her face, then nodded thoughtfully. "Yes, Miss, I'll take you right to him."

After the prostitute, the sergeant's acceptance of Verity's obvious station came as a great relief. She followed him through a mind-boggling array of tents, drilling men, and officers riding purposefully through the maze of an armed camp. The sergeant stopped, pointing a dirt-stained hand toward a large tent.

"That's the Major's hut. I'll speak to his valet for you, if you like."

"Thank you. Please do." Verity pulled her large hood tighter around her face as she turned into the rain. Her thick, chestnut brown hair blew in the cold wind, and her blue-gray eyes lit with a warrior's gleam.

"Ah, Garrett Knox. I have you now."

"A girl to see you, Sir."

The valet peeked in through the flap of the officers' tent to see that his commander heard him. Garrett Knox set aside his dog-eared volume of Emerson.

"Who is it, Ned?" Garrett suspected one of the so-called 'laundresses' of again soliciting his attention.

"Don't know, Sir, but it's a different one this time. Never seen her before. Old Sam sent her. Looks like a lady."

Ned sneezed, then broke into a wheezing cough. "I told you to rest," said Garrett.

"Pretty girl," explained Ned.

"Ah."

"Thought you might enjoy seeing her, sir. A little ray of sunshine, a flower—"

"Thank you, Ned. Is it still raining as hard?" The boy nodded vigorously, and Garrett started to suggest the lady be sent in. *No. That will encourage her to stay.* Garrett had no patience for some infatuated girl with the poor sense to call at such a time.

"I'll be right out."

Garrett donned his overcoat to face the rain. "Where is she?"

"There, Sir." Ned gestured toward a woman waiting beside the muddy road.

Garrett didn't recognize the woman, but her graceful figure intrigued him immediately. He started toward her, but she spotted him and marched across the road instead. An exceptionally bright and refined face looked up at him, brows arched inquisitively, lips curved with the faintest suggestion of disdain.

A flower, a ray of sunshine. . . .

"Major Knox?"

"I am." *Not a wanton,* thought Garrett. *But not exactly a lady, either.*

"Major Garrett Knox, I hereby place you under arrest." She paused. "On behalf of my country!"

No words from a woman's lips ever surprised Garrett more. He stared at the girl, wondering if he'd heard her correctly. The small, pert face glared up at him. Tight waves of reddish-brown hair dusted across her cheek as she awaited his reply.

She looks like an angel. With the tongue of a viper.

"I beg your pardon?"

"You're under arrest," she repeated victoriously.

Garrett's brow rose, his lips tilted with amusement. "For what crime, dare I ask?" Perhaps the girl attempted to gain his interest. Women went to great lengths to enamor him. If this was her purpose, it worked.

The girl's chin lifted. "Sedition. Spying," she amended, as if he might not understand. "You are a traitor, Major Knox, and you're coming with me to pay for your duplicitous crimes."

Garrett nodded slowly. He pressed his lips together to keep from smiling. "Where are we going?"

"Washington."

Garrett nodded again. "Before I go with you—and I'm assuming you have authority to act on behalf of your country—May I ask what proof you possess? Or is proof required from one of your high station?"

"What?"

"What makes you think I'm a spy?"

"Westley Talmadge told me."

Garrett's face darkened. "What do you know of Westley Talmadge?"

"I know he died with your name on his lips, you villain."

"Who are you?" *Maybe I'm dreaming.* The girl reached out and pinched him fiercely, as if the passion of her anger couldn't be contained without physical release.

"His wife," she announced. Garrett eyed her with growing suspicion.

"Westley Talmadge had no wife . . ."

She pinched him again. "We married shortly before he died."

Garrett studied the girl's perfect face. A small nose, well defined, full lips, eyes that could cast a spell over the strongest male heart. Adrian's heart.

"Verity."

"Yes," she answered, slight hesitancy evident in her voice.

"Then we have much in common, Mrs. Talmadge. My brother Adrian died uttering your name. But that won't surprise you, will it? You played those two boys against each other for years. They died at odds, fighting over you."

Verity's face paled, but her lips tightened angrily. "Any grief Adrian had came from you. Westley told him someone in your company betrayed them. He believed this person was responsible for my brother's disappearance."

"Robert Talmadge was killed in battle," Garrett reminded her.

"My brother is missing, not dead. No one found his body."

The wild passion in Verity Talmadge moved something in Garrett, something he had considered frozen, impenetrable, lost. "Mrs. Talmadge, I searched for Robert's body myself—"

"And you succeeded to his command! Reason enough to let the matter be. Curious, isn't it, that you left the Maryland Cavalry to take my brother's place?"

A muscle in Garrett's jaw twitched as his own anger flared. "Adrian and Westley helped in the search for Robert."

Verity appeared unconvinced by his alibi, but she let him continue.

"True, we found nothing, no sign. But countless are lost this way in battle. The fields of Antietam were strewn with bodies, buried hurriedly. I believe Robert lies in such a nameless grave. Buried by Yankee or rebel, you can trust his grave was dug with admiration and honor."

"That's very comforting," said Verity bitterly. "Some damned rebel put my brother in the ground, and you're telling me to take heart. The rebels *honored* him. Was it with honor they shot my husband?" She leaned closer, her eyes blazing. "Was it?"

"As we do, the rebels do, Mrs. Talmadge."

"You defend them. But then, you have close ties to their side, don't you? Your miserable cousin fights under that rapscallion, Lee—"

"Rapscallion. I've never heard that term applied to Robert E. Lee."

"So," voiced Verity triumphantly, "you admire him, do you?"

"I do."

"You don't even bother to deny it!"

"Admiration isn't akin to agreement, Mrs. Talmadge." Garrett had never faced this kind of interrogation before. Irritating, true. But strangely enjoyable.

"Contact with your enemy cousin, perverse loyalty to the rebel commander—"

"Adds up to spying?" finished Garrett. "As for my cousin, Jared's reasons for defending the South—"

"His right to hold slaves, no doubt," cut in Verity disgustedly.

"Jared's loyalty is to Virginia. Not to slavery."

"No, the rebels don't like to talk about that issue, do they?"

Garrett didn't answer. As his thoughts turned back in time, he saw his young cousin's face as they both had fought anger. *"You Northerners can't dictate how we live our lives,"* Jared had claimed, his quick temper barely under control. *"The rights of the state—"*

"State's rights," Garrett had echoed, his own patience tried. *"How long must we hear that tired old song used to maintain control over a subjugated people?"*

"You have no answer, I see," guessed Verity.

"If this issue had an answer, Mrs. Talmadge, there would be no war."

"You don't deny your connection, then?"

"No. Adrian and Westley knew Jared from their days at Eton. Just as Robert and I became friends at school in Switzerland. Do those connections trouble you as well?"

"No doubt Jared used his Southern charm to deceive them, just as you deceived my brother Robert. Eton is in England, after all. Things are different there."

"That much is certain."

"If they'd known your cousin caused Robert's disappearance—"

"Did Westley accuse Jared?"

"Not exactly. I surmised that on my own."

"I see."

"But you exchanged information with someone, a rebel. Your cousin seems the most likely person."

"I can't believe Westley thought this."

"Not at first. He admired you, for whatever reason. But he learned about your dealings with the enemy. Apparently he learned too much, and—"

Garrett stepped menacingly toward her, and Verity hopped backward. "If you try to kill me, I'll scream."

Verity's suggestion tempted Garrett Knox sorely. He took another step, and she scrambled back. She slipped and fell into the mud. Garrett shook his head. For a long while, he just stared at her.

Adrian had spoken of an angel, not a hellcat, but Adrian's judgment of character lacked insight. Garrett assumed that a sweet-faced enchantress had beguiled his young brother, but a new picture emerged. This was no lady bent on winning hearts, then choosing the wealthiest. This was a wild, willful woman, a raging sea. Adrian had been a ship, destroyed on its surface, but the sea had no blame.

Garrett held out his hand. Verity sneered and struggled to her feet without his assistance. "You're not going to kill me," she noted.

"Not just now."

"Ah," said Verity. "Too many witnesses."

"That, too," agreed Garrett. "What now?"

"Will you come willingly to Washington?" she inquired as she shook mud from her black skirt.

"Perhaps." Garrett rubbed his chin thoughtfully. "But these things have an order, Mrs. Talmadge."

"Such as what?"

"Generally, you should report my disobedience to my commander."

"Where is he?"

"He's having dinner in the officers' mess."

"Very well," said Verity. "Come with me." She paused. "Just where is the officers' mess?"

"This way, Mrs. Talmadge. If you'll follow me . . ."

Verity kept a good distance from Garrett's side, scurrying along to keep up with his long stride. She understood now why Adrian refused to believe the truth about his brother, why Westley agonized over his knowledge. Garrett Knox appeared honorable, the very image of perfect manhood.

She eyed him covertly. Broad, muscular shoulders filled out his uniform, visible even through his overcoat. Strong, chiseled features defined his face, as if he had been carved from raw marble, then polished to perfection.

Women fawned over him. Westley and Adrian had regaled her with Garrett's scandalous exploits abroad. Supposedly working for the French government as an engineer, Garrett had left mistresses broken hearted all over Europe. A young princess demanded he marry her. Subsequently, Garrett Knox couldn't return to Yugoslavia, under penalty of death.

"In here," said Garrett. Loud voices came from inside the long tent.

"Those don't sound like officers."

"You should hear the enlisted men."

Garrett held open the door, and Verity walked in. "Which one?"

Garrett indicated a short, whiskered officer, and Verity marched up to him. The officers rose as one, nodding to the young lady. Verity ignored them.

"Colonel Godwin," said Garrett. "This is Mrs. Talmadge, who requests a moment of your time on an urgent matter."

"What can I do for you, Mrs. Talmadge?" asked the colonel.

"Garrett Knox must be arrested. For spying."

Colonel Godwin looked at Garrett. "Spurned mistress?"

"Just crazy." Garrett sighed.

The colonel smiled indulgently at Verity. "Well, my dear, I'm afraid I can't spare Major Knox just now. He's a fine officer, you know. A girl's complaints may seem serious to you, but—"

"The man consorts with rebels. He's given information to the enemy, and caused the death of God knows how many!" sputtered Verity.

Garrett leaned toward her. "I trust you won't pinch the colonel." She glared back at him. She'd contemplated doing just that.

"Yes, yes," said the colonel soothingly. "Be that as it may, I'm afraid I can't let him go. Why don't you go to Washington, my dear? Oh, it's an exciting place right now. A lovely belle such as yourself will enjoy no end of parties, dances—"

"I'm in mourning! My husband died, and it's his fault."

"Poor little thing. Losing your husband no doubt rattled your senses. You'd best get on home to your family."

The colonel seated himself and took another bite of his dinner. Verity had failed. She felt sure Garrett was smirking, but she didn't dare look at him. If she attacked him in front of these men, *she'd* be the one in prison.

"I'd like to collect my husband's things."

"Of course," said the colonel. "You'll have to see his commander."

"That would be me," put in Garrett with subdued pleasure. Verity gritted her teeth.

Verity turned and marched toward the door. She forced herself to ignore the snickers as she yanked the door open. She went outside, into the icy rain, and Garrett followed her. She didn't bother with her hood this time. The rain soaked her hair and dripped beneath her dress.

"Curse you. You tricked me. You knew that whiskered old fool wouldn't believe me."

"It seemed unlikely," agreed Garrett.

"You'll fetch Westley's belongings?"

"I will." Garrett called to his valet, and the boy appeared, wide-eyed with speculation about the young woman at Garrett's side. Ned sneezed, then coughed. Verity stepped back.

"Bring Captain Talmadge's belongings, Ned. His widow is here to collect them."

"His widow, you say?" said Ned. He gazed sympathetically

at Verity, then sneezed again. "I'm sorry, Ma'am. Captain Westley Talmadge was a proper young gentleman."

"Which set him apart from most officers," said Verity irritably. The boy glanced uncertainly at Garrett. "You're kind to say so," Verity amended. The boy couldn't be blamed for serving this steel-eyed devil. "Thank you."

Ned scurried away to retrieve Westley's belongs, leaving Verity in the driving rain, alone with Garrett Knox. "Why didn't you send his things home?"

"I promised Westley that I would keep his gear for his return."

"You knew, you must have known, that he wouldn't return."

"I knew." Garrett drew a long breath, his weariness penetrating into his soul. "There isn't much. A spare uniform, his musket—"

"Give me what there is. It's all I have left of him."

Garrett eyed her doubtfully. "Westley Talmadge was a wealthy man. As his cousin and beloved, you know this."

"Money means nothing. It's not personal. It came to us from some distant relative. Enoch Talmadge is the one who earned it. Westley and I didn't care about money."

"Your motives were pure, or so you say. Yet Adrian and Westley both made fools of themselves over you. They made enemies of each other. Did it take Westley's injury to make you see your true heart?"

"Westley knew I meant no harm."

"Westley Talmadge was smitten with you, as was Adrian. I doubt he'd even hold you responsible for killing his own mother. So his assurance on your character is relatively meaningless."

Verity turned angrily toward Garrett. "They were my friends. How was I to know they'd become foolish, treat me differently when I grew up?"

"How old are you?"

"I'm nineteen."

"Old enough to know men's hearts."

"Old enough to know how silly men can be."

Ned returned with a worn pack and handed it to Verity. "You won't be wanting his musket, too, will you?"

"I will."

Ned looked at Garrett, who nodded. Verity seized the musket. "That's all there is, Ma'am," said Ned.

Failure throbbed in Verity's veins. Once more, she faced Garrett Knox. "For honor's sake, acknowledge your guilt and surrender!"

"No, Mrs. Talmadge. My honor demands that I remain just where I am."

Garrett placed his hands on Verity's slender shoulders, holding her in his firm grip. She squirmed to free herself, but Garrett didn't release her.

"You see, whatever you may believe, I am not a spy. I saw my brother die, I saw my friends crumpled to dust. I stand opposite my closest friend . . . And, yes, he's a rebel. Do you think I want the bullet I fire to find his heart?

"But I stay, leading my men into battle, knowing some will die. I stay, Mrs. Talmadge, because this country is better whole than divided. Because I can't ignore the rights of any man, of any color, to be a man, a free man."

"You speak fine words." If those words moved Verity's heart, she reminded herself that they came from a liar, a traitor. Another thought struck her. "What about rights of women?"

"If your erratic nature is any guide, women are best kept seen and not heard." Garrett sighed. "Though this seems an impossibility at present."

Verity glared at Garrett Knox, her fist clenched into a ball, as she contemplated the joys of striking him.

"On the other hand, a woman such as yourself would make one hell of a soldier. Heaven help the rebels if you took up arms against them."

"Heaven help *you*, Garrett Knox," vowed Verity. "Heaven help *you*."

Verity spun away and stomped through the mud, dragging Westley's pack and his musket behind her. She never looked back. But Garrett watched her as she made her way through the campsite, waved a fierce command to her coachman, then drove away.

"Sir?" Ned's tentative voice interrupted Garrett's thoughts. "The lady seemed a bit high-strung, didn't she?"

"She seemed crazy," said Garrett. Ned didn't argue.

"Pretty as a flower, though. Can't say as I've ever seen her like."

"Nor have I, Ned," said Garrett quietly. "Nor have I."

* * *

Verity sat alone in her hotel room. Once a private home, the noble Roseclift estate now welcomed guests of the more elegant officers. Verity's connection with the Websters had secured her room, but she took no pleasure in the tasteful bedroom tonight.

Verity fingered the desperate telegram from Candace Webster. *Come back at once. My parents trust me to care for you. Robert trusted me.* Verity didn't finish the message. Candace had used emotion to convince her, but it wasn't working.

Robert's fiancée—the only other person who believed he still lived—Candace contented herself with waiting, with nursing in Washington's hospitals. Verity's nature demanded action.

Candace's parents had traveled to London to win support for the Union, to convince the English not to side with the Confederacy. Should Verity decide to stay in Falmouth, Candace couldn't stop her.

Go home, argued her mind. *For what? To wait?* The Union gave up on finding her missing brother. No one believed Garrett Knox spied for the Confederacy. Except Verity. Even Westley hadn't quite believed the obvious.

Verity felt a shade of guilt for misusing her husband's last words. *"It couldn't be Garrett Knox,"* he had told her, delirious with fever, in agony.

"Someone betrayed you and Robert at Antietam. Only Garrett Knox could have done that."

Westley died. Verity closed her eyes and remembered her husband's face. Once strong and handsome, filled with joy, he lay on his hospital bed, thin and gaunt, the color drained from his face. His golden hair fell to his shoulders.

Verity recalled when Westley had returned from school with Adrian Knox. At fifteen, she had been no beauty, but she was a good friend. Westley and Adrian treated her like a companion. They took her fishing, riding. They taught her to shoot. They teased her about her lanky, awkward appearance.

Then came the war, the Southern rebellion. Her friends joined the Massachusetts regiment together, though Adrian's home was in Maryland. They went to war as funloving boys, writing excited letters, thrilling her with possible battles.

Then came Bull Run. Westley and Adrian came home on leave. No longer boys, but men. Everything changed. They didn't want to talk about war. They didn't want to ride or shoot or take Verity fishing. They wanted to dance. Each tried to kiss her. Each declared his love, and asked for her hand.

Candace had said Verity had changed, that she was a woman now, but Verity had felt no different. She could still outshoot both. She didn't want to be a wife. She loved both Adrian, with his wild, reckless manner, and Westley, gentle and kind. But her feelings didn't seem developed enough for marriage.

She put them off, not intending to set them against each other. Yet they left Boston still in love with her, and bitterly at odds with each other. When she next saw Westley Talmadge, he lay near death, wounded at Antietam. She granted his wish and became his wife.

Adrian died at Fredericksburg, and Verity fell into despondency. She left Westley's family in Boston and went with Candace to Washington—never forgetting Westley's last words, and the incrimination of Garrett Knox.

Garrett Knox. The man she once admired from afar, whose exploits thrilled and tantalized her. The man who betrayed her brother and her two best friends. The man who destroyed her world.

"Anger poisons me. I sit here and stew and do nothing. What am I thinking? I tried and failed. I should go home."

A white heat filled Verity's body. "I will not go home. I will not forget the ones I loved, nor accept defeat. There must be a way."

For a long while, Verity sat silently. She eyed Westley's pack, then opened it. She drew out his winter uniform. Tears filled her eyes as she held it up. Verity looked at Westley's musket. She put her finger up to her lip and tapped thoughtfully.

And then she knew. She knew how to destroy Garrett Knox, how to avenge those she loved. Garrett himself had given her the idea. *Heaven help you, Garrett Knox.*

With calm, even purpose, Verity Talmadge rose from the bed. She stripped away her damp, bombazine mourning dress. She stripped down to her soft, cotton drawers. She put on Westley's uniform.

The looking glass told her the uniform was too large, but not by much. It could be altered. Easily. A few stitches here and there, even by a girl who couldn't sew very well. Unlike the breasts of the prostitute Verity met at Stoneman's Switch, her own small ones required little concealment. A cloth tied firmly.

A tiny smile appeared upon her lips.

Garrett Knox walked through the camp of the Massachusetts 20th, heedless of the rain, searching. He wasn't certain for whom he searched, or what evidence he expected to find. He'd been with the 20th since Antietam. Nothing.

His men nodded as he passed. Some saluted. Garrett returned the gesture, then walked on. His mind wandered from his pursuit; he found his thoughts settling on Verity Talmadge. He remembered his brother's wide-eyed infatuation with the girl; he remembered vivid descriptions of matchless beauty and charm.

She's beautiful. Garrett had to agree with that. Her charm, however, escaped him. *Spirit,* he thought. *The woman has spirit. The kind of spirit that makes a man wonder what she'd do in his arms, what she'd do when he kissed her, ran his hands over her lithe body. . . .*

"Major Knox?"

Garrett turned at the unfamiliar voice. A darkhaired man with a broad smile nodded, offering his hand in a friendly gesture. "Dave Delaney, here," he said cheerfully. "Your valet said I'd find you hereabouts."

Garrett shook the smiling man's hand. "I am Garrett Knox. What can I do for you?" The man's smile widened. He seemed eager to make a good impression, to put the Yankee officer at ease. His pleasant manner seemed genuine. Why, then, did Garrett feel certain he couldn't be trusted?

"I'm on the trail of a runaway girl," reported Dave Delaney. "A young, headstrong miss by the name of Verity Talmadge. Got a lead that she headed this way, and that she asked for you. Thought you might be able to point me in her direction."

Garrett hesitated. "May I ask your connection to the lady?"

"Hired by her family, or rather, her guardians, the Websters. Their daughter, Candace Webster, was engaged to Miss Talmadge's brother. I've been hired to find the girl, lest some harm befall her."

Again, the man spoke pleasantly, openly, but somehow, his explanation wasn't convincing. "Miss Talmadge indeed visited me earlier today," said Garrett. "I have no idea of her whereabouts now. I trust she's returned to Miss Webster in Washington."

"Hope so," said Dave Delaney. "I thank you for your help."

The man shook Garrett's hand again. His smile never faded. He left, but Garrett watched him go without pleasure. Would Candace hire a detective to search out Verity? Possibly, but it didn't sound right, though Garrett wasn't sure why.

He wanted to warn her, tell her to take care. As Garrett headed back to his tent, an unfamiliar pang of helplessness taunted him. Verity wouldn't listen to him. She believed him a traitor, and perhaps a murderer. Garrett had no idea where to find her.

A flash of intuition made him hope Dave Delaney didn't, either.

Verity spent the early part of the night sewing, shortening the legs, the arms, tightening the waistband. She tore off Westley's captain's insignia, but left the Mass 20th badge.

Bleary-eyed, she again inspected herself in the looking glass. Her body looked right, but the long waves of chestnut hair . . . Verity retrieved her shears and positioned herself before the mirror.

A moment's hesitation passed while she contemplated her act. Everyone complimented her on her beautiful hair. Reason enough to see it gone. Beauty brought nothing but grief. It drove friends into would-be lovers. It cornered her into a woman's dull life, waiting and waiting and taking no action.

Never again.

Verity parted her hair, then chopped away until it fell into an earthen-red pile at her feet. She disposed of the remnants, then studied herself again. The remains of her hair fell to her shoulders, just as Westley's had done. Just like the soldiers she saw at Stoneman's Switch.

"Perfect." Westley's boots were too big for her feet, however. "I need shoes. I can steal the innkeeper's son's." Her feminine complexion gave her no trouble. She ran her fingers through the windowsill dust and applied it lavishly all over her face.

She settled herself at the desk and composed a letter to the owners of the Rosecliff establishment. She assured them that she was returning to Washington, where she would enjoy the wonderful parties and await the certain ending of the Civil War.

Chapter Two

The white sun battled beyond the gray sky, shining like a cold, distant beacon as Verity Talmadge again entered the Union campsite. Her determination never wavered, though her plans hinged delicately on her ability to pull off a boyish identity.

She developed her plans as she walked. Two hundred soldiers a day deserted the Union army. Lax discipline might be tightening under Hooker, but she doubted anyone would question her supposed transfer from one Massachusetts regiment to another.

A bugle rang out, and a company of drilling men marched by. Verity stopped and stood still as stone as men passed by her. No one took any notice, and she relaxed. Her disguise fooled unthinking men. But what about tentmates? What about Garrett Knox?

Win or lose, she thought. Verity shouldered Westley's musket and made her way to the Twentieth Mass. A very young captain stood arguing with a subordinate, the same burly sergeant Verity had met the day before. The captain seemed relieved when Verity interrupted their discussion.

"Excuse me, Captain," she began, her accent disguised beneath a boyish slur.

"Yes, what is it?"

"I've been transferred to this command."

"Well? Papers?"

Verity bit her lip. "I . . . lost them."

The captain rolled his eyes. "Jesus. Recruits. We'll get it straightened out later. Wait here."

The officer disappeared into his tent, then returned with a long list. "Name?"

Verity froze. In all her considerations, her choice of names had never entered her mind. "Ver . . . um, Verrill." *Very good,* she thought, but the captain sighed.

"First or last?"

"First," said Verity. The captain waited, but Verity's mind went blank. She glanced desperately around, then eyed the sergeant. He held a book about Pennsylvanian agriculture. Verity squinted to see the author's name. *A. Watkins,* in gold letters.

"Watkins. Verrill is my first name."

"I'm sure it's of utmost importance," said the captain. "I am Ethan Hallowell. 'Captain' to you. Welcome to the Twentieth."

"Who's the new man?" asked the burly sergeant.

"Watkins," replied Ethan Hallowell.

"Don't look strong enough to carry a musket, let alone fire one," said the sergeant. "Hell's bells, Hallowell, a light breeze'll knock this boy right over."

Verity's eyes widened indignantly. "I'll have you know I've fought at both Antietam and Fredericksburg, and knocked down a bigger man such as yourself more times than I can count. I don't expect I'll have any difficulty now."

Ethan Hallowell laughed, but the sergeant shook his head. "I'd imagine the only reason you're still living is that you're too damned skinny for a bullet to find. Hallowell, you can't expect us to care for this child."

"Sergeant, we lost seven men last night. I can't afford high standards."

"True enough," sighed the sergeant. "Well, boy, you're in. Can't say as I like it much, but there you are. Don't look more than a speck older than my Orator. You're a feisty one, though, which might get you through, or get you killed."

"He'll stay in your tent, Sergeant," decided Ethan Hallowell.

Verity turned to the sergeant and drew herself up proudly. "I hope to improve your estimation of my ability, Sir."

Despite himself, the old sergeant smiled. "We'll see, Watkins. Now get going. It's time for drill. Still, I expect you're too young to snore much. But don't cause me any trouble. Got that?"

"Yes, Sergeant."

"Most folks call me Sam. 'Cept Hallowell here, and he's a stick-in-the-mud Bostonian, if you get my drift."

Verity wasn't sure she understood, and she felt fairly certain Sam's comment didn't reflect well on her kind. She said nothing, however, and followed Sam toward the drill paddock. She had begun to wonder how she'd keep time with experienced soldiers when a familiar voice called to the sergeant.

"Ho, Sam! A moment, please."

Verity froze. Her heart held, then leapt in fear. Garrett Knox came across the field. *He's spotted me. I'm done for now.* But Garrett paid no attention to the dirty boy at Sam's side.

"What would you think of missing drill this morning, Sam?" Garrett's easy familiarity with his soldiers contrasted with Ethan Hallowell's formal manner.

"I'd think high enough of the idea," said Sam. Verity kept her head low, her cap shading her face. She hardly breathed. Garrett Knox took no notice.

"Muster your best shots," Garrett continued. "I've got a shooting contest planned. Informal. You'll enjoy it."

"Sounds good," said the sergeant with budding enthusiasm. "Any particular reason?"

"I want to find our best marksmen. Make sure they can ride well, too."

"That lets out city boys," scoffed Sam.

"Jeb Stuart and his cavalry have been giving fits to the high command. General Averell wants to give them some of the same. Interested?"

"Sure am," said Sam. "Sounds like a cavalry matter, though."

"Yes," agreed Garrett. "Since I served with the Maryland Cavalry, I've been invited to take part. I thought I'd bring along a few of my own men. Show them what New Englanders can do."

"You're one in a million, Major, and no mistake. Any other officers coming along?" asked Sam, clearly hoping there weren't.

"Just Major Wallingford."

"Oh."

Verity sensed this didn't please the sergeant, though he said no more. Daniel Wallingford was Garrett's stepbrother, a man neither Westley nor Robert had liked. Adrian had halfheartedly defended him, saying Wallingford's legal profession distinguished him.

"I'll have the men ready by the targets. The boys need something to do. Maybe even Watkins here will give it a try. Eh, lad?"

Verity gulped as Sam unexpectedly drew Garrett's attention her way. She ran her hand over her nose and coughed.

"Can you ride, son?" asked Garrett.

"Yes, Sir," mumbled Verity.

"Good. Be there. A half hour, Sam. I want to get started."

Garrett watched the small soldier march away with the sergeant. Watkins. Something about the boy seemed familiar, but Garrett wasn't sure what it was.

Daniel Wallingford distracted Garrett from his speculation. "Did you tell the men about the raid?"

"Seemed eager about it," answered Garrett. "God knows, we all need something to keep us busy."

"True enough," agreed Dan. "Fighting's bad enough, but some days I think the boredom's worse."

Garrett nodded, though it occurred to him that Dan saw a lot more of boredom than fighting. His early command had been as attaché to General McClellan. Just before Antietam, Dan had requested a field command in Adrian's Massachusetts company.

A slight, blonde woman hurried across the field, her somber tweed attire at odds with the mud that grappled with her shoes. Dan Wallingford noticed her. "Isn't that Rob Talmadge's fiancée?"

"Candace," called Garrett. "What on earth are you doing here?"

Candace Webster didn't bother with preambles or small talk. "Garrett, the most terrible thing has happened. What will I do? Dear God, I promised Robert I'd watch her, and now . . ." Candace's voice broke, she squeezed Garrett's arm. "Verity has run away."

"So I've heard," said Garrett.

"Then you've seen her? She had the craziest notion you were responsible for Westley's death, but I couldn't believe she'd go through with accusing you. I promised that when Robert returns, we'll learn the truth, but she wouldn't listen."

Women have a hard time accepting reality, Garrett decided. Candace spoke with conviction; like Verity, she obviously believed that Robert still lived.

"I saw her yesterday," said Garrett.

"So she did come here. And confront you?"

"She did."

"I wrote to her at the Roseclift estate," said Candace. "Then I got a brief note saying she would be 'traveling' for some time to come, and I'm not to worry about her. It was lighthearted, glib, and completely unlike Verity."

"She's not entirely sane," said Garrett.

"You've noticed that, too?" asked Candace seriously. "She was always . . . willful. Headstrong, but charming. After their parents died, Robert spoiled her terribly. Fortunately, she's not manipulative or crafty. She's as straightforward as an arrow. Otherwise, she might have become the most dreadful femme fatale the world has ever seen."

"There was a time I believed that of her," said Garrett.

"Because of Adrian and Westley? No, that wasn't her fault. She considered them playmates. They became men just as she blossomed. You must have noticed how beautiful she is."

"When we met, she arrested me. Her looks weren't the first thing I considered." Perhaps the second, but Garrett wouldn't reveal that to Candace.

"Had you seen her with Westley . . . she'd known him all her life—their fathers were brothers. When he lay on his bed, dying, in agony . . . she sat with him for hours, Garrett. Holding his hand, talking to him." Eyes filled with tears, Candace paused to collect herself.

"At first, she reminisced about their childhood, about fishing and riding together. But that wasn't what Westley wanted to hear. Verity sensed that, and despite every natural inclination, she flirted, she charmed him. And she lied. I've never heard her lie before, but she lied."

"What did she say?"

"She said she'd always loved him, but couldn't bear to tear apart his friendship with Adrian. Oh, I know she cared, about both of them. But it wasn't real love. I know, because of Robert. But Westley didn't know. When she told him that, I thought he might actually recover."

"So she married him," finished Garrett. He hadn't considered Verity tenderhearted. Strong and willful, yes, but not gentle.

"She kissed him, and he died in her arms. Something cracked in her that day. She didn't speak, just sat alone in her room. When we heard that Adrian died, too . . . she turned a bit odd.

"She wanted to fight, to change things. She couldn't just sit and wait. Verity feels things more deeply than anyone I've ever known. It's impossible for her to let destiny unfold without her assistance. That's why she came after you, Garrett."

"She'll come back in a few days," said Garrett. "What I don't understand is why you've come down here. The gentleman you hired to find her paid me a quick visit last night. I'm sure he'll find her."

Candace's fine brow furrowed. "Gentleman? I hired no one, Garrett. Verity hasn't been gone that long . . . and she'd have my head if I sent someone after her."

Garrett's heart beat with an erratic chill. "A man came here last night. He called himself Dave Delaney, and said you hired him to find Verity. I didn't like him. He smiled too damned much."

"That's strange," said Candace, and Garrett saw the information worried her, too. "I know no one by that name, and as I told you, it's too soon to hire a detective. I don't like the sound of this."

"Perhaps your parents hired the fellow," injected Dan Wallingford.

"No, that's impossible," said Candace. "My parents are en route to London. They have no idea Verity fell into such a peculiar mood. In fact, no one but myself knew she'd gone . . . or so I thought."

"I'll bet the girl met up with some young soldier," said Dan. "I've heard she's good-looking. You'll hear from her in a few days, probably on the arm of a new husband."

Both Candace and Garrett frowned at Dan's suggestion. "That hardly seems likely," said Candace. "Her husband has only recently died, Mr. Wallingford. Verity may be willful, but she's not flighty, nor fickle about men. Her nature is very true."

"Her manner didn't suggest pursuit of a new husband to me, either," agreed Garrett. "This whole Delaney business sits wrong with me. I'm not sure why, but I wonder if he's a danger to Verity."

"What could he want with her?" breathed Candace. "Dear God, if anything happens to her . . . if Robert comes home and finds . . . Garrett, we must do something!"

"We can't be sure of her danger," said Garrett, though he didn't sound convinced.

"Of course not," agreed Dan. "Don't jump to conclusions."

"I'll be staying at the Rosecliff until she's found," said Candace. "Call on me there if you learn anything."

Garrett nodded. "I will."

Verity found herself among a group of soldiers, setting up bottles as targets, talking among themselves. *What have I gotten myself into? What was I thinking?* Still, Verity deemed the targets a fairly easy shot. She felt confident she could hit the mark with ease.

This seemed unwise. Going on raids in rebel territory wasn't her plan when she entered the Union encampment. *I'll have to miss,* she thought regretfully. *Damn.* She didn't like the thought of fumbling in front of Garrett Knox.

Sam grabbed Verity's arm. "Lord Above, you're a skinny one, Watkins." Verity made no comment. "You'll be wanting to meet your new mates."

"Yes, Sir." Verity wasn't at all sure she cared about these scruffy soldiers, but she allowed Sam to direct her to a small group of men.

"Over there's Peter McCaffrey. He's from Framingham. Until you joined up, he was our youngest soldier." Sam called to another soldier. "John, got someone for you to meet."

John nodded, but he said nothing. Verity found his wide forehead and narrow chin distinctive. There was something about his arresting brown eyes that seemed particularly knowing.

"John's in our tent, so you'd best get on his good side. Don't say much, but he sure can play."

"Play?" asked Verity doubtfully. Garrett's arrival prevented Sam from answering.

Garrett went to the head of the group. Verity noted his languid grace with peevish disdain. He seemed larger than other men, annoyingly, more confident.

"I need to find my best shots, so those of you who can ride and welcome an outing for a change, step up. We'll see what you can do."

The soldiers took Garrett's contest as sport, with the spirit of a baseball game. The men lined up in disorderly fashion, eager to take their shots. Sam was the first to shoot.

"Watch this, Watkins lad, and you'll learn something."

Sam fired, hitting the bottle easily. "Very good," said Garrett. "You're in."

Sam stepped away, and John took his place, also splintering the bottle. He said nothing, though he smiled enigmatically at Verity. To Verity's surprise, many others failed to hit the target. Ethan Hallowell took aim, and despite loud riling from the enlisted men, he, too, hit the mark.

Verity felt a wave of sympathy for the young officer. For one thing, Ethan reminded her of Westley, with his pale blond hair and golden mustache. More than that, Ethan seemed deadly serious and a little out of place among the farmers and workmen.

"Good work, Captain," said Garrett. "These men need a capable officer along."

"Well, Watkins?" said Sam. "Take your place."

Verity swallowed hard. How humiliating, having to miss her shot! Garrett studied the small soldier.

"How old are you, son?"

Verity hesitated, keeping her head down, loathing Garrett's patronizing tone. "Seventeen," she lied in what she hoped was a boyish voice.

"Fourteen's more like it," said Garrett. "Son, you go back to your mama and leave the fighting to men."

This was too much for Verity. Her pride flew, soaring miles above her reason. "You called for marksmen, Sir. I can shoot a flea off a dog, and I can hit that bottle at twice this distance."

The men laughed at the slight soldier's bravado. Garrett stared at her, his eyes wide, his mouth open. For a sick instant, Verity felt certain her recognized her. Garrett's shocked expression faded to a smile.

"Twice the distance, eh? Well, Watkins, let's see you do it. Otherwise, you go back to where you belong. Today."

Verity bit her lip. That gray-eyed devil had caught her in a wild exaggeration, but Verity stepped forward to back up her claim. With irritating leisure, Garrett had the target moved exactly twice its former distance.

"Take your shot," said Garrett.

Verity studied the mark, her fingers tingling with tension and excitement. Verity lifted Westley's musket, loaded it briskly, took aim, and fired.

To the astonishment of all, Verity's shot shattered the bottle. With a great sigh of relief, and surprise, she turned to Garrett Knox. Garrett stared at the broken bottle. He looked at Verity.

"Do it again."

"What?"

"Again, Watkins. Anyone can get lucky."

Verity glared at him, but she reloaded her musket and shot again. Again, the bottle burst into shards of glass.

"Jesus," muttered Garrett. "What now?"

"I'm in, Sir. Yes?"

He hesitated. He looked around the campsite thoughtfully. "There's not much going on. It might be the safest place ..." Garrett's voice trailed. Verity noticed a cleft in his square chin. It annoyed her.

"Well, Sir?" Verity felt supremely confident now in her disguise. Garrett probably hadn't looked at her very closely when they first met. Her eyes glittered as she set her musket against a stand.

"You're in, boy. Next."

Verity joined Sam and the others. Sam beamed with pride. "What a shot! Watkins, you're a wonder. Did you see that, Hallowell? Don't judge a man by his size."

Sam slapped Verrill's shoulder, nearly sending Verity to her knees. John said nothing, just nodded his approval in her direction.

"You're a fine shot," said Ethan. "I'll give you that. But target practice is a lot different from combat. That's where a man is tested. Not here."

"Yes, Captain." Ethan's words hit their mark, too. Verity had no intention of entering a battle. Now that her disguise proved foolproof, she could easily find evidence against Garrett Knox.

"Watkins!" Garrett's deep voice startled Verity and she spun around to face him. As she did, he tossed Westley's musket toward her. It fell against her leg.

"What'd you do that for?"

"Be ready for anything, son," said Garrett with a restrained smile. He walked away.

Verity picked up the musket and frowned irritably. "Arrogant fool," she grumbled under her breath. Sam overheard her.

"You pay attention to the major, lad. Mark my words. You'll learn what we got in Garrett Knox once the bullets start flying. Ain't a better man in either army."

Verity accepted Sam's admonishment, but inside, she seethed. *I'll pay attention to him, all right. Maybe he's charmed these farmers and blacksmiths. He won't get away with that now. You'll make a mistake, you steely-eyed fiend. And this time, I'll be there to catch you.*

Garrett Knox stood outside his tent, arms folded across his chest, wondering what possessed him to let a girl stay in the army. At least, the army was the last place Dave Delaney would look for Westley Talmadge's elegant widow.

Garrett watched Verity marching alongside John as Ethan drilled them. She never lagged, and she obeyed every command perfectly.

"Robert, my old friend. I hope you'll forgive me for this."

Still, strict army discipline might help Verity Talmadge more than any amount of lady's schooling. Robert Talmadge's pretty sister had never met men like Sam, like John. Blacksmiths, farmers . . . men who worked, and worked hard. Garrett liked the thought that Verity's new exposure would occur under his own watchful eye.

So she had married Westley Talmadge, after all. Hard to imagine that gentle boy would know how to handle Verity Talmadge. Had Westley lived, Verity would have soon wrapped her poor husband around her little finger, then turned his life into a whirlwind of trouble.

Garrett Knox sighed and shook his head. The boy would have loved every minute. Garrett guessed Verity herself might require more than gentle, respectful kisses and an adoring embrace. She needed passion, a skilled touch.

Garrett had watched his army grind from failure to failure, losing men that time would never replace. He wanted to forget, he wanted distraction. The girl marching in disguise hadn't accepted defeat, not yet. More than anything else, this gave hope to Garrett Knox.

Across the field, Ethan's drill ended. Sam slapped Verity's back at a job well done. Even John appeared to say a few complimentary words. Garrett wondered how long the girl could keep her sex a secret from her tentmates. Somehow, he guessed Verity Talmadge would find a way.

Verity saw Garrett watching her. She wondered if he'd guessed her identity, after all. No, he wouldn't let her calmly drill with his men, sleep in their tent. Verity intended to prove him a spy.

Garrett knew that. If he knew the truth, he'd haul her forcibly
from the camp and return her to the Webster's care.

Garrett turned away and went into his tent. Verity relaxed.

"I've got to hand it to you, Watkins. You held up with the best
of us under drill," said Sam. "You must be a mite stronger than
you look."

"Yes. I am." In truth, every muscle in Verity's body ached.
She'd taken more steps than seemed possible. Only pride, and the
fact that Garrett Knox watched, kept her going. "When do we
eat?"

"Ain't that just like a lad?" chuckled Sam. "Always thinking
of his stomach. You come along with us, young fellow. We'll see
you get enough to fill you up."

Sam looked rather disparagingly at Ethan Hallowell. "Anything
else, Sir?"

"That will be all, Sergeant," said Ethan. "Dismiss the men."

"Move out to grub," shouted Sam, and the men dispersed,
leaving Ethan Hallowell standing by himself.

"Aren't you coming, Captain?" asked Verity, though Sam
frowned at the inquiry.

"No," said Ethan, taken aback by Watkins's invitation. "I dine
with the officers. Naturally."

"Thank you for the drill, Captain," said Verity earnestly. "You
did it very well."

"You're . . . welcome, Watkins," said Ethan.

Sam looked doubtfully at Verity. "Come along, Watkins. The
day soldiers start thanking officers for drill is the day Lee best
send his boys over. We'd deserve to be finished off!"

Sam took Verity to his tent, accompanied by John. "You settle
in here, lad. Then come out by the fire. We'll have a supper ready.
Maybe you'll join us for some songs."

Sam made army life sound like a picnic in high summer. It
hardly fit in with Westley's tales of camp life, with barely edible
meals and danger around every corner.

Verity entered Sam's tent, and found it surprisingly homey
inside. The men had built small quarters out of self-cut timber and
cloth coverings. A makeshift chimney rose through the excavated
roof. A fireplace of stones, brick chips, and sod warmed the tiny
hut.

Verity noted the small attempts at furnishings; upside down boxes used as tables, boxes attached to the wall serving as cupboards, and comfortable bunks made from hay and pine boughs. Letters bound carefully, lovingly, lay at bedsides. Something about this touched her heart; to her own wonder, tears sprang to her eyes.

When Verity stepped outside again, she saw more than tents and hovels. She saw a vast city of similar, little homes. Rather than hardened, nameless soldiers, Verity now saw men, each doing his best to live with a semblance of the dignity and comfort he knew at home.

"Over here, Watkins," called Sam. The men gathered around the fire, serving themselves from large pots of stew, drinking coffee. Freshly made bread was served with the stew, and Verity filled her dish with the warm food.

The soldiers joked among themselves, and Verity relaxed as she hadn't for years. As Verrill, she felt totally invisible. Though their conversation tended to be crude, Verity felt more and more at ease.

The winter sun faded beyond the horizon, and the men threw scraps of wood onto the small fire. "It gets cold nights," said Sam, "but we got our own way of warming things up."

John retrieved an old guitar from their tent and sat down to play. "Have a seat, lad," said Sam. "You'll be hearing something you won't never forget."

Other soldiers gathered round, listening in silence to the soft strumming by John's strong fingers.

"Ever heard anything like that in your old company?" asked Sam.

"Never in my life," said Verity quietly.

"He sings some you know, like 'Lorena,' 'Cry of Freedom,' and the like. Most, he made up by himself. Some make you want to dance like a boy courting, some make you near on to cry, but they're all good."

> *"The years ceeep slowly by, Lorena,*
> *The snow is on the grass again . . ."*

Sam fell silent as John's low voice sang the poignant words. To Verity's astonishment, tears formed in the gruff man's eyes.

She wondered if Sam had a wife. Where he lived. What mattered to him, so that he should leave it all behind for this.

> " 'But the heart throbs as warmly now,
> As when the summer days were nigh . . .' "

Garrett Knox stood watching his men, listening to John's mournful song. Verity's attention fixed on him. She wondered if the song moved his heart, too.

> " 'We loved each other then, Lorena,
> More than we ever dared to tell . . .
> And what we might have been, Lorena,
> Had but our loving prospered well . . .' "

Verity's lip curled in irritation. "What's he doing here?"

"Hm?" Sam looked at Verrill Watkins, detecting mistrust in the boy's voice. "What've you got against the major, anyway?"

Verity bit her lip, restraining herself from blurting out the truth. "Well . . . he's not from Massachusetts, is he?"

"No, but then, neither is Abe Lincoln. Don't you trust him?"

"Of course I do, but that's different."

"Major Knox, he's a hell of a horseman. His papa died a few years before the war, calling his son back from France. On his deathbed, they say. The major took over, and produced the best horseflesh to be found north of Virginia."

This impressed Sam. The Yankee cavalry had been ridiculed, but Garrett's deeds were widely known, returning respect to the Union. "Don't know why he left the Maryland Cavalry. Figure it had something to do with Major Talmadge."

"Talmadge?"

"Robert Talmadge. Brave as they come, just like his cousin. Westley Talmadge. Both gone now . . . Major Knox transferred then. Maybe he just wanted to look after his little brother. But the boy died, too. Damned shame."

Verity didn't want to hear any more. Apparently Sam knew nothing sinister about Garrett's motives. She forced her attention from Garrett Knox, and back to the music.

* * *

Garrett couldn't hear Verity's comments, but he guessed she hadn't gotten far in proving his guilt. An idea struck him, and he repressed a grin as he walked to her.

"Watkins." Garrett spoke sharply and Verity jumped.

"On your feet, lad," suggested Sam. Verity rose.

"Yes, Sir."

"I've got a proposal for you."

"Sir?"

"My valet has taken ill. Looks like he'll be going home. Sam's tent is already overcrowded. I'd like you to take Ned's place."

Garrett's invitation left Verity speechless. He smiled and waited. "It's a lot of work. But you'll get a better bunk. It might even get you out of drill, occasionally."

"Would it, Sir?"

"It's just Major Wallingford and myself."

"Ain't you the lucky one!" said Sam enthusiastically.

Garrett smiled as Verity squirmed. She was caught. He'd given her the perfect opportunity to prove him a spy. And he could limit her mischief. It would be altogether enjoyable.

"Very well, Sir. I'd be pleased to take the post."

"Bring your things to my tent, then. You start work in the morning."

Verity followed Garrett to his tent. Dan Wallingford lay on his cot, arms behind his head. "What's this?"

"This is Watkins," said Garrett. "He's replacing Ned, for the time being."

"Is he?" Dan Wallingford sat up. "Good. Here, Watkins . . ." Wallingford tossed his jacket at Verity. "Arm's got a tear. Have it fixed, will you, lad?"

"Yes," replied Verity. Garrett guessed she had no idea how.

Verity fidgeted uneasily, then turned to Garrett. "Is there anything you'd like done around here, Major?"

Garrett pulled off his overcoat, considering the matter. A pile of unopened letters caught his eye—most, if not all, from female admirers. Ned had written brief replies, sparing Garrett the necessity. It pleased Garrett to put Verity Talmadge to the task.

"Those letters need replies," said Garrett. "And I don't have the time."

"Or the inclination," put in Dan. "He wants a woman with more to offer than pretty prose."

Verity glanced between them. "Sir?"

"Major Knox wants you to write brief, impersonal notes to these smitten girls," explained Dan Wallingford, grinning at the farm boy's uncertainty.

Verity sat at the small desk and examined the envelopes. "What do I say, Sir?"

"Tell them he thanks them for their kind support of our nation's cause, and hopes the hardships of war don't touch their sweet natures," suggested Dan. "Isn't that what you had Ned say, Garrett?"

"In essence."

"Very well." Verity opened the first, read a few lines, then turned to Garrett. "This woman, Emma Blake, wants a lock of your hair."

"If he sent hair to every girl who requests it, Major Knox would be bald." Dan grinned at Garrett. "You know how Lord Byron handled this."

"How?" asked Verity.

"Byron sent the enamored miss a lock of his hair, all right. But not the hair from his head," said Dan Wallingford. Garrett cringed.

"I don't think we should bore Watkins with this."

Verity looked suspicious. "From where?"

"Where do you think, boy?" scoffed Dan, shaking his head at Watkins's innocence. "Pubic hair, of course."

"Just a legend," injected Garrett. "Told by schoolboys."

Garrett felt Verity's gaze on him. "Is there anything you'd like to send, Sir?"

"Thank the young lady for her interest, Watkins," said Garrett. Verity Talmadge was more impertinent than he realized. "Remind her it's still winter, and I can't spare any hair . . . at all."

"I'll tell her it's filled with lice," decided Verity, and Dan Wallingford laughed.

"I thought that's why you shaved the mustache, Knox," said Dan. "Ah, Watkins, you'll be a good valet. Too much respect is bad for an officer."

"Too little is bad for a valet," added Garrett. "And I don't have lice, Watkins."

Verity's low opinion of him stung. Garrett wasn't sure why. The girl was obviously crazy. But bright. Garrett had to admit Verity Talmadge had a quick brain, if illogical. A tiny smile curved her lips. Dirt smudged her smooth cheeks, but Garrett discerned the beauty beneath. He intended to keep her in his control, safe from danger. The danger to himself suddenly seemed more pressing.

Verity finished the first note and turned to the next. As she read, she shook her head. She stopped writing and looked over at Garrett. She seemed to be studying his face.

"Watkins?"

"Just checking your eyelashes, Sir. This girl referred to them."

"What of it?"

"She seems to feel they're unique."

"Are they?" asked Dan.

"Everyone has eyelashes," said Verity.

Verity turned back to the letters, and Garrett lay back on his cot. So much for impressing her with his good looks. Garrett never considered his appearance—he accepted female praise without caring.

If he wanted a woman, he made certain she was free from a clinging nature, that she wanted a hearty tumble in bed, without restraints afterwards. This manner of loving had pleased him well throughout his twenty-eight years. Why did it seem inadequate now?

"While Watkins here labors over your smitten followers, why don't you and I pay a visit to our lovely 'laundresses'?" suggested Dan.

Verity looked around at him, bit her lip, and turned back to her writing. Garrett saw Verity holding her motionless pen, waiting. Apparently she'd already learned the true purpose of the laundry girls. Here was one impression he could correct.

"It's been a long war, Dan. But not so long that I'm willing to wait outside the hut of some gritty-toothed strumpet."

Dan Wallingford cringed at this description. "When you put it that way, sleep sounds more appealing."

Verity's pen moved again, dipped in ink to continue her response.

"How about you, Watkins?" suggested Dan with a grin.

The pen dropped, the ink splattered. "What?"

"Surely you're old enough—barely. Hell, if another battle comes, you might not get the chance for a good—"

"Jesus, Dan," cut in Garrett. "Leave the boy on the straight and narrow, will you?"

"I'm not much taken with prostitutes, Sir," Verity told Wallingford, speaking as if to a simpleton. "I understand such women harbor bugs in unfortunate spots."

"God," muttered Garrett, but Dan Wallingford laughed.

"You could be right. Thank you both for destroying my mood. And if you'll both be quiet, I'll get some much needed sleep."

At the mention of sleep, Verity yawned. Garrett felt a wave of sympathy for the girl. He admired her courage, and he didn't want her to fail just yet.

"Get some rest, Watkins. You can finish those later."

"Thank you, Sir. I believe I will."

Verity left the desk and flopped down on Ned's cot. She didn't bother to undress, though she pulled off her shoes. She probably had nothing else to wear, anyway. Dan Wallingford began to snore, and Verity put her pillow over her head.

Garrett smiled as he watched her. What a woman! He'd seen many beautiful women, taken many to his bed. But he'd never met one he couldn't forget. Beauty wasn't enough. Charm wasn't enough. Garrett wasn't sure what Verity had that no other woman possessed, but she fascinated him. The appeal of madness, perhaps.

Verity's small, stockinged feet stuck out from beneath her blanket. Garrett got up and covered them. For a while, Garrett looked down at her sleeping form. Verity Talmadge might be crazy, but then, the world itself had gone crazy, too. Maybe Verity was just the kind to set it straight.

Garrett went back to his cot and closed his eyes. Since the first shots were fired at Fort Sumter, Garrett Knox had been with the Union Army. He'd seen commanders come, fail, and go. He'd seen boys with shaking hands fire muskets at boys in gray. He'd seen them crying for their mothers as they died. What started as a joyous test of honor became a long nightmare.

By tending Verity, Garrett honored his dead friends, his brother. Verity's presence gave Garrett someone to protect, a fate he could control. Until Joe Hooker decided to move against Robert E. Lee across the Rappahannock, there would be no battles. From what Garrett knew of Hooker, warfare didn't seem imminent. Until that time, Verity Talmadge was safe in blue.

Chapter Three

"Rise and shine, Watkins!" Garrett's abrupt tone startled Verity from sleep. She jumped up from the cot, blinked, and stared at him.

Garrett stared, too. Her shoulder-length hair fell around her face, a soft shadow of rich brown and sparkling red. Her lips looked pink and soft—kissable—from sleep. Her blue-gray eyes focused uncertainly. Garrett knew she'd misplaced herself. He watched as her senses snapped back into place.

"Is it morning, Major? It's dark still."

"Reveille has sounded, Watkins," said Garrett, taking pleasure in Verity's muted groan. "It failed to wake you, however. What kind of soldier sleeps through the bugle call?"

"A tired one," grumbled Verity. "I am a bit hungry, though."

"And when you've seen your commander, cleaned your musket—and washed, I might add—you can eat."

"Washing is bad for your health, Major. A good layer or two of dirt keeps the lice away."

Garrett eyed Verity's filthy complexion, wondering how she ever got her perfect skin that dirty. "Bathe, Watkins. One washing for one layer. That should leave you enough grime to fend off the critters."

"As you say, Sir."

"Report to your officer first."

"My officer? I thought you were my commander."

"Not directly," said Garrett. "You're under Captain Hallowell."

"Oh," said Verity. "Good."

Verity left the tent, but Garrett pondered her reaction. If nothing else, a soldier who appreciated Ethan Hallowell might benefit the young captain. Garrett liked Ethan, but the boy had no skill as an officer. He was bright, noble, brave . . . and thoroughly disliked by his men.

Ethan Hallowell, from Boston's finest society, was only nineteen. His good looks and elegant manner captivated local women, though the boy remained oblivious to his effect. His detached, cool reserve soon put the smitten girls off, but Garrett doubted Verity would respond that way.

Garrett considered this possibility with less pleasure. Ethan resembled Westley. Garrett doubted Verity had felt true passion for her dead husband, but she might have felt comfort, ease. Familiarity.

Garrett harbored no illusions about society. He walked through it without interest. He preferred his rugged soldiers; like them, Garrett immersed himself in life. He couldn't simply explore it through art or music or books.

Verity Talmadge was the same. Familiarity and comfort might have an appeal for her. But her true nature was stronger. She'd proved that, by sneaking into the Union Army with her dead husband's musket over her shoulder.

Verity found Ethan Hallowell. He groaned when he saw her. "Don't you ever wash, Watkins?"

"I just did!" replied Verity indignantly. Ethan groaned again.

Sam and John appeared with young Peter McCaffrey. "You called, Captain?" asked Sam.

"Yes, three quarters of an hour ago," said Ethan. "But don't feel any need to respond in haste, Sergeant."

"You can report me again."

"For all the good it does," muttered Ethan.

"I assume you've got a pressing reason for rushing out breakfast," said Sam.

Verity suspected the sergeant took great joy in irritating Ethan

Hallowell. Ethan's light skin flushed, but he did his best to control his emotion.

"I've assigned you picket duty." Ethan looked for a negative reaction, but the soldiers just shrugged.

"Gets us out of drill," said Sam. "Maybe get us some fresh tobacco, too," he added with a nudge at John. John grinned, but Verity looked between them doubtfully.

Ethan's eyes widened, his lips tightened. "None of that!"

"None of what?" put in Verity.

"The captain don't much like our fraternizing with Johnny Reb. Do ye, Cap'n?"

"I do not," said Ethan. "It's against every regulation, every code of war—"

"What do you mean, 'fraternizing?'" asked Verity.

"Well, picket duty ain't exactly thrilling," explained Sam while Ethan fumed. "The rebel pickets ain't far, and most of us—who ain't got a regulations' code book up our backsides—take the opportunity to strike up talk, make a few trades. The rebs want coffee, we'll take their tobacco, whatever—"

"What if they decide to shoot you, instead?" asked Verity, and Ethan nodded.

"Hell, now, Watkins. When the bugles sound, we'll shoot each other right enough. Don't mean we can't enjoy ourselves now, though."

"It means just that," put in Ethan. "You'll do no such thing, Sergeant. No fraternizing. I'll see to that myself."

"How?" asked Sam.

"I'll take the duty with you," decided Ethan. "There will be no unregulated interaction today."

"Aw, hell," mumbled Sam.

"Move out," said Ethan.

John retrieved his guitar and Sam brought coffee. They took an inordinate amount of time preparing for duty while Ethan stewed and grumbled.

"Come along, Watkins," suggested Sam. "It's a fine, misty morning for picket duty. Gets you out of drill."

"May I, Captain?"

Ethan hesitated, but Verity guessed one respectful soldier was worth an army. "Very well, Watkins."

Verity accompanied them, if only to protect Ethan Hallowell from himself. If anyone could distance himself from his soldiers, it was Ethan. Men like Sam and John loved and respected Garrett Knox, but they couldn't see anything good in a man like Ethan. *Ha! How wrong they are,* Verity thought. Ethan wasn't doing much to ingratiate himself, either. He walked apart from his men, his back straight, his movements stiff even as he scrambled down the riverbank to assume picket duty.

"Set up here," said Ethan. "And no slacking."

No, Ethan wasn't exactly a born leader, Verity had to admit. But something wistful and proud in Ethan Hallowell touched her heart. He seemed like a brother, though from the way he treated Watkins, apparently Ethan didn't recognize this.

"You, Watkins, will peruse the far bank to the left."

"Yes, Sir!" said Verity. Ethan eyed her suspiciously, as if checking Watkins's sincerity. Apparently, he detected no guile, so he turned to Sam.

"Sergeant, I expect to know what's going on to our right."

Sam rolled his eyes. "There's six rebs having a drink of fake coffee and chewing on some stale biscuits. Got bacon, too."

Ethan looked across the water. "I see nothing." He lifted his spyglass. "Where?"

"In them bushes."

Ethan adjusted his glass, but shook his head.

"Hey, Reb!" Sam's voice boomed across the misty Rappahannock. "What you got for breakfast?"

"Biscuits and bacon fat!" shouted back a rebel. "Ain't got no coffee, though. Just this poison broth."

"Ain't that a shame? Got some fine brew over here."

"Got a bag of Virginia's finest!" called the rebel. "Trade!"

"Send it over."

"Hold there!" exclaimed Ethan. "This is just what I meant to prevent!"

"Just a bit, Reb," called Sam wearily.

"What's the problem?" asked the rebel.

"Officer."

"Oh."

"There will be no trades," insisted Ethan. "For God's sake, Sergeant. These men are our enemies."

"What do they want?" Garrett Knox joined Ethan's pickets. He took a cup of coffee and drank. He seemed casual, unaffected by the fraternization that troubled Ethan.

"The disillusionment of our forces," said Ethan.

"Coffee," said Sam.

Garrett nodded, but a tiny smile flickered on his lips. "We're trying to reunite the country, Captain. Not sunder it forever."

Ethan didn't argue. Verity recognized his youthful respect for Garrett, and her heart expanded with pity.

"Do you like cigars, Captain?" asked Garrett.

"No."

"What about bacon?"

Ethan hesitated, and Garrett smiled. "What have you rebs got for those who don't smoke?"

Verity stared at Garrett Knox in astonishment. "You can't be thinking of trading with them, Major. Captain Hallowell says it's against the rules."

"Rules?" asked Garrett, his brow arched as he looked at Verity. "If we attended to rules, what would we say about your . . . age, Watkins?"

Verity bit her lip. True, rules meant little to her. "That's a 'maybe,' Sir."

"We've got a fine slab of bacon," called the rebel.

"Deal," said Garrett.

The pickets leapt into action. Sam readied a small raft, put a bag of coffee on it, and pushed it out into the river with a long pole. Across the Rappahannock, the rebel did the same. Both men waded out to make the exchange.

John prepared a small fire to cook the bacon. Despite himself, Ethan Hallowell waited eagerly for his portion. Verity sat beside him and chewed happily on the cured meat.

"It's very good," she said thickly. Sam smoked a cigar thoughtfully, and John began strumming his guitar.

"That's fine music," called a satisfied rebel picket. "Almost as fine as this here coffee."

"Fine cigar," called back Sam.

"You Yanks don't seem so bad. Where're you from?"

"Massachusetts," said Sam. "All over the state."

"What'd you do back there?"

"Farming," said Sam. "John here was a blacksmith."

"Same as me," called the rebel. "Hey, what do you boys think of dancing?"

"Like it fine," called Sam.

"Dancing?" asked Ethan. He closed his eyes.

"We're dressing up as fine folk and busting in on a ball tonight," the rebel told them. "Got a good officer over here who treats us better than most. He's letting us in, and we'll show the ladies that a blacksmith and a farmer can put any blue blood to shame on the floor."

"That seems unlikely," muttered Ethan.

Garrett Knox set his coffee aside. "What officer?" Verity saw his smile, the twinkle of recognition in his eyes.

"Knox."

"Jared," said Garrett quietly.

"A relative of yours?" asked Verity knowingly.

"I can't think of anyone else who would instigate a party infiltration like that."

"How about you boys come over and join us!" shouted the excited rebel.

"Certainly not!" exclaimed Ethan.

"I don't think these uniforms will inspire much congeniality from the ladies," laughed Garrett.

"We'll fix you up as civilians," called the rebel. "Leave the blue over here, and we'll have ourselves a fine time of it."

"I think not," said Ethan. He glanced at Garrett, who seemed to consider the offer with surprising seriousness.

"It would be good to see Jared," said Garrett. "But I'm afraid I'm fairly well known over there, civilian clothes or not."

Garrett turned to Ethan. "You go, Hallowell. Take the men and make a night of it."

Ethan Hallowell's mouth dropped, his blue eyes widened. "Major?"

"Hell, Captain. It's been a long war. When did you last go dancing?"

"Dancing?" said Ethan.

"Dancing, Hallowell. Rebel girls know more about it than your Boston types. I'm not telling you to betray your country's secrets. Just enjoy yourself."

Garrett's nonchalant attitude about socializing with the enemy stunned Verity. She expected a careful cover of his perverse loyalties. She looked around at the men. Sam, John, Peter McCaffrey . . . any one of them might be in league with Garrett Knox. It couldn't be a coincidence that Garrett's rebel cousin arranged this outing.

No wonder it seemed simple and innocent, accidental. It was

well planned! One thing wasn't planned, and that was Verrill Watkins' presence at the rebel ball.

"I could use a little dancing," said Verity to Garrett's great surprise. "Yes, Sir. I'll take you up on it."

Sam laughed, but Ethan was aghast. "What if we're . . . you're caught?"

"You won't be the first to go courting rebel girls in civilian disguise," said Garrett. "The officers may not like it, but they know young men. As long as there's no suspicion of wrongdoing, they turn a blind eye."

"I don't like it," said Ethan. "But if you approve, Major, I'll do nothing to stop them from going."

"I'm counting on you to keep an eye on them, Captain," said Garrett. "We don't want Watkins deserting the Union army for a pretty rebel girl."

"Sounds fun, don't it?" said the youthful Peter McCaffrey. "I don't know how to dance, though. When I'm around girls, I stutter—"

"Don't fret on it, McCaffrey," said Sam. "Take a good swig of whatever spirits you can find, and you'll be dancing right enough."

"Dancing isn't difficult, Peter," said Verity. "I'll explain it to you on the way. Just be respectful and polite to the girl. That's what matters."

"What would you know, Watkins?" laughed Sam.

"I know women." Verity's comment brought greater mirth from the other soldiers, not least from Garrett Knox.

"You see what I mean, Captain?" said Garrett. "These men need you. Watkins needs you. See that this arrogant lad stays out of trouble. We don't want a Virginia belle's daddy forcing him into a wedding. If you see my cousin, give him my regards."

"Very well," said Ethan, his voice a near groan. "I'll go. Dear God, socializing with rebels. I never dreamed this day would come . . ."

Ethan was still muttering as they started away. Garrett watched the five Yankee soldiers enter the icy Rappahannock. Verity was first to sink in and swim. Garrett sighed heavily as the small band met with the rebel pickets. It would have been enjoyable, to watch Verity at a ball. To dance, to laugh. . . .

Garrett had more important matters to attend to this day. He needed the inquisitive girl away from camp, so that his own actions would go undetected. Verity Talmadge was right about one thing. Their regiment harbored a spy. And Garrett intended to find out who it was before the raid.

"Who've we got here?" asked the rebel picket.

"Name's Sam O'Neill," said Sam. "Here's John, Peter McCaffrey and young Verrill Watkins."

"Pleased to meet ye," said the rebel. "I'm Gordy Dyer, and these are my mates." Gordy eyed Ethan with obvious misgivings. "Who's he?"

"Hallowell," sighed Sam. "He's here to make sure we behave ourselves."

"Officer," said Gordy, with no more respect than Sam showed.

"This outing will take place within the bounds of propriety," said Ethan. "I'm here to see none of my men stray from acceptable grounds."

"Meaning you couldn't keep 'em on the Northern side, so here you be," laughed the rebel.

Ethan fingered his Colt revolver.

"What've you got for clothes?" asked Verity. At the sound of her voice, Gordy Dyer's brow rose.

"You ain't old enough for dancing, little one. Hell be damned, I thought we rebs fought 'em young. You ain't more than a sprite at best."

"A sprite that can shoot the flea off a dog—them being his own words," put in Sam. "Don't go crossing Watkins, Reb, or you'll get one ugly surprise."

Verity puffed visibly at Sam's praise, and her lip curved dangerously. The rebel shook his head, but he took pains to offer the small Yankee no further offense.

"Captain Knox done provided us with fancy clothes," said Gordy.

"Knox, eh?" said Sam. "Our Major Garrett Knox is his cousin. Told us to send regards."

"Garrett Knox," said Gordy. "Fine man, that. Damned shame he's on the other side. Most of us thought he'd fight for the South, being Maryland born and raised.

"There's more than one way of serving one's chosen country," put in Verity. Sam glanced her way, but she said no more. "Will this Jared attend the ball?"

"Well, if he don't, half the ladies of Fredericksburg won't show up."

"Why not?" asked Verity.

"The young gent's got a way, boy," sighed the rebel. "He's a lion on the field, and you know how ladies love lions."

"Do they?" asked Peter McCaffrey. Verity noticed a slight stammer already in the boy's voice.

"They like a good heart and gentle manners more," she reassured the nervous boy.

"That's right, McCaffrey," said Sam, though he didn't sound convinced himself. "Get yourself into these civilian duds, and we'll set out for the time of your life."

"What time does the ball start?" asked Verity as she stripped off her Union jacket.

"It starts when we get there," said the rebel.

Verity hid behind a bush and hurriedly dressed in the rebel's clothes.

"What're you doing there, Watkins?" called Sam. "You got something the rest of us don't?"

"The need for privacy," she responded without hesitation, appearing again clothed as a civilian.

"Damn, wash the boy's face," groaned Gordy Dyer. "They ain't thinking we're fancy folk if we go in looking like that!"

With no choice, Verity rinsed her face in the river. She pulled her cap low over her forehead and her curly hair shaded her face, but they all stared at her in surprise.

"He looks like a girl," said Gordy. "And a right pretty one."

Verity froze. One choice only presented itself. She made a tight fist and flung herself violently at the rebel. Stunned by the small Yankee's fury, the rebel fell backwards. Verity landed on him and punched him as hard as she could.

"Enough!" commanded Ethan. No one listened, but Sam pulled Verrill Watkins off his rebel counterpart.

"Told you, Reb. Don't go provoking Watkins."

Sam held Verity back as Gordy struggled to his feet and rubbed his chin. "Begging your pardon, lad. Don't mean no harm."

"Your apology is accepted, Sir," said Verity. Sam released her.

"Still, you do look a bit . . . young. We gotta do something to fix you up.'' The rebel considered the matter. ''I know!'' He fumbled with his pack, produced a razor and grabbed a portion of Verity's hair. ''Hold still.''

Verity complied while Gordy trimmed tiny bits of her hair. The others watched while the rebel made a slight mustache over Verrill Watkins' lip with the hair and a bit of sealing wax. Seeing the results, Sam laughed.

''Well, there's a sight. But it suits you. If you were a mite taller, and a whole stretch cleaner, you'd look—'' Sam paused, his eyes narrowing as he studied her features. ''You look like Robert Talmadge.''

''Do I?'' asked Verity, her heart moved by the connection to her missing brother.

''You could be his little brother,'' said Sam, and John nodded.

''Major Talmadge and Watkins have absolutely nothing in common,'' said Ethan. ''Perhaps around the eyes. But their natures . . .''

A very tall rebel officer stood watching the unkempt group. ''What have we here?'' His voice was soft, low, with a faint trace of humor.

''Captain!'' exclaimed Dyer. ''Well . . . the thing is—''

''Yankees,'' said Jared Knox. He studied the group. ''Spies, perhaps?''

Gordy Dyer cringed, and Verity wondered if she would spend the war in a rebel prison. Ethan Hallowell groaned and closed his eyes.

''We came with a message from your cousin,'' piped in Verity, though her voice shook. ''Garrett Knox.''

Jared ambled down the bank to join them. Verity looked closely at him. He was younger than Garrett, blond, with an angular face and a sweet expression. He was slightly taller than his Yankee cousin, though lighter of build. Both had the same knowing gleam in their eyes.

Besides Garrett, Jared Knox was the handsomest man Verity had ever seen. Not just handsome, either. Her brother had been handsome, aristocratic, and noble. It was that knowing, strangely sensual gleam that set Jared and Garrett Knox apart from other men. No wonder the two had wreaked havoc among Europe's women.

''You're Garrett's soldiers?'' asked Jared, his interest raised by the small soldier's words. "He's with a Massachusetts company now, I've heard."

"He moved from the Maryland Cavalry under mysterious circumstances," said Verity.

"He's a damned fine officer," cut in Sam hurriedly. "Couldn't ask for a better. Not unlike yourself, if your men are right." Sam watched Jared Knox hopefully. A slow grin appeared on the rebel officer's face.

"Spies, or would be revelers?" asked Jared.

"We came to dance," said Verity.

"That's good," said Jared. "Because the only things you'll spy tonight are pretty girls."

"Maybe we should head back," suggested Ethan Hallowell without much hope.

"An officer?" guessed Jared.

"Aye," sighed Sam.

"We'll have you back before tomorrow's dawn," promised Jared. "Follow me."

Jared led the group to a sprawling Georgian mansion on the outskirts of Fredericksburg. Virginia belles flitted about in gowns the likes of which Verity had never seen. Handsome officers with lavish whiskers led the beautiful women in graceful dances.

"It's a far cry from what we've been seeing," muttered Sam. John said nothing, as usual, but he shook his head, a sardonic smile upon his lips.

"What beautiful folk," murmured Peter McCaffrey. "The men dance real well, d-don't they?"

"Hell's bells, McCaffrey. They ain't seen nothing," said Sam with a wink at Verrill Watkins. "Just wait 'til you boys hit the floor. Ladies won't know which way is up."

"A frighteningly realistic appraisal," said Ethan.

Verity wondered if Garrett's reasons for sending his disguised men into rebel territory had something to do with their pride. Sam had told her about General Burnside's Mud March earlier in the winter; how wagons disappeared in the mud while the rebels laughed and taunted them from across the river.

The Union army floundered. They bravely sacrificed their lives at Fredericksburg. For nothing. The rebels danced and laughed.

The Confederacy had won, decisively, almost every battle so far. The Virginians exuded victory like the right of royalty.

Without Jared's presence, the pickets' messy group would have been turned away without hesitation. But when Jared introduced them as his bravest soldiers—and their brothers—not an eyelash was batted.

"There you go, men," said Jared. "You're in, and no one will question you now. Dance to your hearts' content. But please, spare my reputation by behaving yourselves. Especially you, Watkins."

The sun lowered behind the mansion, and long shadows filtered across the wide lawn. Lamps glowed from every corner, hanging from trees, glistening on small pools.

"What now?" groaned Ethan when Jared left them.

"Dance, of course," replied Gordy Dyer as he surveyed the vast collection of young women. "Officers don't know nothing."

"Aye, you've got a point there, Gordy," agreed Sam. He caught the eye of middle-aged widow and smiled. She smiled back, and Sam went to dance. John took a young woman to the floor, too, and eased into a waltz with surprising grace.

Verity stood with Peter McCaffrey and Ethan. A slight, red haired girl passed by, and Peter sighed. "Ask her to dance," prodded Verity.

"I can't," whispered Peter, his face coloring bright orange at the suggestion.

"Of course you can." Verity shoved him toward the girl. The girl nodded before Peter spoke, and led him toward the floor.

"I hope he listened to my instructions," said Verity to Ethan.

Ethan didn't reply. Verity looked at him, and saw his open mouth, his wide, dumbstruck eyes. She looked in the direction of his gaze. A slender girl stood fanning herself, watching the dancers. Dark brown curls fell around her face, her hair bound in a feminine chignon behind her head.

"She's pretty. Do you know her?" Verity waited for an answer. None came. "Captain?"

Ethan stared at the girl. "Know her?" His voice trailed. The girl looked his way, and Ethan snapped to his senses. "No, of course I don't know her, Watkins. What makes you think that?"

"You were looking at her as if—"

"Oh, dear," mumbled Ethan. Verity saw the pretty girl walk toward them. Ethan's face colored. He looked off toward the lanterns on the pond.

The girl stood directly in front of him. "Do I know you?"

"I was just wondering the same thing," said Verity.

"I don't believe we've met," stammered Ethan.

"Dance with me," said the girl.

Ethan's blue eyes widened. The girl held out her hand. Ethan took it and walked as if in a dream toward the dance floor.

So, he's human after all, thought Verity. She liked the way the rebel girl took charge of the situation. So much for docile Southern belles. Verity looked around for Jared Knox. He was dancing, too. Verity found a table of punch and assorted cakes and stuffed the best into her pocket.

"Do you dance, too?"

Verity looked around, then down, and saw a tiny young woman with thick spectacles. "Not very well."

"Oh." The girl's face fell, though she tried to hide her disappointment. She was very plain. Verity felt a wave of sympathy.

"I wouldn't want to embarrass you by my lack of skill."

"You want a prettier partner," sighed the girl. Verity cringed. "I thought, being young and small yourself—"

"I'd love to dance with you." *This may be the most humiliating moment of my life.* Verity seized the girl's gloved hand, trying to remember how to lead.

Actually, leading came easily to her. Verity remembered when Adrian Knox first taught her to dance. *Let me lead, Verity,* he complained. *You're the girl.*

Verity took gleeful control of the small woman and spun her around the room. She saw Sam with his widow, he laughed and nodded as they twirled by.

"You're a wonderful dancer," said the tiny woman. She sounded surprised, and a bit breathless.

"Thank you," said Verity as the music ended. She released her partner and headed back for the punch and sweets. The small woman followed her.

"My name is Mavis Graham. What's yours?"

"Verrill Watkins," said Verity. "Pleased to meet you, Miss Graham."

"Mavis," said the woman shyly. Verity eyed her doubtfully.

Jared Knox joined them at the punch bowl, and Mavis gasped, averting her eyes as if a prince stood beside them. "Enjoying yourself, Watkins?" asked Jared as he ladled punch into a crystal cup and drank.

"A fine party," said Verity. Though Jared danced with many partners, no one seemed to hold his attention long. Girls flitted purposefully near him, but he didn't notice.

"You've certainly got a vast selection of ladies here," noted Verity impertinently, but Jared sighed.

"Ah, but where is the one who remains in my heart beyond the dance floor, Watkins?"

A small sigh escaped Mavis Graham's lips, but Jared didn't notice. "Maybe you need a girl who's a little less agreeable," suggested Verity. "Or maybe you've just seen too many beautiful, adoring women, and no one has the power to intrigue you anymore."

Jared looked at Watkins. He didn't seem irritated by Watkins' direct assessment. "There was a woman," said Jared. "I saw her only once, on a dark, rainy night. But try as I might, I can't forget her."

"Who?" asked Verity, surprised by Jared Knox's confidence.

"I don't know her name. All I know about her is that she's a Yankee spy."

"A spy!" exclaimed both Verity and Mavis together."

"A spy, Watkins. That happens in war."

"So I've heard," said Verity. "How did you meet this woman?"

"I didn't meet her," said Jared. "But I nearly caught her that night. She had no fear. She even dared taunt me before she rode away." Jared sighed again. "My sweet enemy."

"You didn't see her face?" asked Verity.

"I felt her presence."

Jared's words resonated through Verity. As if she understood the underlying passion of his sentiment. "You don't look much alike, but you remind me of your cousin."

"How so?" asked Jared.

"I'm not sure exactly. He doesn't seem quite . . . normal, either."

Jared laughed. "Normal can be dull, Watkins. But I expect you know that."

"True," said Verity. Mavis looked between them doubtfully.

"Enjoy the party, Watkins," said Jared. "It's been good, and refreshing, to speak with you."

Jared returned to the dance floor with yet another belle, but Mavis uttered a deep, drawn out sigh. "He's magnificent, isn't he?"

"He's not exactly what I expected." Verity liked Jared Knox. That didn't mean she trusted him, however. She could picture Jared and Garrett plotting the Union's demise. Somehow, though she couldn't imagine either arranging Robert's death.

In a blinding flash of certainty, Verity knew. She struggled to find proof of Garrett's guilt, yes. But she also searched for evidence of his innocence. She wanted to prove Westley's faith in Garrett justified. She wanted to drive away all doubts. She wanted to be free . . . Verity's lips parted. Her breath stopped. . . .

I want to be free to love him.

"Is something wrong, Verrill?" asked Mavis.

"God, yes," groaned Verity. Mavis seized her arm and leaned closer. "I mean, no."

But now she knew. She knew why she couldn't truly love Adrian or Westley. She had been waiting for Garrett Knox. The day she learned Garrett might have betrayed her faith, Verity's love turned to hatred. She had denied her old feelings. They resurfaced with the force of lightning.

"Do I understand correctly that you know Captain Knox's Yankee cousin?" asked Mavis.

"Why do you say that?" snapped Verity with a curtness she hadn't intended.

"You said Captain Knox reminded you of—"

"Oh, yes. That. Well, I've seen Garrett Knox before. Briefly."

"Girls here still talk about him, arguing over which Knox is handsomer," said Mavis. "Of course, I've never seen Garrett, so I wouldn't know. It's hard to imagine anyone better than Jared, though." Mavis bit her lip. "Oh, I'm sorry! How thoughtless of me. You're quite attractive, too, Verrill."

"Thank you," said Verity.

"I expect when you're older, you'll be handsome," said Mavis. "Maybe you'll even grow a real mustache."

"I doubt it," muttered Verity as Mavis walked away.

What a peculiar night! Dancing with a tiny, bespectacled Southern belle, listening to Jared Knox's personal confidences, watching Ethan Hallowell crumble beneath the gaze of a pretty rebel girl . . . worst of all, and strangest, realizing that her real goal in the Union army was to prove Garrett's innocence. . . .

No, I won't let myself love him. Not until I know which side he's on. A child's infatuation is one thing. I loved the man I imagined, not the arrogant officer back at Stoneman's Switch.

As Verity Talmadge watched the Southern dancers, the War Between the States took a whole new turn. . . .

The excitement of the rebel ball passed for Verity. Unfortunately, it showed no sign of slacking for her comrades. Peter McCaffrey was still dancing, a wide smile on his freckled face. Sam and John sampled the foodstuffs.

Jared Knox showed no sign of any covert activity. Verity guessed he wouldn't get much opportunity, anyway. Pretty belles surrounded him constantly. With that many women fawning over him, Jared wouldn't make much of a spy.

Verity's heart warmed when Jared led Mavis Graham in the Virginia Reel. *He's got a kind heart.* Mavis glowed. For the first time, Verity understood the appeal of Southern men. Tenderness, combined with the suggestion of passion. And joy.

"You're quite a dancer, Watkins," said Sam. "When you took to the floor with that little sprite, I thought for sure you'd crush her toes. Once again, you proved me wrong."

"I told you I could dance."

"That you did. Dance and shoot. Is there anything else you can do?"

"Plenty," Verity assured him. "But just now I'm a bit bored. When do we go home?"

"Home? Hell, boy. Stoneman's Switch is a far cry from 'home' for all of us."

"Maybe so. But this place is farther." Farther from Garrett Knox, too.

"You could be right," agreed Sam. "We might best get a move on." He looked around. "Where's Hallowell?"

"He was dancing," said Verity.

"Hunt him up, Watkins. John and I want one more spin with the ladies, and then we'll get on back to Hell."

Verity went in search of Ethan. He wasn't in the ballroom, so she went outside. Couples walked arm in arm, but Verity saw no sign of Ethan Hallowell or his rebel girl. Verity followed a path toward a little pond. She crossed a small, arched bridge. And there she found Ethan.

He stood, tall and handsome, holding the rebel girl in his arms.

With infinite grace and tenderness, Ethan bent to kiss the girl's mouth. Verity hid behind a bush so as not to embarrass them. The kiss stopped, and Verity began to extract herself from hiding.

"I love you, Bess Hartman." Ethan's voice sounded low and richer than usual. Verity slid back behind the bush.

The girl touched Ethan's mouth. "And I love you, Yankee."

Verity's mouth dropped. Maybe they knew each other, after all. But Ethan's reaction surpassed Verity's.

"Yankee?" He released the girl. She just smiled.

"I'm not a complete fool," said Bess. "Don't fret, Yankee. I won't turn you in. I just don't want you thinking I don't know."

"Then why—" Ethan's voice trailed.

"The first moment I laid eyes on you, I loved you," said Bess simply. "And a few seconds afterward, I knew you were no Southerner. Something tells me your name isn't Beauregard Keats, either."

Beauregard Keats, thought Verity in dismay. Ethan would choose Keats. She shook her head.

"Ethan." Ethan was smiling now. "And not Keats."

"Well?"

"Hallowell. I'm a captain in the Twentieth Massachusetts, from Boston."

"Of all places!"

"It doesn't matter," said Ethan. "We love each other. You can come north with me, we'll marry . . ."

Having released his constraints, Ethan seemed like a burst dam to Verity. But she couldn't help a sigh of feminine appreciation.

"I can't go north," said Bess. "I love you, Ethan Hallowell. I didn't say I sympathized with your cause. I'm a Virginian. I've got a father, five brothers, six uncles, and more cousins than I can count fighting here."

Verity's heart fell. She felt sure Ethan's did, too.

"Then I'll never see you again," said Ethan quietly. Tears formed in Verity's eyes.

"You will if you cross back over," said Bess. "Send me a message through the pickets, and we'll meet."

"I couldn't take advantage of your sweet, trusting nature that way," said Ethan. For reasons Verity didn't understand, his voice sounded husky.

"You can, and will." Bess moved closer to him, her body touching his. She wrapped her arms around his neck and pulled his head down to hers. The ensuing kiss told Verity the girl was right.

Another couple came along the path behind Verity's position in the bush. The way Ethan was kissing Bess, Verity doubted either would hear. If Ethan were discovered . . . Verity scrambled from the bush, coughed loudly, and Ethan jumped away from Bess.

"Watkins!"

"There you are, Captain." Verity looked pointedly over her shoulder, and Ethan noticed the approaching couple.

"We'd better not be seen together," whispered Bess. "I'll sneak back to the party. You'd best leave with your little Yankee friend here."

Bess seized Ethan's hand and kissed it. Their eyes met, and then she darted through the bushes toward the mansion. Ethan stood transfixed.

"Come on, Captain," said Verity. "Let's get out of here. Sam and the others are waiting for you."

"Are they?" The other couple appeared and looked askance at Ethan and Watkins.

"Beautiful spot, wouldn't you say?" Verity noted in an exaggerated Southern drawl. "We'll just be leaving you to it."

Ethan followed Verity from the pond. Verity studied his distracted expression. "You'd best stay out here, Captain. I'll fetch the others."

"You do that, Watkins." Ethan came to his senses and grabbed Watkins's arm. "Not a word about what you saw. Were you spying on me?"

"No, of course not. I was trying to find you. I saw you were . . . busy, so I waited for you to stop kissing the girl. It didn't look like you had any intention of stopping, so when I heard someone coming, I thought I'd best warn you."

Ethan's face colored to a deep red. "You can't tell the others about this, Watkins." Suddenly Ethan's lack of camaraderie with his soldiers seemed palpable. He was in no position to demand favors. Verity saw his anguish, caught as he was between his desires and his propriety. "Please."

Verity smiled. "I saw nothing but a gentle heart. Your secret is safe with me, Captain. Now, and always."

Chapter Four

Garrett Knox sat in a dark corner of Madame Ivy's brothel, his back facing the customers as he drank from a frothy tankard of ale. Ivy herself bustled between customers. Occasionally she glanced Garrett's way, they exchanged a meaningful look, and she continued with her work.

Skillful strains of music set the mood, played on a perfectly tuned piano. A tall, black man sat playing portions of Mozart's Twenty-first Concerto. Well-dressed women sat beside officers. Occasionally, a woman ascended the stairs on an officer's arm. A certain discretion marked Ivy's establishment. No drunken soldiers patronized Ivy's brothel. Less fortunate men waited in line outside the huts of cheaper prostitutes.

A thin, narrow-shouldered man entered the smoky, warm meeting room and looked furtively around, then took his place at the bar. Ivy spotted him, then took another full tankard of ale to Garrett.

She leaned down as she served the drink. Garrett caught her eye. "That's him," she whispered. "Alfred Spears."

Garrett didn't look, but Ivy went to greet the new customer. "What can I get for you, Mister?" Ivy's robust, pleasant voice was purposefully raised to meet Garrett's ears.

"Bourbon," said the man abruptly.

"And can I interest you in—"

"No. Just drink."

"Very well. Your pleasure is mine." The oft-repeated phrase amused her, though she rarely sold herself.

Garrett stole a glance at Alfred Spears, committing the man's shifty appearance to memory. For the next three hours, both Garrett and Alfred Spears waited. Neither seemed satisfied by the evening's outcome. Midnight passed, and Alfred Spears finally left.

As soon as the door closed behind him, Ivy hurried to Garrett's side. She seated herself beside him and shook her head. "What happened?"

"Damned if I know," replied Garrett. "He sure as hell waited there for someone."

"But that someone didn't show," finished Ivy. "Ah, well. Spying is a course that's not meant to run true."

"Apparently not. Damn. You're sure about this, Ivy?"

"Sure as I can be, Major. Spears didn't take much drink tonight for one reason, and that's because he can't handle it. Soused to the gills, he told one of my girls everything, as I told you. He had a hand in a move or two at Antietam. He's been meeting with an officer, and passing information to the rebs. An unsavory fellow, too, from what my girl said he wanted in bed."

Garrett glanced doubtfully at Ivy. She wasn't known for restraint. "What did he want?"

"A whipping," she told him nonchalantly. "Couldn't make up his mind whether he wanted to do it, or have it done to himself. I sent him on his way—told him if he wanted a spanking, he'd have to get it somewhere else."

Garrett grimaced. "Good."

Ivy scanned Garrett's body thoughtfully, with a clinical expression. "Now, if I was a mite younger, I'd show you a thing or two. Hell, maybe you'd show me. But damned if my back's not acting up again. Guess I spent too much of my youth on it."

"Diligence to craft."

"Maybe I could interest you in one of my belles tonight. It's been a long wait, with no results. I'd hate to think you wasted your night for nothing."

Garrett considered Ivy's offer. She ran a professional establishment, and she treated her girls well. She made certain they knew what they were getting into before they joined, and she kept them clean and healthy afterward. If they choose to leave, then Ivy helped them get started in legitimate jobs.

"I'm not saying I couldn't use your services, but I have some men out on a rebel outing tonight, and I want to make sure they get back without trouble."

"You're as bad as your cousin. Young Jared sent four rebels in Yankee uniforms over the river to visit me last week, though he himself didn't attend, more's the pity."

"I, too, missed a chance to socialize with my esteemed cousin. Jared arranged the event tonight. But I'm sure I'll hear about it. Watkins, in particular, must have watched him like a hawk."

"Watkins? Old Sam mentioned a Watkins, too," said Ivy. "Seemed fond of the lad. I think he's missing his own brood, and his Kady."

"Maybe, but Watkins isn't much like Sam's children," said Garrett. "The lad is a lass, Boston-bred, and as crazy as they come."

Ivy stared speechless at Garrett's casual disclosure. "A lady?"

"More or less. You remember Robert Talmadge?"

"Not as well as I'd like," said Ivy. "A handsome fellow, if a bit removed from my place in the world. Unlike yourself, he didn't seem too comfortable crossing over to my side of things."

"No, Robert was hopelessly honorable. But his little sister is a whole other matter."

"His sister? You can't mean . . . it's not possible!"

"I wouldn't have thought so, either," said Garrett. "The girl marched down here from her safe Boston world, accused me of spying, and placed me under arrest."

"Did she now? I expect she's just trying to get your attention."

"I flattered myself with that notion, too. But I was wrong. Verity Talmadge is dead set on proving my guilt. To that end, she's now cavorting amongst rebels with four unsuspecting Union soldiers."

Ivy studied Garrett's expression. "If she's Robert Talmadge's sister, she's probably a fine looker."

Garrett attempted a careless shrug, and Ivy nodded knowingly. "Something tells me you had a good reason for letting her stay."

"Only while things drag here. The girl's in danger, Ivy. I feel it."

"How so?"

"Strange, smiling fellow came looking for her. He gave a false name. I don't know what he wanted, but something tells me she's safer in the army than out.''

"Smiling, you say? Strange. A while back, a man came in, grinning like a fool. Pleasant as all-can-be. Gave me the shudders.''

"Did he ask for her?''

"Nope. Just wanted a drink. No interest in my girls, either. But who'd think a pretty, Boston girl would come here?''

"No one,'' said Garrett. Ivy's words gave him an idea.

"If things heat up, if we're to move against Lee, I can't let her continue as Verrill Watkins. But I can't send her back to Washington, either. It's a lot to ask, Ivy, but can I leave her here?''

"It's nothing to ask! I'd love to care for the poor, little thing.''

"You haven't met her,'' said Garrett. "But I thank you.''

"Love will find you, Garrett Knox. I've seen that. Neither a wanton nor a lady, and she walks in disguise.''

Garrett glanced at Ivy from the corner of his eye, then took another drink of his ale. "Not ghosts again, Ivy?''

"Scoff if you will,'' replied Ivy. "But those as passed to the Great Beyond move in the Unseen Mists around us. I look at you, and I see Beings mulling around, them as are interested in your fate.''

"Ah,'' said Garrett. "How comforting.''

"There's a brownhaired Englishman around you most often.''

"How do you know he's English?''

"He's wearing a red uniform, got his hair tied back. As identification, I expect. Pretty fellow. A bit like you. Not so rugged and rough, though.''

"I trust that's meant as a compliment.''

"I like tough men,'' Ivy assured him.

"So I'm being watched, am I? I hope this man is forgiving.''

"I hope so, too,'' laughed Ivy. "But it's not just you. We've all got our Guardians. There be links to the past everywhere. I wonder who I'll see flitting around your Miss Talmadge?''

"I can't imagine. Who's the craziest figure in history?''

"Bring her here,'' suggested Ivy. "I'm looking forward to meeting the girl.''

"If General Hooker decides to move against Lee, I'll bring her.''

"Looks like you'll be keeping her a while yet. Things aren't likely to change soon. Fighting Joe Hooker talks big, but he ain't got balls where it counts. And I should know.''

Garrett didn't disagree, but his face revealed his gloom over the prospect of another lousy Union commander. "I know."

"You keep trying, Major. It's darkest afore the dawn, they say."

"Maybe," agreed Garrett. "But I'm wondering if we've got a lot more darkness to come before we ever see the light."

Garrett waited by the Rappahannock for the returning pickets. The first light of dawn peeked above the eastern horizon, and still no sign. Garrett began to wonder if they'd been caught, and what would happen to Verity, when he heard them scrambling down the far bank of the river.

Garrett heard Verity's cheerful voice bidding the rebel pickets farewell, and he breathed a sigh of relief. Clothed again in blue, the Union pickets splashed through the water and emerged on the northern side again.

"Thank God," groaned Garrett, with more emotion than intended. "What took you so damned long?"

"We misplaced Hallowell," said Sam. "And it took Watkins a good long while to find him." Garrett eyed Ethan, who said nothing, though he looked uncomfortable. The morning light spread through the trees just as Garrett turned his glance to Verity Talmadge.

For a long while, he just stared. Tears started in his eyes, his lips compressed, his chest jerked with restraint.

"What's the matter with you?" asked Verity indignantly.

Garrett started to speak. He burst into laughter instead. Garrett's reaction infected the others; they laughed, too. A long while passed as Garrett roared with laughter. Tears rolled down his strong face as Verity waited with her hands on her hips.

"I don't see what's so funny," she said. This brought a howl of laughter from the others. Even Ethan grinned and shook his head.

"That's quite a growth," Garrett managed to utter between convulsions of laughter.

"Do you mean my mustache?" asked Verity. Garrett nodded. "Gordy said it would make me look older."

"Ah."

"The reb dared say Watkins here looks like a girl," Sam told Garrett. "Watkins laid him out and gave him a sound thrashing."

"Did he?" Garrett's eyes watered with amusement. "That took nerve, to challenge Watkins in any way."

"It did, indeed," agreed Verity.

"So," said Garrett as they headed back for the camp, "tell me about your outing. Did you see Jared? And you, Watkins, I trust you danced to your heart's content?"

Verity eyed him suspiciously. "I enjoyed myself very much, thank you."

"Watkins proved himself just a good with a dancing partner as he is with a musket," said Sam. "Quite a gentleman."

"You danced, did you, Watkins?"

"A reel or two," said Verity nonchalantly.

"Danced? The lad took a tiny, bespectacled miss out onto the floor, whirled her around, and put us all to shame." Sam patted Watkins's shoulder proudly.

Garrett pressed his lips together to restrain a new outburst of mirth. "I wish I'd been there." And that was an understatement.

Ethan and the others went to their tents, but Verity continued on with Garrett.

"What about Jared?" asked Garrett.

"He was there," said Verity. "Women surrounded him, like moths around a candle. Don't think he cared much for any. He seems to have set his heart on a Yankee spy."

"What?" Garrett stopped and stared at Verity.

"That's what he told me."

"He told you?"

"Yes," said Verity. "At the punch bowl. I mentioned his assortment of women, and he said he only wanted one. A spy he saw one night. Men are strange, aren't they? Here he's got the choice of Virginia's prettiest girls, and he wants his enemy."

"That sounds like Jared. Although I've never known his romantic attachments to last very long."

"There's always one," sighed Verity. "One you can't forget, no matter how you try."

"I'll promote you to colonel's rank, Garrett. Whatever it takes to get you back where you belong."

Verity hovered outside Garrett's tent, eavesdropping without remorse on his conversation. Brigadier General Stoneman spoke privately to Garrett Knox. The other Mass 20th soldiers waited with interest, but no one other than Verity dared brazenly listen. They waited for her disclosures eagerly, however.

"What's going on in there, Watkins?" asked Sam.

"Ssh," said Verity. "I can't hear when you're talking."

Verity heard the sound of glasses, liquid poured. "Thank you," said the general.

"I prefer the cavalry," admitted Garrett. "And that's probably where I'd have the best effect."

"He prefers the cavalry," Verity relayed to Sam. Her face puckered at this. What if Garrett left the 20th?

"Damn," said Sam.

"Damn sure you'd have more effect in my corps," the general told Garrett. "The Federal cavalry is Hooker's top concern. He's withholding my promotion until I prove we're a force to challenge the rebs. Sixty horses in my cavalry came from your farm, Garrett. They're the best we've got. But I need you, too."

Verity shook her head and sighed. "The general's buttering him up."

"Hell's bells," said Sam. "The major's got to look beyond flattery."

"You heard about the exchange between Fitz Lee and our Averell in February?" said the general. "Apparently Fitz's Uncle Robert thought we'd be coming over soon. Fitz Lee came over at Kelly's Ford, routed Averell's regiment, then left a note telling him to put up his sword and go home. Taunted him a bit on his quick retreat, too. Left it with a challenge to return the visit with a sack of coffee."

"How exciting," murmured Verity outside the tent.

Apparently, Garrett Knox thought so, too. "A tempting offer."

"I guessed you'd feel that way, especially since your young cousin was among them. Like you, my friend, Jared Knox is probably bored. It's been a long winter," said the general. "Averell wants the raid tomorrow. We're taking three thousand troopers, crossing at Kelly's Ford, and giving them some of their own."

Verity frowned. This must be the raid Garrett wanted Massachusetts sharpshooters for, the raid she shot her way into as Watkins, and the perfect opportunity to watch Garrett in action. Catch him red-handed.

"You're coming along, aren't you?" asked the general. So much for a firm command. Why everyone gave Garrett Knox a free rein was beyond Verity.

"I wouldn't miss it," said Garrett. "I'm bringing a few of my men along."

"Very good. Maybe the action will inspire you to transfer back to the cavalry."

"That is my intention. I know it's my duty to serve where I'm most effective—"

"What's stopping you? You can lead infantry into a bloodbath, Garrett. I saw you do it at Fredericksburg. I commanded an infantry corps there, too. Won a brevet for gallantry. I know what it's like, and by God, I don't want to see it again."

"I've never seen braver men than those who marched up that hill," said Garrett quietly.

Tears started in Verity's eyes. Fredericksburg, where Adrian died.

"You're a damned good officer, Garrett. But when you face that fire . . . there's not a man alive who can make a difference. Do you think that won't happen again? Antietam, Fredericksburg . . . The rebs aren't quitting. Hell, right now they're winning the war."

"It will happen again," said Garrett, and Verity's heart chilled.

"Then go where you can make a difference. On horseback, reconnaissance, tactical movements . . . not this."

Verity's breath held, Garrett didn't respond at once.

"When my duty here is fulfilled, I'll transfer," agreed Garrett. "But I have business here beyond tactics."

"What business?" asked the general, echoing Verity's thoughts.

"It's too early to say. When the time comes, when I have something to report—"

"Don't take too long," said the general. "The cavalry needs you."

The general started out the door, and Verity hopped back, whistling casually and fiddling with her musket. Sam and the other listeners did the same. They saluted the general, who nodded. Garrett came out of the tent.

"You can come in now, Watkins." Verity bit her lip.

"I was just—"

"Eavesdropping," finished Garrett. "Sam, gather my sharpshooters. Where's Hallowell?"

"God knows," sighed Sam. "He missed drill this morning, if you can believe it. Left a lieutenant to handle it. Not that I'm sorry about his absence, but the young fellow's been acting a mite odd."

"Everyone has moods," put in Verity hurriedly. Garrett glanced at her suspiciously.

"Not Hallowell," said Sam. "Or I wouldn't have thought it, anyhow. Them blue blood's as crazy as they come, for sure."

"That much is certain," agreed Garrett. "Watkins, come with me."

Verity followed Garrett into his tent. "Yes, Sir? About the raid? When do I get my horse?"

"You don't."

"Sir?"

"Have you fought on horseback, Watkins?"

"Not exactly." She'd raced Westley and Adrian on horseback, and won. She'd even shot a musket from horseback, shattering watermelons as she galloped past just to prove she could do it. Adrian had been impressed, but she couldn't tell Garrett that fact.

"I think it's best if you remain here."

Verity wasn't easily put off. Here was a chance to observe Garrett in rebel territory. Maybe he planned a meeting with Jared. Maybe he'd prove himself a hero. Fear didn't enter her heart. She liked riding, she could shoot. . . .

Men died in battle, but Verity had never seen this firsthand. It was illusion, offering excitement and adventure to a girl whose only fear was boredom.

"You're letting Sam and Ethan go," said Verity. "Sam's never fought on horseback, either."

"Young McCaffrey is staying behind."

"Only because he couldn't hit the target."

"You're staying, Watkins. I'm a major, an officer. You're . . . a Watkins. Don't argue with superiors."

Verity's mind twisted around a way to accompany the others on the raid. Obviously, she wouldn't convince Garrett by reason. But if another officer ordered her. . . .

"As you say, Major. Sorry to miss it, though."

Verity found Ethan standing at the edge of the campsite, staring over the Rappahannock. "Have you seen Major Wallingford?" Ethan didn't hear her voice. "Captain Hallowell."

Ethan looked around and sighed heavily. "Watkins. Yes, what is it?"

"I'm looking for Major Wallingford. Do you know where he is?"

"He left me in charge."

"I see," said Verity. "So naturally you're gazing across the river. Are you going over again?"

"Should I?" asked Ethan wistfully. "My heart never came back, Watkins. It's over there, in her arms."

"I think your brain stayed over there, too," said Verity. "You missed drill. I told a lieutenant you ordered him to drill us."

"Thank you, Watkins. That was good of you."

Ethan sounded vague, and Verity felt tempted to slap him, to bring him to his senses. "I hope you don't act this way on the raid."

"The raid?"

"Yes, Captain. The raid. We're going tomorrow morning."

"Are we?" Ethan's expression changed. He looked thoughtful and sad. "Her brothers fight for Virginia. Her father, her cousins . . . what if I killed one of those men?"

"The way you're acting, you couldn't hit an elephant broadside. I wouldn't worry. Pull yourself together, Captain. Bess understands. Remember what you're fighting for."

"The Union, yes."

"No. You're fighting for the rights of all men, whatever their color, to live as free men. For all men to live in honor, each according to their own merit, not by skin color or the land of their ancestry."

"What?"

"The Union means nothing if our purpose isn't the freedom of all men," said Verity. "That's what you're fighting for, Ethan. Now, where's Wallingford?"

"I saw him heading out of camp," said Ethan.

"Which way?" asked Verity. Ethan pointed west.

Verity hunted for Dan Wallingford all around the camp. She passed Joe Hooker's headquarters, and Madame Ivy's notorious brothel. The brothel was suspiciously near the general's headquarters. She asked everyone she passed if they'd seen Wallingford, but they either didn't know him or he hadn't passed that way.

Verity had nearly given up when a dark coach stopped just beyond the camp, and Dan Wallingford got out. Verity waited, hoping to catch him when he passed by. A lean-faced man inside the coach closed the door, and it pulled away, leaving Wallingford by the roadside.

Verity wondered why it didn't deposit him closer to the 20th Mass. Maybe the roads were too rutted for a coach.

Wallingford walked toward her, and Verity called to him. "Major Wallingford!"

Dan Wallingford started at Watkins's voice, his eyes flashing black. A quick smile replaced his angry expression. "Watkins! What are you doing out here?"

"Looking for you, Sir," said Verity. "Having trouble with my horse."

"Your horse?"

"He's gone lame, and I'm afraid I'll miss the raid."

"We can't have that." Wallingford seemed anxious to treat Watkins in a pleasant manner. Verity hadn't noticed any particular affection from Garrett's stepbrother before. "What can I do to help you?"

"I wondered if you could get me another."

"I could, but it's almost dark now, Watkins," said Wallingford. "You'll have to pick him up tomorrow, and that might be too late. We're leaving at dawn."

"I'll catch up if I have to. But I need a horse."

"Very well," said Dan. "I'll see that you've got a mount waiting."

"Thank you. I'm glad you could help me."

"Why didn't you ask Major Knox?" Dan sounded a little suspicious. Verity shrugged casually.

"He's off somewhere. I thought you'd be more inclined to help me, considering."

Dan's eyes narrowed, but he didn't ask what Verrill Watkins 'considered.'

"You won't mention my request, will you?"

"No need. It seems we've reached an understanding, Watkins," Dan added enigmatically, though he didn't sound pleased. "Let's leave it at that, shall we?"

"That's all I'm wanting," said Verity, confused by his tone. "Nothing more."

"Good," said Wallingford. "I'd hate for the situation to grow out of proportion."

Verity walked with Dan back to the campsite. She didn't understand his cryptic words. Maybe he'd been visiting Madame Ivy's brothel, and didn't want anyone to know why he'd left Ethan in charge. He seemed ill at ease, and Verity began to wish she'd asked another officer.

Verity woke with a start. In a flash, she realized the sharpshooters had left without her. "Hell's bells!" She hopped out of bed and yanked on her uniform. Verity raced to the stables and found her horse, a lithe chestnut who seemed intent on his morning hay. Verity tacked him up and hauled him from his breakfast. She scrambled on his back and galloped after the raiders.

Verity caught up to Averell's three thousand troopers at Kelly's Ford. The shallow water made ideal crossing, but as the first horses plunged across, the rebel pickets raised their fire. Muskets cracked and burst back and forth across the river. Men fell, horses stumbled and neighed frantically.

Verity pulled her mount to a halt and stared. Smoke swirled around the lead riders. She saw a horse struck by a bullet. It reared, and the rider fell. Verity couldn't move. The deafening noise, the screams, the shouted commands . . . she was terrified.

"What do I do?" One thing seemed sure and strong, and that was Garrett Knox. She couldn't see him anywhere, nor any of her friends.

Verity's hands shook and her fingers felt numb, but she guided her horse through the rear of the melee. Finally she saw him. Astride a huge bay horse, Garrett Knox calmly directed his men. With precision and logic, Garrett's men surrounded the rebel pickets. The Federal troopers began taking prisoners.

No one seemed terrified. The men seemed calm. Not as calm as Garrett, maybe, but no one felt like Verity. *It's nothing,* she told herself. *They're used to this. I'll get used to it, too.*

Verity decided to hang back until the threat of being sent home was well past. She kept a safe distance behind Garrett and his men, though she kept the group of Massachusetts soldiers in sight. She saw Ethan's blond hair. Sam laughing atop a heavy-boned gray. John rode a scruffy, solid-looking horse that resembled its rider with eerie precision.

A third of the Federal cavalry remained behind to protect the rear. The troops crossed a large pasture and set up a defensive position behind a stone wall. The morning was only half over, and Verity felt as if a week had passed.

Verity waited until Garrett left his men, then joined the others. "Watkins!" exclaimed Sam. "Thought you'd been left behind."

"Problem with my horse," Verity explained, but Sam grinned.

"The major told you to stay behind, lad. You'll be catching hell if he sees you."

"Then he'd best not see me." Verity fingered her musket. "I got Major Wallingford's permission, anyway. And one major's as good as another."

"Like hell," said Sam. "But I guess it'll do. It got you here, anyway. How do you like it so far?"

"Is it over?" asked Verity. Both Sam and John laughed.

"Hell, no. Don't know why Averell stopped us, though. We was doing fine. You'd think a West Pointer would have more guts. Major Knox said the same. He wanted to press on, but I guess Averell's worried about confronting his old buddy, Fitz Hugh Lee."

A rush of exclamation rose throughout the Federal troopers. Verity saw the reason in a flood of terror. Fitz Lee's men galloped toward them.

"Get ready, boy," said Sam. "Send 'em back where they came from."

Verity loaded her musket, but her hands trembled violently.

"March seventeenth," said Sam. "St. Patrick's Day. Hell of a way for an Irishman to celebrate."

Riding four abreast, the rebel cavalry charged the Union position. Verity knelt beside Sam, sheltered behind the stone wall. The motions and commands of drill helped, now.

"Hold your fire." Ethan Hallowell dismounted and paced up and down his line, tall and brave, golden hair shining in the sun. Despite the lack of respect he inspired, every man obeyed his orders.

The rebel horsemen thundered nearer. Verity saw their faces, their grim expressions ... she saw a man with a shovel beard leading them, a young soldier smiling as he charged. . . .

"Fire!" Muskets cracked all around, and a veil of smoke distorted Verity's vision. When the cloud cleared, the rebels were upon them. Verity fired without aiming. Terror motivated her. She didn't wonder if her shot hit anything.

"Reload!" shouted Ethan. "Fire at will."

Musket fire blazed hot like a volcanic rain. Verity loaded and fired again and again. Her actions took on a will of their own though her brain went numb. Verity saw the smiling young rebel nearly upon their line. She stared but couldn't fire. The Union muskets roared, and the rebel fell from his horse. Still smiling.

Verity's heart went cold, her breath stopped. She'd seen the boy die, fall to the earth with a sick thud in front of her. The rebels spun around and galloped away. The blue fire slacked, then ended.

"Well, that was quick," remarked Sam.

"Quick?" It had felt like an eternity to Verity. She still stared at the rebel's lifeless body, lying in a distorted heap among the bodies of horses and men. Some writhed in death's final throes, others lay motionless.

Medics searched the wounded rebels, dragging those still alive behind their lines for what minimal treatment they could offer. Verity couldn't take her eyes from the dead rebel boy.

"What's the matter, Watkins? Did you know the fellow?"

Verity shook her head.

"Doesn't look much older than yourself," observed Sam, assuming this fact provoked Watkins reaction.

Verity's stomach heaved without warning, and she threw up.

"Casualties?" called Ethan Hallowell.

"Just Watkins here, and that ain't serious."

"Good work, men." Ethan seemed remarkably calm, and Verity eyed him suspiciously. Sam looked up at the young captain with misgivings. Ethan wasn't given to complimenting his soldiers' actions.

"Mount up," called a familiar voice. Verity spied Garrett riding toward them. She hid her head, and he didn't notice her.

"Going after them, are we?" asked Sam.

"We are," answered Garrett, his voice ringing with pleasure.

Garrett Knox galloped along the line, magnificent on his powerful bay. Verity watched him ride away.

"What an animal!" sighed Sam. Verity thought the rider more impressive. "Mount up, Watkins. Appears the Major didn't notice you just yet. He will, though. Mark my words, there'll be hell to pay when he learns you've disobeyed him."

Verity didn't answer. She hopped onto her horse's back and fell in line beside John. He smiled and nodded, though as usual he said nothing.

"Where are we going?"

"Looks like the rebs have crossed yonder river," Sam told her, gesturing to a creek that branched westward from the Rappahannock. "Now it's our turn."

"For what?"

"The major's leading us in a countercharge."

"He's *what?*"

"The rebs charged us, now we charge them. Never fought on horseback, have you, Watkins?"

"Neither have you." Verity's fingers went numb, but even as the fear surfaced to squelch her voice, Garrett Knox urged his group into a gallop.

"Forward, Gentlemen!"

"Stay behind me, Watkins," ordered Sam. Verity didn't argue.

They galloped over a mile. It flew by in seconds. Verity kept her balance astride her lithe mount, but that was all. She closed her eyes, expecting death. When the rebels opened fire, her horse stumbled, snorted, then galloped onward.

From horseback, the Union cavalry fired, reined in, fired again, all in a haze of musket smoke. Bullets whizzed by her head. Verity ducked after they passed, a reflex she couldn't control. She never touched her musket.

"Retreat!" came the command, but not from Garrett Knox.

"What?" Verity heard Garrett's angry voice, questioning his commander's order.

"Back to the wall, Major. Get them back."

Verity opened her eyes and saw Garrett wheel his horse around, his face dark with anger. She wondered why. Retreat seemed incredibly sensible at this point. She turned her horse, who seemed equally relieved to be leaving the foray.

They rode back to the stone wall and returned to their former positions. Verity left her weary horse and sat down beside Sam.

"Now what?"

"We wait for their return visit."

"Again?"

"I expect it'll go this way until nearly dark," said Sam. "Don't you think so, John?"

John nodded, but said nothing.

"Oh," said Verity.

"The major didn't like the way it went," said Sam, to John's agreement. "Averell pulled back our charge before we did any real damage."

"That's true," piped in Ethan Hallowell. To his soldiers' surprise, he seated himself beside them, stretching out his long legs and leaning back against the wall.

"You heard something, Captain?" asked Sam.

"Major Knox is in a state of fury," replied Ethan, relishing his information. "The commanders gave him the first charge, free run, then called him back before we'd inflicted significant casualties."

"It felt significant to me," Verity murmured.

"Except for you, Watkins," said Ethan cheerfully. "Fighting from horseback is exhilarating, isn't it? Everything moves so much faster than in the infantry."

"So why'd we pull back?" wondered Sam.

"Averell heard that Jeb Stuart and his artillerist, John Pelham, are on the field. Pelham's here because he was courting a girl, and Stuart can't resist entering any fray."

"How do you know why they're here?" asked Sam.

Ethan shrugged, but his face colored. He offered no further explanation.

Verity considered the day's activities for a while. Nothing made sense. "So what good does any of this do?"

The men stared at her, but no quick answer came. "What do you mean, Watkins?" asked Sam.

"This fighting, charging, and countercharging. What did it accomplish?"

Again, silence.

"We crossed over, set up here, and waited. They charged. We shot, and they ran back to set up across the creek. So we charged them, then came back here. I see dead men, wounded men . . . why?"

Ethan cleared his throat. "Well, Watkins, we're showing them we can hold our own against their cavalry."

"I expect they know that already," said Verity. "And now that we've proven it—"

"Hell, now, lad," spouted Sam. "'Ours is not to reason why—'"

"'Ours but to do or die?'" finished Verity.

"Yes," said Ethan, though he seemed less certain.

"That's not much of an answer."

"Why'd you join up, Watkins?" asked Sam.

Verity hesitated. *To prove Garrett Knox a traitor,* didn't seem a good answer. She thought about what her reasons would have been if she were a boy. What mattered? Verity remembered Robert's words the day he told her he was going to fight. . . .

"I joined to aid in the creation of a country where all men are free. Where all men have the right to control their own destinies, to be the dominant force in their lives, to be responsible for themselves."

Sam, John, and Ethan stared at Verrill Watkins in astonishment. John frowned and shook his head. Sam chewed his lip. Ethan's lips parted. To Verity's astonishment, tears started in his blue eyes.

"Thank you, Watkins," he said softly. "I heard Frederick Douglass say words like that, and my heart moved. In the light of recent events, I'd forgotten. Thank you for reminding me."

Ethan rose and walked away, his face riddled with emotion.

"You don't say," mumbled Sam, and he fiddled with his musket.

"You got a lot to learn, boy," grumbled John, though he didn't explain his objection to Watkins's words.

Verity intended to pursue John's argument, but Garrett Knox walked by, distracting her attention. "Where's he going?" Garrett walked in the direction of the horses. Sam shrugged, and Verity got up to follow Garrett, her musket slung over her shoulder.

Verity watched Garrett as he found his horse, and her breath held. Garrett sighed. "Another futile battle." Garrett laid his broad hand on his horse's muscled neck. The horse nuzzled him, then returned to his feed.

"Nothing changes," Garrett told the horse. "How long will it take to see an end?"

He sounded weary, a pain Verity couldn't understand. Her heart moved with pity. Garrett took a bag from his jacket and stuffed it in his saddlebag.

"Here's to you, Jared Knox." Garrett led the horse away, then tied him to a tree apart from the others.

Verity's heart stopped. No. It couldn't be.

Garrett left the horse and returned to his men. Verity hid herself deeper in the bushes. She covered herself in leaves and branches. And waited. . . .

* * *

Artillery shells flashed and roared overhead as the Union and Confederate regiments exchanged long-range assaults. The afternoon wore on, with an occasional cavalry charge, but Verity remained in the bushes.

It's my imagination. He wouldn't attempt anything this brazen. Just as Verity started to extract herself from her hiding place, a tall, goldenhaired man walked toward her. Verity held her breath. Jared Knox, dressed in Yankee blue, walked idly through the Yankee position . . . he walked to Garrett's huge bay horse.

Verity's breath came in small gasps. Her throat was constricted as tears blocked her vision. Jared's presence revealed the truth: Garrett Knox was a spy.

Jared didn't hesitate. He knew where to look. He opened Garrett's saddlebags and withdrew the bag, then put in another. He chuckled, patted the horse, then disappeared in the forest, heading back across the creek to his own side.

Pain racked Verity, and her head ached. She'd seen it, but she couldn't accept it. How dare Garrett Knox seem so strong, so honorable and brave? How could he speak such beautiful words about the rights of man, then betray them all this way?

Verity squeezed her eyes tight. She saw her brother, she saw Westley as he lay dying, she remembered Adrian Knox—how they all had adored Garrett. How *she* had adored him, even from afar!

Verity loaded Westley's musket. Her expression turned grim and determined as she waited for Garrett's return.

Evening's long shadows crossed the pasture, darkening the creek where the rebels held their position. Garrett went to his horse, opened the saddlebag, and found Jared's gift.

"Stop right there! Don't move!"

"Oh, no. Not—"

"That's right, Major. You're done for, this time."

"Watkins." Garrett turned to see Verity scramble from the bushes, her musket poised, her face puckered with fury.

"Didn't I tell you to remain at camp?"

Verity ignored his comment. "Drop your revolver." Garrett did so. "Hand it over."

"The revolver? You just told me to drop it."

"The sack," said Verity. "Do it, now!"

Garrett tossed her Jared's sack, which she caught in midair. Verity adjusted her musket under her arm and tore open the bag. Tobacco leaves fell everywhere. Garrett sighed at the loss.

A slip of paper fell from the bag, too. Verity picked it up. *"Good coffee, better tobacco. Next time, pick your brew more carefully.* Code? Probably marked in acid."

"This has gone far enough. Miss Talmadge, you're going home."

Verity's mouth dropped. "What? You know who I am?"

"Who else?" Garrett took a step toward her, but Verity aimed her musket at him.

"Not another step! I've caught you red-handed. I saw your cousin leave this incriminating note, I saw you leave one for him. If that doesn't prove you guilty—"

"It proves my cousin is fairly critical when it comes to coffee, but little else." Garrett took another step. Verity's hands trembled, but she prepared to shoot him.

"If you're going to shoot me, I'd appreciate if you aimed higher. As you've got it there, you'll blast a hole in my gut. Death is rather slow that way."

Verity adjusted her aim. "I don't want to kill you. So please surrender."

An artillery blast thundered overhead, a parting shot from the rebels across the creek. It overshot the stone wall, careening through the woods behind the horses, splintering branches like firewood.

Wood shattered above her head. As Garrett leapt toward her, a branch cracked and fell. It struck her head, and she collapsed. Garrett's pulse froze.

Garrett didn't wait for Averell's retreat across the Rappahannock. He picked up Verity's limp body and carried her on his horse's back to Falmouth. She wasn't dead—her even breaths told him that—but she didn't stir, even as he galloped through the shallows at Kelly's Ford.

Garrett carried her to safety, but on waking Verity might find her new environment even stranger than the army.

Chapter Five

Garrett carried Verity over to the soft bed. She stirred and opened her eyes. "Are you going to kiss me now?"

Garrett eyed her doubtfully. "Just now, I thought I'd put you in bed."

"But we're not even married yet." No real objection sounded in Verity's voice. "Very well, but I don't think my parents would approve. But they're gone, aren't they? Like Robert . . . all I have is you."

"Your mood has shifted, I gather." The last time he looked into her blue-gray eyes, she had held a gun and threatened his life.

Her lids drifted across her eyes, her black lashes casting tiny shadows over her high cheekbones. Her pink lips curved sleepily. With an astonishing depth of tenderness, Verity pressed her lips against Garrett's.

Garrett's motion stopped when he felt the gentle touch of her mouth against his. He was bent over, about to put her on Ivy's bed. Her lips parted, her tongue flicked to taste him.

She's really lost her mind this time. This knowledge didn't cool his reaction, however. Every nerve in Garrett's body stirred, then leapt to fire. He returned her soft kiss with an ardor he hadn't intended.

"I take it the girl's awake." Ivy's voice startled Garrett, and he dropped Verity onto the bed. A small frown twisted Verity's mouth, but she closed her eyes, seeming to drift back into sleep.

"Ivy," said Garrett, his color deepening when he saw the madam's grin. "She's a bit . . . disoriented."

"I'd say she's got a fair handle on things." Ivy looked down at the girl. "Lord Above, the child is filthy!"

She glanced at Garrett. "You sure this is Rob Talmadge's little sister?"

"I'm sure," said Garrett. Ivy looked back at Verity.

"We'll get her cleaned up. Good bone structure, I see that. A little on the skinny side, though."

"A lot on the crazy side. Take care of her, Ivy. Robert Talmadge was a good man. The girl nearly got herself killed today, because I hadn't the sense to send her back where she belongs."

"By the looks of it, she don't belong in Boston, either."

Verity opened one eye and looked between Ivy and Garrett. "Boston? Am I in Boston? Good. Then it was all a dream."

Her face scrunched up as she considered this. "How much was a dream? Are Adrian and Westley still alive? Is Robert downstairs? I suppose he's readying himself for an outing with Candace?" She clucked her tongue disapprovingly, then peered at Ivy. "Who are you? A nurse? Have I been sick?"

"I'm the owner of this establishment," said Ivy. "You got a little bump on the head, Sweetie."

"A big bump on the head," corrected Garrett. "A tree nearly took your life, girl. And maybe saved mine."

Verity looked confused, then furious. "You!"

Verity struggled to sit up. Her eyes spun around in their sockets and she fell back onto her pillow. Garrett shook his head. "I guess she remembers."

Verity turned a glaring eye to him. "I remember. What'd you do with the note, you villain?"

"A minute ago, she was kissing you," Ivy laughed. "A girl's heart is nothing if not fickle."

"I never kissed him. How absurd! That was a dream." Garrett smiled knowingly, and Verity's cheeks flushed. She mumbled incoherently and closed her eyes.

Garrett stood beside her bed. "I've got to go, Ivy. Keep her here, and see that she doesn't leave until I decide what to do with her."

"Decide? I thought you were sending her back to Boston."

"Maybe. If I could be certain of her safety there—"

"What else can you do?"

"God knows."

"She can stay here, but I'm not sure I've got the power to control her."

"Where am I?"

Verity looked around the room. Garrett watched her eyes narrow in utmost suspicion at the burgundy velvet upholstery. She sniffed, probably at Ivy's strong perfume. Her eyes narrowed still more. "Where am I?"

"I'll leave you two alone." Ivy hurried from Verity's bedroom, and Garrett sighed.

"You're in a bedroom. At Madame Ivy's brothel, quite near General Hooker's headquarters—"

"What?" Verity shot up in bed, shocked beyond further words.

"Ivy's brothel. I couldn't think of anywhere else to bring you."

"So you put me in a brothel? No, I can't be here." Verity struggled from the bed, put her feet on the floor and tried to stand. Her knees buckled, and Garrett caught her.

"You *can* be here, and you are." Garrett set her back on the bed, but he didn't let her go. Verity swallowed hard.

"Release me," she ordered.

"I thought you might want to kiss me again."

"I did no such thing."

"Ah. Must have been my imagination." Garrett sat beside her on the bed and eased the covers back over her body.

"If you knew about me and Watkins . . . why'd you let me stay?"

"Because you're in danger, Verity."

"From you?"

"Not from me, you little idiot. As tempting as it's been, I've resisted the impulse to kill you. A man calling himself Dave Delaney appeared the night after you arrested me, looking for you. Told me Candace hired him to find you."

"She wouldn't dare!"

"So she said. He went to her, too, saying the authorities were after you. She convinced him you went to Paris."

"Why Paris?"

"For the latest fashions, and to be courted by princes."

"That hardly seems likely. I hope this Delaney person doesn't know me."

"I hope so, too."

"I still don't see the threat," said Verity. "What could he want from me? Does Candace think he had something to do with those letters I received after Westley died?"

"She mentioned that," said Garrett. "I'm not sure, either. It's just a feeling I got, speaking to that smiling man. Something tells me he's more likely to hurt you than any rebel."

"So you'll let me stay." It wasn't a question.

"Now that you've accepted my protection, I see no reason—"

"Who says I've accepted that?"

"I assumed." Garrett sighed. Where Verity Talmadge was concerned, assuming anything was a mistake.

"Did you tell the men about me? I suppose it won't ever be the same with them, will it?"

"I haven't told them yet, if only because I'd have to explain why I let you stay."

"They wouldn't be my friends anymore, would they? It is so pleasant, to live with them. You can't imagine, because you're not a girl. Men treat you differently. As Verrill, they accepted me."

"This is a frightening thought, but I understand you."

"It was awful, though," she went on. "The battle. I was most ill, you know. I vomited."

"Did you? How revolting," said Garrett, though he smiled. "If I'd known you were there . . . tell me you didn't ride in the charge."

"I did," said Verity. "I closed my eyes through most of it. I guess I'm not as brave as I thought. I knew how to shoot from horseback. Adrian taught me."

"Did he? What in hell was that boy thinking?"

"That was before the war really started, before Bull Run," said Verity. "They were excited, then. Nothing had changed."

Verity fell silent. Garrett pushed a tangled lock of hair from her brow. "You're brave, Miss Talmadge. Bravery seems to be lack of sanity, and you've got that in force."

Verity didn't argue. "Today, I thought that, too."

"You're not a usual young lady, for certain."

"That's true. I liked it better here than in Boston or Washington. Candace nurses at the hospital, but I wasn't a very good nurse. We waited and waited. I hate waiting. We heard about Antietam, and we waited for the lists. You have no idea how long it takes every day to pass. We heard about Robert, and time stopped . . . two days later, we learned Westley was shot, too.''

"You've been through a lot, Verity.''

"I've never understood how Westley got shot when the battle was supposedly over.''

"No? Well, I'll tell you something, Miss Talmadge. No one understood. They said it must have been some rebel sharpshooter taking his last shot as we backed off. But I know damned well the rebs were no where around then.''

"What are you saying?''

"I'm saying that you're right, Verity. There is a spy in my regiment. But, as God as my witness, it's not me.''

Verity's eyes widened. "Why should I believe you? I saw Jared Knox with your horse. He left a note.''

"Which was just as it seemed, a note to a cousin. It must have looked suspicious to you, and it's a wonder you didn't shoot him then and there—''

"I wanted you, not him.'' Verity's cheeks flushed and Garrett smiled.

"I'm glad. Jared is as dear to me as a brother.''

Verity cleared her throat, looking tense. "You say there's a spy. Who?''

"If I knew that, I'd arrest him and go back to the Maryland Cavalry.''

"So that's why you're in Robert's regiment?''

"Robert told me something was wrong. He hinted just before Antietam that he knew something, but he wasn't ready to say. Then he disappeared. Adrian was worked up about something, too, but he told me he wanted to handle it himself. Westley told him someone was spying. They fought about it, then Westley was shot in the back . . . that shot came from a soldier in blue.''

"You have no idea who it was?''

"None.'' Garrett paused, but he didn't say more.

"You can't send me away,'' decided Verity. "I can help you find out who—''

"Absolutely not. No. If anyone can botch up my investigation, it's you.''

"Maybe I wasn't so impressive today. But Verrill Watkins can find out a lot that you can't. Everyone pays attention to you. I'm virtually ignored.''

"That may be true. My rank makes me visible. But I can't risk your safety again."

"I won't go into battle again, I promise. I saw enough today to last a lifetime. But you can't send me home. You can put me on a train, but you can't keep me on it all the way to Boston. I'll come back, and sneak in again. I had no trouble the first time. This time, I won't get caught."

"I won't send you home. You'll stay here, with Ivy. Where I can check on you as I see fit."

"You can't mean to leave me in a brothel," said Verity. "I hope Ivy has a sure lock to keep me in. Otherwise, I'm not staying a minute. I'll be back in my regiment just as soon as I please."

"And if I decided to warn the men about you?"

"You can't warn every regiment in the army."

"Oh, yes, I can."

"I'll make up a new disguise."

"No need, Miss Talmadge. I'm going to regret this, but I'll keep you with me, where you can't get into any more trouble."

Verity's eyes brightened. "You'll let me stay?"

"For a while. But I want your word, your solemn promise, to stay out of battle."

"Given!"

"Very well," sighed Garrett. "I'll assume, however foolishly, that you have the good sense to stay out of the fighting."

"I do." Verity's face tightened thoughtfully, her lips curved to one side. "I would have sworn I'd be braver. But I was terrified. I couldn't think straight, and I could barely shoot."

"Miss Talmadge, you've just described how every soldier feels the first time he finds himself in battle. You're no different. You didn't run, which is better than some. You didn't crack, possibly because you're already over the edge. A man, or a woman, gets used to battle. You do what you have to do."

"Maybe so," said Verity. "But I thought it was the end of the world. The others stayed so calm. Sam even seemed to enjoy himself. And Ethan, I know he has mixed feelings, but he never faltered."

" 'Mixed feelings?' " said Garrett.

"Oh, well . . . it's nothing. I just admired him today, that's all."

Garrett studied Verity's guilty expression. So she 'admired' Ethan Hallowell, did she? Garrett withstood a tremor of jealousy. Despite his doubts, Garrett liked the young officer. Ethan fought well, and a certain innocence marked his character. Appearances could be deceiving, however.

"How long will I stay here?"

"Until I'm satisfied that you're well."

She puffed an impatient breath. "What will it take to satisfy you?"

Garrett's brow lifted, and he smiled. "That remains to be seen."

"I feel a little weak. A day or so here might be pleasant. Of course, I can't go downstairs."

"Why not?"

Verity's eyes widened. "My parents are watching me. From the Otherworld. I'm sure of it. Can you imagine what they'd think if they saw me wandering around a brothel?"

"I know Robert didn't care much for it."

"My brother never went into a brothel."

"Oh, yes, he did." Garrett saw her face whiten, and he patted her shoulder. "For a glass of beer, Miss Talmadge. He was thoroughly horrified by the 'invitations' he received. And loyal to the end to Candace."

"I should hope so. Maybe Candace is a bit dull, but she truly loves him. Anyway, I'm not worried about Robert watching me, because he's not dead. Only Mama and Father can see me from the Other Side."

Verity looked pale. Garrett didn't want to argue with her. Not now. But the chances of Robert Talmadge still being alive were nil.

"I know you don't believe it," guessed Verity. "But he'll come back one day, and everything will be all right."

"No rebel prison listed him as captured."

"They made a mistake, perhaps. I know my brother very well. I would have felt his death. He was my father, my mother . . . everything. I *know* he's alive."

Verity spoke with such conviction that Garrett almost believed her, despite overwhelming evidence to the contrary. "I hope you're right. Until we know for certain, one way or another, I suppose both are true, and neither. But the fact remains, we may never learn what happened to your brother."

"If we never learn, that means he died," said Verity. "So we'll learn. You'll see."

Garrett rose from her bed, though he found it surprisingly hard to leave her. "Ivy offered you a bath. I suggest you take it. If I let you be 'Watkins' again, you can go back to your grime later."

"I might wash," said Verity. "Though I rather like a more natural look. I haven't had to brush my hair a hundred times, nor fiddle with dresses and corsets and stockings. I like men's drawers much better. And trousers—do you know what it's like to wear a crinoline?"

Garrett laughed. "I can't say that I do, no."

"I'm not pretty now." Verity sounded pleased with the assessment. "Nobody notices me, no one acts foolish. Praise God, I don't have to act like a lady."

"That must have been a severe trial," said Garrett. "And one accomplished only with great effort."

Verity nodded her head vigorously. "It's good of you to understand. Adrian and Westley wanted me to wear fancy dresses and say girlish things—after they came home from Bull Run, anyway. I hated it. I like to say what I think."

"I've noticed that."

"A lady has to flatter a man, no matter what kind of idiot he is. Pretend she doesn't know half what he knows. Even when she knows twice as much. I'm not naturally flirtatious."

"I've noticed that, too."

Garrett wondered if Verity's tongue once loosed, could be silenced. "Miss Talmadge, your charms are deeper and more lasting than beauty. When a man finds a perfect diamond, he wants a perfect setting to complement it. Maybe, if the man were truly wise, he would leave the diamond alone."

With that, Garrett seized Verity's dirty hand and kissed it. "I'll be back to check on you. In the meantime, behave yourself. Ivy's a friend of mine. Treat her with respect, even if you don't value her profession. She has a good heart, and that's what matters."

Garrett Knox left Madame Ivy's brothel, took a few steps, and walked straight into Candace Webster. Dressed in solemn New England gray, her pale blonde hair bound neatly at the back, Candace looked as respectable as Verity Talmadge seemed wild.

"Garrett!"

"Candace," said Garrett, hoping she didn't know the nature of Ivy's building. "Have you heard anything?"

A full-breasted woman sauntered out of Ivy's front door and

waved at Garrett. Her dress and attitude left no doubt as to her profession. Garrett smiled weakly and hurried away with Candace.

"I must speak with you," Candace said breathlessly as Garrett rushed her away from the brothel. "Privately."

"Have you a coach?"

"I left it near the campsite. One of your men said you'd gone toward the brothel. Of course, he didn't refer to it as a 'brothel.' He hemmed and hawed and said 'salon,' finally. How lucky I found you!"

Candace spoke with no condemnation, just practical relief at her good fortune. Garrett cringed. He wanted to say, *'It's not what you think,'* but Candace didn't give him the chance.

"That man, Dave Delaney, came to visit me at the Roseclift!"

Garrett stopped. "What did he want?"

"He said the 'authorities' had learned of Verity's disappearance, and put him on the trail. He used a different name this time, Jake Martin, but I'm sure it's the same man."

"How do you know?"

"He smiled constantly. Very pleasant, charming. I didn't trust him."

"Sounds like the same," agreed Garrett. "What did you tell him?"

"I told him Verity had gone to Paris. He seemed doubtful, but he didn't question me further. I said I was visiting relatives here, to explain my presence."

"Good," said Garrett. "I have a suspicion he's not working alone, though. He won't believe your story for long."

"I know. If we only knew where she was! I'm so worried."

"She's all right, Candace."

Candace eyed Garrett suspiciously. "You know where she is."

"I do," he sighed. "Go back to Washington, Candace. Speak visibly about Verity's trip to France. Write letters. If we can convince these people she's gone, so much the better."

"But what about—?"

"She's safe, I promise you."

Candace looked back at the brothel, she looked at Garrett. "Not . . . ?" She shook her head as if she couldn't bear to know. "Have I your word?"

"While I live, no harm will come to her."

Candace studied Garrett's expression intently. "You care for her, don't you? I'm not surprised. Quite frankly, I suspected you might be the man for her, even after she decided to arrest you. It won't be easy, Garrett Knox. But if anyone can tame Verity Talmadge, it's you."

Verity slept through the night, and didn't wake until the following afternoon. The scents of roast chicken and biscuits roused her from the depths of sleep. Verity opened one eye and looked around the room. Ivy set a tray of food beside the bed.

Verity snapped her eye shut, hoping Ivy wouldn't speak to her. Ivy opened the door, then closed it again. Verity sat up, and Ivy laughed.

"Looks like you're ready for supper, Honey." Verity bit her lip in embarrassment. She hadn't meant to offend the woman. She just didn't know what to say to a madam.

"I'm a little hungry."

Ivy put the tray on Verity's bed, and sat beside her. "Eat up, then." Ivy watched as Verity devoured the meal.

"So you're Robert Talmadge's little sister, are you? I understand you married his cousin. Westley, wasn't it?"

"Did you know him?" asked Verity.

"I ... saw him, and young Adrian, once or twice." Ivy's casualness seemed forced. Verity set her fork down and met the woman's eyes. Ivy looked away.

"You can't mean—no."

"They was boys," explained Ivy gently. "Don't think either one knew what they was doing. Got themselves real liquored up first, too."

Verity swallowed. Then an angry expression tightened her small face. "I don't believe it."

"Aw, Honey, that was in the first days of the war, back when I'd set up shop in Washington. Before Bull Run. They was so eager to be men, back then. Don't you fret on it. A young fellow needs to know what he's doing when he takes a bride. That's all."

"Why? A girl isn't supposed to know. A man and woman should go to their marriage bed untarnished."

"If you think good loving tarnishes a man, you're a sight more innocent than you look. Hell, now. You don't want no boy rutting on you without a notion of what he's doing."

Verity paled. Ivy laughed and slapped Verity's covered knee. "Don't mean nothing, Sweetie. I'll tell you another thing—"

Verity wanted to interject, *"Please don't,"* but Ivy wasn't to be stopped.

"I saw those two boys a time or two, gave them my best girls."

"God," groaned Verity.

"They went home on leave, then came back as dewy-eyed and in love as I've ever seen any man. Both of 'em. Wanted nothing to do with any of my girls after that, though they came in for drinks. Westley said he'd found the woman of his dreams, in the most unlikely place. Adrian told me the same. Unfortunately, they picked the same girl."

"What did he mean, 'unlikely?'" said Verity indignantly.

"Well, looking at yourself, I'd say that's obvious. But somehow they both figured you'd make a good wife. I told them you don't change a woman to suit yourself. Neither listened, and they set to arguing about which one you preferred.

"Westley seemed to think you were his right, being relatives, but Adrian said you'd have two-headed children if you married your cousin."

"That was a rather disgusting argument," agreed Verity. "Adrian told me that, too."

"Sounds like those two boys put you through hell." Ivy's face looked sympathetic, kind. Verity relaxed in her company. Her own mother died just after Verity's birth, her father died before she reached ten years. Maybe Ivy wasn't quite the proper type, but Verity liked her. Ivy seemed motherly, in the same way Sam seemed like a father.

"I never understood it. I felt so guilty, not feeling what they wanted me to feel. If I loved one, I'd hurt the other."

"Looking at you now, I don't understand it, either," said Ivy with a laugh. "But you've got something, or Garrett Knox wouldn't be falling over his feet to take care of you."

"He's just protecting me because I'm Robert's sister."

"You think so? I wonder. Still, Garrett's not a boy. You'd best remember that. He's a man. A handsome man, with a powerful build and a damned sure idea how to use it."

"Use what?"

"His body," said Ivy. "If you catch his eye, you'd best be prepared for a night you ain't never going to forget."

"I think you're mistaken." Verity's cheeks flushed, her breaths came shallow. "As you said, I'm not terribly appealing right now."

"Didn't stop him from kissing you."

Verity squeezed her eyes shut and grimaced in embarrassment. "I'm awfully afraid I kissed him."

"And set his fires on high. Do you know what girls around here would give to have him look at them the way he looks at you?"

"He thinks I'm crazy."

"He may be right about that. Still can't keep his eyes off you, though. Garrett Knox has his pick of women, that's true. But he's never met his match. He's never been in love, I'd guarantee that. When he falls—there's a sight I'd like to see."

"He won't fall in love with me." Verity sounded forlorn. "Not after all I've done."

"We'll get you cleaned up," decided Ivy as she rose from Verity's bed. "That's the first thing to be done. Ain't no man wanting to touch you when you look like that."

"I could use a bath."

"And a louse check," added Ivy. "Though hopefully, you haven't been here long enough to pick up the critters. You strip off that uniform, and I'll have it laundered for you. There's a robe in the wardrobe. Wear that until I find you a pretty dress."

Verity waited until Ivy left to pull off her uniform. She stood naked in front of the looking glass, surveying her reflection with intense scrutiny. Her breasts hadn't changed since she taped them. Still small. Her stomach didn't look soft and feminine anymore, however. It looked firm. Verity frowned. A man wouldn't like that. Her legs had a more defined shape than before, too.

Verity put on the robe and sat on her bed, miserable. *I'm making myself look like a man, when I should be eating and plumping myself up.* "Oh, hell. What does it matter, anyway? I'm meant to be—a Watkins."

Verity bathed, but it took a while before she dared put on Ivy's dress. The chemise was a cream-colored satin with a fine lace fringe. The corset seemed scanty, and it squeezed her small breasts high, but no one would see that, or the black silk stockings. But the dress . . . a deep blue velvet, lined with black satin with an impossibly low bodice.

Verity suspected the designer intended to reveal full breasts. Hers weren't full, but they were high and firm. Squeezed by the corset, they seemed terribly visible to Verity. She looked at herself in the mirror.

"Well, I just can't leave this room, that's all."

Still, Verity found her image curiously appealing. Her neck looked long and graceful. Her breasts seemed much larger than they really were. Her waist looked very small. Verity turned and examined herself from the side. She liked the effect. It suited her better than the drab dresses worn by Boston's finest ladies.

She found herself wondering what Garrett Knox would think. Her hair fell just above her shoulders, still damp from washing. The curls were tighter without the heavy length, and fell around her face in disarray. Verity pushed them away, but they fell back in place.

The door opened, Verity's breath caught. She bit her lip, expecting Garrett, but Ivy walked in instead. Verity's face fell, but Ivy just stared.

"Lord Above, but you're a vision!"

"Am I? I feel rather naked."

"Yes," said Ivy. "That's what I meant. Lord, the price I could command for you!"

Verity's eyes widened in shock, but Ivy just patted her shoulder. "Don't worry, Honey. Garrett Knox would have my head if I so much as suggested the notion. Still, you'd make a fat lot of money." Ivy sighed. "I suppose you're not in need of cash."

"I am not." Verity was horrified by the image of seeing herself.

"I suppose you're better to look at than you'd be at pleasing a man."

"Why?"

"Do you know anything about pleasuring a gentleman?"

"No," Verity admitted. "Of course not."

"I suppose your young husband was too sick to treat you right, so you don't know what you're missing."

Verity didn't answer. She affected a cold, distant expression, but Ivy paid no attention.

"Still, looking like that—more's the pity you aren't using what you've got." Ivy sifted through Verity's hair, her face thoughtful. "Let's see what I can do with the pretty curls you've got left. Sit."

Verity did so, though she wasn't sure why she listened to the impertinent madam. Ivy seized a brush and worked through Verity's knotted hair. By the time she finished, Verity's earthen-red hair gleamed, light reflecting off the waves like the sun on a red sea.

"That's better," said Ivy. "I'll do it up in a knot, and we'll see . . ."

She proceeded to form a chignon at the nape of Verity's neck, taking care to leave bursts of chestnut curls framing the girl's face. Verity surveyed her reflection, then shook her head.

"You've left it too curly. You're supposed to brush it straight and flat, Ivy. Mrs. Webster said so. I had to wet my hair and pull it straight. And Westley's mother said curls are sinful."

"Didn't want you getting boys hard, that's what," finished Ivy.

Verity looked around at her. Ivy sounded matter-of-fact, decisive. "What does that mean?"

"God's nightgown, girl! Your mama didn't teach you nothing, did she?"

"My mother died when I was two," said Verity. "Mrs. Webster oversaw my female education. But she never said anything about hard boys."

"Not the whole boy, just his member."

"Member of what?"

Ivy rolled her eyes. "His private parts, Sweetie. There are other choice words, but Major Knox would slice me in quarters if I told you."

"Oh," said Verity. "His penis. I see."

Ivy laughed and shook her head.

"Why would that be hard? It's just a little thing, isn't it?"

"Now that depends," replied Ivy. "When a man wants a woman, when fire rages in his blood, it all centers there. Rises up like a pillar, if you're lucky, and if he's well-endowed."

"For what purpose?" Such questions Verity always wanted to ask now came easily. "Does this precede copulation?"

"It does," said Ivy. "He gets you all ready—if you're very lucky—then fills you with his mighty staff. Together, you drive yourselves into the sweetest oblivion you'll ever know, until you both climax and he spills his seed inside you."

Verity stared at Ivy as she tried to picture this. Garrett's face emerged in her mind. She imagined his body without clothes, his 'mighty staff.' Verity's face flushed hot and pink, and she looked away.

"As I told you earlier, it helps if the man knows his way around a woman, inside and out. Boys, now they take you before you're ready, and it ain't much of a time, for sure. One, two, and it's over, leaving you wondering why you're there. Some men never get beyond that.''

Verity adjusted her position in the chair. "What do you mean, 'ready?' ''

"You look at his face, and you want him," said Ivy. "Your body knows this, and it prepares itself."

"How?"

"You get wet between the legs."

"Do I?" asked Verity in surprise. "I don't think so."

"Next time you're near Garrett Knox, you pay attention to the signs. Go find a woman who don't react to him that way, and I'll show you a woman numb from the neck down."

Verity was too confused to be embarrassed, though she sensed these were things her family wouldn't want her to know.

"Boston society wouldn't like you much, Ivy."

"Not in public, anyway," said Ivy.

"It didn't like me, either," said Verity. "The Websters tolerated me, but Westley's mother told him not to marry me."

"Did she, now?"

"Yes. The old crow. Westley sent her away, and wouldn't let her come back."

"Good for Westley." Ivy stood back and examined the results of her work. "You're a beauty, all right. Come downstairs with me, Honey, and enjoy yourself."

"I can't go downstairs!"

"Hell, now. You think I fixed you up so you could sit in your room? Don't worry. My customers haven't started in yet. But you can meet a few of my girls, and Jefferson."

"Jefferson? Who's that?"

"Jefferson Davis."

Verity's eyes widened. "Not—?"

"Not the rebel President, no," Ivy laughed. "Though they've got the same name. This one's a different sort, for sure. Colored piano player. Wants to fight, but no regiment here will let him."

"Because of his black skin? That makes no sense."

"Right enough," sighed Ivy. "Some folks forget what we're fighting for."

"Not for long." Verity rose. "I *will* join you in the parlor, Ivy. Thank you."

Verity marched toward the stairs, purpose in every step she took. Ivy followed behind. "I had a feeling."

"Mr. Davis? I wonder if I might speak with you."

Verity stood behind the piano player. He was playing a portion of Beethoven's "Moonlight Sonata." He stopped and turned slowly to look at her. They scrutinized each other silently.

Jefferson Davis had the most perfect, chiseled, beautiful face Verity had ever seen. He looked like a king, tall and lean, with an imperious, somewhat condescending expression. His eyes were black, his lips sculpted and full. His skin was a deep, midnight brown, and his black hair gleamed in the lamplight.

"Who in hell are you?"

"Verity Talmadge."

Jefferson Davis assessed her further, utmost suspicion in his expression. "What do you want?"

"I—I thought I might be able to help you."

"No." Jefferson turned back to his piano, picking up the sonata just where he left off.

Verity placed her hands on her hips. "You wait just a minute, Sir. You might look like a king, but you've got the manners of a knave. Turn around and speak to me this instant, do you hear?"

Jefferson played a few more notes, then turned. "Yes'm, Miz Talmige," he drawled in an exaggerated fashion.

"That's better," said Verity, deliberately irritating him. His black eyes flashed, and she smiled. "Forgive me for interrupting you. I can see you've got a rapt audience here." Verity looked pointedly around the empty room. One of Ivy's girls walked by and yawned.

Jefferson made a face, but made no comment. "What you be wantin', Lady?"

"I be wantin' to smack you. To think, I considered getting you into my regiment. I'd end up shooting you myself!"

Jefferson's expression changed in a flash. "What do you mean, *your* regiment? You're a girl." His accent changed from a South Carolina drawl to something that sounded almost Maine-ish.

"Each to his own, Mr. Davis." Verity turned her back to him and gazed around the room.

"If you've got something to offer, say it, and be done," he commanded. Verity hummed.

"Tell me," he warned. Verity hummed louder. "All right. I humbly beg your forgiveness. I might have been rude."

Verity peeked over her shoulder. " 'Might have been?' "

"I was rude. Sorry."

"Good enough." Verity sat down beside him on the piano bench. "Ivy says you want to fight. Is that true?"

"For all the good it does me."

"Why do you sound like you came from Maine?"

"I was born in South Carolina," Jefferson told her, drawling excessively, and drawing out each word. "I . . . moved to Brunswick, Maine, and lived with a Scottish linguistics professor and his little girl." Jefferson's voice changed again, making 'professor' sound like 'professah.' "You want to hear a Scottish brogue?"

"Not right now, thank you," said Verity. "What are you doing here? I can't believe your professor would want you living in a brothel."

"Probably not," agreed Jefferson. "But I have to earn some wages until someone lets me in. My best friend's gone back to Boston to join that Colored regiment, the Fifty-fourth."

"Why didn't you go, too?"

" 'Cause I don't think they'll see much fighting. Here's where the war is, in Virginia. I want to do my part. The professor died, and his little girl got sent to Virginia, where she's taken up spying for the blue."

"She's spying?" Verity thought of Jared Knox and his Yankee spy. "No, it can't be," she muttered. "Was this girl pretty?"

"Prettiest thing I ever saw. Not so different from yourself."

"Why were you so rude when I spoke to you, if you think I'm pretty?" asked Verity. Jefferson looked young, no more than twenty. He sounded decidedly flirtatious now.

"Thought you wanted me."

"For what?"

"My tall, lean body, my handsome face—for those mystiques attributed to men of color."

Verity remained completely blank, and Jefferson laughed. "Apparently not known by all. I'm sick of Ivy's girls wanting to find out by me. As if I'd have to pay for a girl. Ha!"

Verity decided Jefferson Davis possessed matchless arrogance, but then Garrett Knox entered the brothel. Her heart fluttered as he smiled at one of Ivy's girls. The girl sighed and batted her eyes. Her hips swayed. Garrett accepted it all as his due.

"Well, here's your first hurdle, Mr. Davis." Verity rose from the bench and called to Garrett.

"Major Knox! Over here, if you please."

Garrett stopped, turned, looked around, and his jaw dropped. Verity hoped his look was appreciative. Ivy watched them from behind the bar, a wily grin on her face.

"What do you think, Major?"

Garrett's vision moved slowly from the top of Verity's head to her satin slippers. She tapped her foot impatiently beneath her wide skirt.

"Verity?"

"Of course. Who else? I need to speak with you on an urgent matter." She paused, but Garrett didn't move. He just stared. "Well?"

"What matter?" His voice sounded strange, and Verity wondered why.

"Mr. Davis here wants to fight." She looked down at Jefferson. "You can shoot, can't you?"

"I can shoot the flea off a dog."

Verity beamed. "See? Just like Watkins! Can he join your regiment?"

Garrett looked between them. "Davis, is it? I've heard you play. You're very talented."

"Will you let me fight?"

Garrett hesitated, and Jefferson issued a derisive snort before turning back to his piano. "Just what I figured." He began an angry version of the "Moonlight Sonata."

Verity shook her head. "You misunderstood."

"Didn't 'misunderstand' nothing, Girl."

"I can get approval from Colonel Godwin," said Garrett. "But the men, now that's up to you, Davis. Tomorrow morning, you be at the Twentieth Massachusetts drill site."

Jefferson stopped in mid-chord. "What?"

"I'll give you your chance. But it's the men you'll have to convince. They're not set to accept you, I'll warn you of that. We've got more than a few Irishmen, and they're not disposed to accept men of color. They think they've got it bad enough in Boston without competition from you. Some of them are just plain thickheaded."

"They'll let him join," said Verity with utmost confidence. "Ethan will, I know. He joined because of Frederick Douglass."

"Don't have Frederick Douglass sleeping in the next bunk, though, does he?" put in Jefferson.

"And Sam, he's like a father. John won't mind, and even if he did, he wouldn't say so, because he doesn't talk."

"I'll be there." Jefferson didn't sound enthusiastic about the prospect of acceptance. "Giving them a choice, now that's a clever way of saying the decision's already made."

"That remains to be seen, Davis," said Garrett. "They might be pigheaded, but only a fool turns away a soldier with as much to win as you've got."

"As I said, I'll be there. And then we'll test your pretty words."

"Not to worry," Verity intoned cheerfully. "Tomorrow, you said? Good. I'm feeling much better."

Jefferson Davis eyed her doubtfully, and Garrett breathed deeply, resignation echoing in his sigh. "I take it Davis knows your unique situation."

"No," said Jefferson.

"I dressed up like a boy and joined Major Knox's regiment," said Verity. "Apparently he knew, but he let me stay anyway."

"Why?" Jefferson looked askance at the Yankee officer.

Garrett sighed. "God knows."

"It's a long story," said Verity.

"I'm thinking I can guess part of it." Jefferson winked at Garrett and turned back to his piano. "So there's a girl in blue. Tells a tale, don't it? Ever heard of the *Marriage of Figaro?*"

"Mozart's opera?" asked Verity. "A boy dresses up as a girl to be near his lady love, isn't it?"

"Something like that." Jefferson began to play a strain of the opera's music.

"Very nice," commented Verity. "But I don't see the connection."

"Blind as well as crazy," muttered Jefferson, but he didn't stop playing.

"Would you care to dance, pretty wench?"

Both Garrett and Verity startled when a deep voice spoke behind them. A thin, gaunt man stood behind Verity, his bloodshot eyes raking over her with blatant lust. "I want this one tonight, Ivy. Get her ready."

"Not tonight, I'm afraid," said Garrett. "She's mine, bought and paid for."

Ivy stepped between them. "Perhaps I could interest you in one of my other girls, Mr. Spears."

Jefferson stopped his music and watched the unfolding scene like a spectator, looking from one player to the next with expectant glee. Verity cast a reproachful glance his way.

"Get done with her and send her down."

Verity grimaced in disgust, but Garrett slid his arm around her waist. "I've paid for the night. I don't intend to throw away good cash for a quick tumble."

"Look, Major, I've only got an hour to kill. Let me have her first, and I'll double your pay."

"A tempting offer," said Garrett.

"What?" Verity gasped, but Garrett's arm around her waist tightened in what she guessed was a comforting manner.

"I think you'd better find another," Garrett suggested.

Spears reeked of alcohol, Verity felt faint from his breath alone. "Like a pretty officer, do you, whore?"

Garrett's jaw hardened. "I'd be leaving, if I were you."

"Leaving? Hell, I want a piece of her, too." He reached out for Verity's breast.

In one swift, clean motion, Garrett caught the man by the collar, showed him to the door, then tossed him unceremoniously to the muddy ground outside. The girls cheered. Jefferson Davis laughed, but Verity stood shaking by the piano.

Garrett adjusted his sleeves, then returned, smiling. He seemed unusually pleased with himself. "I'm afraid you're attracting too much attention, my dear." He held out his arm for Verity. "Shall we adjourn to your quarters?"

"My quarters?"

"Your bedroom, my sweet. Where you'll show me the night of my life, and weave memories to last a lifetime."

Verity couldn't answer. Jefferson Davis returned to *Figaro*. Verity placed her hand on Garrett's strong arm, and walked with him toward the staircase.

Part Two
On Fields of Fire

"... this is not destiny
But man's own willful ill."
—*Julian and Maddalo*, P. B. Shelley

Chapter Six

Garrett led Verity up the stairs. "Are you going to stay with me all night?" she asked.

"Would you rather Alfred Spears accompany you?"

"No—how do you know his name?"

"He's a spy, working for someone, though I'm not sure it's the rebels."

Garrett kept walking, but Verity stopped. Garrett looked around and saw her heading back down the stairs. "Where in hell do you think you're going?"

"Do you mean to tell me that man may be responsible for what happened to Westley and Robert? And all you thought to do was toss him out the door?"

Garrett bounded down the stairs and caught her arm. Verity struggled, but he held her fast. "I'm almost afraid to ask, but what do you intend to do?"

"I'm going to kill him."

Garrett rolled his eyes and groaned heavily. "You really are crazy, woman. Just when I think you're as far gone as you can get, you go one step farther. Alfred Spears is *a* spy, not necessarily the one we're looking for. I suspect he may deal with the person responsible. I'm hoping he'll lead me to the bastard who shot your husband and Robert—"

"Robert wasn't shot."

"Maybe not. Either way, if you go shooting Alfred Spears, you're destroying the only lead I've found."

Verity considered this. Her face puckered thoughtfully. Her lips twisted to one side. Garrett watched her expression, his heartbeat quickening. How could a woman so odd be so alluring? His vision wandered from her delicate face to her breasts, squeezed high by the dress, her soft skin glowing in the lamplight.

"Very well. I won't kill him. Yet."

"That's very comforting." Garrett eased her back up the stairs.

They entered a narrow hallway leading to various bedrooms. Chairs upholstered in red velvet lined the hall. Garrett's gaze followed the line of chairs, past the bolted doors.

"Oh, no," Garrett groaned. Verity didn't respond.

An officer sat on the last seat, his trousers down around his ankles, while one of Ivy's girls knelt in front of him. The girl's hand was wrapped around the man's erection while she—

"No," murmured Verity. "It's not possible."

The girl sucked the man's staff vigorously, making loud, slurpy noises while her head bobbed up and down. The man's head tipped back, and he groaned. Verity backed up and bumped into Garrett.

Garrett didn't think. He just wrapped his hand over Verity's eyes and yanked her down the hallway toward her room. The girl stopped her performance and looked around at Garrett. Verity twisted her head away from his grasp and stared at the couple.

"I can handle two of you, no trouble," breathed the prostitute eagerly. "Especially a man who's built like you."

"Thank you, no." Garrett shoved Verity through her door, then locked it. Verity just stood, her face blank, as she considered what she'd just seen.

"What were they doing?" Verity's voice revealed utmost suspicion.

Garrett had no idea how to respond. "They were . . . um . . . Do you really need to know?"

"Ivy said a man fills a woman with his mighty staff." A harsh groan from Garrett cut off her words. Verity's eyes narrowed, but she continued. "I didn't think she meant the mouth."

"A simple variation," said Garrett.

"Your voice sounds higher than normal."

"Does it?"

"Yes. Why did you cover my eyes? I'd already seen."

"Had you?" Garrett looked around her room, trying to find something to distract her. He spotted the checkers board. "Checkers. We'll play checkers."

Garrett readied the board, then seated himself at a small table. Verity sat down across from him and took the first move. Her eyes never left his face.

"Why did he groan?"

Garrett moved his checkers piece quickly. "Your move."

Verity moved. "Well?"

"Maybe you should ask Ivy." *I'm advising Robert's sister to consult a prostitute.*

"Apparently her descriptions weren't very accurate," said Verity. "Or complete. Why did he groan?"

Garrett didn't meet her eyes as he concentrated on the board, but he felt her piercing stare. "From pleasure."

Verity thought about this while Garrett held his breath. "Do you mean all his fires went to his . . . member?"

"Something like that." Garrett moved another piece hurriedly. "I've got to have a talk with Ivy."

"She said when I kissed you, your fires went on high. Does that mean . . . ?"

Garrett flipped his checkers piece into the air. It clattered onto the floor. He picked it up. "Will you just play?"

"I *see*," said Verity knowingly.

"A young lady does not discuss such matters with a gentleman," said Garrett in his most formal tone.

A short laugh escaped Verity's lips. "As you've pointed out often enough, I'm not much of a lady. As for you being a gentleman . . . ha! And I want to know. Men live a whole different life, one I never suspected. Ivy says even Westley and Adrian came here."

"Jesus," cut in Garrett. "What in the name of God possessed her to tell you that?"

"She respects me."

Garrett looked at her. Verity's chin was high, and her bright eyes gleamed. "Respects you?"

"Yes. She thinks I'm smart enough to face reality. That I'm not a weak, little fool who faints and shudders at the slightest hint of natural behavior. And she's right, too."

"I suppose she is."

"Why don't you want to talk about it? If such things give a

man pleasure, shouldn't women know, so they can be good wives? Your move.''

Garrett moved recklessly, and Verity chuckled. She moved her piece with loud hopping noises over Garrett's, taking his and piling them in a neat stack on her side. "King me."

Garrett doubled Verity's piece, then moved again.

"You're not playing very well." She jumped her piece over three of his. "King me again."

Garrett obeyed.

"The woman didn't seem to mind," Verity added thoughtfully. "She acted as if she enjoyed it."

Garrett took one of Verity's pieces, hoping to distract her. She merely hopped back over his, and continued with her agonizing line of conversation.

"It didn't look all that 'mighty' to me."

"Miss Talmadge—"

"Do all men like that?" she asked. Garrett grimaced. "Do you?"

"That's enough! You win." Garrett rose abruptly from his chair and paced around the room. He felt hot, and he knew he was hard. He adjusted his frock coat to conceal any evidence. If she noticed, she'd mention it.

Verity collected the pieces, neatly arranging them as evidence of her victory. She fell silent, thoughtful. She watched as Garrett paced around the room. He pulled back the curtain, then lifted the window to let cool air inside.

"If you're hot, why don't you take off your coat?"

"This will be fine." Garrett's voice was forcibly calmed.

Verity continued her scrutiny. She adjusted her position in her chair. Restless. Garrett wished he didn't know the reason why, but the look on her face revealed pure, innocent sexual curiosity.

"You're very handsome. Is that why women want to go to bed with you?"

Garrett closed his eyes. *The night of my life. A night spent with the temptress from hell.*

"Ivy says you're renowned as a lover." She knew what she was doing now. She knew she was teasing him. Garrett looked over his shoulder. Maybe it was time to show her the dangers of playing with a man's fire.

"You, Miss Talmadge, have gone too far."

Garrett fixed his gaze on her startled face. He went toward her. Verity leapt out of her chair and backed away.

"Don't you come near me!" She scrambled around the table, putting it between them.

Garrett followed her. His eyes bored into her. A faint smile curbed his lips. He paused, braced his arm on the table's center, then vaulted across, catching Verity in one motion.

"What are you going to—"

His mouth came down on hers, his arms tightened around her. She froze, shocked. *Good.* Garrett felt her tense body soften. He ran his tongue along her lips, parting them to allow his entrance.

She didn't know how to react, but her mouth opened instinctively. Garrett delved his tongue through the soft entrance, across her white teeth, sliding over her tongue.

A wild shudder raced through Verity; Garrett felt it as if it passed into him. She caught his tongue between her lips and sucked gently. His whole body hardened. He wound his fingers in her thatch of hair, cupping her head, bending her back.

Verity leaned against him, eagerly accepting the rhythmic caress of his tongue. Wild lust surged in Garrett's veins. When he leapt across the table, he'd meant to seize her, kiss her, leave her breathless. Show her she wasn't ready for passion. How wrong he was! Her body molded against his, she returned his kiss with a vixen's eagerness.

Garrett's erection burned, ached, strained to meet her flesh. He could take her now, on the floor. They wouldn't make it to the bed. He would thrust into her, drive them to madness. Madness. Verity Talmadge had no hold on reality. She had no idea what it really meant to give herself.

I can't take Robert's sister on the floor, in a brothel . . .

Garrett broke the kiss, and he moved away from her. Verity slumped into her chair and stared at him.

"Does this mean my body's ready for you?" she asked in a small, breathless voice. "Ivy said—"

"Don't tell me," groaned Garrett. "Checkers. Yes. Another game, Miss Talmadge?"

"Very well."

Garrett seated himself at the table and moved first. When Verity took her turn, her hands were shaking. "I've never been kissed that way," she informed him.

"That makes two of us."

"I find *that* hard to believe. Adrian said you had dozens of lovers in France."

"That boy had no discretion."

"Did you?"

Garrett kept his gaze on the board. "A few."

"You're not going to tell me it's none of my business?"

"Would it make any difference if I did?"

"No, probably not. It would just mean you're embarrassed and don't want to talk."

"I don't, but don't let that stop you."

A knock on the door interrupted them. Garrett breathed his relief. "Come in," he called, trying to sound casual and not quite succeeding.

Ivy tried to open the door. "You locked it," Verity reminded him. Garrett was hesitant to move, so she got up and let the madam in.

"Hello, Ivy."

Ivy looked around the bedroom. "You may be the first couple to actually use that checkers board." Ivy looked from Verity to Garrett. "Although it looks like the game has taken a toll on you. Maybe it has erotic powers I didn't realize."

"It's just a little warm in here," said Garrett.

Ivy glanced at the open window, then at Verity. "I'd say it's downright hot. Maybe I'd best leave you two alone."

"There's no need for that," said Garrett, too quickly. "Stay a while."

"Can't," replied Ivy. "Old Sam's downstairs. We've got a lot of catching up to do. Just came to leave you this bottle of wine. Thought you might get thirsty up here. It being so 'hot' and all."

"Thank you."

Garrett took the bottle and Ivy left. He poured himself a tall glass, then a smaller one for Verity. Verity took her portion, but her face was knit in a tight frown.

"Even Sam," she muttered disgustedly. "Doesn't he have a wife, eleven children? How could he? Adrian and Westley were one thing—and you—but Sam—"

"He's not here on business."

"Oh, no? An awful lot of men seem to choose this place for a drink. Aren't there taverns?"

"Ivy is Sam's sister."

Verity's mouth dropped. "But he's so respectable, in a farmer sort of way."

"Don't misjudge Ivy, Miss Talmadge. She and Sam come from a family of sixteen children. She married at thirteen, just to spare her father the burden of feeding her."

"She's married?"

"I think she's still married. If he's still alive. I don't know the full story, but it's not a pretty one. He beat her to a bloody pulp whenever he thought she'd crossed him."

"How could anyone hit a woman as soft and kind as Ivy?"

"It didn't take much to set him off. Maybe she burned the biscuits. God knows. When she became pregnant, he beat her almost to death. She lost the baby, and she fled."

"I guess it was lucky she got away from him, at least."

"It was," agreed Garrett. "But she had no money, no way to fend for herself. She took to selling herself to buy food."

"How horrible!"

"Maybe. But somewhere along the line, Ivy learned that men aren't all like her husband. She learned that men can be vulnerable, even weak. Rather than vindictiveness, Ivy gave love. She also learned she could choose the kind of man she'd cater to. And later, she taught her girls the same."

"She has a good heart. I still think she deserves a better life than this."

"You may be right," said Garrett. "But she believes her services contribute to the Union's cause."

"How so?" Verity paused. "I don't suppose this is what President Lincoln meant by service."

Garrett smiled. Verity had a good sense of the ridiculous, which set her apart from most women in society. It might be, despite her youth and sheltered upbringing, that he'd found a woman who looked at life the way he did. Except that he wasn't crazy. Yet. He took a sip of wine. "Ivy sees frightened boys. By her arts, she convinces them they're men. That may be the only touch of womanhood a lot of them see before they die."

"Like Adrian and Westley."

"Since you know," sighed Garrett. "I spotted those two fools in line outside a filthy strumpet's hut, dead set on losing their virginity. God knows what disease they'd have picked up, so I directed them to Ivy."

"You. I should have guessed."

Verity turned back to their game. Garrett collected himself and played better this time. "I suppose your fires rise easily," she mused as Garrett took her farthest piece.

"I like to think not."

"Why can't you go back to Yugoslavia?"

"Is there nothing my little brother didn't share with you?"

"I expect there's a lot. I've only heard the slightest of your escapades."

"Good. As for Yugoslavia . . . a young and willful princess learned that I was 'enjoying,' shall we say, the pleasures of one of her ladies-in-waiting. The foolish girl felt insulted, and wanted me for herself. I refused, and she told her father I'd seduced and betrayed her."

"Truly?" asked Verity excitedly. She paused. "Young and willful, you say? That sounds like—"

"You?" finished Garrett. "No, she wasn't much like you. She was spoiled and selfish. You're just crazy. You're not manipulative, either. I can picture you doing a lot, but not squealing to your father."

Verity considered this. "I wouldn't, it's true. I don't like it when women use wiles to get their way."

"You'd prefer to stomp in and make your demand straight on."

"Yes," agreed Verity. "That's what I'd do. I'd prove to you I was better than any lady-in-waiting."

"How?"

Verity considered the matter before answering. "I'd fix myself up first. Then I'd find your room, climb in your bed, and do what Ivy's girl did."

"God, why did I ask!"

"Would that work?" A sly smile grew on Verity's face as she scrutinized Garrett's reaction.

"Quite possibly." Garrett met her eyes. "You're too damned beautiful for your own good."

"Don't be ridiculous. I'm not beautiful in the least. I'm dressed like a tart—"

"It may surprise you to learn your appearance tonight isn't exactly offensive to a man's eye."

"No?" A flash of warmth flooded Verity's cheeks. "My hair is half cropped off."

"All the better to frame your sweet face."

She moved her checkers' piece. "King me," she said weakly. Garrett did so, but his eyes never left her face.

Verity took a gulp of wine, then poured herself another.

"Go easy on that, Woman. It's not water."

"I'm thirsty." She drank again. Garrett shook his head. Verity pulled out Ivy's carefully placed hairpins. Her hair fell loose to her shoulders, around her face.

Garrett forced his attention to the checkers' board. He seized the opportunity to jump Verity's pieces. "King me, at last." Verity dutifully doubled his piece.

"A better fight." She took another large mouthful of wine. "I suppose there's a knack to it." Verity's voice sounded a little thick, and she slurred slightly.

"I think you've had enough." Garrett moved the wine bottle out of her reach. Verity drained her glass and calmly reached for his. She drank that, too.

"A knack to what?" he asked. Verity stood up, retrieved the wine bottle, and sloshed a portion into her glass.

"What's the matter?" Verity bumped back down into her chair. "This wine is very relaxing. Tasty, too."

Verity looked up at Garrett, her lids heavy, unwittingly seductive. "What did you ask? Oh, yes. I remember. *'A knack to what?'* Sucking a man's member, of course. I'm obviously better at checkers than you, so I couldn't have meant that."

As proof, Verity jumped her piece over Garrett's. Unsteadily. She knocked several onto the floor. "Oh, hell. We'll have to start over."

"I think not. You go to bed, girl. That wine went to your head."

Verity rose rather unsteadily, held her head high, and walked to the bed. She sat on the edge, bounced comfortably, then fell back. Her hoopskirt stood up like a tent.

Good. Maybe she's out for the night. Garrett pulled off his jacket, threw it over a chair, then wondered where he would sleep.

Verity sat up. "I can't sleep in this dress." Before he said a word, she tugged it off her shoulders, unbuttoned the back, and slid out of it. She stood up and began to fumble with the corset. "Petticoat and crinoline first."

She untied the hoopskirt and stepped out of it. Garrett couldn't turn his eyes away. Verity's slender body defied its trappings. She popped apart the hooks of the corset, pulled off her stockings, and tossed it all aside. Garrett's vision fixed on her long, shapely legs.

Her little toes curled as her feet sank into the thick rug at the bedside.

Clad only in the satin chemise, Verity sat back on the bed. Small, round breasts defined themselves beneath the exquisite material, with pert nipples visible and painfully enticing.

"Have you any idea what you're doing?"

"What?"

"Fanning my fires," said Garrett, his voice a near groan. "Get in the bed so I can't see you."

"What's wrong with me?"

"Not a goddamned thing."

Garrett sank into the armchair. It wasn't comfortable, no doubt rarely used in Ivy's boudoir. He adjusted his position. He was stiff and hard. "Not unlike this chair."

"What did you say?"

"Nothing."

"You're not going to sleep in that chair, are you?"

"Would you prefer me in bed?" He shouldn't have asked.

"Yes. I would like you to kiss me more."

"You're drunk."

"I am not!" Verity sat up again, her expression disgruntled and indignant. "I feel very light and pleasant."

"Soused to the gills," remarked Garrett.

"Not at all." Verity's eyes narrowed. "So you're spending the night there, are you?"

"That is my intention." Verity's lips curved in the most seductive smile Garrett had ever seen. "Don't—"

Verity slid off the bed, walked across the room, then settled on his lap. "I want to kiss you."

"A day ago, you wanted to shoot me. What's next?"

"That remains to be seen."

"God, no," he begged as she bent to kiss him. Garrett closed his eyes, fighting his reaction. He felt her small hand on his face, guiding him toward her. He felt her soft breaths. Verity's open lips brushed across his, teasing, enticing him. Her tongue slid along the firm line of his lips, dipping in at the corner, tasting him.

Garrett trembled with the force of restraint. She bit him, very gently. Tugged at his mouth. She squirmed around on his lap so that her legs straddled him. Her chemise pushed up above her thighs. Garrett saw her long, slender legs, and he forced his eyes shut again.

Verity wrapped her arms around his neck. She kissed his square jawline, his neck. Soft sighs escaped her lips as she leisurely explored every angle of his face with her kiss.

"I'm not a saint, Verity."

"Heaven knows."

"I can't dishonor your brother and your husband by taking you like a common whore."

Verity sat back. "Who said anything about 'taking me?' I just want you to kiss me."

"Up!" he thundered. Verity hopped off his lap.

Garrett rose, towering over her. "You, woman, are the most devilish creature the world has ever produced! You do not torment a man this way, Miss Talmadge. You don't strip off your clothes, stand there like an angel of sex, sit on his lap, drive him mad . . . all for a damned kiss!"

"No?"

"No! Do you know, have you any idea, what you've done to me? Do you know how hard I am?"

Verity looked down at his crotch. "Sure enough." She paused. "That," she said with a quick gesture, "looks bigger than the other man's."

"He didn't have you torturing him all night."

"It's barely ten o'clock."

"Back to bed."

Verity obeyed, settling herself against the pile of down pillows. She watched as Garrett sat back in the chair. "I want you inside me." No coquetry sounded in her voice. Just a practical assessment. "I think that's why I'm so damp. Ivy says that's what happens when you want a man."

"Desire," said Garrett, his voice unrecognizable through his constricted throat, "is one thing. Good sense is quite another. Should you give in to this . . . impulse, you'd regret it. This moment is best kept for a husband."

"My husband died. And he didn't keep 'this moment' for me, did he? My heart flutters when you're near. Did you know that? My knees feel weak, my fingers tingle. I didn't know before, but that's desire, isn't it?"

"It is."

"You desire me, too."

"God help me, I do."

Verity swung her legs from the bed again, letting the chemise slide up over her thigh. She crossed the floor, a slight smile on her lips.

"What are you doing?" asked Garrett. "No—" Garrett sprang out of his chair, but she touched his face, then rose up on tiptoes to kiss him. She drew back, assessing him thoughtfully.

Her gaze lingered on the bulge beneath his trousers. Her lips curved mysteriously as she reached to touch him. She ran her finger along the hard ridge, then cupped its length in her hand. Garrett couldn't move. Blood throbbed in his veins, centering mercilessly where she touched.

"Verity . . ." Garrett's voice trembled with warning.

"If I kiss your lips, this happens. If I kissed you here, what—?"

"I would explode."

"I want to lie with you, Garrett Knox. There are many reasons why we shouldn't. Only one that we should." Her hand slipped to his concealed erection, her fingers defined its shape. "Two, if you count my body's desire."

Garrett just groaned. "You're drunk."

"I'm not. I felt a bit giddy for a while, but not anymore." She looked up at him, reasonable and young and beautiful. "I want you because everyone I loved is gone, and you are so alive. I think that if we lie together, I will be alive, too."

Garrett studied her expression, and he understood. "You need me."

"I do."

"Society would frown." He couldn't repress a smile.

She smiled, too. "We'll keep it to ourselves, shall we?"

Garrett hesitated. They were the same. "I never did care much for the constraints of society."

Garrett scooped Verity into his arms, then carried her to the bed. Verity didn't speak nor move as he pulled off his loose shirt, discarded his trousers. She longed to see him undressed. The sight defied her imagination.

Verity had known men all her life, better than she knew women. No man came close to Garrett Knox's power. He radiated masculinity, assurance. Strength. His male organ stood poised, the emblem of his raw, forceful nature. When he moved, every muscle supported him in perfect grace. Even when he bent to kiss her. . . .

Verity's lips parted to receive his kiss. She expected wild, unrestrained passion, but Garrett touched her gently. His kiss teased, hinted at more, titillated her with pleasure. Verity touched the hard flesh of his shoulder. She felt power throbbing beneath his skin.

Garrett lowered himself to the bed beside her, throwing aside the covers to bare Verity's body. He ran his hand over the satin chemise, circling her breasts, teasing her with the possibility of intimate touch. He kissed her mouth, her face, her throat. He slipped his hand beneath the chemise, running his touch along her hip to cup her bottom.

"Garrett—"

"You're not sobering up, are you?"

Verity frowned. "I told you—I'm not drunk."

"Then what troubles you? You know that with your word, I'll stop."

"I'm afraid, if you touch me that way . . . I'm not sure what I'll do. I might cry out, or move, or do something you don't want me to do." She paused, looking into his dark gray eyes. "What if I like this too much?"

Garrett smiled. "Society will frown, but I'll keep it to myself."

Verity giggled. "Are you sure you won't mind?"

"I'm sure. Verity, there's nothing you can feel, or scream, or do, that I won't relish, I promise you. You can claw at my back, you can sink your perfect teeth into my shoulder, you can wrap your legs around me and make any demand that strikes you."

"I'd never bite you."

Garrett kissed her throat. "Don't speak too soon."

Garrett slid the chemise over her head and tossed it away. Verity had skinny-dipped many times with boys, never noticing her own nudity, but that was before she grew up. She felt acutely aware of her womanly body now.

"You are lovely," he told her huskily.

"Am I?" Verity glanced down at her body, wondering if it had changed since she looked in the mirror. No, no change. "I never wanted to be pretty before. But it's good you think so."

Garrett touched her mouth and kissed her cheek. "I think so."

Verity didn't know how to please him now. Her nature felt more at ease when in control, but Garrett seized mastery of her body. He watched her face as he traced a line across her collarbone. He circled her breast, over the soft flare of skin as it rose to the summit. His finger grazed her nipple, and a quick breath expanded her rib cage.

Verity's eyelids fluttered shut, Garrett intensified his touch, back and forth across the taut nipple, then the other. She didn't expect his kiss. When his lips brushed over the firm peak, she caught her breath in surprise.

Garrett flicked his tongue against the tip, circling and teasing until Verity's breaths came in rushed gasps of pleasure. He sucked gently, then moved to the other breast. For a moment, he rested his cheek against her, then sat back to look at her.

"You are the most exquisite sight I've ever seen."

Verity couldn't answer. She trembled, and the world spun around them. She lost sight of what she was, where she was . . . everything.

Garrett ran his hand all along her leg, then he caught her foot and lifted it. To her surprise, he kissed each toe. A strange, tender gesture from a man whose strength seemed boundless. Verity's toes curled, and a small giggle escaped her lips.

"You're not ticklish, are you?"

"A bit."

Garrett's eyes darkened. "I'll have to learn where else you harbor sensitivity."

Verity didn't understand, but he grinned, pressing kisses up her legs, taking exquisite time with the backs of her knees. His tongue touched the surface of her skin, lightly, and Verity's nerves twitched with delight.

Garrett lay back beside her, cradling her body against his, his arm wrapped around her. He ran a feather-light touch along her thighs, skimming over the thatch of soft, reddish-brown curls between her legs.

Verity gazed at him uneasily. "Should you touch me there?"

"I don't know." Garrett sounded gravelly, almost hoarse. "Should I?"

Garrett continued his gentle caress. His finger dipped deeper between her legs. Verity shuddered, turning her head against his chest. He played, barely touching, teasing her. When his finger met her moist, slippery entrance, a deep groan sounded in his throat.

"I warned you." Verity guessed her condition pleased Garrett.

He kissed her head, her face. She heard the loud thump of his heart, his short, ragged breaths.

"So you did." Garrett dipped his finger inward, just parting her secret entrance. She squeezed mindlessly around his probe. Garrett's whole body jerked with restrained lust.

"If your finger feels this good, what will—?"

Garrett kissed her with sudden passion, stopping her words, as if he couldn't bear to hear her sensual speculation. His finger delved inside her again, finding her maiden's veil, widening it.

Verity arched beneath his skill, deepening his touch, squirming against his hand. "I can't spare you a virgin's pain, but maybe I can make you forget it."

"I'm not afraid of pain, Garrett Knox. I'm not afraid of anything anymore."

Garrett withdrew his finger, pleased when she gasped in exasperation. He found the tiny bud at her feminine apex and circled it with a light touch. Verity's breath caught. A low, raspy moan erupted from her throat.

"What are you doing?" With her head tipped back, she caught her lip between her teeth. Her eyes closed.

"I'm making you feel half, a quarter, of what your kiss did to me."

"How did you stand it?"

"I didn't," he replied, his lips close against her ear. "That's why I'm here."

Garrett teased her beyond words, until she writhed and gasped, and cried out in mindless pleasure. He held her at the brink of perfect surrender, her every breath a plea for satisfaction.

Garrett's skill taught Verity how much she wanted him inside her, filling her. She learned she wasn't complete unto herself, as she had once believed. She needed him to reach the pinnacles he now offered.

"It's not enough," she murmured. "I want all of you."

Garrett smiled, but he continued teasing her, slowing while she whimpered in agonized delight. Verity's whole body quivered, and her hips arched toward his hand.

Garrett positioned himself above her. He waited as her face flushed with passion, as her breasts rose and fell with sharp breaths. He guided his shaft toward her opening. Verity felt his length, smooth and thick, between her legs. She felt the rapid throb of his pulse, the heat of his staff against her sensitized, damp flesh.

He let the tip enter her. She clasped his shoulders, her hips circled him. "My love . . ."

Garrett's body pressed inward. Verity tensed when he parted her maidenhead, but the pleasure of his full entry obliterated discomfort. Garrett sank into her body. He filled her until his shaft met her womb, until she squeezed tight around him.

Verity thought he pierced into her very core. She had never imagined a man's length would go so deep inside her. It seized control of her soul, all her senses. Commanded her.

A primitive instinct drove her to resist his complete control. Until Garrett moved. His penetration eased, and he withdrew to shallow depths, then entered again. White-hot friction sent currents of desire surging through Verity's body, even into her toes. Her eyes rolled back in her head, and a long, shuddering moan burst from her lips.

Garrett didn't demand acquiescence. Instead, he answered her most secret desires, filling every need that lay dormant in the recesses of her mind. He cupped her slender hips, urging her into motion. Verity's reaction soared with wildfire speed. She undulated beneath him, twisting around his engorged shaft, pleasing herself with the fiery sensations.

Verity turned her face to his. His mouth found hers. Their tongues met, mimicking the rhythmic joining of their bodies. She wrapped her legs around Garrett's, holding herself close against his body. Her undulations quickened, striving higher and higher.

Garrett withstood her eager demand—he turned his face into her hair, his lips against her neck.

Magical, white light sparkled through Verity's senses. A sensation so powerful it seemed beyond endurance gripped her. Her lips parted, her teeth sank into Garrett's shoulder. The sensation burst into raging fullness. Her body quivered and shook, and her toes stiffened. A wild cry shivered from her throat.

Garrett poured the full force of his desire into Verity's quivering body. She felt its heat inside her as her own spasms stilled. His body relaxed, though he supported his weight on his elbows. His body filled hers, and peace surrounded them.

"Dear God, I really bit you."

A low chuckle met her ears. "As I warned you, my sweet vixen. You're not the kind to take a man's desire passively."

"And I screamed, more or less."

"You did."

"I'm really not a lady, am I?"

Garrett kissed her face, still deeply engorged inside her. "Ladies hold very little interest for me. A man can't reach the place I just found if his woman isn't there with him."

"Where were we?"

"Heaven."

"That's not the way the Websters' minister described it."

"Each man to his own heaven," replied Garrett. "But if it's not like this, I don't want to go."

Chapter Seven

Garrett woke with the dawn's first light. Reveille sounded in the distance, but he made no move to rise. Verity slept in his arms, tucked comfortably against him. Garrett kissed her head, but she didn't wake.

The night of my life . . . No woman ever touched him this way. Garrett stared at the ceiling, remembering how his desire rose, exploded, abated. Only to rise again. Verity learned quickly. She sought pleasure. She delighted in his.

Now what? Garrett considered the matter, wanting his decision made before she woke. He couldn't gauge the danger Dave Delaney presented her. His instinct told him it was substantial, but he couldn't be sure.

I'll let her be Watkins a few more days, until I've decided what to do with her. How to keep her safe when I'm in battle.

Verity stirred in his arms. She kissed his chest sleepily, then smiled up at him. "Good morning," she whispered. Garrett brushed her hair from her forehead.

"Good morning, Angel."

Verity seemed changed in the morning light. He'd taken a wild, young seductress into bed. A woman with new maturity woke beside him, her languid smile revealing her satiation.

This woman could be my wife.

"Did I hear bugles?" she asked.

"I'm afraid so."

Verity fought sleep, then sat up heedless of her nudity. "We'll have to hurry."

"Why? Dan will handle muster." Garrett felt sated, but seeing her bare flesh, her sleepy eyes . . .

"Jefferson. You promised to get him into your company. You didn't forget, did you?"

"It slipped my mind, yes. He's not as interesting or compelling as you, My Sweet."

"What did Ivy do with Watkins's clothes?" muttered Verity as she left the bed.

"Back from the world of dreams." Garrett sighed as Verity pulled on trousers, then wrapped a cloth around her breasts.

Garrett dressed just in time to answer an impatient knock on the door. Verity tied her shoes as Garrett admitted Jefferson.

"What's keeping you?" Jefferson held a musket, though he wore civilian clothes.

"Slow down, Davis," advised Garrett. "Let the men have breakfast first. We want them calm before I introduce you."

"I hope they serve bourbon with grub, then." Jefferson looked between Verity and Garrett. "I suppose you two didn't get much sleep. Wonderful! And you're the ones I'm trusting to get me in. Pull yourselves together."

Verity flushed with embarrassment, but Garrett seized the young man's arm. "A slightly less . . . infuriating manner might serve you better this morning, Davis. We want to get you in, not see you hanged."

"Lynched," corrected Jefferson. "Don't want me getting uppity, eh?"

"So much for good advice," sighed Garrett. "Davis, treat other men the way you wish to be treated. Be polite, give them a chance to prove themselves worthy. That's what *you* want, isn't it?"

Verity gazed admiringly at Garrett, but Jefferson rolled his eyes. Garrett looked between them. He saw youth painfully evident, hope unconcealed by cynicism, despite Jefferson's abrupt manner.

An old weight returned to Garrett's heart. So much rested on his shoulders. So much he couldn't change. They were waiting, and they had no one but him.

"If you don't get moving—"

"We're ready," piped up Verity. Jefferson turned and marched down the hall. Verity exchanged a glance with Garrett. They both shook their heads.

"This may not be the best idea I've had."

"It may be among the worst. Still," said Garrett just as Jefferson shouted *"Move!"* to them from the stairs, "if he fights with half that much intensity, the war may not last through the spring."

"Men, I'd like your approval on a new recruit."

Garrett addressed Ethan's company outside Sam's tent after they returned from breakfast.

"There's an able-bodied man who wants to fight with us, if you'll agree to have him."

"If he can shoot and stand his ground, we'd damned sure let him in," said Sam. "We added young Watkins here, and he's a slight bit stronger than he looks, but we could use another shot. Hallowell's company is dwindling to next to nothing."

"That's not my fault," interjected Ethan.

"Of course not," said Verity. "You're a very good officer. But this isn't a large company."

"Where is the fellow?" asked Sam.

"Mr. Davis," called Garrett. "The men would like to meet you."

Jefferson Davis appeared around the tent corner. In a flat second, only Verity's face remained smiling. To a man, the soldiers let their mouths drop open. No one said a word. Garrett knew their reaction wasn't what Verity hoped. Jefferson, too, looked strained and defensive.

It was exactly what he had expected.

"This is Jefferson Davis." Garrett waited for the inevitable laughter about the name to die down before continuing. "He's been searching for a company willing to allow him to join in battle. He has my approval. That doesn't count for much if the men who'll fight beside him don't agree. I invite you to allow a noble heart its right to honor."

Garrett stood back and allowed the men to digest his request. He saw Verity's shock and indignation at the men's reaction. He saw her straighten. He saw Verrill Watkins emerge, and knew that facet of her character was as real as his lover.

"Well, it's fine with me. And it should be with the rest of you, too. After all, Mr. Davis has more to gain by fighting this war than any of us. I think he should be allowed to take part, lest the whites say the black man doesn't own his freedom because his blood wasn't shed in its defense.''

Garrett listened to Verity's fierce words, and his heart moved. *I love her,* he thought. *This woman will be my wife.*

Verity left her place in roll to face each man. ''You, Ethan Hallowell. Isn't this why you joined? You listened to Frederick Douglas. Here he stands. Life isn't simple. You decide. Are you a North man, or will you yield to the slaveowners in the South? You've got one chance to do what's right. Your soul, Captain. Hear its voice.''

Garrett didn't understand Verity's passionate challenge to Ethan Hallowell, but apparently Ethan did. ''I am honored to welcome you, Mr. Davis.'' Garrett heard pain in the young man's voice, but no regret.

''Good. And you, Sam O'Neill. You're Irish, and we all know what that means. Of course, if you deny him, you're rightly saying you're here fighting for nothing. And that would make you look like a fool. And you're no fool, Sir.''

''Watkins, your tongue could confuse an arrow.'' A slow grin broadened Sam's bearded face. ''If the boy can prove his shooting, then I'm for giving him a chance.''

Sam's word tipped the scale on Jefferson's behalf. Peter McCaffrey relaxed, though he peered suspiciously at the black man.

Jefferson Davis, however, wasn't impressed. ''I'm twenty years old, Sergeant. I haven't been a 'boy' for many years. Unless you prefer 'Old Fool' to 'Sergeant.' ''

Verity bit her lip, and Garrett shook his head. Sam took an angry step forward, followed by John, who appeared unusually set for a fight. Verity hopped between them.

''Now look here! Let Mr. Davis prove his skill on the range. Give him a target and see what he can do.''

Verity turned to Jefferson, who glared at Sam and John, equally ready for a fight. Garrett watched in amazement as Verity tried to appease them all. ''Sam calls everybody 'boy.' I'm sure he meant no disrespect. Please, Mr. Davis. Take your musket and show us what you can do as a soldier. That's what matters.''

Verity had managed to prevent, or at least stall, what was developing into the possibility of an ugly brawl. Now Sam stepped back, tugging John along with him. Jefferson readied his musket.

''To the firing range, then,'' said Garrett with a sigh of relief.

John set up the firing line well behind the spot where she had proved Verrill Watkins's ability. "Oh, no," muttered Verity, anger tightening her features, but Jefferson made no comment.

Verity started to raise her objections to the injustice, but Garrett caught her eye and shook his head. "Watch."

Jefferson lifted his musket, aimed without long study of the target, then fired.

The group fell silent, staring in disbelief at the results of Jefferson's perfect shot. Verity clapped her hands, and Garrett smiled.

"Boy, you can fight alongside me any time," remarked Sam. "Just keep it pointed at the rebs."

Jefferson eyed Sam without smiling.

"Oh, hell! Like Watkins here said, I call everyone 'boy.'"

Verity glanced at the sergeant doubtfully, but Garrett shot her a warning glance as Sam eased from the potentially sticky situation.

"But I can see you're sensitive about it. I'll just have to think of something else to call you." Sam thought a minute, then chuckled. "Jefferson Davis, is it? Now that's a name to be reckoned with, to be sure. Mr. President, it is! You'll be known as the President from here on in."

Ethan stepped forward to congratulate Jefferson. "Welcome to our company. You can stay in Watkins's bed, since he's attending Major Knox."

Jefferson seemed to relax a little, though he still appeared aloof. Sam and some of the others offered hesitant welcome to Jefferson, who accepted their words with a detached reserve. He didn't insult anyone, which Garrett considered lucky. John turned away and left the group in disgust.

"Where's he going?" asked Verity. "John seems so tolerant, usually. I can't believe he'd deny a man his rightful place."

"I wouldn't have thought so, either," said Garrett.

"Do you think it will work?"

"If they give him a chance, and if our Mr. Davis controls his anger, yes. He's got courage. The men will see that when the time comes."

"I wonder if Jefferson feels the same misgivings about sharing living quarters with white men that they feel about him?"

Garrett nodded. "Most likely, yes. Let it work itself out, *Watkins*. This situation won't perfect itself in a day."

"At least, we got him in," said Verity.

"We did. But you are the reason it went as smoothly as it did.

Without your well-chosen words, we'd be in the middle of a battle right here.''

Verity smiled, her eyes twinkling with memory.

"Don't do it, woman," he whispered. "Lest these men think I've taken a shine to Watkins."

"Maybe you can take me to Ivy's again," she suggested in a low voice.

"I'm afraid I've got a meeting with Colonel Godwin tonight."

"Can't we meet afterward?"

"It'll go late, Verity." Seeing her downcast expression, Garrett smiled. "Believe me, this isn't the way I hoped to spend the night, either."

Mail arrived at the camp that afternoon, and men rushed forward when the courier called their names. Sam read his with a grave expression.

"Is something wrong, Sam?" asked Verity. At first, he didn't seem to hear her. "What is it?"

"My boy, Orator, who I mentioned to you."

"Is he all right?"

"That's the thing. I don't rightly know. This here's from my wife, Kady. She tells me the boy's taken off unawares to her. No one knows where he's got to."

"You mean he ran away from home?"

"Seems so." Sam paused. "A bullheaded, Irish lad like that— no telling where he's got to. Just thirteen, but he's sure he's a man. Thinks he's ready for anything, he does. Even the army."

"We'll look for him, then," decided Verity. Sam nodded, but both knew how difficult it would be to find one thirteen-year-old boy in the vast Federal army.

Garrett and Dan returned after midnight, but Verity waited. "What happened?" she asked, startling Dan, but Garrett drew a long breath before answering. Verity saw from his expression that Hooker's speech had disheartened him.

"We've enjoyed the exuberance and fine wine of our brilliant commander," said Dan as he loosened his cravat. "Intended on Hooker's part as a rousing address calling on our readiness to participate in the greatest victory any American army ever forged. Major Knox saw the evening otherwise.''

"Did you, Sir?''

"Hooker has made no secret of his intention to drive past Lee into Richmond,'' said Garrett. "But, no, his bluster doesn't convince me. In fact, it terrifies the hell out of me. I'm afraid we'll be placed on another field of battle where we can't win. And Robert E. Lee knows a great deal better how to manipulate that field than Joe Hooker.''

"At least, he's not hesitant,'' offered Dan.

"Not yet, no,'' said Garrett. "Hooker doesn't respect the genius and daring of the commander facing him. His overconfidence might bring about another Union disaster like Fredericksburg.''

"Well, he certainly sounds sure of himself,'' remarked Dan.

"Too damned sure,'' said Garrett. "Not for nothing was Lee President Lincoln's first choice to lead the army. He hasn't found another to match. McClellan spent his time posturing, wasting months. Later, Burnside wasted lives. I fear Hooker may throw them away in a rash action yielding nothing but grief.''

"What do you think he's got planned?'' asked Dan as he stretched and sat down on his bunk to remove his boots. "He wasn't specific on that count.''

Garrett shrugged. "Something brilliantly complex and perfectly simple. So original Old Marse Robert would never dream of such daring.''

"We'll be moving soon,'' speculated Dan. "Might have gone already, but the rain's been delaying the cavalry.''

"No doubt Lee's already heard the rumors,'' said Garrett. "Hooker isn't hard to read.''

"Oh, dear,'' muttered Verity. "Maybe he's gathered enough men—''

"There aren't enough men for the assaults they order,'' interrupted Garrett. The emotion in his deep voice sent chills of apprehension along Verity's spine.

"They order thousands of us against unassailable positions. We're mowed down like wheat in a field. They hold us back from attacking where and when is wisest, then too late hurtle us against rebels who only need load and fire to repel our shattered forces.''

"You don't have much faith in our fearless leader, do you?'' laughed Dan.

"Not much, no,'' admitted Garrett. "Hooker could use a little more fear. Then he'd set his plans accordingly. I don't trust a man who thinks the enemy isn't going to show up.''

For a full week, late meetings delayed Verity and Garrett from enjoying their new passion. Verity lay restless on her cot, waiting for his return. The month of April wore on. With the bright flush of spring, rumors ripened about Joseph Hooker's long awaited attack on Lee's Army of North Virginia.

Garrett attended a meeting with Dan Wallingford and Colonel Godwin. Verity heard John singing outside, the mournful *"Johnny Has Gone for a Soldier."* Verity thought of Robert, and tears misted in her eyes.

She felt lonely, painfully aware of Garrett's absence. They'd found little time alone, and she lived for the silent exchanges, the meaningful looks.

"He won't be back before midnight." Verity put on her shoes and went to join the others.

Sam sat by the small fire, whittling a piece of softwood into nothing. Jefferson paced, then sat down. Verity seated herself beside him. He seemed to enjoy her company, never revealing her secret to the others.

Ethan appeared out of nowhere. "Where in hell have you been, Hallowell?" asked Sam. "If you leave that puny lieutenant to our drill once more, I'm liable to wring his scrawny neck. God's nightgown, I thought *you* were bad. He's worse."

"That's true," agreed Verity.

Ethan didn't explain his whereabouts, but Verity hadn't seen him since the afternoon of the previous day. His expression seemed strange, even more distracted than usual. Verity recognized his mood. He met her eyes and a small grin appeared on his lips. Verity shook her head, but she smiled, too.

"Damn, I wish we'd get moving," grumbled Jefferson.

"I hear they're preparing marching rations," said Ethan. "It looks like we're headed somewhere."

"You heard anything from the major, Watkins?" asked Sam.

"Only that he thinks we'll be marching soon." Verity, for one, wasn't eager to leave the comparative safety of camp. She doubted Garrett would let her accompany the men, anyway. Despite her better judgement, Verity felt a tug of regret.

Though spring brought its usual beauty to Northern Virginia, it rained almost continually. Brief respites in the downpour served to taunt the men in blue with the possibility of action. Across the river in Fredericksburg, assured of their invincibility rebels called to the Yankee pickets.

"We've drilled and drilled 'til I don't think I can drill anymore," Jefferson complained as he chewed on a piece of hard-tack. "I hope they'll order us somewhere soon, or I'm likely to head on over that river myself to take on the rebs."

"Why don't you just march on back to the jungle you came from, boy?" muttered John, ostensibly under his breath.

Verity gulped as Jefferson turned toward the scraggly musician. Their eyes locked in virtual combat, hate flickering in a visible light between them. John and Jefferson had come close to blows often since Jefferson joined the company.

"You need some lessons with that miserable old guitar," said Jefferson. Ethan winced, and Verity's heart quickened nervously as John slowed his strumming to glare at Jefferson.

"What would some swamp-running ape know? Go back to your whorehouse piano, boy, and leave the fighting to men."

"That's enough." Ethan looked helplessly to Sam, but the sergeant kept whittling and didn't look up.

"Sam," urged Verity.

"Let it be, Watkins," said Sam.

Verity hopped up from her seat as Jefferson rose and moved menacingly toward John. "No!"

But Jefferson didn't attack John, as Verity dreaded. Instead, he seized the guitar from John's hands and sat down beside him to play. John started to wrest his instrument from Jefferson's control. The sudden ring of music stopped him.

An exotic, pulsing surge emanated from the old guitar. Unknown rhythms emerged through Jefferson's skill, leading his ragged audience to unfamiliar worlds of raw glory.

John was astounded. The black man had taken the guitar he had made himself and produced melodies he'd never imagined. Despite his fury, John's mind was already forming lyrics and harmonies to the music Jefferson produced.

Jefferson stopped and handed the guitar back to John. John took it almost gingerly, as if seeing it for the first time. No one else spoke, watching the moment unfold between those two.

"Well, President, you sure can play, I'll give you that. Where'd you learn guitar?"

"Never touched one before," answered Jefferson. "I learned it from watching you. Added my own touch, of course, but I just followed what I saw you doing. You're a damned fool ass, but your music doesn't show it."

Garrett spoke to Verity as soon as he entered their tent. "Take the night off, Watkins." Their eyes met.

"What? You're giving him the whole night?" questioned Dan.

"The boy's been working hard, Dan. I think we can do without him, don't you?"

"Guess so," said Dan. "I did have a few things for the boy to do, though."

"Tomorrow." Garrett's eyes met Verity's. "As for myself, I'll be paying a visit to Madame Ivy's grand establishment."

"Wish I could go with you," sighed Dan. "Godwin's got me on duty tonight."

"A shame," said Garrett, his eyes still on Verity's. "Watkins, you can go now."

"Thank you, Sir." Verity darted from the tent, making a beeline for the brothel. Rounding a corner, she bumped into Ethan Hallowell.

"Watkins! What are you doing out so late?"

"I'm on a brief leave. And you?"

Ethan blushed. "I've given myself a leave, as well."

"You're crossing the river again?"

"Again? How did you know?"

"A gleam in your eye," said Verity. "Did you see her?"

"I saw her," said Ethan. "She's more beautiful than I remembered, especially without . . ." He caught himself, bit his lip, but Verity smiled.

"And you're going again tonight? Isn't that a little risky, Ethan?"

"Maybe. But we're headed out tomorrow, Hooker's orders. I've got to see her one more time, Watkins. I never thought about it much before, but I could die. I've got to convince her to marry me, especially after we . . . well, after we were so close."

"You think she might have a baby. Don't worry, Captain. You'll be a good father."

Ethan blushed furiously, but he didn't deny Watkins's guess. "I hope so."

Suddenly Verity realized the significance of Ethan's words. "Heading out? You mean the army? Where are we going?"

"We're moving west, trying to get around Lee, as I understand it. The enlisted men aren't supposed to know, but it's no secret. As a matter of fact, I heard it first from Gordy Dyer."

"The picket? Ethan, you shouldn't talk about war things with the rebels. It might be taken wrong. I know you meant no harm—"

"I didn't," Ethan assured her. "He told *me*. Anyway, I must go if I'm to meet Bess at the right time."

"Enjoy yourself."

"Perfect bliss, my little friend." Ethan took Watkins's hand, shaking it vigorously. "Thank you, Watkins. You can't know what your friendship means to me. I learned from your words that I can be true both to the woman I love and our national cause."

"I take it Bess understands your position."

"She does," said Ethan dreamily. "She feels its does credit to my honor that I serve the Union to the best of my ability. She still loves me."

"Love is a higher law," agreed Verity. "Never let it go."

Verity hurried to the brothel, washed, then allowed Ivy to dress her in a black velvet gown. Far from a somber mourning dress, the velvet plunged over her breasts, hugged her waist, then flared gracefully to the floor.

"No jewelry," decided Ivy. "Bare skin attracts a man more than any diamonds or pearls."

"Does it?" asked Verity as she gazed at her reflection. "I think this is more shocking than the blue dress you gave me."

"That was tame. This is meant to set a man on fire. Sit while I fix up your hair."

Verity sat at a vanity table, fiddling with a vast array of bottles and jars while Ivy combed her hair. Verity picked up a cut crystal bottle. "What's this?"

"Oil of the Gods," said Ivy.

"What's it for?"

"Well you should ask. It contains a special oil, direct from the Far East. When massaged into a gentleman's skin, it brings relaxation and . . . other things."

"What other things?"

"Now, that depends on where you apply the potion. You'll have to use your imagination on this point."

Someone knocked on Ivy's door. She stuck her head out, then

turned back to Verity. "He's here. Handsome as a king, rugged as a barbarian warrior."

A wild tingle coursed along Verity's nerves, centering in her fingertips. "Do I look pretty?"

"Like an angel and a devil wrapped in one," Ivy assured her. Verity wasn't sure this was the effect she wanted, but the madam opened the door before she could consider it further.

Verity peeked out of the dressing room and saw Garrett. He wore full dress uniform, even a sabre having at his side. He saw her and held out his hand. A smile curved the firm line of his lips as she came to him.

"You're lovely tonight, my lady."

"Thank you."

At a cue from Ivy, the new pianist struck up a rather faulty waltz. Neither Garrett nor Verity noticed its inadequacies. "Would you care to dance, my love?"

"I would."

Garrett drew her into his arms, easing her into a slow, graceful rhythm. This time, Verity had no difficulty following. Garrett led with skill and assurance, stilling Verity's own impulse to take over. She flowed in his arms, her eyes on his, as they glided around the room.

Neither spoke, though their eyes burned with the promise of the night to come. Their bodies touched lightly, but Verity knew he was aroused. His strong hand gripped hers, while his touch on her waist made her feel like a feather.

"It's time for this dance to continue . . . upstairs."

Verity nodded. The pianist played on, oblivious to the fact that his audience had departed. Garrett led Verity up the stairs. She smiled when he checked the hall first.

"All clear."

Verity chuckled. "I don't know what you think I'm going to see that I haven't seen already."

Garrett glanced back at her. "Nothing you won't find out from me." He grinned and held out his hand for her.

Garrett led Verity to her old room, but stopped before entering.

She eyed him doubtfully. "What are you doing? Aren't we going in?"

Garrett smiled at her eagerness. "We are." He lifted her into his arms. "But we're going in my way."

He kissed her lips, then carried her over the threshold. Garrett kicked the door closed behind them, then bore her to the bed. He set her on her feet, then cupped her chin in his broad hand.

"Have you any idea how I've longed for another night with you?"

"Yes."

"Vixen."

Garrett ran his finger along Verity's collarbone, then across the soft skin above her breast, sliding along the lace-edged bodice. He delved into the cleft of her bosom, then drew out a small bottle of liquid.

"What's this?"

"Oil of the Gods," said Verity. "At least, according to Ivy." She took the bottle from his hands. "Shall we try it and find out?"

Her offer puzzled Garrett, but Verity began undressing him. His senses leapt with anticipation when he felt her deft fingers touch the heat of his skin. Verity pulled off his coat, then pushed his shirt over his shoulder.

She kissed his shoulder, tasting his skin. She tossed aside his shirt, then turned her attention lower. Her eyes fixed on his, she slid his trousers off his hips, down to his ankles.

Garrett's pulse surged when she wet her lips. She slid her hand down his stomach until she met his masculine length. She wrapped her fingers around the swollen girth, squeezing sensually, massaging him while he stood spellbound before her.

Garrett's lust had compounded over the week without her. It leapt beyond anything he'd known before. Verity released him, stepped back, and slowly undressed. Garrett watched as each creamy inch of her was revealed. She dropped the straps of her satin chemise, smiling when a soft groan escaped his lips.

"Lie down."

Garrett willingly complied and lay back on the bed to await her.

"Roll over."

"You're a bossy wench."

"That shouldn't surprise you." Verity climbed astride him, the soft flesh of her bottom brushing tantalizingly against the back of his thighs.

Garrett glanced over his shoulder as Verity opened the crystal bottle and poured some of its fluid into the palm of her hand. It smelled of almonds and spice, an exotic scent. She applied the rich oil to his back, easing her fingertips into his flesh, playing with the taut muscles until they relaxed beneath her touch.

Deeper and deeper she stroked him, his skin slick with the potent oil. Verity worked her way down to the small of his back, kneading and massaging as Garrett moaned his approval.

"This is pure heaven, My Dear," he murmured lazily. When Verity began massaging his firm buttocks, he knew the heaven had just begun.

"Lie on your back now," she whispered, and she leaned forward to kiss his face.

Beginning at his chest, she worked her way down. Each muscle tightened and relaxed beneath her fingers. She stroked over his chest, then traced a line downward across the taut cords of his stomach.

Verity again poured the scented oil into her palm and eased to the heart of Garrett's need. Garrett groaned as she took his hardened staff into her hand, caressing him gently at first, then with firmer strokes. Over and over, she ran her hand along the heated shaft, teasing the blunt tip with her fingertips, then returning to explore the entire length.

"Do you like this?" she asked, her voice low and husky as her own desire soared.

"I do indeed, Sweet Angel. I do indeed."

"I want you, Garrett Knox."

"I am yours to command, woman." Garrett placed his hands on her hips, then guided her into position above his heated erection.

Verity rose above him, then lowered until the tip of his staff met the moistened warmth of her sex. A harsh groan tore from his throat as he drove his hips up, sinking his length deep inside her.

Verity gasped in surprise, pushed upward by the force of his entry. She braced herself on his chest, then began a rhythmic ride of absolute pleasure. She tipped her head back, surrendering fully to the wild sensations.

Her fingers dug into his chest, her whole body quivering as she writhed in her ecstasy. With shuddering force, he spilled his seed against her womb, filling her with desire, with the essence of his life.

Verity clasped his shoulders, holding him close. She slid off his body and lay close beside him. "First you bite me, then claw my flesh," he noted as he examined the scratches on his chest.

"I didn't mean to," she told him earnestly. "That won't stop you from—"

"Quite the contrary. All women should learn your art of sexual oblivion."

"Is that what it is? I do lose control of myself, I'm afraid."

Garrett gathered Verity into his arms and kissed her forehead. "You do, my Sweet Angel. You do."

Verity contented herself a while, lying in Garrett's arms, her eyes closed. "When I'm with you, nothing else seems to matter," she said drowsily. "It's hard to believe there's a war."

"I've watched you all week," said Garrett. "Drilling, eating grub, listening to—and telling, I suspect—ribald jokes. I wondered if I'd lost my mind. Watkins—that's not what I imagined when I considered the woman I'd make my wife."

"What did you imagine?" Verity turned in his arms to look at him.

"When I was seven, I told my father I would marry a large woman and squeeze a lot of babies out of her."

"Dear God!"

"Later, I imagined a helpmate, companion of sorts. A woman who liked horses, sex. Of course, I imagined marriage in the distant future."

"I do like horses and sex. I don't know about the baby squeezing thing, though."

Garrett laughed, and suddenly Verity realized the impact of his words. "What do you mean, 'wife?' Do you want to marry me?"

"Are you proposing, my Sweet Flower?"

Verity blushed. "No! I only meant—"

Garrett didn't let her finish. He sat up, naked, his dark skin warm in the lamplight. "Then I'd better hurry, lest you again seize the gentleman's role and beg for my hand." Garrett left the bed and knelt beside it, drawing Verity's hand to his lips.

"My dearest love, will you do me the great honor of becoming my wife?"

"You're naked. You can't ask me to marry you when you're naked."

Garrett seized his cravat, tied it around his neck, and took her hand again. "Well?"

"I'm naked, too."

"I don't mind."

Verity wrapped the blanket around her body, then returned her hand to Garrett's. "You may continue."

"Then, Miss Talmadge, grant me your hand. I can't live with you in my heart if you're not beside me in life as well."

"Are you sure you want me beside you?"

"I'm sure."

"Then I accept." Verity dropped her blanket and slid onto the floor, safe and loved in Garrett's arms. They kissed, and she pulled off the cravat. Garrett lifted her back onto the bed.

"Can we marry this soon?" she asked as they settled back into the warmth of their covers. "I'm in mourning, after all. I wouldn't want to dishonor Westley, even if our marriage wasn't complete."

"This is war. Such things as mourning periods fall to the wayside in light of more pressing situations. Ours may be considered urgent."

"Because we're marching out tomorrow?"

"How did you know that? I know rumors flood the campsite, but most hint at another assault on Fredericksburg."

"Ethan told me."

"How did he know?" Garrett sounded serious, even suspicious. But Verity saw no reason to keep the truth from him now.

"A rebel picket told him, when he went to see his Bess."

"Bess?"

"Ethan met a girl at the rebel ball. They fell madly in love, and he's gone to see her a few times."

"Has he?" Garrett's suspicion mounted, but Verity couldn't guess why.

"It isn't so surprising, is it? You're the one who sent him over. Ethan is surprisingly romantic."

"He fell in love with a girl, a rebel girl, in one night?"

"Yes."

"Does she know his allegiance?"

"She guessed. I overheard them, you see, when I went looking for him. It was almost as if they knew each other before. Very romantic."

"Are you sure they didn't?"

Verity began to sense the direction of Garrett's doubt. "You can't think Ethan Hallowell would be dishonest?"

"Men aren't always what they seem, Verity."

"I thought you like him."

"I do. As did Robert. And Westley."

"No." Verity sat up. "You don't think Ethan was responsible for—no. For what reason?"

"If he's involved with a rebel girl, that may be reason enough."

"That's ridiculous. I told you they just met." Verity's brow furrowed angrily. "If I'd known you'd be so foolish, I wouldn't have told you."

"Our first argument?"

"Hardly our first," she replied without looking at him. "Or have you forgotten when we met?"

"I'll never forget." Garrett smiled at her, and Verity's heart fluttered. Her anger fought against her love, and she fixed her eyes on a rumple in the blanket.

"Ethan is my friend. You mustn't accuse him, Garrett. He's vulnerable, in a peculiar, stiff way. And he admires you so. It would crush him."

"He matters to you."

"They all do. My life was so empty—you can't imagine. Now I have purpose. I belong. Sam is like a father, though a different sort from my own. John is a quiet uncle with a knowing gleam in his eye. Jefferson seems like my little brother, even if we're a different color."

"And Ethan Hallowell?"

"I suppose he reminds me of Westley," said Verity. "Only more fussy, tenser. I feel the need to protect him, though I'm not sure why. I see him, and I think he's standing on the edge of some dreadful precipice. I know he'll fall. It's just Ethan's nature to fall. And I wonder if he'll get up again. I can't stop him from falling, but maybe I can help him after it's over."

"All this, in Watkins," sighed Garrett. "If they only knew!"

"They wouldn't be my friends anymore. I don't want them to know."

"You have a surprisingly tender heart, my love. Candace told me this, but I never guessed the depth."

"I'm not tender," scoffed Verity. "I just think they need me. Jefferson needed me, and now he's fitting in very well. I know

Ethan will need me, too. I don't know why or how I know this. I just do."

"So you intend to stick around?"

"Of course! You don't mean to send me away, do you?"

"Until I find out what Dave Delaney wanted with you, I'll keep you near. Whether you stay as my wife or Watkins remains to be decided. Wives, after all, stay with officers at camp. Still, if we marry now, your presence will be known."

"Well? Make up your mind!"

"If we marry, your masquerade is over," said Garrett. "If we wait, the ruse stands a while yet."

"If we wait, we'll still do this, won't we?"

"We will." Garrett took her hand and kissed it. "There's another matter to be considered, however. After these nights of unrestrained passion, my child might already grow in you."

"That's true." A baby hadn't occurred to her, but she felt suddenly ripe, full. A woman. "I would like that. Unless you intend to squeeze it out of me."

"I'll leave that to nature. You must watch the signs, Verity. If you're pregnant, I want to know, so I can keep you safe from disease and danger."

"I've had every disease as a child," said Verity. "There's nothing left for me to catch."

"Good, but don't strain yourself. I'll have to keep you out of drill."

Verity rolled her eyes. "I'm very fit. And they ride pregnant mares, don't they?"

"You're not a horse."

"I'm sure it's better to be strong."

Garrett didn't argue. "When I leave tomorrow, you'll stay here with Ivy."

"I want to go with you."

"You know I can't let you do that," said Garrett. "I want your word, Verity. You'll stay."

Verity didn't want to march with the army. She didn't want to see battle. She lay back in Garrett's arms. "I'll stay."

"Good. I don't want to worry about you when I lead my men."

Garrett closed his eyes, edging toward sleep, but Verity lay long awake. *When I lead my men . . .* Garrett would enter battle again. What if something happened, what if no one saw, no one was quick enough to help him?

No, he's fought many times without injury. Verity tried to sleep. What if the spy, the traitor, wanted Garrett dead, too? If only she could follow along, invisible, out of danger! Just to be sure things went well, that Garrett stayed safe, unharmed.

What can I do? Nothing. I'll stay with Ivy, do as I'm told. He'll be my husband soon. I must learn to obey.

Chapter Eight

Garrett left before daybreak. Verity stood at Ivy's door, tears glistening in her eyes. "You'll be careful, won't you?" she asked, though it seemed a weak, forlorn question.

"I'll come back. How could I not, when I have you waiting here, dressed like that?"

Garrett kissed her cheek, he held her close, cradling her head against his shoulder. Verity wrapped her arms around his waist, unwilling to let him go. All night the thought of his danger had tormented her. By morning, the threat became a certainty.

"You need me," she whispered. "Let me come with you. As Watkins. I'll stay in the rear."

"No, Verity."

There was no use in argument. Garrett's mind was set. He kissed her again, then drew away. The eerie call of bugles rang from around the campsite. The smoke from morning campfires hung low in the frosty, cool air. A foggy haze blanketed the ground as men formed into their companies.

"It looks like rain," said Ivy.

"Naturally," replied Garrett. "When the Army of the Potomac moves, it rains. Always."

"It's not a good sign," said Ivy. "I don't like it. The spirits don't like it, either."

"Spirits?" asked Verity doubtfully.

"Them as wait beside us, our Guardians," Ivy told her. "They're in waiting for disaster. I feel it."

Garrett met Verity's eyes and shook his head. "With that encouraging word, I must go."

"I love you." Verity's soft whisper rang through the morning air. It hung as an eternal promise.

Garrett cupped Verity's chin in his hand, then kissed her lips. "I love you, too."

He turned around. He left. Garrett didn't look back, but Ivy stood in the doorway with her arm around Verity's waist. "He's walking into darkness. He's strong, but it's not enough."

"What do you mean?"

"I mean, he's leaving the light behind, Little Miss. I see him, and he's brushing up too close to his own downfall—"

"Ivy," warned Verity. "Speak plainer. This doesn't have anything to do with Spirits, does it?" *Spirits from heaven, or from the bottle?*

"He'll risk his life for another. The other will be saved. If no one comes forward to help, your Major Knox will most probably die."

"No! Ivy, that's crazy. You can't know that."

"I have the gift of sight. It ain't sure. Hell, it's failed me enough in the past. Didn't warn me about that husband of mine, nor show me a way to save my baby. But when it shows itself, I listen."

"You see all this about Garrett?"

"The light around him darkens." Ivy looked closely at Verity. She backed away, and looked again. "That light remains around yourself."

"Then I can help him."

"God forgive me for saying so, but yes. Get yourself back in boy's clothes and go after him. Just don't tell him I advised you."

"He won't let me. He made me promise."

"You can't keep a promise to a dead man."

Dressed again as Verrill Watkins, Verity fell into line beside a Minnesota company. "Who's this?" questioned an irritated lieutenant.

"Verrill Watkins," said Verity. "I'm afraid I missed my company, so I thought I'd march along with yours until I catch them up."

The lieutenant eyed her insignia. "Twentieth Massachusetts, eh? They're a whole regiment ahead. You won't be catching up until we get there."

"Get where?" asked Verity. A few of the soldiers nodded at her inquiry.

"God knows."

The Minnesota regiment marched out, joining the long procession westward. Verity soon found herself awash in the swelling blue lines. The rain began, soaking into the rutted path they followed. Mud sucked at her boots. The weight of eight days rations and forty rounds of ammunition nearly crumpled her to her knees. Verity resisted the temptation to discard her knapsack along the roadside.

Onlookers watched the long, blue files pass by, but she heard few cheers of praise. Rain drizzled down on the soldiers as they slogged through the mud.

"We can't go on like this," muttered Verity.

"Hell, boy. It's less slow going than Burnside's Mud March last winter. We'll make it."

"Wonderful." *Why did I listen to that crazy madam? We'll turn back. Garrett will be fine. Unlike myself, if he learns what I've done. . . .*

The weather cleared by noon. In the sky above, an observation balloon shuffled about in the gusting winds, its attempt to scout out Confederate positions obviously thwarted. Garrett sighed. "Science in its glory."

"What the hell is that?" asked Sam.

"Professor Lowe's observation tactics at work," replied Garrett.

Garrett stared up at the balloon as the wind drove it farther and farther from its target. How many rebels waited for their Yankee foe this time? Led by a man of wisdom and courage, the rebels hadn't faltered yet. Hooker imagined that leaving a few regiments in Falmouth fooled Robert E. Lee. But no such tactics had fooled the rebel commander yet.

"I hope he's seeing more than we are down here," put in Jefferson who trudged along beside John.

Garrett sighed and urged his weary horse onward. "For myself, I hope he's seeing less."

The army erected pontoon bridges over the Rappahannock, then went into bivouac north of the crossroads. Everything went according to Hooker's plan. Verity made her way from the Minnesota regiment to the Massachusetts divisions. Spirits were high. Most praised Hooker's cleverness in removing his army secretly to Lee's flank.

At last, the rebels would be forced to take on the Union's greater numbers on Federal terms.

Morning for Ethan's company came before dawn. Verity slept in a stolen blanket, miserable on the wet, lumpy ground. Waking, even this early, came as a great relief. She rose, stretched. . . .

"Watkins!"

Verity jumped. Sam had spotted her. "Sergeant," She began weakly.

"You're an indomitable little fellow, ain't you? The major told us you was down with the sickness."

"I got better." How convenient that Garrett had used illness to explain Watkins's absence.

"I hope you don't got nothing we'll be catching."

"That seems unlikely," said Jefferson. "Something tells me the major isn't aware of your presence."

"No," replied Verity casually. "I don't think we need to bother him about that just now."

"I'd like to talk to you, Watkins," said Jefferson. "Alone."

He seized Verity's arm and led her away from the others. "Now look, girl. I'm the only one who knows what's going on here. Since you've seen fit to disobey your man, I'll be taking over in his absence."

"You're very conceited," noted Verity. "I helped you get in, and now you're betraying me."

"Betraying you? Ha! I'm saving your crazy hide."

"I have no intention of fighting, Jefferson." Suddenly she wondered why not. She could shoot as well as any of them. She had experienced one battle already. She didn't like it, but as Garrett said, she did no worse than other first-time soldiers.

Jefferson saw her expression, and his dark eyes narrowed. "You stay out of it."

"We're on picket duty," announced Ethan Hallowell. "Of all the insulting tasks . . ."

Ethan's announcement distracted Jefferson. "We won't see much fighting," said Jefferson disappointedly. "I guess you can stay, Watkins."

"They wanted a small company," Ethan told them as explanation for what he considered a lesser task. Despite the close proximity to the enemy, the pickets rarely shot at each other.

"Let's get moving," said Ethan. "Sam, John, Jefferson, McCaffrey. And you, Watkins, since you've seen fit to disobey orders once again."

Verity accompanied the men into the dense woods. Ethan searched for an advantageous position along the western line. "How are we supposed to see anything in this thicket?" asked Verity as they filed through the trees.

"Use your ears, Watkins," advised Ethan. "Much can be heard that can't be seen."

"And my nose, I guess. That's not terribly reassuring," she replied. "I hope the rebels haven't washed lately."

Sam laughed. "What would you know about washing, boy?"

Ethan organized his small company along a ridge in the forest. Verity sat on a fallen tree branch. Sam went farther along the ridge with Peter McCaffrey, while Jefferson and John circled the immediate area.

"What are we supposed to see?" Verity asked Ethan.

"We're now west of the Federal position. General Hooker is headquartered at the Chancellor house. We're a lookout. We're to note anything and everything that might be suspicious. Specifically, any sign of rebel movement. Which is why we're to maintain our silence."

"Oh," whispered Verity. She kept her eyes focused through the trees. "They'd have to come awfully close."

"Then we'll have to be awfully quick," said Jefferson as he paced along the ridge.

"I thought Lee was southeast of here," said Verity. "What would he be doing way over on this side?"

"Outflanking the flank," said John grimly as he finished surveying the area.

Verity's heart began to thud. Silence descended around their position, broken only by occasional pipings of birds and the stealthy motions of woodland creatures. Verity sat on the log until her legs ached from the tedium and her bottom was numb from the hard seat.

Morning wore on. They heard the first explosions of artillery, the *pop* and *whoosh* of musket fire.

Jefferson began to fidget. "What's going on back there?" Long waits while others clashed in deadly combat weren't why he had suffered indignity and prejudice to enter the army.

Garrett might be in that firefight, and Verity was stuck in the middle of the forest with no way to help him. All grew nervous as they waited. Finally, Ethan left to find out what was going on.

When he returned less than an hour later, he was plainly confused. Sam left his post to question Ethan. "What's going on?"

"Have you seen Major Knox?" asked Verity.

"As a matter of fact, I have," replied Ethan. "He said the early fighting went well. Hancock's division and General Couch's held a good forward position, keeping the rebs back. They wanted to move in."

"That sounds promising," put in Verity.

"Indeed," agreed Ethan. "But it seems Fighting Joe Hooker inexplicably ordered them back to defensive positions. Major Knox says Hooker let the fear of Lee get the better of him. When I left, the commanders were trying to convince Hooker to pursue the rebs, but I don't think they'll get far."

"I don't understand," said Verity. "I thought we came to drive Lee back, not the other way around."

"So we all believed," sighed Ethan. "It seems Lee has defeated Hooker mentally. Major Knox told me to put you all on special alert. Anything can happen now."

The eerie silence returned. All eyes stared through the thick forest. The soft green and gold shards of light lent a beguiling, calm beauty to an increasingly hostile environment. The distant thunder of a battle gone curiously awry met their ears.

After a time, the slightest movement of squirrels overhead caused startled alert. Ethan decided to take action. "I want to send out scouts. Quietly. Two of you at a time go forward and see what's up. I don't like this. It's too quiet."

"Let me go," said Verity. She was stiff from sitting. Moreover, she couldn't stand the long wait, the inactivity, while her mind agonized over what happened beyond her reach.

"Very well, Watkins," said Ethan, just as Jefferson said, "No."

"I'll go with you, Watkins," decided Jefferson. "With that dirty face and my ebony skin, who's better suited to hiding in shadows?"

Ethan hesitated. "I'm not sure about this."

Verity and Jefferson headed off through the trees without his consent. Verity heard Ethan muttering about officers lacking real authority. She began to wonder what possessed her to think venturing forth was such a good idea. But Jefferson clearly enjoyed himself.

"How do you know your way around forests so well?" Verity whispered as he picked his way through the dense undergrowth.

"I made my way north through these woods. Slept in caves, holes, whatever . . . when you're hunted by dogs and angry white men, you learn to move swiftly and noiselessly through whatever's in your path. I'll tell you, though, I never expected to be hunting rebels with a crazy white girl."

"For the last time, I'm not crazy."

Jefferson laughed softly, and moved on.

A curious apprehension surfaced in Verity. Jefferson seemed to feel it, too. Even the soft sound of a swaying bush seemed dangerously loud. They approached another ridge, and Jefferson indicated they should keep low. Verity crouched as they moved closer. Both moved from the shadow of one tree to another.

On their knees, they crawled to the rise of the slope. Brambles and pine needles pierced through Verity's trousers to scrape her legs. She didn't try to pull them out. The even trampling of marching men met her ears, just beyond the next rise.

"What is it?" Verity whispered.

"A force of rebels," replied Jefferson. "Listen. Not a sound of cups banging, nothing. They're sneaking in around us!"

"Will they come this way?"

"Doubt it. They're not far enough around our western flank yet. I'd guess they'll go all the way up, then cut in to push our line back in on itself. Lord, we'd better get back and warn them."

With as much stealth as possible, Jefferson and Verity returned to Ethan. Verity scrambled up over the last ridge, skirted down the bank, and ran directly into Garrett Knox.

"What in the bloody name of God are you doing here?" Garrett was obviously forcing restraint to his voice, but she could see the fury in his face. Verity suspected he wanted to yell, to wrap his hands around her throat, to toss her into the air and back to Boston.

"Watkins is on picket duty," said Ethan in surprise.

"Watkins," growled Garrett as he stepped toward Verity, "is a woman. And the damned craziest, most disobedient and monstrous woman that ever lived."

Verity backed away, wounded by Garrett's rage. Ethan, Sam, and Peter McCaffrey stared at her, aghast. Jefferson sighed and shook his head, but John just smiled as if he'd always known.

"A girl?" said Ethan weakly.

"Of a sort." Garrett's eyes bored into Verity's smudged face. "Gentlemen, allow me to present Verity Talmadge."

"Talmadge?" asked Sam, staring at her in utter disbelief. "Not—"

"Yes. Robert Talmadge's sister. Westley Talmadge's widow. And my fiancée."

"What?" John spoke up, his low voice ripe with amusement. The men chuckled.

"Now if that don't beat all," muttered Sam.

"Now that you all know," cut in Jefferson. "We've got bigger things to worry about than the major's pretty lunatic. The rebs are moving around us, and at a quick pace, too."

"Did you see them?" asked Garrett.

"No, Sir, we didn't. But we heard them, plain as anything. Men marching, and a large number, too. There's no mistake."

Verity nodded in agreement, but she didn't dare to speak.

"I've been hearing rumors like this all day," said Garrett. "No one at headquarters is listening. I don't know what they expect, the fools. We had them." His fist clenched, and he punched the air. "Hancock wanted to advance. We were ready. That idiot Hooker called us back. I'd like to know where his brilliant plans are now. He's pulled us back into trenches, giving Lee every opportunity to re-position his army."

"What do we do now?" asked Verity.

"Well," said Garrett as he considered the matter. "If you're right, then the rebels will cut through somewhere beyond here. If they do, there'll be a goddamned rout."

"Not again," groaned Ethan.

"Again," said Garrett. "Get back to the regiment, men. There's no good staying here. Maybe they'll listen to your warnings, but I doubt it. It may be too late now, anyway."

"What about me?" squeaked Verity.

"I'll deal with you later," said Garrett in a low, threatening voice. "But for now . . . men, I have to ask you a favor. I'm expected at headquarters. Watch her for me. And don't expect she'll heed your commands. Apparently, such obedience is beyond her. If the battle comes, sit on her, tie her to a tree. But don't let her fight."

Garrett mounted his horse and rode swiftly through the woods toward the Chancellor house. "Move out," said Ethan, but he didn't look at Verity. Sam, also, walked apart from her as they returned through the woods. John said nothing, but he grinned. Verity didn't dare to speak to them. Jefferson walked beside her, a silent comfort when her heart felt ready to explode with sorrow.

The 20th Mass was entrenched near the rear of the Union line. All seemed to share their confusion about the purpose and value of their current positions. A few minutes after they entered the trenches came the sudden explosion of musket fire, far to their right.

The hidden rebel army came crashing out of the forest, bearing down on Hooker's right flank. Though the waiting remainder of the army couldn't see the results, no one imagined the outcome would be successful.

By nightfall, a horrible rout had taken place. Wounded and terrified men poured in around the waiting encampment. Robert E. Lee had done the unthinkable—he split his smaller army, and won. The right flank collapsed.

The cries of wounded men mingled with the mournful wails of whippoorwills. Night descended over the Union army.

Verity sat by herself, chewing on a piece of salted meat. No one spoke to her. She fought tears, but her pride kept her from sobbing. Her grief gave slow way to anger. How could Garrett hurt her this way? True, she had disobeyed him, but for his own good.

If I tell him Ivy's spirits said I had to go, he'll lock me away forever. Damn. Verity peeked over at Ethan, who still carefully avoided looking her way. Sam whittled and John sang. No one spoke to her.

Garrett hadn't returned to check on her. *I guess the wedding's off,* Verity told herself miserably. Jefferson sat down beside her.

"Well, Watkins, the game's up, I'd say."

Verity sniffed and nodded. "I'm glad you're still speaking to me, at least. Thank you, Jefferson."

"Well, now, I don't think about women like those fools do. My mama had more gumption and courage then twenty white men. I expect if she was still alive, she'd be fighting, too."

"How did she die?"

"Beaten to death," said Jefferson as he took a bite of hardtack.

"What?" Verity's face paled.

"Our master had her beaten when he found out she was teaching our young folks to read. Of course, that might have had something to do with what she had them read."

"What?"

"Uncle Tom's Cabin."

"Still . . ."

"She fought back, too," remembered Jefferson. "She slugged that bastard, kicked him—kicked him where he'd feel it."

"Good," said Verity. "If die we must, die fighting."

"Two of a kind, you are," said Jefferson. "Thought the minute I met you, you were like my mama."

"Thank you, Jefferson."

Jefferson left to find his accordion, then sat down beside John. "You knew, didn't you, President?" said Sam, accusation evident in his voice.

"I knew."

"I suppose your kind don't have the same regard for women," said Sam.

"No. We know them a lot better than you do," replied Jefferson. "We see them for what they are, not for what they're supposed to be. Take a look at your own wives, your daughters. There's a spark of our Watkins in their eyes."

"That is impossible," said Ethan. He lowered his voice. "She's not normal."

"I am, too!" Verity couldn't stand it anymore. She leapt to her feet, placed her hands on her hips, then stomped over to face them.

"Normal? Normal, Ethan Hallowell? If we discuss normalcy, where would your—" Verity paused. No, no matter what he thought of her, she cared for him. She wouldn't betray him.

"Never mind," she grumbled. "I'm not normal. My brother disappeared, then I watched Westley die. Do any of you know what it's like to be powerless?'' Jefferson's brow rose, but the others fidgeted and didn't meet her eyes.

"No, I thought not. I didn't want to wait anymore. I wanted to do something, so I did. Girls can't do things, so I dressed up as a boy. If it's normal to sit and wait for life to unfold, I don't want to be sane.''

"You ain't got to worry about that, girl,'' said Sam. "But have a seat. You're reminding me of a school teacher that used to scare the hell out of me. Sit.''

Verity sat. "Thank you.''

"So you're marrying the major, are you?'' asked Sam. "Don't know what he sees in you.''

"I'm a good shot,'' countered Verity. She raised a brow as a warning.

"And a damned good wrestler, too,'' laughed Sam. "Lord, if Gordy Dyer knew a little sprite of a girl had knocked him down—''

"No wonder you danced so well,'' added Peter McCaffrey.

"That's how I knew the girls would like you, Peter,'' said Verity. The boy smiled and blushed.

Ethan finally looked at Verity. "I can't believe Westley married you. Even if you're Major Talmadge's—no. Thank God he's dead, if only to spare him this disgrace.''

Verity glared at Ethan. "Robert isn't dead. He was betrayed by a spy or a traitor, but he's not dead.''

"A spy?'' asked Peter in a high voice.

"A spy, Peter,'' said Verity. "Westley, my husband, told me one of your company, possibly, had betrayed my brother.''

"That's true enough,'' said Sam. "I suppose you thought to ferret out the wrongdoer and bring him to justice? Ain't that like a girl?''

"You know?''

"Hell, it don't take much to figure. I've always suspected Hallowell here.''

"*What?*'' gasped Ethan.

"Calm yourself, Captain,'' said Sam. "I just hoped it was you so we'd be rid of you.''

Ethan fingered his Colt revolver. "What a relief!''

For the next two days, the Union army fought and retreated while most of its great force remained unused. Though the roar of artillery fire and discharging muskets filled the air, Ethan's company was removed from the fighting.

With pick in hand, Verity worked with the others on the entrenchment. She tore into the ground while fear grew in her that this bit of earth was all she had to protect her from the advancing rebels.

The men hadn't completely accepted her, but even Ethan relaxed in her company. Garrett checked on her, said a few cold words, then departed. Verity's heart ached at his rejection, but she kept her misery to herself.

"Watkins," began Sam. Then he shook his head. "Sorry, Miss Talmadge. If that hole gets any deeper, you're going to disappear."

"Sounds good to me," said Jefferson. "Keep digging, and see if we don't make it to China before dawn."

"I don't see what good this does," Verity remarked as the cool darkness of evening settled around the toiling soldiers.

"If the bullets start flying around here, it'll be a good place to hide your head," Ethan told her as he directed their activities.

Embarrassed by Verity's efforts, Ethan lent a hand shoveling beside her. Garrett came by to check on their progress and was suitably impressed.

"Well done, Captain."

"I hope it serves the purpose," said Ethan.

"It keeps Miss Talmadge occupied, at least," said Garrett. Verity didn't answer, and she didn't look at him as she continued to dig. She couldn't stand to see his cold expression.

General Hooker rode along the line, splendid on a white horse. Despite what already seemed a disaster, he seemed confident as he inspected the lines. A trail of officers followed the commander, and soldiers cheered as he passed by, but the atmosphere plummeted as soon as he was gone from view.

"He looks confident," remarked Jefferson.

"God knows why," replied Garrett darkly. "You, Miss Talmadge, will come with me."

Verity dropped her pick. "Where are we going?"

"We need to talk."

"My ditch isn't finished."

"Come."

Verity followed Garrett behind the line, to where the horses were kept. Garrett checked his mount, patted the horse's nose, then finally turned to Verity.

"Well? How goes it, My Sweet?"

"I had to follow," sputtered Verity. "I know you're angry, and you have every right to be—"

"Yes? Go on."

"Ivy said you're in danger."

"Ah," said Garrett. "A prostitute would know these things. Please, please, don't tell me this has something to do with spirits."

"A bit."

"And the men? Have you lost their friendship forever, or have they come to realize you're no different now than the Watkins they knew?"

Verity stared up at Garrett. "You did it on purpose, didn't you? Is that why you haven't come to talk to me?"

"I wanted them to see what I see—a brave woman who cares for them. A person they love, whether you've shocked them or not."

Tears glistened in Verity's eyes. "Then you're not mad at me anymore?"

"I could kill you. Or kiss you. But not when you're dressed like that."

"That's probably pretty sound."

"When we return, however, things will change. You'll become my wife, wear a dress, and stay within my sight at all times."

"As you wish," she replied in a sweet, demure voice.

Garrett laughed. "How big a fool would I have to be to believe you?"

That night, Garrett assigned Ethan's company to picket duty. They took up positions along a small creek, across which were their Confederate counterparts. Despite the ongoing battle, picket duty remained relatively safe. Verity was pleased to be free of the dank trench, especially since Garrett accompanied them.

Across the narrow stream, the shadowy forms of rebel pickets were visible in the rising moonlight. "You Yanks ready to go home yet?"

"Hell, no," yelled Sam. "We're having a grand old time with you Johnnies."

"You Yanks got coffee over there?" shouted one of the rebels.

"Why do they always want coffee?" muttered Verity. "It puts holes in your stomach, and keeps you awake all night."

"You rebs want coffee, you're going to have to come on over and get it!" shouted Garrett in a booming voice.

A silence followed, and then another voice shouted back excitedly from across the dark mist. "Garrett? Garrett Knox?" A tall man emerged from the darkness of the trees. "Is that you?"

"It is indeed, Cousin!"

"Not Jared Knox again," said Verity. "He appears at the strangest times."

"Truce!" called Jared. "You Yanks give us a moment! If you've got coffee, Knox, we've got tobacco. I'm for a trade if you are."

"Truce it is," Garrett shouted back. "Davis, hand me that sack of coffee."

Verity watched Garrett head out into the icy stream. Ivy's words returned to haunt her. *He's walking into darkness.* Verity knew Jared Knox wouldn't hurt his cousin, but what if another rebel spotted the Yankee officer?

Without further consideration, Verity splashed out into the shallow stream. It curled black around her feet, and it seeped into her boots and up to her knees as she waded after Garrett, but the footing was mercifully firm.

Across the way, Jared Knox came down a steep embankment and into the swirling water. Garrett met his cousin in the center of the stream. They faced each other, then embraced.

"A strange way to arrange a family reunion," said Jared.

"Neither of us lacks for companionship," agreed Garrett. "I see you've stepped up in rank."

"Now there are two called 'Major Knoxes.' One for each army. Whoever wins, our name will sit well."

"What inspired the promotion?"

"Riding a good horse in Fitz Lee's raid," said Jared. "How goes it with you, Cousin?"

"I haven't found much to appreciate in war. Though your side may feel differently."

"A battle won isn't a war. And we've lost something more valuable than a battlefield. Stonewall Jackson died today."

"How many more? Robert Talmadge, Westley Talmadge . . . Adrian."

Jared's face paled. "Adrian? No. When?"

"At Fredericksburg," said Garrett. "Leading a pointless charge at Marye's Heights."

"I was there," murmured Jared. Garrett knew he wondered if his shot found his cousin's heart. Garrett clasped Jared's shoulder.

"In war, there is no fault."

"Much has changed, hasn't it, since we parted to take up arms for our respective lands? That we still meet as brothers says much."

"Much I tried to tell you at the war's beginning, if you recall. We are two parts of a whole, my friend. One day, you may see this for yourself."

"Ah, but the learning is long," said Jared. "And lonely."

Garrett laughed. "When have you ever been lonely? Can it be you miss the swirl of Richmond's balls? Or is it the Yankee spy who tugs at your heart?"

"I take it Watkins reported on our meeting."

"Watkins," began Garrett. "There's a story in itself—"

A flash of blinding light shattered the conversation, a shell tore through the trees above the stream. The light reflected on the surface of the stream. Verity screamed, but it landed harmlessly in the trees behind the Union pickets.

"The war intrudes," said Jared. "Farewell, my friend. Take care."

"And you, Jared Knox."

Jared's voice betrayed no fear. "I always do."

The two men embraced again, and Garrett headed back across the stream. Verity followed, still shaken by the shelling.

"What's the matter with you? I'd think by now you'd be used to artillery fire."

"I thought it was coming for you, and that you'd die saving Jared."

Garrett's eyes narrowed. "Not Ivy?"

"I guess it's just her imagination." Verity followed Garrett up the bank, scrambling up behind him just as a large group of men moved in through the trees.

"They're coming!" shouted Sam. "Ready arms, men!"

Verity froze. Another company of rebels approached, shadowy forms moving toward them.

"Back to the line," ordered Garrett. "Get out of here, Verity. Now." Garrett moved forward to lead his pickets.

Verity gulped, gripping her musket, but she backed away. Jefferson, John, and Sam took positions to fend off their attackers. Verity watched in horror as the much larger band of rebels came toward them.

"Take your shots, then move back," ordered Garrett. "Ready . . . Fire!" Garrett fired his revolver, then drew his saber. Close, hand-to-hand fighting was something they had all drilled for, but an action rarely seen in combat.

The muskets blazed, answered by rebel fire. "Back, fix bayonets," commanded Garrett. Verity scrambled farther back, but she readied her musket to fire.

Ethan's small company moved back, took positions, and fired again. "Fire!" The muskets cracked again, the rebel fire returned.

A piercing scream rose above the musket fire, cut off with a final groan. The sound ripped through Verity's heart. Through the smoke, the smoldering leaves, she saw Peter McCaffrey fall to the ground. He didn't move again. The rebels charged, their own bayonets ready.

Jefferson Davis ran toward Peter's body, oblivious to the mass of rebels who jumped toward him. "Get back, Davis!" shouted Ethan Hallowell.

"Christ Almighty, he's a goner," yelled Sam. "It don't matter now, Davis. Get back here!"

Jefferson picked up the dead boy's body, throwing him over his shoulder. Ethan's company opened cover fire. Muskets blazed, but Jefferson carried the boy back toward the line. A rebel leapt toward him.

Garrett drew his saber and ran forward to help Jefferson.

"No," breathed Verity. The moment came. Darkness surrounded him. She fixed her bayonet and raced toward the rebels.

Garrett held the rebel pursuit back with the skill of his saber alone, then knocked a rebel to the ground as the man drove his bayonet at Jefferson.

Ethan, Sam, and John joined the fray, followed by Verity. "Get out of here!" Garrett ordered. But he didn't retreat. He held the ground while Jefferson stumbled toward the others. Garrett fired his revolver, then moved back. Too late. A rebel charged toward him, the bayonet pointed at Garrett's back.

Verity fired. A perfect shot. The rebel's musket shattered, sending the man to his knees. Garrett made it back to the line.

"Back!" Garrett grabbed Verity's arm and pulled her along as they raced through the trees. Jefferson Davis still carried Peter McCaffrey's body when they reached the Union line. After the fierce resistance of the Yankee pickets, the rebel skirmishers withdrew, disappearing back into the dark, misty wood from whence they came.

Verity collapsed in the safety of the Union trench. Garrett knelt beside her. She expected to endure his fury, but Garrett just took her hand.

"It's over," he told her gently. "It's all right, now."

"Peter," she whispered. Jefferson sat beside the boy's still body. Crying. Tears ran down his perfect face as he held the dead boy's head in his lap. John and Sam stood behind him. Ethan shook his head and walked away.

"Is he really dead?" Verity asked in a small voice.

Garrett nodded. "For Peter, the war ends."

Chapter Nine

The next day, Ethan's company received orders to withdraw from its entrenchment. The final retreat across the river began slowly. A heavy rain had washed out the makeshift bridges, now hastily repaired for the crossing.

Bodies of the fallen clogged the retreat, but Jefferson insisted on bearing Peter McCaffrey back to Falmouth. The rising stench of death sickened Verity. If Averell's raid had horrified her, the real results of battle were overwhelming.

Verity tried not to look at the swollen faces of the men lying by the roadside. As she stumbled along, she tripped and fell headlong across the body of a dead soldier, his face frozen in the grim mask of death. The back of his head was missing, and blood covered his red hair.

Suddenly Verity recognized the rebel picket—Gordy Dyer. Her empty stomach heaved in revulsion, and she stood gagging by the roadside.

Garrett picked her up and set her on his horse. "It's over," he told her, but the rebels still pursued the retreating Yankees. "We've got to move on."

Garrett gave Verity strength and courage when nothing else could. He walked beside her, leading the big horse. They retreated further, the road choked with wounded. As they plodded along, a harsh cry ripped through the air, so filled with pain and grief that Verity's heart nearly stopped.

The anguished cry came from Sam. Garrett led the horse forward to see what had befallen the old sergeant. Sam had fallen to his knees beside a small soldier's motionless body. John stood beside him.

"My boy, my boy! Damn this war, damn the bloody rebels. Damn Hooker. Damn them all!" he wailed, sobbing as he lifted the lifeless form into his arms.

The men remained silent, though John placed his hand on the old man's shoulder. Jefferson and Sam bore the bodies of the young soldiers. No one spoke as they re-crossed the swollen Rappahannock.

By mid-morning of the next day, the Army of the Potomac headed miserably back to Falmouth. No one knew why or how they had lost again, or even when their victory turned to defeat. But the war's end seemed farther away than ever.

Verity lay in Ivy's boudoir, her head cradled on Garrett's shoulder. Rain battered the window and rattled in its shutters. They hadn't spoken, just taken the room Ivy offered, locked the door, and made love with a ferocity and passion neither had experienced before.

Verity had felt safe in Garrett's arms, but a chill swept through her as her body calmed, leaving her once again at the mercy of her thoughts.

"It seems so pointless," she said. Garrett glanced down at her. "Not—?"

"No." Verity smiled and kissed him. "Not this. I meant the fighting. Peter is dead, Sam's son, too. Westley, Adrian. Have we accomplished anything? Have the rebels?"

Garrett didn't answer at once. "I love you, Verity Talmadge. I love you because you see things straight on, and deal with them that way, too. No pretense, no pretty embellishment."

"If I could think of embellishment, maybe I'd try."

"Maybe," said Garrett. "But you're right. We haven't accomplish a damned thing. We lost another good boy. But you're right. The rebels win, but the war goes on and on. I saw that in Jared's face. They're winning the long defeat."

"How can so many good people keep killing each other?"

"Because we're the bravest, most honorable damned fools that ever lived."

They didn't talk about the war anymore. Verity lay gazing into Garrett's metallic gray eyes. He ran his thumb back and forth across her cheek.

"I admired you from afar, you know," she told him. "Adrian told me about your escapades in Europe, how you refused to dwell in society. I decided you were the man I would marry."

"I can't think of anyone else for you," said Garrett. "Nor for me, for that matter. When I think of marriage, I see a husband always watching his words, keeping his true nature from his wife lest he harm her with shock. Men fight, they kill, they drink until they can't feel, then go home on leave and tell their wives fairy tales about the war."

"You can tell me fairy tales if you want, but I doubt I'll believe you."

"I wouldn't insult your intelligence with lies, my love."

"Good," said Verity. "I suppose I don't know what a marriage is supposed to be, anyway. I don't remember my parents together. The Websters never say anything that isn't couched in propriety. They call each other 'Mr. Webster,' 'Mrs. Webster.' I guess that's better than a man calling his wife, 'Mother.' "

"True," agreed Garrett. "My father called my mother 'Lorelei.' "

"Why? I thought her name was Katarina."

"It was. He named her for the Sirens of the Rhine, the Lorelei. The Pennsylvania Dutch are actually German, you know. *Deutsche.* He met her while buying a horse in Pennsylvania from the Amish."

"The Amish let her marry outside?"

"Not willingly. My father convinced her, and then stole her away."

"How romantic!" sighed Verity. "Were they happy?"

"They were, as I remember, though she didn't live long. She lost three babies before Adrian. She died when I was seven, when Adrian was born."

"And you took care of him."

"My father grieved a long while," said Garrett. "My mother's death took something he never regained, though he remarried a few years before he died."

"Dan's mother?"

"Mildred. A good woman, cheerful. She was more a nurse than a wife, but she took care of him while I lived in Europe. She manages Fox Run in Maryland, more or less. She lives there and keeps it running, anyway."

"You like her?"

"I do," said Garrett. "She treated Adrian well."

"And Dan? You don't seem particularly close."

"By the time our parents married, we lived on our own. I was in Europe, Dan was practicing law in Washington. Adrian knew him better than I did, though he still handles legal matters for my estate."

"Oh." Since Garrett's opinion of his stepbrother seemed favorable, Verity kept her own feelings quiet. "I suppose you don't have much in common. He doesn't have the capacity for mischief the way you and Jared do."

"'Mischief?' My dear woman, your estimation of my cousin may be accurate, but as for myself—"

"Yugoslavia, Garrett." Verity's eyes twinkled, and Garrett let his defense slide.

"There was a time when I lived my life without restraint. Jared joined me in France, wide-eyed and innocent from boy's school in England—"

"And you corrupted him."

"I broadened his horizons," corrected Garrett with a grin.

"He seems so happy," said Verity. "As if the war hasn't really touched him."

"Well, he's on the winning side," Garrett reminded her. "But you're right. Jared Knox draws great pleasure from life, and he shares it lavishly with his men, with those women he deems desirable. Though his temper might be considered equally powerful."

"Truly?" asked Verity. "Did you ever fight?"

"We didn't come to blows. Unlike you and the rebel picket," said Garrett. "But we engaged in numerous arguments over North and South, state's rights . . ."

"What about slavery? How can he justify that?"

"To my knowledge, he never has. In fact, Jared remains strangely silent on that subject, saying only it will end in its own course."

"Ha. Not bloody likely, when it profits them that way."

"As I replied myself," agreed Garrett. "It's the one thing he's never been open about, as if something about the issue comes too close to touch. It's sensitive with all Southerners, but for Jared . . . there's something he keeps to himself. God knows what."

"Robert said ending slavery was the one thing worth dying for," said Verity. "I agreed, but I never thought about it much. When Sam asked me why I joined, I quoted Robert." Verity fell silent. She sighed.

"Robert Talmadge was the best, most honorable man I ever knew," said Garrett. "He lived his ideals. Sometimes I thought he was too good to survive."

Tears formed in Verity's eyes. "He was good enough to overlook my shortcomings."

"And mine," added Garrett. "But never doubt, my love. Your brother would be proud of you today."

"What? Lying here with you, in a brothel, having just left battle?"

"I don't think Robert expected conventionality. Or I wouldn't admire him as I do."

"At least you're speaking of him in the present tense," noted Verity. "I've made some headway."

"Until we know otherwise, I'm willing to believe he's still alive."

"Good."

"There's something we need to discuss, Verity." Garrett sounded serious, so Verity sat up to listen.

"What?"

"Ethan Hallowell."

"Ethan? What about him?"

"There's a good chance he's the traitor that killed Westley—"

"No."

Garrett took her hands. "He was there, every time. According to your own evidence, he's involved with a rebel girl. I like the boy, Verity, but no one knows another's heart."

"I don't believe it."

"Ivy heard his name spoken by Alfred Spears."

"That's hardly evidence."

Garrett studied Verity's angry expression. "You were more than willing to believe in my guilt. Why do you think Ethan Hallowell incapable of such an act?" Garrett sounded a little jealous, but Verity wasn't in the mood to appease male pride.

"I fantasized about you, I knew you as a romantic figure from afar. But I know Ethan as a friend. There's no way he'd betray anyone."

"Robert and Westley knew him as a 'friend,' too."

Verity's lips tightened angrily. "Why do you suspect Ethan, anyway? It was Wallingford who got him promoted. Why not your esteemed stepbrother? He's a lawyer, after all. That in itself is condemning."

Verity's disrespect for Dan Wallingford revealed itself, but Garrett didn't seem offended. "I considered that possibility. Not that any evidence pointed at Dan, but he's certainly got better connections than Ethan."

"And?"

"And nothing. For one thing, he was with me when Robert disappeared. No one knew where Ethan was."

"What about Westley?"

"Ethan found your husband's body. Dan wasn't in the area."

"Where was he?"

"On his way to Washington."

"Maybe."

Garrett's jaw hardened. "You're not being reasonable, Verity. Ethan Hallowell knows your identity. Dan has no idea who you are. I'm telling you this because—"

"Because what? You think he'll try to kill me? For what reason?"

"Because Ethan Hallowell is your cousin."

Verity stared at Garrett, her lip twisted to one side. "That's ridiculous. I never knew Ethan in Boston. We're not related."

"Yes, you are. Ethan and Westley were brothers. Which explains why they resemble each other so closely."

"That's not possible."

Garrett rolled his eyes. "It's possible. Your uncle, Cabot Talmadge, fathered Ethan, two years after Westley's birth."

"How do you know?"

"Robert confided this to me before Antietam. He thought that neither Westley nor Ethan knew, but apparently the matter was mentioned in Cabot Talmadge's will. Leaving the possibility of Ethan inheriting the fortune that now rests solely with you."

"Ethan is a bastard?" asked Verity weakly. "But he has sisters."

"Much older sisters," said Garrett. "All blackhaired and tiny.

Ethan is tall, blond. Verity, there's no doubt. Maybe he doesn't know.''

"He knows.''

Garrett eyed Verity doubtfully. "Are you sure?''

"I'm sure. It's in everything he does. Poor Ethan.''

"Does your sympathy for him extend to your husband's murder?''

"Ethan loved Westley. He's mentioned him several times.''

"I told you, you can't know another's heart.''

"I know Ethan. And I love him.''

"Indeed.''

Verity's confidence in her own judgment soared. "I understand now, everything. Why I have to protect him. Westley wants me to.''

Garrett drew a long, patient breath. "You've been around Ivy too much. Westley is dead.''

"Exactly. So he can't help. He knows I will. He wants me to make things all right for Ethan. And I will.''

"God,'' groaned Garrett. "This isn't why I told you.''

"I know. You think I'm in danger. You're wrong. I have a purpose, Garrett Knox. I'm to protect my brother-in-law! My cousin.'' She faced Garrett like a defense attorney. "You will not accuse my cousin of any dishonorable act.''

"I will accuse him if evidence warrants.''

"Evidence doesn't warrant a damned thing here,'' said Verity.

"I'm watching him.''

"You'd best watch yourself!''

Verity and Garrett looked away from each other, fuming with their conflicting anger, their equally determined wills.

"Verity, I warn you. Have a care around Ethan Hallowell. If you die, a vast fortune will go to him. And his rebel lover.''

"Bess Hartman is a very nice girl.''

"Hartman?'' Garrett's voice was a near groan.

"I think that was her name,'' said Verity. "Why?''

"Because Thomas Hartman is one of the most notorious rebel spies in the Confederate army. He rides with Mosby's Raiders. You've heard of them, I presume. Tom Hartman disguises himself as a Union soldier, takes his place in whichever Yankee company pleases him, then turns it upside down. The man spies at will.''

"Ethan doesn't know.''

"Like hell."

"It's a coincidence. Or maybe Bess is playing him for a fool. I'll have to warn Ethan. If she's using my cousin, she'll find herself in a pickle, mark my words."

Verity started out of the bed, but Garrett yanked her back. "You're not saying a goddamned word to Ethan Hallowell, you little fool! Jesus, have you no sense at all? As my wife, you'll obey me in this, woman."

"Obey?" mocked Verity. "If you think you're going to order me around, you'd best think again, Garrett Knox. I have a purpose in this life, and by God, you're not stomping it out of me just because we like each other in bed!"

"Like each other?" Garrett's gray eyes gleamed as he pulled her into his arms. His lips curved dangerously when Verity gasped. He kissed her, licked her full lower lip. He ran his thumb across her hardening nipple.

Verity's fury threatened to give way beneath desire. She felt the damning liquid between her legs, the vortex of need awaiting him. Her breasts ached where he touched. She heard his low chuckle as she stifled a moan.

Garrett's sexuality overwhelmed her, but suddenly Verity knew it was a battle more than a seduction. She twisted her head away and met his burning gaze.

"Will you spare Ethan?"

"No."

Verity pulled from his embrace, though it seemed as if she left her real self in his arms. "Then we have nothing more to say to each other . . . or do. Until you come to your senses and apologize, our wedding is off."

The words caught in her throat, and she nearly choked when she heard herself call off their marriage. She wanted to say, *I didn't mean it,* wanted to swallow her rash words. But Garrett let her go, his face darkened with anger.

"Very well. Until you can be reasonable, I see no reason for us to marry. You will, of course, report to me if you find yourself pregnant."

"I will." Her voice came like a proud whisper, but Verity's heart throbbed. Why did he have to anger her this way? Why couldn't he see that Ethan needed her?

*   *   *

Verity's loyalty to Ethan Hallowell stunned Garrett. He recognized his own jealousy, but he couldn't understand her illogical mind. He knew she'd lost her parents, her brother, her two best friends. Maybe in some peculiar way, Verity considered herself responsible. As if she should have been with them, as if she could have saved them.

Garrett knew, because these same thoughts had motivated him to leave the Maryland Cavalry and take his place with the Massachusetts fighting men. He understood Verity, all right. Too well. Verity believed strength carried responsibility, just as he did. But whether Ethan Hallowell deserved her protection, Garrett couldn't know.

Neither spoke as Verity tugged on Watkins's clothes. "You're not going back."

"Perhaps I should just hunt up this Dave Delaney myself," said Verity meaningfully as she continued to dress.

Garrett lay back on Ivy's bed, resigned to Verity's stay in the army. "I take it you're returning to camp." His throat felt raw and dry. He would sleep alone in a brothel this night.

"I see no reason to stay." Verity paused, and Garrett knew she expected his apology. He refused. "Very well." She paused again, allowing him a second chance. His refusal deepened. It was he who deserved an apology. "I'm going."

She hesitated when she reached the door, looking back at him. He stared at the ceiling. Verity opened the door. Slowly.

"Verity."

As she closed the door, her eyes widened hopefully, expectantly. "Yes?"

"Be careful. Don't put yourself at anyone's mercy."

Verity's face puckered angrily. She looked away. "I already have," she muttered. "Yours."

Verity left, and Garrett lay motionless. Every muscle in his body ached. She was gone. He should have known they were both too volatile to enjoy a peaceful love. Too strong. Mildred said he needed a passive woman, a woman who wouldn't cross him.

But passive women had no power to arouse his passions. Passive women didn't bite his shoulder in ecstasy. They didn't claw his chest and moan his name. They didn't dress as soldiers and fight in blue. And they didn't risk their lives to save a friend.

* * *

Verity wandered through the Mass 20th, her heart throbbing miserably in her breast. Garrett was mad at her, and she was mad at him. She forced her mind from their fight, and reflected on what she had learned. Ethan was her cousin, her only living relative— if Garrett was right about Robert.

She found Ethan sitting alone on the bank of the Rappahannock. Verity sat beside him, but neither spoke. To her wonder, she saw tears in his blue eyes.

"What happened, Ethan?"

"She won't marry me," he told Verity in a tight, constricted voice. "Her brother found out about us and forbade it. I had her convinced. But she's not pregnant. She still loves me, she thinks that when the war ends, everything will work out."

"Maybe she's right," said Verity without much hope. This war would never end.

"You know better, Watkins. Sorry, Mrs. Talmadge."

"Verity."

Ethan smiled and looked down at her. "I can't believe you were married to Westley."

"He was my best friend," said Verity. "He was the kindest, fairest person I ever knew—except for you."

"I didn't know him in Boston. But when we marched across that cornfield at Antietam, he was the only thing that kept me going."

Verity recognized Ethan's subdued emotion and she took his hand, squeezing it gently.

"We survived that bloodbath because of his skill," said Ethan. "It can't have been easy. That was the day your brother disappeared, and Westley took over his command for the battle. But he never let it show. He led us and he kept us alive. And then he got shot, afterward. I couldn't believe it. I found him, you know."

"So I've heard," said Verity. "That must have been horrible."

"It was a bad wound," said Ethan. "But I thought he'd live. I always thought I'd see him again."

Verity felt certain now that Ethan knew about his parentage, but Westley hadn't known. He would have liked Ethan, but he never mentioned his younger brother as he lay dying. Westley, who longed for a brother, never knew he had the best of all.

"Why aren't you with the major?" Ethan deliberately changed the subject, and Verity understood.

"We had a bit of a row." After all, if she couldn't tell her cousin, there was no one else.

Ethan looked at Verity and shook his head. "I can't imagine why. But women are nothing if not irrational."

"Thank you very much," said Verity. "I might say the same of men."

"Why can't it be easy? Love, I mean. It slams you in the face when you least expect it, then eats away at you. I want a child with Bess, but only if I can live as its father."

Ethan said this with particular emphasis, and Verity's heart ached with sympathy. "You'll have another chance."

"I could use a drink." Ethan pulled a bottle from his haversack and popped it open. He took a long drink, then passed it to Verity. Realizing he had offered liquor to a lady, he snatched it back. "I'm sorry! I keep forgetting who you are."

Verity seized the bottle and drank. "I keep forgetting who I am, too."

"No wonder. If I looked in the mirror and saw that face, I'd forget, too."

"Again, thank you." Verity passed the bottle back to Ethan. Already, the burning liquid eased her troubled thoughts. A small smile on Ethan Hallowell's face told her he felt the same.

Two hours later, Ethan and Verity lay on their backs, side by side, giggling at nothing. An empty bourbon bottle lay cast aside in the dirt.

"It's a pleasant night, isn't it?" slurred Verity cheerfully. "Just like home in the summer. Makes one want to go for a dip, doesn't it?"

"A dip?" asked Ethan. "You mean bathing?"

"Didn't you ever swim at night?" asked Verity.

"No."

Verity sat up. Her head was already swimming; she forced her eyes wide open to see. "Let's go for a little swim, Ethan."

"Now? I don't have bathing gear."

"God," groaned Verity, "You don't wear bathing dress at night, you idiot. It's pitch black out here. It's not like we'll see each other."

"You don't mean—No. We can't." But Ethan was already tearing off his uniform. "Then again, why not?"

"You had a very limited childhood," said Verity as she also undressed.

"I did, indeed. Actually," said Ethan as he tossed his uniform aside and headed for the river, "my father never liked me much."

Verity followed him. "That's probably why you're so incredibly successful leading other men."

"Wretch." Ethan splashed into the river and sputtered at the cold.

The cold water cleared Verity's senses somewhat, and she swam circles around Ethan. "It's more fun without clothes."

"That's what I told Bess."

Both Ethan and Verity cackled at this. "You're making lewd jokes to a lady," said Verity happily. "You've really stooped, Hallowell."

"I have, indeed."

Morning came, and Verrill Watkins hadn't returned to his tent. "Where in hell is that brat?" cursed Dan Wallingford. "I have got work for him."

"He never came back?" questioned Garrett. His pride kept him at Ivy's, but he had never slept. Damn.

"No, and I can't find Hallowell around anywhere, either. I've got him scheduled for drill."

"I'll find them."

"Them?" asked Dan, but Garrett didn't answer. Half in fear, half in jealousy, he headed off to search the campsite.

Ethan wasn't in his tent. The other captains hadn't seen him since the previous evening. Garrett wondered if Verity and Ethan had deserted. He headed to the bank of the Rappahannock.

There they lay. Bare flesh shining in the morning sun, side by side. Naked. Garrett couldn't move. He couldn't shout, nor grab Ethan by the throat, nor toss Verity over his shoulder. He just stood, staring at his woman lying with another man.

Ethan lay on his stomach, arms folded, his long, lean body poised comfortably. As satisfied as a child. Verity lay curled up beside him, her arm just covering her breast, a smile on her face. The empty bourbon bottle between them caught Garrett's eye.

He'd seen the effect of liquor on Verity Talmadge, and his heart quailed.

"What in hell is going on here?" Garrett's booming voice shot through both Ethan and Verity. They jumped, saw each other and screamed. Neither noticed Garrett, so horrified were they to be stark naked in each other's presence.

"Don't look, Watkins!" Ethan's face flushed to flaming red as he scrambled into his uniform.

"I'm not looking, you idiot." Verity hunted around for her discarded clothes, then dressed in a flash.

Garrett watched the two in horrified amusement. If they became lovers in the night, it happened in a drunken spree, and it hadn't changed their essential relationship. Not that this was entirely comforting, but Garrett was old enough to know how such things happened between men and women.

He never attached sacredness to sex. Why, then, did his heart ache with brutal force? Why did he look away as Ethan Hallowell pulled trousers over his lean body? A decidedly handsome body that may well have sampled the unique pleasures of the only woman Garrett ever loved.

Dressed, Ethan turned palefaced to Garrett. He looked ready to die, to suffer the most evil consequences. "This," he began weakly, "isn't what it seems."

"No? What is it?"

Ethan and Verity looked at each other. "I don't remember," Ethan admitted.

Verity's eyes wandered upward. "No. Neither do I. We were having a nice conversation. You offered me bourbon—"

"You took it," corrected Ethan.

"You suggested we go swimming," continued Verity.

"You suggested."

"Whatever." Verity peeked over at Garrett, a guilty expression on her face. "Of course, if you hadn't cast me aside—"

"Cast you aside? I believe it was you who called off our wedding."

"Did you?" asked Ethan. "Why?"

"Never mind," said Verity with a quick, warning glance at Garrett. Garrett said nothing. Right now, he didn't care if Ethan spied for Robert E. Lee himself. Lying naked with Verity seemed a far more dangerous crime.

"Hallowell, you're late for drill."

Ethan nodded, grabbed his hat, then seized the opportunity to leave. He hurried toward the campsite, leaving Verity alone with Garrett. "I suppose I'm late, too," she offered, but Garrett stepped toward her, blocking her escape.

Verity bit her lip nervously. "I'm sorry, Garrett. I didn't mean to embarrass you."

Garrett looked past her, over the river toward Fredericksburg. "You aren't beholden to me, Verity," he told her quietly. "Your first lover isn't necessarily your last. You weren't designed to be a simple maiden. Maybe I couldn't love you if you were. God knows, I've known enough women in my life. There's nothing you can do that I can't forgive."

Verity's eyes widened in shock. "We went swimming! That's all. We didn't—"

"You said yourself you don't remember. Apparently, neither does Hallowell."

"That's true. But I'm sure—"

"It doesn't matter."

"It would matter to me!"

"We'll speak no more of it."

She stared at her feet. "Are we still engaged?"

"If that is what you wish."

"It is."

Verity looked sick and miserable. Apparently, the bourbon didn't settle well. A reluctant smile crossed Garrett's face. "Coffee, my sweet, might serve you well this morning. And breakfast."

"I can't eat."

"You'd better."

Chapter Ten

Another month passed, and the crest of spring rose and flowered all around. Chancellorsville became a dim memory, felt but not mentioned as the tide of days marched on. For Verity, it was no more than a nightmare remembered vaguely. Her relationship with Garrett concerned her more.

Though they maintained their engagement, Garrett made no effort to meet at Ivy's brothel again. He seemed unusually busy with command, kept late at meetings with the depressed General Hooker. Rumors ran rampant that Lee was moving his army north. The camp buzzed with speculation about Hooker's next move.

"It's not Hooker who's calling the shots now," Ethan told them as they sat outside Sam's tent. "It's Abe Lincoln himself."

Verity lay on her cot, her hands folded on her chest. Her brow puckered thoughtfully as she awaited Garrett's return from his meeting with Colonel Godwin. She heard him outside the tent.

"Aren't you coming, Dan?" Verity frowned at Garrett's question. Garrett used Wallingford as a buffer between them. They shared a tent, but Verity never saw him alone. She caught glimpses of his chest, his legs. Occasionally, she stole a glance at his firm buttocks when he undressed. A sultry heat swamped her body even at the thought. . . .

"Thought I'd go on to Ivy's," said Dan. "Care to join me?"

Verity sat up in bed. *Don't you dare.* Her breath held while Garrett contemplated his answer.

"Not tonight, Dan." Verity breathed a long sigh of relief.

"Can't think of a better way to end it than lying between the soft thighs of a willing wench."

Verity grimaced at Dan's description. *Willing wench, indeed.*

"Good-night, Dan," said Garrett with a laugh. Verity heard Dan walk away, but Garrett didn't enter the tent. She glared at the entrance, waiting. She knew he stood outside. She heard a drawn out sigh of resignation, and Garrett walked in.

"Not sleeping, Watkins?"

"Verity." Verity rose from her cot, standing no more than an inch away from Garrett. He backed up to remove his jacket. She closed in. "You don't have to call me Watkins now. No one's here."

"I keep forgetting." Garrett tossed his jacket aside. He avoided looking at her.

"I thought we should talk." Verity's eyes burned into his face, willing him to look at her. He didn't.

"Should we?"

"I think so." She waited. No response. "Well?"

"What would you like to discuss?"

"Why you don't want me anymore."

Garrett's eyes flashed to Verity's face. "What makes you think I don't want you?"

Verity made a sputtering noise, then pinched Garrett's arm. "Don't you dare! Don't you dare answer me with a question!"

Garrett rubbed his arm, but a grin spread across his face. "Must you always be so violent? No wonder we're losing the damned war. Put the female of the species in against the rebs, and we'd win tomorrow."

Verity drew up indignantly. "I'm not violent."

Garrett looked down at his arm and lifted a dark brow. "I beg to differ."

"You haven't answered my question, Garrett Knox. I've sat around here for almost a month, waiting for you to come to your senses. I assumed, since you're a man and foolish, that you harbored sensitivity about my escapade with Ethan. I suppose I wouldn't be entirely pleased to find you naked with another woman—"

Garrett laughed. "I shudder to think what you'd do. But I doubt you'd stop at pinching."

"I might shoot."

"You might." Verity started to speak, but Garrett cupped her chin in his hand. "Verity, I'm not angry about the night you spent with Ethan. I'm not angry at all."

"Then why . . ."

Garrett released Verity's chin and sighed. "You and I gave in to passion. I was ready. You weren't."

"I was ready. Didn't you notice? Ivy said—"

Garrett cut her off. "Not physically."

"Then what in hell are you talking about?" Verity placed her hands on her hips, ready to pinch should he anger her again.

Garrett turned away.

"Well?"

"If you haven't noticed, you tend to leap into things before thinking."

"I do not."

Garrett's brow rose again. "No, *Watkins?* How much thought did you give your stint in the army? Averell's raid? Chancellorsville? Did you think at all before you poured bourbon into your little body and stripped in the company of a young and probably quite virile man?"

"Ethan again," noted Verity. "It comes back to that, doesn't it? You're jealous!"

Garrett's back straightened. "I'm just making a point, Verity. You don't think. You act. You experienced your first real lust with me. You leapt in to learn what's there. You think you love me. You're willing to marry me. How do you know?"

"How do I know? What do you mean, *'How do I know?'* I know because I know, you idiot. Just the way I know I love Ethan like a brother, the same way I loved Westley and Adrian. I know, because when I look at you, my heart wants to explode."

"You need time—"

"I need you."

"You are a special creature, Verity Talmadge. Unique. God knows, I've never met anyone like you. You give in to impulses most women won't even talk about. Maybe we're right for each other. I believe we are. But you can't know. You're too young and inexperienced. You're blinded by lust right now. You think you should love me, that you should marry me, because we shared a bed.''

''That's ridiculous—''

''You need time to know for sure.'' Garrett was adamant, and Verity relented.

''How much time?''

''I'm not sure. But I'll be here when you're ready.''

Verity drew a long breath, but then she touched his face. ''I'll wait, a little while. But you're wrong, Garrett Knox. You think I don't know myself. I do. I became Watkins because it's the only thing I could do to be true to myself. I think that's what honor really means, to be true to your soul's voice. That's how I know you're the only man for me.''

''For your sake, as well as mine, I want you to be sure. We won't stay in Falmouth forever. When the time comes for the army to move, we'll talk again.''

Marching orders were passed down the next morning. Not a minute too soon for Verity. Word came of Lee's progress north. He'd gone much farther than the Union commanders guessed. The nervousness pervading Washington was thrust on the Army of the Potomac. They ceased being the pursuers and became the defenders of their own ground. Pennsylvania.

It was late in June, and Virginia was irrepressibly hot, especially to the New Englanders who would have been enjoying spring's pleasant days back home. A deep, sweltering summer had eclipsed spring entirely. Even at daybreak, it gave signs of becoming an unbearably hot day to come.

Sam's company assembled outside their tent, waiting for Garrett's instructions. Since the army was about to move, Verity assumed Garrett would mention their future together. But Garrett was busy organizing his men, and they found no time alone. Verity suspected he avoided her, but she couldn't be certain.

''What now, Major?'' called Sam. Jefferson Davis tossed his musket in the air and caught it.

''Lee's headed north through the Shenandoah Valley,'' Garrett told them. All around was the bustle of forming companies, officers giving orders. A general sense of excitement pervaded the atmosphere.

"We're to stop him before he reaches Washington, and moving quickly, too. I hope you men are ready for a march."

"We sure are," said Sam. "It's high time we met the Johnnies on our own ground." Antietam Creek in Maryland had faded to memory, but New Englanders generally considered Maryland 'the South,' anyway.

Garrett looked out over the rising mists of the Rappahannock. "They may come to wish they'd never left these banks at all."

The march started at mid-morning. Endless columns of infantrymen began walking toward their far off homes. Twenty miles were covered the first day, despite the heat. Men fell from exhaustion and cramped muscles, but Verity suffered little beneath the blazing sun.

As they marched, groups of soldiers acquired food from the little farms along the way. Some companies brought along cows for slaughter that night. Despite her experience in battle, Verity felt sorry for the beasts and obstinately avoided eating the meat. The others teased her mercilessly.

"Where do you think the salt pork comes from?" taunted Jefferson as he finished his lean cut of beef.

"I know perfectly well where it comes from, Jefferson," Verity replied. "A pig. But I don't have to spend all day marching alongside a pig, nor look into its big, brown eyes, either. I'm not eating anything I've met."

Jefferson laughed, but Verity wasn't swayed by his amusement. Still, the smell of roasting meat tortured her empty stomach. She sat chewing on hardtack, wondering if she had been hasty in her kindness.

For three more days, they marched north. The landscape grew more and more majestic. Grain ripened in fields, and cherries ripened in orchards. The soldiers stuffed the cherries into their mouths and pockets while admiring the large, splendid barns dotting the rolling countryside.

As they journeyed into Pennsylvania, local farmers set up food stands in anticipation of the passing army. Verity had saved every cent of Watkins's pay. She bought milk, bread, a nut cake, and a pie, all of which she carefully bore to the evening bivouac.

"Why in hell are you buying all that?" asked Jefferson as she returned from doing business with yet another roadside merchant. "Don't you know those devils set their prices ten times their worth?"

"I don't care," said Verity. "I'm sick of army food. My insides are half gone from all this coffee. Tell me you wouldn't like some milk for a change, or a slice of this cherry pie?"

"Don't fret yourself, President," John said, breaking his usual silence to make a rare comment. "Those prices will come down. They'll be begging us to stick around when Bobby Lee heads this way."

Garrett joined them for Verity's cherry pie. "It seems we have a new general."

"Who this time?" asked Ethan.

"George Meade has replaced Hooker."

"I wish they wouldn't change them on us right in the middle of an operation," said Ethan.

"Meade seems a sensible fellow," replied Garrett. "He'll face up to Lee better than some."

The 20th Mass was part of General Hancock's Second Corps. They reached Taneytown at noon. A messenger rode along the line from the west, bearing news all found interesting.

"The First and Eleventh Corps have engaged Lee," he told Garrett breathlessly. "About fifteen miles west of here, in a town called Gettysburg. Our wonderful General Reynolds was killed, and the rebs drove us back through town, to where we're dug in now. Waiting for you folks. It looks like Hell."

"We'll be there before dawn," said Garrett. The messenger rode on, and Garrett called to Ethan. "We'll be marching most of the night, Captain."

Verity's heart sank. Once again, battle loomed around the corner. They pushed westward and the moon rose. By midnight, even Verity was staggering as she walked. They stopped and got a few hours sleep, but they rose before the sun and began again toward Gettysburg.

Just before dawn, the Second Corps filed into their respective positions along a rise which faced a large, rolling field. The Union army was spread out along a ridge that trailed down from Cemetery

Hill, stretched nearly two miles like an arm toward the little hills beyond the pasture.

At the point where the slope was lowest, the army situated the batteries of heavy artillery, supported by a Pennsylvania regiment. South of the Napoleons began Hall's line, which included the 19th and 20th Massachusetts regiments.

"What do you think of it, Major?" asked Ethan when Garrett came to inspect the company's position toward the left of the regiment. Ethan seemed eager to please Garrett, but Garrett appeared increasingly pained about dealing with the young officer. Verity cursed male jealousy.

"Looks promising, Captain. For once, the situation may be in our favor."

"They'd be fools to cross that field at all," said Ethan.

"Maybe. But Lee came north for a fight. I doubt he'll leave after his successes yesterday."

Garrett turned to Verity. "It's time we had a talk, Madam. Come with me."

Verity followed Garrett from the line. They walked up the hill a way, then sat together beneath the shade of a large oak.

"It's time, Verity. You need to make up your mind. There's a battle coming, and I don't want you in it. I want you back in a dress, I want your future secured. If not with me, then—"

"What?" asked Verity in astonishment. "And I don't have a dress. I suppose I can get one in town, but right now, they're too distracted by the rebels . . ."

Garrett drew a long breath. "Verity, you're digressing. I'll give you one hour. If you're ready to be my wife, then we'll marry."

Verity started to tell him she was ready, but Garrett stood up and walked away without another word. Verity wandered along the line, absentmindedly considering Garrett's strange words. From their positions with the regiment, she knew that both Ethan Hallowell and Garrett watched her.

Garrett saw Verity walking toward him, ambling among men who had no idea of her identity. He knew she had formed her answer, and he couldn't resist the fear and hope that surged inside him. He drew a breath.

A small man approached, glancing furtively left and right.

Garrett recognized Dave Delaney, despite his new goatee. "What in hell are you doing here?"

"You know me, Major. You know what's going on."

"I do." Garrett wasn't sure that he knew anything, but better Delaney think so than not.

"I'm in deeper than I meant to get," Dave Delaney said hurriedly. His face paled, as if he recognized someone. Someone dangerous. "Damn-nation," he muttered. "Hell ain't trickier than this. Meet me up by the Napoleons. At the half hour."

"I will."

The spy's eyes fixed on Ethan Hallowell before he hurried away.

Verity saw Garrett with a small, suspicious looking man. She joined Sam and Ethan, but Ethan stared at the little man. "I know him."

"Who?" Verity turned in the direction of Ethan's furious gaze.

"That man speaking with Major Knox. Westley pointed him out to me . . . at Antietam Creek. He's a spy. If you'll excuse me—"

"Ethan! Where are you going?"

"I'm going to have a talk with the bastard."

"I don't think that's such a good idea, Hallowell," said Sam. "If he's what you say—" Ethan left before Sam finished.

"Aw, hell," muttered Sam. "Blue blood's got the sense of a pea."

"If anyone can turn the world upside down and let it land on himself, it's Captain Hallowell," added Jefferson.

John shook his head and rolled his eyes. "We owe him."

"That we do," agreed Sam.

Tears puddled in Verity's eyes at their surprising loyalty to her cousin. "Well, let's help him."

"Too late," said Sam. "There he goes!"

"Ethan, no!" Verity started after Ethan, followed by Sam, Jefferson, and John. Ethan broke into a run, catching Dave Delaney at the crest of the hill. A cornered spy might shoot first, listen later. And Ethan wasn't in the mood for offering leeway.

"Hallowell!" Garrett's booming voice reached Ethan, but the young man didn't stop. Even Dan Wallingford noticed the commotion, and he, too, started after Ethan.

Ethan backed the small man against a bent tree. Dave Delaney shuffled his feet, stuffing his hands in his pockets. Verity bit her lip hard. Ethan was accusing the man of spying—she knew it. Delaney glanced left and right, nervous.

Verity heard Ethan's voice as it rose. "I've never forgotten your face. That stupid smile. God damn you, you killed my brother."

Verity raced up the hill with the men. Ethan's anger wouldn't wait. If the spy recognized the fury beneath the cool exterior . . . "Ethan!"

Garrett Knox was running, too. "Hallowell!"

Ethan grabbed Delaney's collar and shoved him hard against the tree. Verity noticed the spy's hands, still in his pockets. Why?

"Ethan, he's got a gun, a gun!" Verity's shrill voice rang over the fields, and Ethan heard her. Just as Garrett reached the cannons, Dave Delaney jerked his small revolver from his pocket and aimed at Ethan's gut.

Ethan Hallowell was quicker. He twisted aside, aimed his own revolver, and fired. Dave Delaney fell dead.

Garrett leapt toward him. "Hallowell, no!"

"Didn't I tell you?" groaned Jefferson. "There goes the whole damned world, right smack on Hallowell's head."

Ethan stood over the body, shocked but not sorry. Verity stared down at the lifeless spy. "He almost killed you," she whispered. "Why?"

"Because I accused him of killing Westley."

"Did he?"

"I don't know."

Verity stood loyally at Ethan's side, but Garrett's face was grim as he arrived to examine the body. Dan Wallingford came up beside him, shook his head, and turned to Ethan. "Well, Hallowell, you've done it now."

"Done what? That creepy little man tried to shoot Ethan."

"Quiet, Watkins," snarled Wallingford. "This doesn't involve you."

"Like hell! I'm a witness. We all are."

"That's right," chimed in Sam. "Saw the little bastard pull a gun on the Captain. Hallowell had no choice."

"A man's got the right to protect himself," added Jefferson.

Ethan's eyes misted at his soldiers' unexpected support. "Thank you, men."

"Your loyalty is admirable," said Dan, though his lip curved scornfully beneath his handlebar mustache.

"When an officer is worthy, we know it," said Verity. "And when he's not . . ." One brow rose as her gaze moved up and down Wallingford's body, her lip curled disparagingly, prime disgust evident on her expression.

"Watkins—"

"It's all right, Watkins," said Ethan. "It can't be too hard to prove this Delaney a spy. He admitted as much before he tried to shoot me."

"Did he indeed?" mocked Wallingford. "Well, Garrett. What more proof do you need? I told you this boy was up to no good. Hell, Adrian and Westley Talmadge thought so."

Verity froze. Fiery hatred filled her soul. She stepped toward Dan Wallingford with murderous intent. "They thought no such thing. Westley Talmadge died in—"

"Watkins!" Garrett's harsh voice cut her off, and Verity bit her lip.

"Hallowell's relationship with Watkins here might be suspect, too," added Wallingford. Verity had no idea what he meant, but Ethan grimaced. "The Greeks did it, after all. And they're both . . . pretty."

"Oh, for God's sake!" boomed Sam. "Ain't been none of that! We all know Hallowell's got a girl. He ain't got no 'specially fond feelings for Watkins here."

"A girl?" asked Wallingford.

"Shut up, Sam," said Jefferson. Sam clamped his lips together and said no more.

"What did the Greeks do?" asked Verity suspiciously.

"Never mind," said Garrett. "Keep to the point, Dan. If you've got something to say, that is."

"You can't think I had anything to do with spying." Ethan sounded like a Boston aristocrat again, indignant that his honor might be questioned in any way.

"You know what you have to do, Garrett," said Wallingford. "I've warned you, and now it's too late."

"You? What the hell do you know?" asked Verity. "You promoted Ethan to captain, after all. You thought well enough of him then."

"That was my way of keeping an eye on him," said Wallingford. "I've had suspicions for some time, though Major Knox hesitated to believe the import of my find."

Garrett didn't speak, but Ethan's face paled. "You think I'm a spy? That I had something to do with Robert Talmadge's death? With Westley's? No.'' His voice sank to a whisper. "No."

"That seems likely," said Dan. Verity made a fist.

"Why?" asked Ethan.

"For a fortune, boy," said Dan. "Westley Talmadge was your brother."

All color drained from Ethan's face, but Verity whirled at Garrett and erupted in fury. "You told Wallingford?"

"Robert Talmadge told us both," said Garrett.

"Robert, you fool!" Verity punched at the air, as if her brother's tall body were in reach. Both Garrett and Ethan smiled despite their predicament.

"Is everyone in this bloody army aware of my shame?"

"There's no shame, Ethan Hallowell," insisted Verity. "Except on the blackhearted villain who set you up this way."

"This boy must be arrested now, Garrett," said Dan. "He's in your command, but if I must—''

"There's no need, Dan. I'll handle it from here." Garrett's tone brooked no quarter, and Dan relented.

"Very well. I'll trust your judgement will outweigh whatever loyalty you hold for this villain. I'll inform Colonel Godwin that Hallowell's out of action. You can handle the rest."

Wallingford left, and Verity fingered her musket, eyeing his back like a target. "I can't believe you let him get away with that."

Garrett didn't answer. He faced Ethan instead. "I'm sorry, Captain. Until this gets straightened out, I want you in the rear. Consider yourself under temporary arrest, and I'll keep you out of shackles."

"You don't believe Ethan . . ." Verity fumed. "You wanted my answer. Well, you just gave it yourself! I can't marry a man who would destroy my cousin."

"Verity—''

"What the hell is going on out there?" interrupted Ethan.

A concentrated force of Confederate soldiers moved across the wide pasture, flowing across the field like a gray tide.

"Here they come," said Garrett. "A mass of rebels are attacking the Round Tops. I guess this is their second wave."

Despite Ethan's confinement, they all hurried back to their line together to watch the battle's progress. Half a mile to their left, a large mass of Third Corps soldiers moved inexplicably forward, repositioning themselves out beyond the Union line.

"What's going on?" asked Jefferson Davis.

"Damned if I know," said Garrett.

Ethan shaded his eyes from the sun. "Those are General Sickles's men, aren't they?"

Garrett nodded. "They are."

"What of it?" questioned Verity, but suddenly she knew. A large mass of General Sickles's Third Corps soldiers moved forward toward the oncoming rebels. They had broken the continuity of the powerful Union line to reposition themselves in the position of a sitting duck.

Garrett shook his head. "General Sickles isn't famed for his good sense. He shot his wife's lover, after all. It won't be long before he'll be driven back."

"Seems the high command agrees with you, Major," added Sam. "Look."

Messengers from General Meade galloped down the line, calling frantic orders to send Sickles back into place. Too late. Clouds of dust and smoke rose in the midst of the massing men as the rebel army crashed upon the wayward Yankees.

Men and horses fell, blown as if by violent winds to fall like leaves on the ground. Too horrible to watch, impossible to look away. Beside Verity, Garrett swore, and the others stared at the unfolding tragedy.

Worse came. Between the earsplitting barrage of artillery fire came the rebel yell. Across the field of golden wheat, a huge amassment of men in gray appeared. The armies met and clashed, and the Union line fell back.

"Can we join them, Major?" asked Jefferson plaintively.

"Wait for your orders, Davis," advised Garrett, but his fists clenched with helplessness.

Within two hours, General Sickles had fallen and his forces were driven back. Reinforcements joined the Third Corps, and finally drove the rebels back across the stricken field of grain.

It was early evening now, and as the shadows lengthened attention remained focused on the battles in the low grounds, the hills, and the orchards to their left. Garrett called their attention to a new, more immediate threat.

"Ready yourselves, men," he ordered. "We've got company coming."

Loaded muskets were set aside, extra muskets were passed forward from the rear.

"Who will lead my men?" Ethan sounded hurt, but proud. Garrett hesitated.

"We want Hallowell." Sam spoke up, his bearded chin set in a determined, Irish expression. A faint smile crossed Garrett's lips.

"Very well."

"Thank you, Major!" Ethan's eyes gleamed as Garrett handed him back his Colt revolver.

"Just for the battle, Captain. Report to me when it's over."

"What about me?" questioned Verity.

"You, Madam, will report to the rear. Now!" Verity didn't move. Garrett's eyes flashed. Verity's shoulders slumped.

"I can fight."

"God knows," said Garrett.

"They're going to break through down there," said Jefferson excitedly. The crest of rebel attackers neared the Union line just down from the Second Corps position.

"General Hancock seems aware of that," replied Garrett.

As they watched, General Hancock galloped toward their position. Young and greatly admired, Hancock's presence lent confidence to the men who followed him. He shouted to the commanders of the lower divisions, who in turn shouted to officers along the line.

"Move your divisions south to plug that hole," he told Garrett as he rode by.

"We're in," called Garrett. Jefferson laughed, but Verity felt sick.

She stood alone, watching her friends and her lover race toward their enemy. And suddenly, she saw more than her own life. It was her country's future at stake. Something greater than herself hung in the balance, something even greater than the fate of those she loved. She could have a say in its outcome. In a strange way, Verity Talmadge felt honored to be there at all.

Fear turned to resolution. Musket in hand, Verity took off after her friends.

Verity caught up with Sam. Garrett raced on ahead of them. Half a mile seemed a day's march in the midst of battle. In an attempt to stall the rebel advance, a regiment of less than three hundred Minnesotans were sent forth to engage. Verity recognized the men with whom she'd marched to Chancellorsville.

The tiny regiment moved forward to face a force of nearly two thousand. Bayonets fixed, the Minnesotans charged into the center of the Confederate line. The rebels fell back, then came on, pummeling the Yankees with concentrated fire. The Union soldiers were ripped apart, but they held on long enough for the Second Corps to take position.

"Down on the crest, men," yelled Garrett.

Verity knelt beside Sam and fired into the ranks assailing the devastated Minnesotans. "Jesus, woman, you are crazy," shouted Sam, but he laughed as he fired his musket.

The rapid blue fire drove the Southern brigades back. With no reinforcements, the rebels withdrew. A cheer rang along the crest. Verity's own high voice rang among them. Called upon to perform the impossible, the Minnesota regiment staggered back at less than a fifth of their force. Because of them, the Union line held.

The celebration didn't last long. To the north, a line of Georgians attacked, and Verity followed her company back to support the defenders. This time, the defending divisions had the attackers outnumbered. The assault fell back. Verity never fired her musket, and the Georgians withdrew before Ethan's company reached their original position.

"I can't believe they'll try that again," gasped Jefferson. "Oh, no! Not—"

Garrett followed Jefferson's stunned gaze. "Verity."

"Hello, Garrett," said Verity. "I was just—"

"Fighting," finished Ethan. "Fighting. No, we're not related. We can't be. God forbid, what if insanity runs in the family?"

"Verity," said Garrett again. "Verity." She suspected he couldn't think of anything bad enough to say.

"Must have a Celtic ancestry," offered Sam thoughtfully. "That explains it. Hallowell's plainly English," he continued in disgust. "But you, Missy, your mamma must have been—"

"She was Scottish," said Verity.

"As I said. A Highlander, no doubt. Still, you done well, I've got to say. You sure can shoot. The major here, he'd feel better if you weren't quite so bold, and you've shaken poor Hallowell's respectability, but that can take a few knocks without doing no harm. He's too respectable as it is."

Ethan's jaw firmed at this, and Verity smiled lovingly at Sam. Spy or no spy, bastard or not, Ethan Hallowell remained a gentleman.

Chapter Eleven

The 19th and 20th Massachusetts regiments were lined up just to the left of the cannons. Across the pasture, the rebel army occupied Seminary Ridge, hidden in the trees while Robert E. Lee planned a decisive victory.

Verity spent the night with her company, refusing to speak with Garrett until he freed Ethan. Ethan remained under Garrett's guard, but at least he wasn't in shackles. Verity knew Garrett and Dan Wallingford argued about the matter, but so far, Garrett had the upper hand.

Verity broke her silence to question Garrett on the outcome of the argument. "Well? What about Ethan?"

Garrett exhaled and shook his head. "What do you expect of me, Verity?" Garrett seemed tired, as if he hadn't rested. Verity felt a pang of guilt for interrogating him.

"I expect you to free an innocent man."

"Besides loyalty, have you any reason to believe Ethan is innocent?" asked Garrett. Her lips twisted into a frown, but she didn't answer. "No. I thought not."

Verity looked away. "You let him lead us yesterday."

"'Us,'" he repeated. "'Us.' You will never fight again, Madam."

Verity cocked her head, her lips curved. Garrett's expression matched hers and he held up a dress. "I acquired this from General Hancock's very respectable wife. Wear it."

Verity examined the dull garment and groaned when she noticed the corset and stockings Garrett had located. "I don't like it."

"I'm not giving you a choice, woman. Aside from Ethan's poor, boggled soldiers, you're unknown in this army. They see a boy soldier. One of them. In this dress, my sweet, you'll be a woman once more. Just try to join the fray in a dress."

Defeated, Verity snatched the dress from Garrett's hand. "I see. You've planned this."

"You've got a half hour to dress. I want that face scrubbed and your hair brushed."

"A half hour?" asked Verity. "What's the rush? It's fairly quiet this morning. I know they're fighting over at Culp's Hill, but there's nothing going on here."

"Not yet," said Garrett ominously: "Now, do as I say. And hurry."

Verity obliged Garrett's request. She found a jug of water, rinsed her face, and she brushed her hair. She disappeared into a surgeon's tent, then emerged clothed once again as a woman. The dress wasn't like Ivy's racy garments. It was brown and cream, very plain, with a high neckline.

Mercifully, Garrett had forgotten shoes. Verity wore the shoes she'd stolen from the innkeeper's son, pleased with her secret defiance.

As Verity walked back toward her friends, she had the curious feeling that she left her true self in Watkins' identity. This sedate, feminine woman wasn't her at all.

"Can we help you, Ma'am?" asked Sam politely. Verity rolled her eyes.

"No."

Garrett allowed Ethan to remain with the men, though technically he was still under arrest. He looked up when she approached and doffed his cap respectfully. Verity eyed him with misgivings. Sam was whittling, and John strummed his guitar. Only Jefferson grinned and winked.

The men gaped as Verity hiked up her skirt and sat crosslegged beside them. "Don't look at me that way, Sam. I'm just not in the mood for teasing."

Sam's eyes widened. "Miss Talmadge! I didn't recognize ye all getted-up like that!"

"It wasn't my idea," said Verity gloomily.

"I take it the major's finally got his way with ye," said Sam with a grin, but then he paled. "Meaning with your dress, and not your particulars—"

This sounded even worse, and Sam bit his lip. Verity smiled despite her frustration. "I know what you meant, Sam. What's going on with the rebs, anyway?"

To the discomfort of the men, Verity flopped back and lay looking up at the sky.

"Our side has driven the Confederates off Culp's Hill," Ethan told her.

"Does that mean we've won?"

"Hell, no, Watkins," answered Sam. "It just means we don't have so much to worry about from our backside when old Marse Robert comes at our front."

Verity sat up. "What do you mean, 'front?' I thought they tried that yesterday, and failed?"

"They was testing us," said Sam. "No, Missy, the real fight's yet to come. Though I hear a little band of Mainers kept the rebs from overrunning us all yesterday, up on them hills," he added, gesturing toward the Round Tops. "Bayonet charge."

"Good for the Mainers," said Verity.

Garrett joined them, seating himself next to Verity. "I see you've finally obeyed my word," he observed as he surveyed her appearance. He brushed dirt and grass from her back and sighed. "A man can only hope for so much, I suppose."

Verity yawned and stretched, looking out across the undulating countryside. The sun peeked in and out of hazy clouds. "It's going to be hot today," she noted as she gazed toward Lee's invisible army.

A farmhouse sat in the midst of the battlefield, intact despite the blood on the ground. At the bottom of the slope beneath the 20th Mass were skirmishers from Ohio, Vermont, and Maine, waiting for the chance to delay the next oncoming attack. A fairly steady popping sounded from their muskets as they exchanged shots with the rebel sharpshooters.

"It's beautiful here," said Verity. "Peaceful. This morning, I thought I'd never seen a more beautiful land than this."

Garrett looked at her. "I thought that, too."

"Maybe it's over," said Verity, but Garrett gazed across the field toward his Southern foe.

"It's not over."

"Lee's got something planned, make no mistake," said Sam.

"Then why's he waiting so damned long to start at us?" asked Jefferson. His active nature wasn't suited to sitting around waiting to be attacked.

John set aside his guitar. "Maybe it's a mighty good plan."

Verity took a deep breath and gazed sleepily across the rolling, green fields. Garrett allowed her to remain with her friends until signs of battle arose. They played cards, but the low hum and buzz of nearby bees suggested sleep for a drowsy afternoon. Verity yawned and leaned back against the stone wall.

"Your turn, Missy," said Sam.

Verity forced her attention back to her cards.

"There she goes!" A wild shout vibrated from the New York regiment beside the 20th Mass, picked up and echoed by others. An artillery explosion rent the air. The battle had begun.

Verity jumped to her feet, but Jefferson yanked her back down. "Keep low, you little idiot." As he spoke, the whole Confederate artillery line seemed to explode in one blast.

Just past one in the afternoon, shells hurtled toward the Union line. Verity crouched low behind what seemed a very inadequate stone wall. "Garrett told me to stay in the rear. I've disobeyed him . . . again."

"Don't go worrying about the major now, Watkins," said Sam. "You're as safe here as anywhere. Look. Them shells are flying right past us. Clean over our heads. It's the rear they're hitting, not us. Stay put."

Verity fingered the stone wall. "If only we'd fixed this up when we had the chance."

"This wall won't make much difference if it's hit dead on by a shell," said Jefferson.

"Wonderful." Verity closed her eyes.

Behind them, colossal explosions crashed and shook the earth. Verity's teeth rattled when an ammunition chest was hit. "Where is Garrett?" Verity forgot her own fear and started to rise.

Ethan caught her and pulled her down beside him. "You stay put, little cousin. Major Knox is fine."

"Listen up, girl," added Sam. "The major's down like us, if he's got a lick of sense. That's the best any of us can do."

Verity agreed, but her eyes filled with hot tears. Their last words had been cold, bitter. She hadn't told him she loved him. And she did love him.

"If one's going to hit you, you won't hear it coming," said Jefferson in an attempt at comfort.

"President," sighed John. "Pipe down."

The earth shook as barrage after barrage crashed into the Union position, but as Verity got used to the deafening explosions she realized that most overshot their target.

"Looks like the Johnnies are aiming high," commented Sam cheerfully. He seemed totally unaffected by the hellish blasts. Verity wondered if he'd lost his mind. But Sam showed no fear of death now.

"Look there," directed Jefferson. "There's your Major Knox."

Verity saw Garrett with Dan Wallingford, sheltered with a group of officers. Her fear eased. Wallingford was smoking a cigar, but he seemed more rattled than the rest.

"That bit of slime Wallingford seems to be suffering, anyway," she noted.

"He probably thinks the rebs should take better care of their own," remarked Ethan. Seeing the others' reaction to his comment, Ethan shrugged. "Forgive me. Bitterness is no excuse for groundless accusations."

"You got reason, Hallowell," said Sam. "But groundless? I wonder. Aye, I wonder indeed."

Verity wanted to pursue Sam's enigmatic comment, but the constant thunder prevented further conversation. The heat combined with terror became unbearable, and Verity began to think she would die of thirst before a cannon blast ever got her.

Garrett appeared beside them, smiling as if they endured no more than a summer thunderstorm. To the delight of all, he held out a filled canteen of water.

"Drink what you can," he advised. "God knows what's coming next."

"Next?"

"Hell, yes, Watkins," broke in Sam. "You don't think the rebs are smashing us like this for nothing, do you? Hell, no. They're softening us up, and then they'll come on over to clean up the mess. Ain't that right, Major?"

"No doubt." Garrett sounded almost casual. "But if they think we're shattered by this bombardment, they'll be disappointed by the results."

"Why?" Verity felt shattered, anyway.

Garrett shrugged. "Not doing much damage. Oh, it's loud, all right, but it hasn't hit our big guns. We'll have plenty left when they come over."

"Why hasn't the artillery fired back?" asked Ethan.

"We're holding off, trying to lead them over," said Garrett. "We'll let loose a few volleys before long."

The Union guns opened fire with a deafening roar. Disregarding danger, General Hancock rode along the line, encouraging the troops and inspiring confidence wherever he went.

"It seems for once we've got a leader ready to fight," commented Garrett.

"But Meade's our leader," said Verity. The commanding general occupied a small house in the rear, but he hadn't been seen recently by the fighting men.

Hancock rode on, and the men cheered. Garrett watched their commander appreciatively. "Not up here."

The cannonade lasted for almost two hours before the shelling finally eased. An ominous silence descended over the battlefield. Men stood and stretched. Verity shook the dust from her skirt.

Smoke lifted in the air and drifted away over the hills, clearing the field that lay between North and South. "Ain't that a sight?" sighed Sam.

On a hill by a clump of trees, artillerymen cleaned cannons and reloaded canisters. The men hurriedly prepared, but Verity stared out over the field toward Seminary Ridge. She spotted the swell of the gray line as it rose from behind the first crest.

"They're coming." Verity's voice died down as she realized the enormity of Lee's onslaught.

"My God," murmured Ethan, but his voice was drowned out by a rising chorus of shouts. All had seen the same sight. Robert E. Lee made his final move. And a more stunning display had never been seen by anyone.

A line of skirmishers preceded the Confederate column, followed by a huge amassment of perfectly ordered ranks. Regimental flags unfurled, they marched as if on parade. Slowly and steadily they came on, gray and butternut.

"So many . . ." Verity was mesmerized by the mystical precision of the Confederate movement. "We'll be overrun."

Verity had been speaking to herself, but Sam heard her voice and laid his hand on her back. "The largest waves strike the shore only to fall back again to the sea," he said in a low, deep voice. The men nearest stopped working and stared at him in surprise.

"Hold fast, men. We are not sand. We are the rocks and boulders of Pennsylvania. The North. If we stand firm, no power on earth will move us. If we stand, no death before nor after will have been in vain."

Verity wondered if another spirit spoke with Sam's tongue, and a strange chill ran along her spine.

"Get those muskets loaded," ordered Ethan. "The Nineteenth will be reloading for us, passing the weapons up. I want a steady stream back and forth." As he spoke, he loaded a second revolver.

Garrett hesitated, then drew a long breath. "I'm sorry, Hallowell. You're to report to the rear."

"Why?" cut in Verity. "He led us yesterday."

"For one thing, I want him to keep you in your place," said Garrett.

"It's all right, Verity," said Ethan. "I understand."

Ethan turned and walked away, but Verity's eyes blazed with anger. "You can't do this to him. It's cruel."

A moment ago, she had longed to tell Garrett Knox how much she loved him. But now Ethan walked away, his head bowed, his shoulders slumped beneath tortured pride. "How could you?"

"Has it occurred to you that Ethan Hallowell might be in as much danger as Westley, as Robert? Where better than a battle to kill a man without suspicion?"

"Why?"

"I don't know. It's just a feeling. Now, go. I don't want you up here, either."

Verity refused to budge. Garrett turned back to his men as they worked feverishly, loading muskets and stacking them, entrenching to await an onslaught that might end this day forever.

Verity stood beside Ethan, waiting among the stretcher bearers. Many women worked here, but Verity felt her real place was with her friends. It seemed an eternity while the gray soldiers came on, closer and closer, up and down over the undulating fields.

Sporadic artillery fire began again, but no one paid it much heed. All eyes focused on the slowly advancing Confederate columns. The Union batteries fired, blasting amidst the gray, but still the rebels came on, heedless of the sudden gaps.

Across the field they came, drawing ever nearer. As the rebels crossed the diagonal road that split the pasture, a small regiment of Ohio skirmishers darted boldly out to fire at the rebels' left flank. The flank faltered, falling to their rear. Along the ridge, men in blue cheered.

Verity heard John's deep voice, raised in surprising emotion. "Hurrah for Ohio!"

"John was born in western Ohio," Ethan told her. Verity looked up at her cousin. He stood tall and proud beside her, condemned unfairly by the man she loved. Verity took his hand.

"You love them, don't you?"

"I do."

The Confederate force came on. Like a great wave breaking upon jutting rocks, it passed over the Union skirmishers, continuing on toward the blue shore. The Massachusetts men aimed their muskets and waited for the command to fire. Hands clenched, Ethan trembled.

Sam knelt behind the rock wall, with John beside him. Jefferson gathered a stack of loaded muskets passed to him by the supporting 19th, and also readied himself. Garrett walked down the line studying the ranks, looking for weakness.

Verity couldn't stand it anymore. She couldn't leave Garrett to face that fire without her. "I've got to go." Ethan tried to catch her, but Verity darted forward, dragging Watkins' pack, heedless of the soldiers who blocked her way. She shoved her way through the mass of men, and ran to Garrett Knox.

"Verity! Jesus, get out of here." Garrett pulled her into his arms and kissed her mouth. "Go."

"I can't leave you." Her eyes were wide, filled with tears.

"I love you, Verity Talmadge." Tears formed in Garrett's eyes, but he smiled. "If you'd obey at least one command, please, go back."

Ethan raced up behind her. "I couldn't catch her—"

"It's all right, Hallowell." Garrett turned and surveyed the oncoming rebels. Five minutes away. Maybe. Garrett looked back at Ethan Hallowell. For a long moment, Garrett held Ethan's steady gaze.

"Report to your command, Hallowell," he said at last. "The men need you."

"Yes, sir!" Ethan jumped into readiness, but Verity's tears swarmed her vision, then fell to her cheek.

"You, Watkins, will report to the rear with the stretcher bearers."

"Yes, Sir," said Verity. "Ready for anything, Sir."

Verity looked at the men she'd come to know, to love. Sam turned to her, smiling. John nodded her way. Jefferson held up his long, gifted hand in a still wave, and Verity raised her own in salute.

Ethan had gone down the line to position his company, but he returned to Verity and drew her aside. "What is it, Ethan?"

Ethan drew a letter from his jacket and handed it to her. "If I should fall," he began quietly, "be sure this reaches my Bessie."

Verity nodded, unable to speak as she took the letter. She rose on tiptoes and kissed his cheek. "I am now, and always will be, honored to be your friend and cousin."

Verity reached into Watkins's pack and drew out a golden pocket watch. "This belonged to your brother. He gave it to me just before he died. I think Westley would want you to have it now."

Ethan swallowed hard, and he took the watch. Without a word, he turned back to his men. Garrett watched them, then turned away. A soft touch on his shoulder brought him back. "Garrett—"

"Verity, get out of here. Please." Two minutes. Firing would begin.

"You'll be safe?" She asked the impossible, and she knew it. "You'll be careful?"

"I will." A promise made of wishing.

Verity wanted to obey, but she couldn't move. Very gently, she reached and touched his face, the slight cleft in his chin, then rested her hand over his heart. "I love you so."

Garrett closed his eyes. "That is all I want to know."

"Never forget."

"Go."

Verity's tears blinded her, but she obeyed him this time. Without looking back, she scrambled through the throngs of soldiers and made her way to the stretcher bearers. Cannons roared and crashed overhead, but Verity didn't notice. All her soul was focused on the group remaining by the wall.

When the Confederates reached two hundred yards, the blue line rose and fired. Blazing smoke poured from the muskets. The rebel front line reeled. Flags fell. Screams of wounded men slashed through the air. Canisters blasted in the rebel midst, creating huge gaps, but the flags rose again in other hands and again they came forward.

Confederate sharpshooters took shelter behind the rocks, then pelted the 20th Massachusetts with deadly fire. The men of the 20th rose in response. Verity heard wild shouts, battle cries. "Fredericksburg, Fredericksburg," they bellowed as they fought the reeling attackers. Six months ago, it was they who made the valiant charge into death.

The chant brought images of dead comrades, men whose spirits would soon be joined by their Southern counterparts.

Garrett fought beside Sam and Jefferson. They poured fire into the enemy ranks, and again the rebels fell back. Blue and gray intermingled in mortal combat as the rebels renewed the desperate charge. No longer regiment against regiment, it became company against company, then man against man.

Verity held her breath as she watched. She left her position and moved forward. Garrett fired a musket in one hand, then whirled and shot his revolver. Men of both sides fell all around, and bayonets glinted in the afternoon sun.

John used his spent musket as a great, swinging club. Jefferson wielded his bayonet like a knight's lance. Shouts and agonized screams blended into a mortal clamor. Cannon blasts shook the ground where men fought hand to hand.

Ethan's company held its own, but then a shell crashed and exploded in the midst of the 20th. Sam's large body hurtled backward to fall in an inhuman pile. Ethan staggered back as several more shells exploded in rapid succession, wreaking heavy devastation in the regiment.

Verity's world stopped, then flew. "No!" She ran forward, her dress whipping around her ankles. She reached the height of the slope. Through the thick smoke, she saw Garrett. . . .

He fought alone, desperately, while Ethan's company regrouped behind him. Verity swayed, gripping her sides as she watched him. He knocked a rebel back, but another leapt toward him, aimed—and Ethan Hallowell pushed Garrett out of the way.

Verity's vision blurred. The world jerked to a stop. She saw spraying blood and flesh. She saw Ethan fall. Jefferson bounded toward him, shooting as he ran. Rebels fell. John smashed another, and Garrett lifted Ethan into his arms.

The success of the Confederate charge hung in the balance. A regiment of untried Vermonters turned the tide. They swung in around the rebels, firing as the smoke rose. They marched as if on drill, pummeling the rebels into defeat.

General Hancock was struck, but he refused to leave the field. Confidence surged along the Union line as reinforcements swept down to join them. That was the end; white cloths brandished all around. Soon the Union soldiers had more rebel prisoners than they could handle.

Ambulances swarmed behind the lines, pulled by heavy-boned, steaming horses. Filled with wounded. John and Jefferson together carried Sam's body. Garrett carried Ethan to the rear, and Verity met them there.

"He's not dead. To hell with the damned stretcher. I'm bringing him to the surgeons right now."

Verity took one look at Ethan and her heart quailed. His sweet face contorted with agony, and blood soaked his trousers. His legs hung in a weird semblance of normalcy.

"This way." Verity shoved her way toward the surgeon's tent. At least, Ethan wouldn't have to wait to be attended.

John and Jefferson lay Sam on the ground. Verity saw the sergeant's body lying there, still . . . she heard his words in her mind as she ran toward the surgeon's tent: *If we stand, no death before or after will have been in vain* . . .

Dying men thronged outside the surgeon's tent. Groans rumbled the walls inside. Some wept. Ethan made no sound, but his teeth clenched with the sheer effort of will. Garrett put him on a table, then called a surgeon over to examine him.

"Christ, Major, I can't waste my time here. Both legs are shot up, too much blood. He's a goner. Put him with the gut wounds."

Verity swayed, but Garrett grabbed the surgeon's arm and the man winced. "A gut wound is terminal," said Garrett in a voice that rang with such deadly calm that the surgeon's face paled. "Broken legs can heal. You will attend him. Now."

The surgeon looked nervously at John and Garrett, then at Jefferson, who stood clutching a musket. The surgeon didn't argue. He cut open Ethan's trousers and shook his head.

"Blasted right through, here, above the knees. Jesus, how many times was he hit? That's musket fire."

"We know what it was, you idiot," sputtered Verity. "Fix him."

"All I can do is amputate. Both legs. He won't make it, though. Too much blood loss."

Verity started to cry. Tears flooded Jefferson's brown eyes, too. John looked away. But Garrett wasn't moved. "We'll take care of him. You do your job, and we'll keep him alive."

Ethan opened his eyes, he tried to speak. "Westley," he whispered. "My brother. Please believe—"

"I believe you, Captain," said Garrett gently. "You saved my life. God knows, you had no reason. Be quiet, and save your strength."

Ethan complied, though he had little choice. But when the surgeon retrieved a bloody saw, a shudder twisted his shattered body.

"No," breathed Verity. "Ethan—"

"We've run out of chloroform. You'll have to hold him down, Major," said the surgeon as he positioned the instrument.

"Verity . . ." Ethan's voice came as a choked whisper. "She can't see . . . the men, I don't want them to—"

"We'll go," said John.

"Come on, Watkins." Jefferson grabbed Verity's arm and pulled her away. Verity looked back over her shoulder. Her senses reeled as she saw Garrett lean over Ethan, bracing his arm across the boy's chest. In his hand, Ethan clutched his brother's watch.

Before she turned away, Verity's eyes met Garrett's. The tears in his gray eyes pierced her heart.

* * *

Verity stood outside the surgeon's tent with Jefferson and John. No one spoke. The many screams and agonized groans drowned out Ethan's voice, but they knew. Minutes passed. The sun settled and cast its final shadows while they waited. The sky darkened beneath rain clouds, rain began.

Verity sank to her knees, weakened by a day too horrible to comprehend. Stretcher bearers raced to and fro, in and out of the tent, carrying the dead and the barely living. Jefferson and John stood like grim statues, faces blank, saying nothing.

Finally, Garrett emerged from the tent. His face was white. Verity rose unsteadily to her feet. She touched his arm. "Ethan?"

"He's alive, barely." Garrett closed his eyes, tipping his head back, letting the damp air cool his throat. "He passed out for the last of it. But it's over."

"What can we do?" asked Verity in a tiny voice.

"They're giving him morphine, though they don't have enough to make much difference. I've got him on special care, and he's got us looking after him. There's not much else we can do."

Dan Wallingford approached the tent, and Verity gritted her teeth. Jefferson made a fist, and John fingered his musket. "You men made out all right, I see," said Dan, taking no note of their combative postures. He eyed Verity. With her hair bound in a chignon, in a dress, he saw no sign of Watkins.

"Who have we here?"

"Verity Talmadge," said Garrett. "Found at last."

"You don't say!" exclaimed Dan. "What brings you here, Miss Talmadge?"

"I've been . . . nursing," replied Verity with a quick glance at Garrett.

"Heard Hallowell entered the fray and got shot up," said Dan. "Died?"

"No," said Garrett in a controlled voice. "But he lost both legs."

"Better than hanging," said Dan. John lifted his musket.

"If anyone hangs—" began Jefferson, but Garrett cut him off.

"It's over, Dan. Your proof is gone. There's nothing on this earth that will make me turn that boy in now. You know I don't believe your accusations. Let it pass."

Dan hesitated. "I don't like it. But he's certainly suffered enough. In my mind, however, the matter of the spy is settled."

Dan left, and Garrett drew a long breath. "That didn't exactly clear Ethan's name," said Verity. "But it's enough."

"Dan is a lawyer," said Garrett wearily. "That isn't necessarily indicative of good judgement."

Chapter Twelve

Garrett had Ethan moved to a smaller tent, where Verity tended him. Jefferson and John checked on him often, but the army remaining in Gettysburg labored in burial duties. For once, Verity was glad to get out of Watkins's responsibilities.

The beautiful farmland of Gettysburg stank. Dead horses rotted in the sun. Dead men lay in bloated clumps, reeking in the ninety degree heat. The surgeons' tents were worse. The rotting flesh of half-living men cursed every breeze. Flies swarmed in the stagnant air.

Verity returned to Ethan's side after yet another bout with nausea. Ethan had woken, but he didn't speak. He just stared at the tent fold. When Verity held his hand he squeezed it, so she knew she gave him comfort. But he didn't speak.

Jefferson and John entered the tent, weary from the loathsome task of collecting and sorting dead men. "What's going on?" asked Verity. "Where are the rebels now?"

"Gone," sighed Jefferson, and John shook his head in disgust.

"We had them." John's comment echoed many Verity had heard since the rebel charge.

"Should have followed it up," added Jefferson. "But Meade just sat here, licking our own wounds. And Lee's gone, now. Headed off in the night. No word that we'll follow."

Tears started at the corner of Ethan Hallowell's closed eyes, running down his temple to disappear in his matted, blond hair. "It's not over."

The first words he had spoken, wrenched from his body in agony. "Don't think about that now, Ethan," Verity advised. Jefferson nodded and patted Ethan's shoulder.

"The war's over for you, Captain. You can fetch your lady out of Virginia and haul her on back to Boston. Let the damned war go on without you."

"That's right." John patted Ethan's head in an awkward gesture of affection.

But Ethan's face hardened. "I'll never go back to Boston."

Verity didn't like the tone in his voice. It frightened her. "You and Bess will find a better place to live—"

"I'd like to speak with you alone," said Ethan. "If you men will excuse us, please."

Jefferson glanced at John, who shrugged. "We're expected back on burial duty," said Jefferson gloomily. "Sam's due to be put in the ground at dusk."

Ethan nodded. "I'll be there."

"What?" asked Verity. "How?"

"Major Knox has arranged my attendance. I'll be there."

"I knew you'd pull through, Captain," said Jefferson, his youthful spirits uplifted by Ethan's announcement. He patted Ethan's shoulder again, then left with John.

Ethan's manner didn't reassure Verity, though she wasn't sure why. "Why did you want to talk alone?"

"I want you to write a letter for me. Each word as I tell you. No questions."

Verity found paper and ink, then sat at Ethan's bedside. "I'm ready. For Bess?"

"Yes." Ethan hesitated. "The particulars of mailing are set down in the letter I gave you before the fight. I assume it's still in your possession."

"Of course."

"Tell her I've had a change of heart, and desire to end our engagement."

Verity dropped the pen. "I will not!"

Ethan's eyes met Verity's. He was fighting tears, but Verity refused to relent. "You can't do this, Ethan. Wait until you feel better. You've lost your legs. Don't cut out your heart, too."

"It's over, Verity. It's best forgotten. Please, understand. It's over."

"It's not over, Ethan Hallowell. I won't let you do this. You mean so much to me, and I won't let you do this."

Ethan seized her hand and kissed it. "It can't be. It was never meant to be. Do you understand? You think I'm alive. I'm not. Please, accept my will in this. Please."

Verity lifted his hand to her cheek. "I'll do what you want."

"Then do this last thing for me, and forget."

"Forget?"

"Forget about me. About everything. Leave this damned war, and go back to being a woman. Marry Major Knox. And forget me."

Verity didn't know what to say, how to change his mind. She looked around the dark tent and saw Garrett watching them. Maybe he could convince Ethan. Garrett turned away and left the tent.

"Here it is." Verity handed Ethan the note. He perused it, checking her words for accuracy as if he suspected she would cheat him of his ending with Bess.

"Are you sure it's what you wanted?"

"It is."

"It will kill her," warned Verity.

"It will set her free."

Verity folded the letter and rose from her seat. "You need to sleep, Ethan, since you're going to Sam's burial tonight. Rest."

"There's one more thing."

Verity turned back. "What?"

"Destroy the first letter. There's no need to burden Bess with what might have been. I want your word in this."

"Given."

"Tear it up."

Verity did so. Carefully. Into four even pieces that didn't obscure one word. "Done."

"Thank you."

Verity left Ethan alone, went outside the tent, and put the two letters together. She retrieved another piece of paper and began writing a third letter to Bess Hartman.

* * *

Verity found Garrett overseeing a group of rebel prisoners. A young colonel approached with more rebels. "Major Knox," he called when he saw Garrett. "What shall I do with these gentlemen?"

"If they're willing, they can aid in burial duty," said Garrett.

"Very good." The colonel turned to his prisoners. "If you men desire, you may aid in the final resting of your brethren, even as we lay our own into the soil. Do you agree?"

The Maine colonel's gentle manner surprised Verity. Possessing innate dignity, he granted the same even to his enemy. "Who are you?" she asked impertinently.

The colonel turned and bowed. "Joshua Lawrence Chamberlain, Ma'am. Colonel of the Twentieth Maine. Before that, professor of rhetoric at Bowdoin College in Brunswick."

"Brunswick," said Verity. "That's where Jefferson lived. He's a black soldier who fights with us—"

"Us?" asked Chamberlain with a glance at Garrett, who sighed and made no comment.

"I mean, the Twentieth Mass," corrected Verity. "My brother's regiment, before he disappeared. And my cousin's, now."

"Ah." Colonel Chamberlain eyed Verity's guilty expression. "They say a rebel woman was found dead on the field after Pickett's Charge. Apparently, she disguised herself as a soldier and followed her husband into battle. They died side by side."

Verity's eyes widened. "A rebel woman fought, too? I mean—"

"Say no more, young lady." Joshua Chamberlain smiled. "I can't bear to know."

"That's probably pretty sound," agreed Verity. "Anyway, as I was saying earlier, Jefferson lived with a professor from Bowdoin College. I don't know his name."

"Gordon Reid," said Chamberlain. "He took in several young men. Two lived with him and his little girl for many years. But I never met your Jefferson."

"He's here," said Verity proudly. "He fought yesterday."

"Making our victory more honorable," said Chamberlain.

"Pardon me, Colonel," drawled a rebel prisoner. "This is all just chummy between you Yanks, pretty girl and all. But what about burying our mates?"

"Major Knox has informed me that those of you with wounds will be tended. The others will be fed. You will certainly be granted the right to bury your dead."

Chamberlain paused, and a strange, wise expression crossed his face. "I look forward to the day we again stand as brothers on this, our common soil. Men who fight with such honor and bravery are better as brothers than enemies."

"If all Yanks were men such as yourself, Colonel, that might be possible," said an elderly rebel.

One of the rebels studied Garrett with interest. "Knox?" he asked. "Garrett Knox?"

"I am," replied Garrett.

"Then I served with your cousin."

Garrett's throat tightened, and Verity held her breath.

"Jared?" he asked in a restrained voice, but the rebel nodded sadly.

"Young Major Jared, yes. Led his men out in yonder peach orchard. Never came back," mourned the rebel.

"No," whispered Verity, but Garrett didn't utter a word. He stood as if made from marble.

"Jared." Garrett's voice cracked, and he said nothing further.

"I'm sorry, Major," said Colonel Chamberlain, but Garrett nodded stiffly and turned away.

Verity started to follow him. Another thought struck her and she seized the rebel's arm, interrupting Chamberlain.

"Never came back, you said?"

"Young Jared led the attack through the peach orchard," said the rebel. "His company got separated from the bulk of the army out there. He didn't return, nor did any of his men."

"Then you're not certain he's dead!" exclaimed Verity, but the rebel sighed and shook his head.

"Many lie unaccounted for, Miss. Many lie up there, hidden in the rocks. We mourn Jared. He was brave and strong. But when a man doesn't come back from those fields of fire, it's safe to say he's gone forever."

Verity wasn't convinced. "Couldn't he be injured, maybe with a broken leg or something?"

"We've searched the hills and fields for such men," Colonel Chamberlain reminded her.

"Not completely," argued Verity. "There might be a chance."

Joshua Chamberlain smiled, a sad, gentle smile, then turned to the rebel. "Do you know the area in which your Major Knox fell?"

"Sure do," replied the rebel, but he eyed the Yankee colonel doubtfully. "Can't be thinking any damned Yankee's going to any effort to find a Virginian."

"Then you're thinking wrong," said Chamberlain. "Young lady, please tell Major Knox that I've arranged for a party to look for his cousin. He may want to join the search."

"Yes, Sir!" Verity started away, then turned back and grabbed the colonel's hand, kissing it with surprising force. "Thank you."

Joshua Chamberlain's eyes gleamed with dry wit. "My pleasure."

Verity dressed again as Verrill Watkins, muddied her face, then darted off in search of Garrett. She found him standing by the shattered clump of trees, alone beside the silent cannons. A hot wind blew his dark hair, and his opened uniform jacket fluttered carelessly. He stared south, and Verity knew he cried.

"Garrett." She spoke softly, and he turned. Despite his silent tears, Garrett smiled and shook his head when he saw her.

"You're indomitable, aren't you? Was a dress too much to bear?"

"A bit," agreed Verity. "But Watkins has returned for a purpose."

"I'm almost afraid to ask," said Garrett. "Let me guess. You disapprove of Meade's strategy, and you're heading off after Lee's army yourself."

"No. Just one piece of it. I got Colonel Chamberlain's permission to look for Jared. He told me to find you."

Garrett met her eyes. "Let's go."

Verity and Garrett joined the group Chamberlain organized. Chamberlain eyed Watkins suspiciously, but he didn't recognize the young Bostonian nurse who pressured him into the futile gesture of searching for one dead Virginian.

"I hope you locate your cousin, Major," he said without much enthusiasm. "At least, he'll find a fit burial this way."

"If he's really dead," piped in Verity.

"Thank you, Colonel," said Garrett. "If a fit burial is all I can give him, that I will do."

Chamberlain sighed. "I wish you luck."

* * *

They walked for hours, crisscrossing the fields, hunting through boulders and rock piles seeped in blood. The peach orchard had seen incredible devastation, but the rebel prisoner recognized no one from Jared's company.

Bodies lay in contorted heaps, clothed in blue and gray. The Maine soldiers kept a respectful silence as the Virginian picked through the fallen men. Verity stuck close to Garrett's side as he searched for Jared.

The others held handkerchiefs over their noses to keep out the stench. Garrett took no notice. He dreaded finding Jared Knox lying amidst that gruesome collection of dead men. But he kept looking.

The piles of bodies, blue and bloated in the sun, the stench of death . . . Garrett's eyes closed, and he saw Jared's face, young and filled with joy. The power of life. In a flash, Garrett remembered all the days of their youth. Jared as a small boy when Garrett led him on their first pony, racing across the fields at Fox Run. The wild days of revelry in France. The day they said farewell, and took up arms for their respective lands. . . .

Every time he saw blond hair, his heart stopped, but Garrett kept looking, turning bodies over, setting them gently back into place.

The rebel prisoner turned a man over, and a crumpled picture of a woman and child fell to the earth. Verity picked it up, then choked back a cry. Garrett took the picture from her hands, a photograph of a young woman and a child.

Garrett put his arm around Verity's shoulders, but she shook her head. "We should go back now," he said. "This is hopeless."

"No. I'm all right."

Just as Verity straightened and took a drink from a Maine soldier's canteen, the rebel called out. "Over here!" Garrett's face paled, but he left Verity to examine the rebel's find.

Hidden behind a thicket and a large boulder were several bodies. "These here were Major Jared's men, all right," said the rebel. "Here's Buckingham . . . That's Jimmy Liddell over there." The rebel's voice faded as he knelt beside his dead comrades.

"Is Jared . . . ?" began Verity, but her voice shook.

Garrett steeled himself and examined the fallen men. "He's not here," he said, both relieved and resigned to Jared's uncertain fate.

"Shells hit here dozens of times," said a Maine soldier. "No man could live through this. Lord, look at this place. I thought we had it bad up on Little Round Top."

Despite the horror of the scene, Verity examined the dead men. Her courage astounded Garrett. "Wait a minute! This man hasn't been dead as long as the others."

"That's Jimmy Liddell," said the rebel, tears misting his eyes. "Even in death, the boy's got a likable face."

"You're right, boy," said the Mainer. "Look, his wounds have been tended."

"And here's something else," noted the rebel. "No letters in his coat, no pictures, nothing. Like he done give it all away to somebody, just afore he passed on. Jimmy, he was a good boy. He'd want his folks to have his gear, and he wrote enough letters to fill a book."

Verity seized the dead rebel's canteen. "This has been refilled!"

Garrett stood still as stone. He felt his heart's uncertain quickening. He knew the man who would stay amidst a deathly shelling to tend a wounded comrade. "Jared."

"Maybe he's around here, too," said Verity excitedly.

"He might have hid out," agreed the rebel. "Ho! Major Knox! Can you hear me? It's Danny Madden calling."

"Even if he was here, he's long gone by now," offered the more reasonable Mainer. "We had troops all over this area just this morning. Yesterday, we weren't searching that hard. Too damned tired, begging your pardon," he added with a nod to the rebel.

"If he could, he'd have left last night," guessed the rebel. "Probably headed south on his own."

"Jared wouldn't stay here after the boy died," agreed Garrett. "And he wouldn't relish a stay in a Yankee prison camp, either."

"None of us would," said the rebel. "But it's better than this . . ."

Verity and Garrett returned to the Union camp at dusk. John and Jefferson carried Sam's body to the burial ground, standing silently by the hole in which he would forever sleep. Ethan was already there, his legs covered by a blanket. He sat very straight, but not quite as stiff as he once had been.

"Ready for the service, Major?" asked Jefferson.

"Not yet, Davis. Wait a few more minutes. I'm expecting someone."

"Who?" asked Verity. Before Garrett could answer, Ivy came toward them, dressed in solemn black, a black handkerchief clutched in her hands.

"Ivy!" said Verity in surprise. Ivy's eyes were red and swollen, puddled with tears. She squeezed Verity's hand, then nodded to Jefferson, who gently touched her shoulder.

"I knew it was coming," said Ivy in a broken voice. "Last time I saw him, I knew. When his boy died, Old Sam lost the will to live."

"We may begin now," said Garrett. Ivy looked up at him, pressed her lips together, then hugged him. Garrett kissed her forehead.

"I found a priest," said Jefferson. "Even speaks Latin, or so he claims."

"Thank you, My Dear," said Ivy. "Sam held the faith better than most, though he kept it to himself."

Ivy turned to the men gathered at Sam's graveside. Others of the 20th joined them, caps held in dirty hands, silent and respectful of the sergeant who led them through so many torturous battles.

"I can't tell you what it means to have you all here," said Ivy. "He spoke of most of you, and he loved you all. He never had a friend better than John. From Jefferson, he learned a black man is just like other men, and in your case, anyway, a whole lot better. Aye, loved you, he did.

"Even this pretty young officer here," she added with a smile directed at Ethan. Ethan eyed her doubtfully, but Ivy touched his blond hair in a motherly gesture.

"Aw, Little Prince. Old Sam had a soft spot for you, whether he showed it or not. Said you was as stiff as Boston made 'em, and just as brave as they come. Said there weren't a captain in the army he'd rather follow when push came to shove."

"Sam said that?" asked Ethan in wonder.

"He did. Said he'd been lucky with his officers. Young Adrian, Westley, Robert Talmadge. But I think his words were, *'It's that stick-in-the-mud, Hallowell, who's most likely to give his life for one of us.'* It looks to me like Old Sam was right."

Ethan looked down, hiding the tears that formed in his blue eyes. Verity touched his shoulder.

"Sam was a wise man," sighed Garrett. "God knows, we'll miss him."

"That we will," agreed Jefferson.

"And you, Garrett Knox," continued Ivy. "You've got to know that Sam thought the Good Lord made one man in the image of his finest. And that was you. Said if you took Hercules, St. Patrick, and King Arthur, molded them together, and set them to life, you might come up with a fellow half what you're worth."

Verity sniffled and bit her lip at what she considered an accurate assessment of Garrett Knox.

"I don't know about the St. Patrick part, Ivy," said Garrett with a grin.

"I questioned that, too," admitted Ivy. "Guess he just wanted to include something Irish in your makeup. Told him you was half-German, the other half mostly English, but he thought you must have an Irishman hiding back there somewhere."

Ivy turned last to Verity and touched her cheek. "And you, Little Miss. Sam told me if the force of Nature herself took a human shape, she'd be you. You brightened the darkest days after he lost his boy. Gave him hope. God knows why, but maybe there's more hope today in madness than in sanity."

A low chuckle rumbled from John to Jefferson, passed from man to man, and soon all around Sam's grave were smiling. Even Ethan's expression lightened. Then, as the Irish priest spoke in Latin, the men lowered Sam's body into the earth.

Ivy threw in the first dirt, and the men of Ethan's company pitched the heavy blanket of soil until Sam was joined to the earth. As the sun set over Gettysburg, John sat by the grave with his guitar and sang a final tribute to his brother-in-arms.

A summer breeze lifted the stench from the campsite, but Verity's stomach refused to settle. She couldn't be sure when a wave of nausea would crash through her, making her race off to vomit. At first, she attributed her sickness to the stench of death and rotting animals, but when she sat in the cool shade, retching and groaning, Verity began to wonder.

Ivy found her, sitting with her head in her hands. The madam patted Verity's back. "What's ailing you, Little Miss?"

"God, I don't know. I feel horrible. Then just when I think I'm really dying, it goes away. I try to eat, and after two bites, I'm sick again.''

Ivy studied Verity's face. ''How long since you've made use of dousing strips?''

Verity thought carefully. ''Since before Chancellorsville, I think. That was the hardest part of pretending to be a boy, but I managed all right. It's been a while. I just forgot about it. I guess my body really thinks I'm a boy.''

''Not likely,'' said Ivy. ''I expect it knows better than your peculiar brain what you are. And you'd best start listening to its signs. Honey, you're carrying the major's little one.''

Verity's eyes widened, her mouth dropped. ''A baby?'' Ivy nodded, and a slow, womanly smile grew on Verity's face. ''Do you really think I'm pregnant?''

Verity didn't wait for an answer. She hopped to her feet and clapped her hands together. ''I'm pregnant!'' she announced loudly. A soldier passed by and tripped at the young lady's shocking declaration.

Ivy laughed. ''You'd best be remembering ladylike decorum.''

''Oh, hell,'' grumbled Verity. ''You may be right.''

''The major will be wanting to hear this first, and not from one of his soldiers.''

''Garrett,'' sighed Verity. She closed her eyes dreamily, imagining the two of them holding a baby, loving each other. But Garrett's attitude toward her seemed distant now. Nor had he exhibited any desire for her since he caught her naked with Ethan. Ethan. . . .

''Damn,'' said Verity. ''The way he's acting, he'll probably think it's Ethan's baby. Hell's bells, men can be so ridiculous.''

''Young Ethan's?'' asked Ivy. ''Why would the major think that?''

Verity shrugged carelessly. ''Oh, Garrett found us by the river one morning. Naked. We'd had too much bourbon, you see, and—''

''Naked?''

Verity's brow rose at the madam's shock. ''We went swimming.''

''Naked? You and that sweet-faced, firm-bodied captain?'' Ivy paused to issue another gasp, then shook her head. ''You sure Garrett didn't rip the boy's legs off himself?''

''Ivy! Of course not. Garrett was very understanding. Ethan and I are related.''

"You were related to your last husband, young lady."

"True," agreed Verity. "But—"

"But nothing. You get yourself to the major, go down on your knees—"

"And beg his forgiveness?" speculated Verity haughtily. "I think not. Ethan and I are friends, not lovers. I shouldn't have to apologize for something I haven't done."

"When I say, get down on your knees, I ain't talking about 'forgiveness.' "

It took a while for Ivy's meaning to dawn on Verity. When it did, her cheeks flushed crimson. Still, Verity had tired of Garrett's standoffish behavior. The thought of convincing him pleased her.

Verity's stomach churned, and she flushed with a sickly heat. "Not again," she moaned, allowing images of Garrett's unbridled lust to fade away. She clasped her hand over her mouth and ran toward a clump of bushes.

An hour later, Verity went in search of Garrett. She'd gone over her announcement several times, but her imagination provided a wide assortment of pictures. Garrett's smile. A wide grin. Clenched fists and fury. Steely silence.

Verity fought her frightening imagination, and found Garrett entering Ethan's tent. She joined him, but both stopped when they saw his empty cot. "No . . ."

Garrett seized an orderly. "Where," he asked in a threatening, deep voice, "is Captain Hallowell?"

"Gone, Major," said the orderly. Verity's face blanched, but Garrett's grip on the man's arm intensified.

"Where is the captain?" Garrett asked again.

"Thataway," said the orderly. "Out back of the tent. Just put him in the ambulance."

Verity and Garrett exchanged a doubtful glance. "Then he's not dead," said Verity.

"Not yet," replied the orderly.

Verity followed Garrett to the ambulance. In amongst crowded piles of limbless, bandaged men, Ethan lay. John stood by the cart horses, holding the harness reins in defiance of the driver. Jefferson had the man cornered against the cart.

"You ain't taking the captain," said John. He sounded final, resolute. Jefferson nodded. The driver seemed leery of the black soldier, and looked helplessly to Garrett.

"This is unacceptable, Major," the driver said in a high voice.

"Damned sure," said John.

"What's going on?" A faint smile curved Garrett's lips.

"They've stuck Captain Hallowell in this ship of the dead," explained Jefferson. Verity cringed at his usual bluntness.

"Listen, the boy insisted on heading out." The driver lowered his voice before continuing. "They're mostly goners on that cart, all right. Even if they make it to Washington—and most won't—they'll just end up in a cramped hellhole with other men, waiting to die. Men like the captain, who don't have much to live for, anyway."

"Ethan has plenty to 'live for.'" Verity turned to Garrett. "Why would he do this? He seemed better."

"I don't know." Garrett went to the back of the cart and called to Ethan. A faint cough was his answer. "You listen to me, Captain. I told you we'd have you at Fox Run."

"No," answered Ethan. "Tell the men. One last command. Let me go."

"Ethan! Come with us to Maryland." Verity fought tears, her voice shook.

"You can go back to Boston," added Garrett. "I can arrange that."

"No. Do you think I want to return to my 'father' as an invalid? Dependent on the care of a man who owes me nothing? I'm a reminder of shame."

Ethan sounded weak, but he still had plenty to say. He also sounded determined to leave his companions. Only the sight of Westley's pocket watch in Ethan's hand gave Verity hope.

"You stay alive, Ethan Hallowell," she warned. "And don't think you can hide out once you reach Washington, either. Once I'm settled, I'll find you. Maybe then you'll listen to reason."

Ethan didn't argue, but he sighed heavily. Verity knew the boy expected to die. Wanted to die. "Are you sure—"

"You're a good man, Major Knox. Please, I ask you—let it be."

John released his hold on the harness horses, and Jefferson reluctantly backed away from the frightened driver. Verity reached for Ethan's hand, but he was too far away.

"I will find you," she vowed. "Maybe you don't have anyone in Boston. But you have me."

The ambulance rolled away toward Washington, pulled at a slow pace by the straining horses. Jefferson and John turned away, both looking as defeated as if the battle of Gettysburg had been lost, not won. Verity stood with Garrett, watching the ambulance spitting up dust into a gloomy cloud.

"Everything's falling apart." Verity sighed, her shoulders slumped. "I feel like I'm on an iceberg, clinging to survive. And now it's breaking up into little pieces. Sam's piece went under, now Ethan is floating away. Jefferson and John are going back to war . . ." Verity looked up at Garrett. He stared into the distance, his face unreadable.

"What about you, Garrett? Are you going, too?"

"I've decided to rejoin the Maryland Cavalry. We're moving out tomorrow morning, at dawn."

Verity's face paled. "Tomorrow? Aren't we going to your estate together?"

"I've asked Ivy to accompany you. And Mildred's expecting you, or will be once she gets my wire. But I can't go with you, Verity. My duty is here."

He doesn't want to marry me, after all. Tears puddled in Verity's eyes. Even Garrett was leaving her. Tomorrow. Going back to war.

"I thought you wanted to find the spy."

Garrett looked down at her. "Ethan Hallowell was my only lead. Everything pointed to him. I think he's innocent. If not, then he's paid. Dave Delaney is dead. You're safe. I need to go where I'll be the most use. That means horses."

"What about me?"

"What about you?" Garrett was smiling, but Verity thought he looked sad. Her lips curved into a frown and she lifted her chin.

"You don't have to marry me, if you don't want to." Verity peeked out of the corner of her eye to see his reaction.

"I want to."

A tiny breath of relief escaped Verity's lips. "Good, because I'm pregnant."

This wasn't the way she planned to tell him. Verity bit her lip. So much for the romantic build up.

Garrett's mouth dropped. His gray eyes widened until they were almost round. "Pregnant?" His voice sounded tiny.

Verity looked up at him. "What's the matter with you? For a while, we did nothing else. At least, until you went into a jealous fit and abandoned me."

Garrett barely heard her. "Pregnant?" His voice sounded even smaller.

"Yes, pregnant. I'm going to have a baby. Your baby. And don't you dare wonder if it's Ethan's. Because I'm still quite willing and able to pinch you."

Garrett smiled at her threat, but he didn't comment on her accusation.

"Why aren't you saying anything? You don't look any of the ways I pictured."

"What did you picture?"

"Boundless joy, enraged fury. That sort of thing."

"How about shock?" suggested Garrett.

"You shouldn't be surprised . . ." Another wave of nausea swept through Verity. "Oh, hell. Not again."

Garrett arranged for Verity to stay in a farmhouse not far from the battlesite. "Just for a day or two, until you're well enough to move."

"What if I stay sick for the whole nine months? The doctor says it's the baby making me feel this way."

Ivy joined Garrett at Verity's bedside. "It'll pass sooner than that, Honey. It's just your tum getting used to a little visitor, that's all."

"*A little visitor.*" Verity's face softened, and a smile curved her lips. Her expression contorted from a sudden pang, and she felt the green wave again. Garrett passed her the much-used bucket, and Verity threw up.

"This is your fault, Garrett Knox." Verity lay back in the bed and groaned.

"I thought you were happy about the *'little visitor,'*" said Garrett with a laugh. Verity peeked at him through one eye, but a reluctant smile appeared on her face, despite the green.

"I am."

"So where's that priest?" Ivy looked out Verity's window and tapped her foot. "I told him it was urgent."

"A priest, indeed!" Candace Webster marched into the room, her face lit in a bright smile. "Verity's parents would want her married in a Unitarian ceremony. To that end, I've brought Dr. Malcolm with me from Washington."

Verity sat upright in bed. "Candace! What on earth are you doing here?" The Unitarian minister entered the bedroom behind Candace. He looked both pained and embarrassed to be there at all.

"I wired her after the battle," said Garrett. "I thought you'd like her to join you on the journey to Fox Run."

Candace seated herself on the edge of Verity's bed. "I'm staying there with you, too." She squeezed Verity's hand. "We'll wait together for our men to come home from war."

Dr. Malcolm issued a polite cough. "If everything is in order, shall we proceed?"

"Are you ready, Verity?"

Verity considered her stomach's uneasy peace. "I think so. One can never be entirely sure. We'd best hurry."

Garrett stood beside her bed and took her hand. He wore a fresh uniform, he had washed, and a saber hung at his side. He looked impossibly handsome. Verity didn't dare look in a mirror. She wore a borrowed nightdress. Her shoulder-length hair fell in unkempt curls around her face.

Holding a bible, the minister cleared his throat and began the ceremony. "Gathered as we are—"

"Wait one damned minute, there, preacher!" Jefferson Davis burst into the bedroom, yanked off his cap and took his place beside Garrett. "Thought you'd need someone standing up for you, Major. John figured you'd need music. So here we are."

John carried his guitar slung over his shoulder. He nodded politely to the ladies and the minister, then seated himself cross-legged on the floor. "Begin."

The minister's pained expression intensified, but he returned to his speech. When it came time for Verity to repeat her vows, Garrett leaned toward her. "If you would do me the honor of saying, 'I do,' rather than vomiting, I would be much obliged."

"I do." Verity barely got the words out before she snatched the pot from her bedside.

* * *

"Well, that was a wedding, for damned sure," commented Jefferson. Verity lay on her bed, married at last to Garrett Knox. Her dream had come true. She'd never felt worse.

"Yep." John played tunes on his guitar, but none seemed to have much point. "A wedding."

"Garrett looks splendid." Candace eyed Verity, then shook her head. "It's a sunny day."

Verity winced at the sunlight streaming in the window. She covered her head with a pillow and uttered a long, drawn out noise of pure misery.

Ivy took matters into her own hands. "Child, you got to get beyond this moaning and groaning. You got to eat, and keep it down. Think about what you got, and not what you're losing."

Verity sat up. "You're right! Sam died, and I'll miss him. But now he's with my parents, with Adrian and Westley. With his son. Ethan's gone, but he'll be back. Jefferson and John have more to do, but I'll hear their music echoing in my brain forever."

Verity's eyes brightened and she touched Garrett's hand. "We have a baby." For the first time, the idea of pregnancy seemed real. "A baby."

Verity's stomach settled. Color returned to her face. "You'll come back to me, Garrett Knox. I'll be waiting. God knows, I hate waiting, but you'll come back. You'll all come back. The iceberg is breaking up, it's true. But we're all headed for the same shore."

Part Three
Hearts of Fire

"They shall return
More than they were,
And ever ascending,
Leave all for love."
—*Give All To Love*, Ralph Waldo Emerson

Chapter Thirteen

Culpeper Court House, Virginia
April, 1864

Garrett sat alone in his tent reading Verity's letter. The Army
of the Potomac was camped north of the Upper Rapidan river,
sprawling like a makeshift city around Culpeper Court House.
Across the river, Lee's Army of Northern Virginia lay in wait at
Orange Court House.

A man of action had finally taken command of the Union army.
Ulysses S. Grant was now their leader. There would be no end to
the war without final and total victory—or defeat.

Mail had been severely delayed, taking weeks or even months
to reach the soldiers in the field. Garrett studied the date of Verity's
mailing. The twelfth of February. The day of his son's birth. His
son. *Caleb Robert Knox.* Verity's handwriting looked strong and
sure, as always. Apparently giving birth hadn't weakened her.

Garrett held the small, square photograph in his hand. He hadn't
looked at it yet. He closed his eyes, and he saw her face, lying
beneath him in Ivy's boudoir. He saw her laughing, teasing him.
He remembered her surprise when he first kissed her. He remembered when she kissed him good-bye before Pickett's Charge at
Gettysburg.

Garrett opened his eyes and looked at the picture. It had the same solemn feel that photographers insisted on when posing their clients. Looking closer, Garrett saw that Verity hadn't completely mastered the dignified expression. Her eyes twinkled, almost life-like, as he gazed at her distant face.

Her lips curved, ever so slightly, as if even now, a war away, she could tease the man who loved her. Her hair was brushed, indicating Candace's careful hand, pulled back and bound behind her head. Garrett discerned the faint ripple of curl around her face, a tendril or two escaping to brush her cheek.

Garrett's gaze moved slowly down over her seated posture. Over the swell of breasts that appeared larger than he remembered. Down to her arms, and the child held up like a Madonna's babe.

Garrett swallowed as he allowed himself to examine the little boy. A proud face, even with his head propped up by his mother's hidden hand. A peculiar cap clamped over his ears and around his cheeks. The boy looked tolerant, as if he'd already learned to put up with his mother's strangeness.

Garrett's heart warmed and constricted simultaneously. Verity Talmadge Knox looked more beautiful than he remembered, even squeezed into the restrictive frame of photography. With her hair pulled back, wearing a respectable, dark-colored dress. Gloves. How unlike Verity to wear gloves!

He hadn't seen her since Gettysburg. Without him, Verity had grown great with child, then endured the agony of childbirth. She'd suckled the babe, awakened in the night at his cry. She'd learned every facet of his estate, wandered the lush grounds. Without him.

Garrett stared at her face in the blurry image. Watkins with a baby. Garrett smiled, but his eyes brimmed with hot tears. *God, how I miss you.*

A year had slipped by . . . Garrett could almost hear John's guitar, his low voice singing, *"The years creep slowly by, Lorena . . ."*

Occasionally, when he missed Verity too much, Garrett searched out his old regiment and sat by their campfire. John was still there, and Jefferson. But it seemed lonely without Sam, without Ethan Hallowell issuing stiff, by-the-book commands that no one listened to . . . without Watkins.

"Garrett?" Dan Wallingford spoke as if for the second time, and Garrett looked up.

"Sorry, Dan. Didn't hear you come in." Garrett set the photograph aside. Dan hadn't stayed with the Massachusetts 20th, either. Not much of a horseman, Dan became an attaché on General Meade's staff, and now served U. S. Grant. He seemed less happy with his new commander.

"You looked a few miles away." Dan eyed Garrett's letter, then noticed the photograph at Garrett's side. "Another letter from the wife?" Dan's tone was faintly mocking, as if his stepbrother's marriage diminished his own bachelorhood.

"I have a son."

"Congratulations." Dan offered his hand, and Garrett shook it. "First of many, eh? I'm assuming it's the first, anyway." Dan chuckled, but Garrett looked at him askance.

"I'm a careful man, Dan. When I want to be."

"I guess Rob Talmadge's sister was marrying material, at that. What happens to the Talmadge fortune, anyway?"

Only a lawyer would consider this. Garrett sighed. "It's split between Verity and Ethan Hallowell."

"What in hell will Hallowell do with that kind of sum?"

"What any other man would do." Garrett's jaw tightened, his lips formed a straight, irritated line. This expression often darkened his face in his stepbrother's company.

"So he's still alive, is he?"

"As far as I know, yes. Verity had a hard time locating him. Actually, it was Jefferson who learned Ethan's whereabouts. Davis heard from another wounded man where Hallowell was kept."

Dan shook his head in wonder. "Never understood what made those men so loyal to Hallowell, anyway. Especially that colored fellow. Then again, it's the Boston Brahmin types he's got to thank for his elevated position."

"Jefferson has himself to thank for his 'elevated position.' He is a hell of a soldier, Dan, and the best shot in the regiment. Next to Watkins, that is." Garrett's face softened with the memory.

"Watkins. What ever happened to the lad? I remember seeing him once after the Gettysburg conflict, so he wasn't killed. But he just disappeared after that."

Garrett wasn't sure why, but he had no wish to discuss his wife's escapades with Dan Wallingford. "I'm not sure. As I recall, the boy took sick and went home."

"Back to Massachusetts?"

"I expect so."

Dan nodded, but he didn't seem satisfied with Garrett's answer.

"Well, well. It doesn't matter." Dan stood up. "Won't be seeing you much for a while. Got myself transferred back to Washington."

"Why is that?" asked Garrett. "Things should start moving soon. Grant seems a man of his word, and he wants Lee's army. We'll be making a push toward Richmond soon."

"But his real goal is the army in between," said Dan. "Bound to be a hell of a bloody fight. Just what we've been waiting for, eh? Sorry to miss it, but Washington has need of cooler heads."

Garrett watched Dan go, then turned back to Verity's letter. He could feel the coming battle. He could feel Lee waiting, ready to take on the worst the Yankees could throw his way. This time, Garrett knew the Yankees wouldn't defeat themselves. They wouldn't be satisfied with winning a battle such as Gettysburg. U. S. Grant wanted the whole damned war.

"Should you be going out this soon?" Candace held Caleb as Verity tied her bonnet and pulled on gloves.

Verity rolled her eyes. "For heaven's sake, Candace. It's been almost three months. I've been riding, haven't I?"

Candace groaned. "Yes."

"And I've walked all over this estate. I know every path, every field. Did you know Garrett built little stone benches on the woods' path to the river? Adrian carved his name in practically every tree. I've found the little duck blind where Garrett's great-grandmother gave birth to Garrett's grandfather."

Mildred Wallingford Knox appeared in the hallway behind Candace. She was wringing her pudgy hands together, her face written in utmost distress. Despite the woman's emotion, Verity felt tempted to laugh.

"Dear Heart, please, please reconsider this mad venture. You can't go to Washington, not alone!"

"I'm not going alone, Mildred. Ivy's coming with me."

A low, tragic moan escaped Mildred's lips at this announcement.

Verity hadn't expected to like Dan Wallingford's mother, though she knew both Garrett and Adrian had been fond of her. Mildred took everything seriously, as if respectability mattered more than life.

But Mildred herself was so comical that Verity found her merely amusing. She chastised Verity often, and without force. Since

Verity came from a 'good' family, Mildred considered her worthy. Mildred's relationship with Ivy was quite another matter.

"Ivy knows her way around Washington, Mildred." Verity restrained her pleasure when Mildred started fanning herself.

No one actually said the word, 'prostitute,' but Ivy made no secret of her former profession.

Candace didn't offer any objections to Ivy's presence, which surprised Verity. Though she liked Robert's fiancée, Verity had considered her dull and conventional. Since traveling to Maryland from Gettysburg, Verity had come to realize what a unique and steadfast person her brother loved.

"I'll be back late tonight. Candace will feed Caleb and put him in his crib for naps. Don't worry, Mildred. And make sure Ethan's room is ready. The one on this floor, not upstairs. He'll need a bath, a louse check—"

"Dear heaven." Mildred started to sway, fanning herself with vigorous strokes.

Ivy appeared behind her and slapped her on the back. "Looking a little shaky, ain't you? Brace up, Mildred."

Mildred's face flushed pink with anger, but Ivy took no notice. "Ready, Mrs. Knox?"

"I just don't feel certain of this, Dear Heart." Mildred folded and unfolded a handkerchief. "I know you said this young man is, or was, a gentleman. But he's an invalid now. Both legs— Dear God! What does that do to a gentlemanly temperament, I wonder? He may be bitter, hardened by life's little wrongs . . ."

Despite Jefferson's carefully written instructions, Verity had a difficult time finding Ethan's boarding house. "Maybe Jefferson got the wrong directions."

Ivy studied the letter. She smiled at Jefferson's firm hand and the small, accurate drawings of buildings and landmarks. "A map like this one's got to get us somewhere, I'd say."

"Oh, no . . ." Verity's voice trailed. Ivy looked up at the building which drew Verity's pained attention. In a cluster of identical, wood buildings was a dilapidated, two-story house—if it could be called a house. The windows were boarded shut. Dirty laundry hung off the rafters. Flies swarmed around garbage bins outside the front door.

A little sign indicated, Boarding House. Underneath was scrawled, *Invalids and Cripples, Cheap.*

Ivy and Verity looked at each other. Their driver looked up at the dismal house, then back at the ladies. "Maybe I'd just better drive you ladies back on home now."

"No." Verity lifted her skirt and climbed out of the coach. She stared up at the dark windows. Ethan can't be in there. No living man could be in there. She resisted the powerful temptation to turn around, get back in the estate's lush coach, and head home.

"Lord, I hate to think of that pretty captain lying in there," said Ivy.

"He can't be." Verity's determined steps took her to the front door. She pulled a dirty string. A bell clanged unpleasantly inside the dark house.

A long moment passed while Ivy and Verity waited. Ivy snatched the bell and rang it twice. The door creaked open, exposing the hardened, ugly face of a woman in white.

"What'ch you want?"

"We're here to call on Captain Ethan Hallowell of the Twentieth Massachusetts. We were led to believe he lives here."

"Yeah. What of it?"

Verity's expression hardened. Never had she taken such an intense dislike to anyone as to this woman in white.

"You are called . . . ?" Verity's voice rang with Boston elegance, with regal self-assurance. The woman issued a derisive snort.

"Nurse Abigail."

"Ah. You're a nurse. I see. Somehow I missed your wealth of education and experience, that tenderness that generally enhances your trade. Where is Captain Hallowell?"

Nurse Abigail glanced back into the darkened corridors. "Which one's Hallowell?"

A tobacco-stained, squirrelly man appeared from another room. "What'd you ask?"

"I believe she bellowed, *'Which one's Hallowell?'* "

The squirrelly man shrugged, spat, then eyed the length of Verity's body. His lips parted in a lecherous smile, revealing pointed, yellow teeth. "He's in there somewhere."

"Ah. How comforting."

Nurse Abigail failed to notice Verity's sarcasm and the subsequent combative gleam in her blue-gray eyes. Ivy patted Verity's arm in a soothing gesture. "May we see the gentleman?"

"It'll cost you."

Verity began to twitch. "Cost us? We're here to visit Captain Hallowell, not purchase him!"

"Ain't paid his board this month. You got ties to the boy?"

"He's my cousin."

"Then pay up."

Verity's hands gripped her crochet bag. Her fingers clenched around a wad of money. Ivy took the money and smiled in forced manner.

"How much, did you say?"

"What you got?"

Ivy started to count the bills.

"Don't matter. Gimme that there."

Ivy glanced at Verity, who nodded. Ivy closed her eyes as if in prayer.

"Now then, if you would be good enough to direct us to Captain Hallowell."

Verity edged through the door, though Nurse Abigail seemed reluctant to admit them. Standing on the same level, Verity towered over the woman in white.

"Don't got a lot of room," said Nurse Abigail. "One at a time."

"Ivy, wait out here, will you?"

"I'll just do that. Maybe even wait out in the coach, if you don't mind."

"As you wish. Nurse Abigail?"

"Follow me."

Verity entered a room so dark and musty that the light piercing the boarded windows stung her eyes. Verity's heart labored. She heard the soft groans of fevered men, languishing in the stifling heat, suffering. Ethan. . . .

Verity looked around. Dark shapes lay unattended, some so still Verity wondered if they were dead. The room smelled bad enough to harbor dead men. The flies swarmed eagerly, tormenting men too weak to brush them away.

Worse than the surgeon's bloody tents at Gettysburg, this room allowed no hope, no future. . . .

"Ethan!"

Verity's shrill cry erupted with such force that she almost startled herself. She panicked. Verity had never panicked before, but she did now.

"Ethan! Ethan Hallowell, where are you?"

Verity darted around the noisome room, knocking things over in the darkness, tripping on bedpans filled with urine. Her breath came in short, seized gasps. Verity's senses reeled. *He's my cousin. I've got to protect him. He's falling. . . .*

"Ethan!"

Nurse Abigail eased back toward the door, but Verity spotted her trying to escape. Verity seized the woman's scrawny arm, pinching until Nurse Abigail gasped in pain. "Where is he, you old crow? Tell me now, or so help me God—"

"Here."

Verity dropped the nurse's arm. The cracked voice came from the farthest corner of the room, the blackest corner, where the minimal light from the window holes didn't penetrate at all. Verity made her way toward the voice while Nurse Abigail slithered from the room.

Verity saw the cot, saw a body lying on it. The smell of urine and rotting flesh, even of dried stools, swamped her nostrils. A dumpster not far from the bed explained the odors. Verity couldn't move. "Ethan?"

"Watkins."

A violent sob slashed through Verity's stomach, she bent over as it gripped her. *He's really here, lying in filth.* Her cousin. Her friend. She had promised to take care of him. She tried, but he refused to be found. This man who saved Garrett's life.

Verity spotted the window closest to Ethan's bed. Boarded up, shutting out all light. Verity kicked a pile of rubble out of her way and latched onto the loosest board. She yanked. It didn't budge. "Damn you all to hell, you bloody bastard, let go!"

The board quivered, then popped loose. Verity tore wildly at the others until the soft afternoon sun broke through the gloom. She took several gasping breaths to ease her shaking.

Verity forced iron control on her will. She went to Ethan's bedside. She found a two-legged seat and sat down, balancing herself on her own legs to keep from falling.

"Ethan . . ." She didn't know what to say.

"You shouldn't be here." As if he hadn't spoken in a long

time, Ethan's voice grew in strength after a few words. Despite the squalor, he looked better than Verity had feared. He was thin, but not quite emaciated. A dirty blond beard covered his face. His hair hadn't been trimmed since before Gettysburg.

"You look like a Viking." Verity tried to speak pleasantly, in a light and familiar tone, but tears swamped her vision. Her throat constricted.

Ethan's dry lips cracked toward a smile. "Like their *berserkers,* I assume. How did you find me?"

Verity suspected Ethan was crawling with lice. But she touched him, anyway, brushing his matted hair from his forehead.

"Jefferson found out where you were. A man he knows came here looking for a place to recuperate. He recognized you, though God knows how. Jefferson heard about it, and wrote to me."

"Then you've heard from the men? How are they? Did you marry Major Knox?"

Verity's heart eased. Ethan had plenty of questions. He still cared. "Jefferson writes as often as he can. He and John are still in your old company, but they say it's not the same without you. And yes, I married Garrett. Right after you left Gettysburg. I had a baby, too. A little boy. Caleb."

Ethan looked up at her. "Watkins, a mother. Will wonders never cease?" He squinted, as if he hadn't seen even dim light in months. An expression of surprise, even wonder, appeared in his eyes. "You're beautiful!"

"Thank you, Ethan." Verity paused. "Why do you say that with such shock?"

"Forgive me. I didn't mean . . ." Ethan Hallowell was still a gentleman, after all. "It's just, well, I remember when you finally put on a dress that you were attractive. In a Watkins sort of way." Ethan's cracked smile broadened a little. "I thought Westley and Major Knox loved you for your spirit only. I was wrong. The major must be a happy man today."

"I haven't seen him since Gettysburg." Verity's shoulders slumped. "He was given leave last November, but General Hancock wanted him for something, so he couldn't come home. He's never even seen Caleb."

"He'll come home. He's got you waiting."

Verity's heart sank. "It's been so long. I feel so helpless, Ethan. Anything can happen. I can't help anyone." Verity looked down at Ethan. "Except you."

Ethan eyed her suspiciously. "What do you mean?"

"I'm taking you out of here, and bringing you back to Fox Run. We'll arrange things with that devil in white—"

"No."

"Ethan, I'm not giving you a choice."

"No."

Verity clutched Ethan's shoulder. If she had to pinch him, she would. "Ethan . . ." Ethan stared at the ceiling. He wouldn't go, no matter how hard she pinched him.

"Why not?" Verity saw Westley's pocket watch at Ethan's bedside. The only thing he had kept. Her throat choked on tears.

"I will stay here, where I belong."

"Rats don't belong here!"

Ethan took Verity's hand. He kissed it, and his tears fell onto her skin. Verity's fingers wrapped tightly around his. "You're my cousin, Ethan, my brother-in-law. You're my friend. Do you think Westley would ever forgive me if I left you here?"

"Westley Talmadge is dead, Verity. Gone forever."

"Westley is dead, that's true. So now he knows what he didn't while he lived, that he has a brother. He always wanted a brother. Did you know that, Ethan Hallowell? But I should call you Talmadge, shouldn't I? Because you're Cabot Talmadge's son." Verity paused. "Did you ever meet your father, your real father?"

"Once," said Ethan. "I was twelve years old, but the moment I laid eyes on him, I knew."

"I'm not surprised. You look just like him. Even more than Westley did. Except Uncle Cabot wasn't so stiff as you."

"Apparently not."

Verity snatched her hand from Ethan's. "Uncle Cabot was a good man. He took us all fishing, he let me ride like a boy—"

"I knew it started somewhere."

Verity ignored Ethan's comment. "He was a good father, too. Westley's mother, on the other hand, was almost as awful as your Nurse Abigail. A smile never touched Aunt P's lips."

"P?"

"P, for Prudence. We called her 'Aunt P,' just to irritate her."

"Prudence," said Ethan. "Naturally. Are you making this up?"

"No. Aunt P complained about everything. All she cared about was her social position. I loathed her. I know men are supposed to hold their mothers in high esteem, but even Westley couldn't bring himself to say a good word about her. We all wondered why Uncle Cabot married her. I think Uncle Cabot wondered, too.''

''Is this leading somewhere?''

''Yes. Uncle Cabot and Westley took me for a picnic in Boston Common after my father died. I remember it, because Robert was away, and I was very lonely. I had to stay with the Websters because Aunt P didn't want a girl around. Anyway, Westley and I were playing by the pond, and we saw Uncle Cabot talking with a woman. They were laughing, and I remember Westley saying he wished his mother had been like her.''

''My mother?'' guessed Ethan. ''What makes you so sure it wasn't another in a series of mistresses?''

''Because when she left, Uncle Cabot didn't say a word. He took us home. Westley told me that later he saw his father crying.'' Verity saw Ethan's expression. ''She looked something like your Bess, with curly, brown hair and big eyes.''

Verity waited. A flash of doubt made her wonder if Ethan's mother was blonde.

''It was my mother.''

''Thank God.'' Verity breathed a sigh of relief and Ethan smiled. Verity took his hand again. ''Your parents loved each other, Ethan. They wouldn't want you to suffer this way. Maybe your supposed father didn't care about you, but Cabot Talmadge did. He put you in his will, after all.''

''I don't want his money.''

''Which is why you can't pay your board here. So come to Fox Run with me. Ethan, please.''

''No.''

''Damn! You're so stubborn. You cut off Bess, you cut off your friends . . .''

Ethan flinched at the mention of Bess Hartman's name.

''It still hurts, doesn't it? She still loves you, Ethan.''

''How do you know?''

Verity hesitated, tempted to confess about her correspondence with the rebel girl. In Ethan's present condition, it probably wouldn't profit her much. ''I know women.''

Ethan closed his eyes. ''Please, Verity. Leave me now. I'm tired—''

''I can see why. All this lying around in squalid darkness would wear anybody out.'' Verity fought the desire to shake him.

''When I look at you, I see all the things I can never have—''

"Good! Maybe you'll start wanting them again. The only person who can say what you 'can't have' is you."

Verity rose from her stool, and it collapsed. She kicked it aside vigorously. "I'm tempted to drag you out of here. I'm not sure Ivy and I can do it alone. But if I leave you here, you'll die."

"No, Verity. Please . . . I'm dead already."

Verity's heart quailed at the tears in Ethan's eyes. "You're not dead, Ethan Hallowell. But maybe it'll take you a while to realize that." She paused. Ethan was stubborn, but no more stubborn than Verity herself. He might refuse today, tomorrow. But sooner or later, Ethan's life would demand its rightful existence.

"I'll go, for now. But I'll be back, and I'll keep visiting you until you see reason."

Verity kissed his hand just as Nurse Abigail returned. "Wouldn't touch him if I was you. Got lice."

From across the room, a raspy voice called out. "Water. If you please, Ma'am, water."

"Ain't time," snapped the woman in white.

Verity Talmadge turned, slowly. Ethan must have recognized her expression, because he reached to catch her skirt, to stop her. "Oh, no . . ."

Verity eased her skirt from Ethan's grasp and aimed at Nurse Abigail. "The gentleman requested a drink."

"Ain't time, lady. But it's time you high tailed it out of here. I got work to do."

Verity picked her way across the filthy floor until she stood directly in front of Nurse Abigail. Verity moved slowly around the woman in white until she blocked her exit from the room.

"*Work to do.*" Verity glanced pointedly around the filthy room. "I can see that. I trust it will be thoroughly accomplished before my next visit. In two days."

"You watch yourself, Girlie. You may think you're high and fancy, but this here's my house." Nurse Abigail noticed the open window. "What's going on with my windows?"

"Can't afford glass?"

Those wounded men who weren't feverish or sick took notice of Nurse Abigail's predicament. Verity felt like a Celtic chieftain, brandishing a sword against evil.

"Look here, Lady. You'd best be moving out, right now. I'll be calling the old man if you don't."

Verity's eyebrow rose. "You and I seem to have reached an

impasse. I say you'd best clean up this filthy pig sty. You refuse.
I say you'd best start treating these men with the honor and respect
they deserve. It's plain that's beyond your present capacity.''

"Git . . . out!''

"Don't threaten Watkins—'' Nurse Abigail didn't notice
Ethan's quiet suggestion, but Verity felt a surge of pride. She
grabbed Nurse Abigail's dirty collar and plunged her backward
against a boarded window.

Several astonished gasps and croaks told her the men were
watching. Nurse Abigail attempted to cry out, but Verity clamped
her hand over the woman's mouth.

"I wouldn't. Because, you see, I'm well versed at violence.
True, I haven't used it in a while. But breaking your neck would
be no trouble at all. So you'd best listen. Do you agree?''

Nurse Abigail gave a semblance of a nod.

"Good. This is the arrangement I offer—I won't kill you.
If . . .''

Nurse Abigail's eyes widened. "This house, starting in this
room, will be cleaned. These gentlemen will receive proper care.
You will clean their bedpans every time it's necessary. You will
open their goddamned windows and let them breathe real air.
There will be fresh flowers by their bedsides. You will fetch them
books, arrange for their mail . . . you will make their lives pleasant
in every way.''

Nurse Abigail swallowed as if death might be preferable. Verity
increased the pressure on her throat. "Is that understood?''

After a pause, the nurse nodded. "Again, good. My associate
outside will inspect your cooking facilities. These men appear
underfed. That will change. I expect good meals, served three
times a day.''

Verity paused, glaring at the woman in white as if she might
choose to kill her, anyway. "If this is acceptable, you will nod.
But not before I tell you that I shall return at least once a week
to check on your progress. Between that time, my associates will
inspect. You can expect visits from Miss Candace Webster, as
well as Mrs. Mildred Wallingford Knox.

"Should you attempt any form of intimidation toward these
gentlemen, I will return and kill you. I assure you, I'm quite
capable of killing.''

The look on Nurse Abigail's face said she had no doubt. Verity grudgingly released the woman in white. The woman coughed. "You got nerve, girl."

Verity stepped back as if the woman harbored something more loathsome than lice or disease. Disgust and contempt glittered behind Verity's teary eyes. Her chin trembled as she mustered her outrage into speech.

"Do you know who these men are? Do you know what they did before they ended up here? They looked death straight in the eye, and they went on. They stood over fallen comrades, and kept going. And one man in this room put himself in front of another, because he's too good to do anything else.

"These are the men you've kept in darkness, you old sow. You've got the honor of tending them now, as they find their way back to the lives they deserve. Treat it as such, or so help me God, I'll come back here and rip your lungs out."

Verity's eyes glistened with tears. She looked over at Ethan. He looked shocked, but she also detected a restrained smile. "Good-bye, Captain. See that this woman behaves as I've directed. If she doesn't ..." Verity's eyes returned to the nurse. "She knows."

The men lying in the dark room turned their eyes to the hole Verity had ripped in the wall. Verity spun past Nurse Abigail and headed out the door of the squalid dwelling to fetch Ivy for her inspection.

Chapter Fourteen

Cold Harbor, Va.
June 2

Sixty thousand Union soldiers were lost in one month. Since the fifth of May, U. S. Grant had driven the Army of the Potomac in relentless pursuit of Lee's Army of Northern Virginia. The war had been bad from the beginning. Antietam saw more blood in one day than any other field. Fredericksburg, Gettysburg. . . .

Nothing could ever erase what he'd seen since Grant led his blue army into the Virginia land known as The Wilderness. Horrendous slaughter. The woods burning, devouring the dead and the dying of both armies.

On to Spotsylvania. The battle culminated at the aptly named 'Bloody Angle.' Bodies upon bodies were driven into the mud, death upon death. Lee seized a defensive position, then Grant hurtled his forces at Lee's well-fortified position, to a bloody repulse. Grant moved on, trying to move around Lee's army, toward Richmond. But Lee moved his mobile army quicker, and entrenched first.

Garrett replayed the scene in his mind, over and over. They moved southeast. For four days, the armies skirmished across

Totopotomy Creek. Grant lost over two thousand men before moving on. The armies raced toward Cold Harbor. Lee got there first.

Now the scene would be replayed. Garrett felt it, dreaded it, but nothing he could do would change the outcome. Night fell, and Garrett endured a weariness he'd never known before. Mind-numbing battle scorched his soul.

He'd done well with every command given him. He was called back from the cavalry to lead an infantry division in Hancock's corps during the battle of The Wilderness. His losses were fewer, his positions stronger, than most. When his colonel was killed at Spotsylvania, Garrett took over, and won the previously lost Yankee position.

It didn't matter. He'd seen so much death that he felt dead himself. Artillery shells lit the night, fiery streaks of death in the sky. The sound would echo in his brain forever. Garrett looked toward Cold Harbor, toward the Chickahominy river and its mired swampland beyond.

After all this time, Garrett marveled that he still admired Robert E. Lee. Other men hated their enemies. They used that hatred to drive them into battle. Garrett fought because he still believed in victory. He fought because the men who followed him put their lives in his hands. They needed him. He fought because he was strong enough to fight, to lead, to do whatever it took to bring his soldiers through the fire alive.

Garrett turned away from the sight of Cold Harbor. He walked aimlessly through the hastily laid camp.

"Ho, Major!" Jefferson Davis waved his cap, lifted his musket in the knight's salute. This man wasn't defeated. But Garrett knew Jefferson's victory had come when Verity Talmadge convinced the men of the 20th Mass to let him fight.

"How are you men faring through this picnic in hell?"

"Seen more of Virginia's pretty countryside than I ever want to again," said Jefferson.

John strummed his guitar. "What about you, Major? How's your lady and that son of yours?"

"As far as I know, Verity and Caleb are well. Mail isn't particularly reliable these days."

Jefferson nodded. "Damned sure. We haven't heard from your girl since she cleaned up Hallowell's boarding house."

"This, I hadn't heard."

"She found our good captain living in a putrid swamp of a

place, or so it sounds. She 'discussed' the matter with the house
matron, and things seem to be rectifying themselves. Of course,
we read between the lines and saw Watkins holding a musket to
the 'matron's' head.''

Garrett smiled. He hadn't smiled in a month, maybe longer. He
closed his eyes and thought of Verity. Jefferson noted Garrett's
expression and patted his shoulder.

"We'll be getting out of this soon, Major. Don't you worry. It
can't go on like this much longer.''

"I hope not.''

At dawn, Grant sent three corps at the rebel line. Sixty thousand
men in blue advanced to challenge the men in gray. Robert E.
Lee was ready. In less than one hour, seven thousand Union soldiers
had fallen.

Verity felt restless. She'd spent the morning walking with Caleb
around Garrett's estate. She found the duck blind where Garrett's
grandfather had been born. Verity seated herself there as if she
might draw strength from Garrett's ancestors. She gazed across
the Potomac, watching sea birds dive and twirl toward the sun.

"Garrett . . .''

Caleb slept in Verity's arms. The day promised to be hot, but
the breeze over the Potomac cooled the air. Verity's restlessness
refused to abate. She got up and headed back for the estate house.

Verity approached the front entrance. Oak trees lined the carriage-
way, spreading right and left around the front garden. More subdued than Southern plantation houses, Fox Run was still the most
beautiful home Verity had ever seen. The straight front, the huge,
arched doorway. Two wings swung back toward a long, sloping
field. Pastures to the left, a healthy forest to the right. The stables.

Home.

Verity sighed and started up the long walk. It could never really
be her home without Garrett.

Verity found Candace waiting in the foyer. Her face was white,
and she reached for Verity's arm as if to steady her. Mildred and
Ivy stood behind her, expressions pained, sympathetic. Even the
house servants stood by, waiting like stoic guardians.

"Take the baby, Ivy." Candace's voice shook, but she controlled her expression. Ivy took Caleb from Verity. She said no word.

Verity's arms hung limp at her side. She felt like a child. Like the child she had been when told her father had died. "No."

Candace squeezed Verity's arm. "A message came while you were out. Garrett is in Washington." Candace's tone left no doubt. Verity shook her head.

"Why?"

"The message came from Jefferson. General Hancock's corps made a frontal assault on General Lee's position in a small, crossroads town called Cold Harbor."

"General Hancock leads infantry." Verity's voice shook. "Garrett is with the cavalry now."

"Garrett led the first division—"

"No—"

"While waiting for his men to retreat, he was shot just above the heart."

"He's alive, Honey." Ivy stepped forward and took Verity's other arm. "He survived the cart ride into Washington, and that kills a lot of men itself."

Verity couldn't feel her limbs, and she couldn't force breaths into her chest. It seemed as if she were buried alive. "It's not a bad wound, then?"

Candace drew a tight breath. "Jefferson says the wound is severe. But Garrett Knox is a strong man. He's lived this long. He's in the Armory Square Hospital now. It's one of the best in Washington. I'm sure—"

"The hospital. Do you know what the men say before they're sent to the hospital, Candace?" Rage directed at no one seized a violent shudder through Verity's muscles. "They say 'goodbye.'"

Mildred burst into tears. Whimpering, "Oh, dear. Oh, dear," she ran from the front hall and hurried up the stairs to her room. Verity stood motionless, staring at the letter in Candace's shaking hand. Jefferson's smooth, strong print. . . .

"Have the coach brought around."

Verity arrived at the Armory Square Hospital at midnight. The coach left her off outside the long hall. A nurse tried to stop her as she marched in the door. One look at Verity and the nurse scurried away.

The room was long and narrow, but the beamed ceiling was reasonably high. Windows separated the cots, some open to allow in the cool night breeze. White cots, with lanterns. Some men lay silently, some slept. Some read well-worn letters while nurses and orderlies passed to and fro.

Verity walked down the corridor, looking left and right, her eyes casting off face after face as she searched for Garrett Knox. *If he's not here . . .* Verity shoved the thought away. *I'll find him. I won't give up. I'll find him.*

At the end of the long hall, Verity saw a man sitting by a wounded soldier's bedside. She noticed his eccentric clothing, his long hair and unkempt beard, but it was his voice that caught her attention and held her spellbound.

"And over all the sky—the sky! Far, far out of reach, studded, breaking out, the eternal stars."

The man finished his poem, then sat back. Garrett Knox lay on the cot, his eyes closed, his face pale, without expression. He hadn't shaved in months. Verity had never seen him with a beard or a mustache. His hair was longer than before Gettysburg. There were lines around his eyes that hadn't been there before. Dark Viking.

Beneath his open shirt, Verity saw a heavy bandage wrapped around his chest. Even in the lamplight, she detected the stain of blood.

Verity's hands shook, and her leg muscles quivered so violently she could barely take a step closer.

The man noticed her and rose from his stool, bowing awkwardly. "Evening, Ma'am." He nodded at Garrett. "A relative of yours?"

"My husband." Verity's voice was almost inaudible. The man took her arm and gave her his seat. "Are you a nurse? Will Garrett be all right?"

"Well, now. He just arrived, so I can't say for certain what his chances may be. He hasn't opened his eyes yet, though I've been talking to him some, trying to bring him around. He's breathing all right. A little fast, maybe."

Verity sat on the stool and touched Garrett's forehead. Almost a year had passed since she gazed at his strong, handsome face. A year while she stared at his childhood portrait, while she wandered through his house, touching objects his hands had touched, holding his letters until the ink faded and smudged.

"Are you staying nearby until your husband recovers, Ma'am? I know of a few good boarding houses that cater to soldiers' wives."

"I'm staying here."

The man smiled. "I thought so. I came here when my young brother was wounded at Antietam. Didn't like what I saw at the hospitals. Thought I'd lend a hand. Still, they die. Still, they die."

Verity's shoulders slumped. "My first husband was killed at Antietam. My brother has been missing ever since . . ."

Verity glanced back at the man. He looked peculiar, but his eyes flashed with an intelligent blend of pathos and passion. "What poem were you reading to him, Sir?"

"One of my own, actually. Haven't named it yet. Just a verse. Maybe I'll add more later."

Verity turned her attention back to Garrett. Her eyes flooded with tears. Garrett's strength amid his pallor touched her more than anything else. That he, of all people, should be in need. . . .

"I liked the part about the 'eternal stars,' " said Verity wistfully. "You must be a very good poet."

"A better poet than a nurse, I'm afraid."

"I'll remember your words forever. What is your name?"

"Walt Whitman."

Verity turned her attention back to Garrett. "He would hate a hospital. How can he rest and heal here, with sick and dying men all around? He needs to go home."

Walt Whitman hesitated. "I doubt he could stand a long journey."

"It's not long." Verity felt a wave of excitement. "Just a way up the river, and the road is quite even and straight."

"Let me talk it over with one of the surgeons, and we'll see."

Verity turned back to Garrett. The surgeon would agree. If he had any skepticism, Verity would remove it. Garrett Knox needed her, at last. He needed his home. If she had to carry him on her back, Verity would get him there.

Garrett's surgeon seemed relieved to let a dismal case out of his hands. "Take him home, Mrs. Knox. He'll do as well there as anywhere. At least, he'll get a better burial than most on his own property.''

Walt Whitman overheard the surgeon's gloomy words. He helped the orderlies carry Garrett to the estate coach, then pressed a book of poems into Verity's hand. "Don't worry, Mrs. Knox. The surgeon is lacking in imagination. He's seen too much death to envision anything else. You take your husband home, you open his windows and let the air from his own land touch his face. That's what most of these boys want. Home.''

The poet's words encouraged Verity. She sat holding Garrett's head on her lap, stroking his dark hair, talking to him. He didn't wake, but he seemed no worse when they arrived at last at Fox Run. His body still struggled against a fever, but neither Garrett nor the infection seemed to own the upper hand.

The coachman located three stablehands, and they prepared a stretcher to bear Garrett into his home. Candace came out and held Verity's hand. "Ivy and I fixed up the downstairs room, the one you got ready for Captain Hallowell. We can take good care of Garrett there.''

Verity nodded. "That's good. As soon as he's well enough, he can move upstairs. To his own room. To our room.''

Garrett's head flopped to one side as the men lifted him onto the stretcher. The coachman pushed Garrett's head back into place, and Verity burst into tears.

"Take him inside,'' Candace instructed the men. She wrapped her arms around Verity, but Verity didn't feel her touch. Sobs racked her body. She'd maintained her strength, and she'd brought him home alive. Now her emotion burst to the surface, shattering her. She crumpled to her knees and buried her face in her hands.

"Verity, darling. He's home now. We'll care for him. You must be strong. Garrett needs you.''

Verity looked up. Her wet, plaintive face pierced Candace's heart. "What if I can't help him?''

"Then God Himself could make no difference.''

Candace, Ivy, and Verity took shifts watching Garrett, cooling his brow with a damp cloth, changing his bandage and soaking his wound. Verity refused to leave his side until Candace reminded her that Caleb needed her, too.

"If you get sick, both your men will be without you.''

That was enough. Verity forced herself to rest. She ate, she tended her son. Then she sat at Garrett's bedside, reciting poems from the book Walt Whitman had given her.

Ivy used abilities from her former profession to organize the other women's activities. She supervised the kitchen, the stable hands, the household servants. Never had Fox Run been managed so effectively as now, beneath the madam's control.

Candace handled the crisis with reassuring calm. Her natural tendency to cleanliness kept her fiddling with Garrett's wound, changing his sheets. She spent hours fanning his face. It was Candace who insisted that Ivy shave Garrett's heavy beard.

"For God's sake, Miss Webster, he don't have to be pretty in his sleep," Ivy argued.

Candace remained adamant. "I can't clean his face properly with that beard. I don't see lice, which is fortunate. But it's hot, and a beard just makes it hotter for him. Shave him, Ivy."

Ivy complied, and Verity watched while Garrett's still, handsome face was revealed. "Don't cut him, Ivy," Verity said nervously. Ivy grinned.

"This ain't my first time, Honey." Ivy paused and chuckled. "Hell, you know what they say—there's always blood the 'first time.'"

Mildred entered the room, heard Ivy's comment, moaned, and hurried from the room. Ivy noticed her hasty exit. "You'd think she'd never known a man. Don't that woman have a slew of daughters, and that lawyer-fellow son?"

"I think it's the discussion that bothers her, Ivy," said Candace. "Not the act."

"Bet she did it with her eyes closed."

Candace sighed. "You're probably right."

Verity looked suspiciously at Candace. "Did you and Robert . . . ?"

Candace raised a brow at Verity's indelicate question, then turned back to wipe Garrett's face. "Really, Verity. Some things are sacred."

"Specially when they're done with that pretty aristocrat, Rob Talmadge," added Ivy. Only Verity blushed.

Garrett's fever worsened dramatically through the day and into the night. Despite Candace's admonishments, Verity now refused to leave his side again. Something more than injury plagued him.

He muttered in his sleep. Though Verity understood little he said, she gathered that his last month at war had taken a horrific toll.

His mumbled words brought an image of hopelessness, of continuing despair, of loss repeated over and over without any rest between. A fine sweat broke out over his skin. He tossed his head from side to side as if waging the final battle.

Verity knew she had to bring him hope, that she had to bring him back to Fox Run—not just his body, but his soul. And the only way to do that was to remind him how much he mattered in the world.

"Garrett Knox, please hear me. Please come back. I need you so. I'm so lonely without you. Caleb needs his father. I've done everything I can, but I can't seem to make much difference."

Verity launched into a description of Ethan's boarding house. How brave men lost all hope and languished. Besides Ethan, she'd learned that the other men had no homes to return to. Some didn't want to burden their families with their incapacity.

"I can't let them end this way. No one wants to hear about them, Garrett. I've written letters to our senators, to the Christian Commission. They don't want to think about what happens to these men after the war. I don't know what to do."

"Bring them here."

Garrett's voice startled Verity. She dropped the wet cloth she held to his forehead. Her mouth opened, and her eyes widened. Garrett didn't open his eyes.

Verity's heart raced. "What did you say?"

"Bring them here."

"Garrett! You're awake! Candace, Ivy . . . come here! Garrett's awake, he's awake." Verity clapped her hands. She jumped up from the chair, she seized his hand and kissed it. She bent and kissed his face, though her tears fell down her cheeks and onto his.

Ivy charged into the room. "Saints be praised . . . Look, there's Damian Knox right over the bed."

Garrett opened his eyes. He blinked, as if he saw something behind Verity. Garrett closed his eyes and shook his head. "No, it can't be—"

"What can't be? Oh, it doesn't matter now. You're awake." Verity hugged him, taking care not to bump his wound. "Am I hurting you?"

Verity moved back to check his expression. Garrett looked into her eyes. His eyes widened, and his mouth dropped. Verity bit her lip. Garrett didn't speak. He just stared at her. She'd taken to wearing her hair down her back, bound by a ribbon. It fell well past her shoulders. Escaping strands fell around her cheeks.

She was also plumper than the last time he'd seen her. Verity held her breath. What if he found her unattractive? His eyes cast down from her face to her breasts. Garrett turned his vision back to her face.

"Why are you looking at me that way? Is something wrong?" Verity pushed her hair from her forehead. "I haven't been keeping myself up very well. But now that you're awake—"

Garrett's brow rose. "You've changed."

"Have I?" Verity gulped.

"You're the most beautiful woman I've ever seen."

A smile of pure happiness broadened Verity's cheeks. She took note of his tone and her lips curved to one side. "Why does everyone seem so surprised?"

"Ah, Watkins, I can't imagine."

Verity pressed her hand to Garrett's forehead. "You're cool! Not perfectly cool, but much better."

Candace checked his temperature, then nodded her agreement. "Much better. You're over the worst of it now, Garrett."

"You've won the battle that mattered most, Major," added Ivy. Garrett's face clouded, he closed his eyes.

"Cold Harbor."

"It's over." Verity stroked his hair. "They moved on."

"Where now?"

"Grant made a feint toward Richmond. His real goal was Petersburg. Unfortunately, General Lee got there first."

"Naturally."

"Grant tried to break through and failed, and now the army's set in for a siege."

Garrett considered this for a moment. "A siege sounds wise. It worked for Grant in Vicksburg. A siege may mean the war's end is in sight, after all."

"General Sherman is marching toward Atlanta, they say. To prevent any chance of reinforcements reaching Lee."

"That sounds promising."

"Sherman is quoted in the papers as saying war is hell, and it can't be made anything else."

"That is certainly true."

"Are you well enough to eat?" Verity didn't wait for his answer. "Ivy, have the kitchen prepare a suitable meal."

"The cook has a vat of soup ready," said Ivy. "But maybe the major has a hankering for something more substantial."

"I'll take what you've got. But I've had enough gruel and beans to last a lifetime. I wouldn't mind something to sink my teeth into for a change."

"Got a side of beef ready for roasting!" Ivy clapped her hands together. "Maybe not the whole side . . . just its quarters. It'll take a while, but it'll be worth the wait, I promise you. I'll bring you some soup in the meantime. Get your stomach ready for action again."

Ivy scurried away, and Candace patted Garrett's arm. "I'll leave you alone for a while. But it's good to see you well again, Garrett."

Garrett smiled, and Verity took his hand. "You are better, aren't you?"

"I'm all right."

Verity lifted his hand to her cheek. "I've missed you so. It was almost worth having you sick, just to be able to tend you."

"I'm happy to oblige." Garrett squeezed her hand, but his sorrow didn't seem to lift.

Verity smoothed his hair from his forehead. "You're probably still tired. Maybe you should rest after Ivy brings the soup. Then we'll have a wonderful dinner. I'm a bit hungry myself."

"That's a good idea."

Garrett ate his soup, then slept through the afternoon. He woke refreshed, his fever gone, but his mood wasn't much improved. The ladies served a lavish meal of roast beef and potatoes, complete with wine. Though Garrett ate everything they offered, his spirits rose very little.

Verity sat beside him. Her own appetite had diminished. Something was wrong, something she couldn't comprehend. But Garrett didn't want to talk.

"Are you sure you're all right? I could fetch a doctor to look at you."

"There's no need, Verity. I am fine."

Candace entered the room, Caleb in her arms. "There's someone who wants to meet you, Garrett."

Candace beamed proudly as she carried the baby to Garrett's bedside. Verity bit her lip as Garrett looked at his son. His blond hair was the only thing Verity saw as Candace set the baby in Garrett's arms.

"What do you think?" Candace sounded as proud as a grandmother. "Isn't he handsome? His picture didn't do him justice, did it? Those big, blue eyes, that shiny gold hair . . . he's beautiful."

Garrett stared down at the little boy. Caleb stared back at him. The baby's face puckered when he realized an unfamiliar man held him. A man with a stubbled face, black hair. The man's arms tightened reassuringly, and the baby felt safe. He closed his eyes.

"He likes you." Verity sniffed back tears of happiness. "He hasn't seen many men, and Ivy won't let the stable hands hold him."

Verity saw Garrett's expression change from a father's tentative wonder to sadness. She knew the exact moment he considered his son's hair color. If only she could tell him she remembered that night by the Rappahannock! That nothing happened between her and Ethan besides friendship.

Verity contemplated deceit. Garrett would believe her if she pretended to remember. He would never question her honesty. Verity's face fell. She couldn't lie. She loved and respected Garrett Knox too much to lie.

"The little fellow seems to be asleep. He might prefer his nursery." Garrett handed the baby back to Candace. "Thank you for bringing him in here."

"I just couldn't wait, though Verity said you needed to rest. I knew you'd want to see Caleb. For a man to hold his firstborn son . . . well, that's worth more than sleep, don't you think?"

"Most certainly." Garrett spoke pleasantly to Candace, but Verity's heart throbbed in misery. Candace left the room with Caleb, humming and singing cheerful verses all the way up the stairs.

"You think he's Ethan's baby, don't you?"

At first, he didn't seem to know what she meant. "Ethan's baby?"

"Don't." Verity closed her eyes. "Please don't tell me it doesn't matter."

"It doesn't. You're my wife. Caleb is my son—"

"Whoever's blood may be running through his veins, you mean." Verity hadn't meant to be so abrupt, to let her anger show.

"How can you think, no matter how much I drank, that I could lie with another man?"

A reluctant smile crossed Garrett's weary face. "Finding you naked with Hallowell tended to provoke a few questions."

Verity whirled, but Garrett held out his hand. Her frown tightened, but his hand remained, outstretched. Verity gave him her hand and thumped down into her chair.

"It was perfectly innocent. True, I don't remember things very clearly. I guess Ethan doesn't, either. But I know, no matter what, that I wouldn't have made love with anyone but you."

"Verity, please listen. I accept Caleb as mine. You are my wife. That's all that matters."

"Are you sure?"

"I am."

Verity paused, scrutinizing Garrett's expression. "You still look gloomy. If not doubts about Caleb, then what's bothering you?"

"Nothing." Garrett spoke too quickly, and his jaw hardened almost imperceptibly.

"Why won't you tell me?"

"There's nothing to tell."

Though his wound healed rapidly, Garrett's dark mood showed no sign of lessening. He got up from his bed, but more out of duty than from desire for wellness. Verity's caution around his delicate state grew increasingly strained.

Six days of hard rain sank everyone's spirits, and Caleb showed signs of illness. He slept in Verity's room restlessly, crying out as if in pain. Verity didn't sleep at all. She wandered the halls, rocking him, singing softly.

Candace woke and found Verity walking up and down the hall. "Let me take him a while, Verity. You need rest."

Verity kissed her son's head. It was one thing to leave him in another woman's care when he was well, when he enjoyed the varied companions. But not now. "I'm all right. Maybe tomorrow, Candace. Maybe he'll be better then."

But Caleb's condition worsened by morning. His fever grew. Verity couldn't take a deep breath, and her heart beat in strange little jumps. So many babies died. A fever came, the baby died. In the newspapers, she had read that the rebel General Longstreet lost his three children in a week. Christmas week. To a fever.

Verity took Caleb into the living room and showed him paintings of fox hunts. Usually, even a picture of a long-limbed horse seized the little boy's attention. But now he took no notice. He just cried. Verity felt tense. She wanted to cry, too.

"Give him to me."

Garrett's deep voice startled her. Verity turned and saw him standing behind her, wearing a fresh white shirt open at the throat.

"He's sick," she told him, her voice small and wavering. "I don't know what's wrong with him. He hasn't slept all night. He won't nap now. Ivy says it's just the sniffles, but he feels hot to me. General Longstreet's children died that way."

"Our son won't die." Garrett touched the small head, the soft hair. "Give him to me."

Tears puddled in Verity's eyes. She felt so weak. But Garrett was strong, as always. She placed Caleb in his father's arms. Garrett folded the small figure in the crook of his arm, close against his chest. Caleb stopped crying, studying the dark face curiously.

"Get some sleep, Verity. We'll be all right." Garrett didn't look up. A slight smile touched his lips.

"Are you sure?" Verity's heart ached at the sight of Garrett and his son. The son he considered Ethan's.

"I'm sure."

Verity wanted to stay, to see them together, but something deeper told her this moment was for father and son. If Caleb wasn't safe with Garrett Knox, there was no place on earth to find safety.

"I'll take a little nap," she decided. "If you need me—"

"We'll be fine."

Verity took one lingering look at her husband and her son, then left them alone. As she left, she heard Garrett speaking to the child in his deep, resonant voice. "Having trouble sleeping, are you, little one? I know how you feel. Maybe together we can rest."

Verity tried to rest, but her worry kept her from sleep. After an hour of fretting in her room, she went back downstairs to check on Caleb. Candace met her outside the living room entrance. She held up her finger to her lips, shushing Verity.

"Look," said Candace.

Verity peeked in the living room. Garrett lay on the couch, Caleb sprawled on his chest, secured by his father's large, firm hand. Both slept peacefully. Tears started in Verity's eyes, her heart warmed.

"Back to bed," ordered Candace. "If you're satisfied they're all right."

"I'm satisfied," said Verity. Maybe things would be all right, after all. Maybe.

Chapter Fifteen

Over the next days, Garrett's health continued to improve. He moved around his house without assistance, and he walked outside to see the horses with Caleb. The little boy recovered perfectly from his illness. Now only the sight of his father gave him more happiness than horses.

But something wasn't right. Verity knew it, felt it. It should be better now. But it wasn't.

Mildred insisted on vacating the master bedroom for the couple, but Garrett didn't seem enthused.

"Is there some reason you don't want to share a room with me?"

Garrett sighed heavily and didn't look at her. He just stared out the tall windows, out across the pastures. At nothing.

"My incapacity might prove tedious for you, Verity." Garrett spoke wearily, as if he resisted any explanation at all.

"I see." She didn't see. She didn't understand anything that happened between them since he returned home. Garrett avoided her company. He rarely looked at her. He pleaded weariness, and even when they were alone together, he had very little to say.

Garrett stared blankly, as if his eyes didn't see the sight in front of him, as if he saw something else entirely—perhaps a blank canvas, a veil meant to hide something he didn't want to see.

Verity watched him, and she waited. He offered no explanation, made no attempt to bridge the distance between them. Was it Caleb? Did he truly believe she bore Ethan Hallowell's child? She could think of nothing else to explain Garrett's mood. But even that didn't seem satisfactory, because Garrett seemed genuinely fond of Ethan.

Verity knew Garrett was suffering. Not from injury. Perhaps not even from heartache. Why had he withdrawn from her? Had he stopped loving her in those long, bloody months since Gettysburg?

"What in hell is wrong with you? Have you stopped loving me? You tell me now or else!"

Verity's sharp, emotional outburst startled Garrett. He turned to look at her, his brow furrowed as if he hadn't understood her.

Verity stepped toward him, fully intending to pinch him, to attack if necessary. The dead look in his gray eyes stopped her cold. With a tentative touch, she reached out and placed her hand on his arm.

"Garrett?" Her voice shook. "Did I do something wrong?"

A faint smile, devoid of happiness, touched Garrett's lips. He lay his hand over hers, meant to reassure her. But his touch felt cold, lifeless. "There's nothing wrong, Verity."

"I don't like the way you say my name." Verity's heart ached and her pulse slowed, as a sick tide of recognition flooded through her. "You don't love me anymore."

Garrett released her hand and looked back out of the window. "Love? Can a dead man love?"

"You're not dead." Her voice was so small she could barely hear herself. She hurt. Her stomach hurt. Her throat burned. Tears swarmed across her eyes, burning, too. "What did I do?"

"You've done nothing wrong, Verity. You are the same beautiful woman you always were. Filled with life, with hope. You still have the capacity to bend life to your will."

"Apparently not." Verity choked back tears. "Is it because Caleb resembles Ethan?"

Garrett turned to her, he clasped her shoulders in his grip. "For the last time, no. I will tell you this, and then no more—I have seen too much. Lived too much. Do you understand? No, how could you? Everything I was, everything I had . . . I spent it all. I look at you. I see a beautiful woman, and I see the man I was when I was able to love you. God, how I loved you! I am nothing now, just the shell of the man you knew."

Verity stared in disbelief. She saw the emptiness in the gray eyes. She almost believed he had died. "What happened?"

Garrett closed his eyes, his head tipped back. "I died."

Verity tired of his vague explanations, the ominous tone of his voice. "For a dead man, you're surprisingly warm . . . and strong."

Garrett cut her off with a short, joyless laugh. "Strong? What happens when you reach the limit of your strength? Have you ever wondered, Verity? You're strong. Maybe you're stronger than anyone I've ever known. What happens when you're drawn into something so much stronger that nothing you do matters, your strength fails—"

"Have you been drinking?"

Garrett laughed, a more genuine sound this time. "I wish I had."

Verity lifted her chin. "So, from this I gather you don't love me anymore. Shall we divorce?" Her words came out proud, but her heart constricted. If he said yes, she would die.

"I have nothing left for you, my beautiful wife. I have nothing for our son. Nothing for this estate that I once treasured. Nothing for anyone."

Verity gritted her teeth. "You haven't answered me."

"If you wish a divorce, I will grant it."

The blood drained from Verity's face. "Is that what you want?" She couldn't speak above a whisper.

"I don't want anything anymore . . ."

Verity choked back a sob, and Garrett touched her cheek. "You are the best thing in my life, Verity Talmadge Knox. I love you . . ." Garrett took her shoulders in his grasp again, both holding her close and keeping her away. "I love you, but I have nothing to give you. I love you with the passion of a dead man, who reaches from beyond the grave and cannot touch. Who waits for another time, and fears none will come."

Verity opened her eyes and studied him like a scientist or a physician. "I've never heard you speak this way. What on earth has happened to you?"

"A moment comes when a man sees himself, his world, everything, and he knows his place. For some, that moment is death. For me, it was otherwise."

Verity truly thought Garrett Knox had lost his mind. Her stormy emotion calmed. "You've been through a lot. Your injury has taken a toll. Quite a toll. I think that you need rest.'' Verity paused, examining Garrett's far-off, blank expression. ''Now.''

Verity seized his arm and directed him toward the wide stairs. Candace spotted them. ''Where are you going? Ivy's ordered the cook to prepare a fine dinner. Roast duckling, asparagus—''

''Have it sent to our room.'' Verity shoved Garrett up the stairs. ''And breakfast, too.''

''There was no need to bother the servants with our meal,'' said Garrett. Verity closed the door behind them, watching him as if he might suddenly fall apart and need her to catch him.

''You've overtaxed yourself. Go to bed.''

Garrett complied. He pulled off his shirt, removed his shoes, then lay on the bed, staring at the ceiling without expression. Verity's gaze moved across his body. His wide chest, the defined slab of muscle covered by masculine hair. His powerful arms folded across his chest, his strong fingers interlaced.

A low, sultry heat spread through Verity's loins. After childbirth, her erotic impulses had waned. But after a few months, as Caleb relied on her breast milk less and on Ivy's food supply more, Verity's desire had returned. She dreamt of Garrett nightly, as she had known him before Gettysburg.

She wanted to tell him, to ask that he satisfy this growing hunger. More than anything else, she wanted to be close to him, to lie in his arms, to feel loved again. But Garrett said he couldn't love anymore. He couldn't feel.

Verity eyed him thoughtfully. She hadn't given him much to 'feel' about. She walked purposefully to the vanity table and sat down. She pulled out her hairpins and began brushing her hair. She checked Garrett's position in her mirror. He still stared at the ceiling.

Verity stood up and began undressing. She removed her day gown, her hoopskirt, her petticoats. Garrett paid no attention. She stripped down to her thin, gauze chemise. He didn't look up. Verity's eyes narrowed. With a certain violence, she yanked the chemise over her head. She took a step toward the bed.

A loud rapping at the door disturbed her intentions. ''Brought your trays, Mrs. Knox.''

Verity rolled her eyes. She seized her cumbersome robe from the wardrobe closet, put it on, and jerked open the door. The servant stumbled into the room, steadied the trays, then placed them carefully on the round table by the window. Verity waited impatiently.

"Will you be wanting anything else, Mrs. Knox?"

"Thank you. That will be all."

"You, Major?" asked the servant.

"No. Thank you, Patrick. Not tonight." Garrett didn't look at the man. He still stared at the ceiling.

The servant left and Verity sat despondently at the table. "Aren't you going to join me?"

Garrett glanced at the plates of food, the crystal goblets of wine. Tiny salt shakers, pats of butter. "I suppose I must."

Garrett rose with effort and seated himself across from Verity. For the first time, he noticed her state of undress, saw her discarded clothing. Then he looked at her suspiciously.

Verity picked at her food and didn't meet his eyes. Then she stabbed a sliver of duckling and ate it vengefully. She took a drink of wine. "Watered down," she muttered as she set it aside. Garrett smiled.

"That's probably fortunate."

Verity looked up. "Why?"

"Alcohol has a, well, decisive effect on your behavior, My Dear."

Verity smacked her fork down beside her plate. She rose.

"What is that supposed to mean?" she asked, her voice quivering with restrained anger.

"What?"

"Your remark about my imbibing spirits."

"Oh. That."

"Yes, that."

"When you first—"

"I know exactly what you meant, Garrett Knox. You're referring to the bottle I shared with Ethan. Well, I've had just about enough of that from you! Haven't you ever been intoxicated?"

Garrett started to nod, but Verity didn't let him speak. "I thought as much. And did you make love with whoever was present?"

"I hope not." Garrett repressed a grin, but Verity saw, and her fury leapt like wildfire.

"You're smiling? I wouldn't smile if I were you!"

"Forgive me, Verity. Your meal," he reminded her, gesturing at her untouched plate.

"I'm not hungry."

Verity's anger rose to the surface, and she couldn't stop it. "Damn you!" Before Garrett could react to her sudden outburst, Verity seized her glass of wine and tossed it into his face.

Garrett looked surprised and confused, the white wine dripping off his nose, across his cheek. He calmly retrieved his napkin and patted his face dry. That smile deepened, revealing slight dimples in his cheeks. Nothing had ever infuriated Verity more. She looked around for something else to throw. She grabbed the tiny salt shaker.

"My dear, I beg you to remember that I have only recently recovered from my wounds." Garrett's grin widened, revealing his even row of white teeth.

"Oh! When you're better . . ." Verity sputtered, slamming the salt shaker back onto the table. Then she darted toward the door. "I will be staying in my old room," she informed him as she struggled with the heavy door.

She hesitated briefly in case he wanted to call her back. Verity watched Garrett return to his meal. She swallowed hard. "If you should require me, medicinally speaking, I will be in the next room." She paused. "Good night."

"Good night."

Verity sat in her room alone. At first she was too angry to cry. Then she thought of what she had lost, and she sobbed until her throat ached as if it bled. She didn't understand. Garrett said he loved her, and yet he said he didn't. He made no sense.

Men are insane. Oh, Garrett Knox seems sane, all right. So strong and brave, as if he always knows what he's doing. But he's insane. All men are peculiar. Look at Ethan. Crazy as a coot. What are coots, anyway?

Verity dried her eyes. Ivy understood men. Verity pulled on a nightdress, replaced her robe, and donned slippers. She left her room, headed down the hall, across the staircase landing, and into the east wing to Ivy's room. She knocked. Ivy called, and Verity entered.

Ivy was sitting at her own vanity table, spritzing perfume here and there, fussing with her hair and nightdress.

"What are you doing up and about, Little Miss?" asked Ivy

in surprise. "I thought you'd be enjoying your husband's big, hard body tonight."

"Oh, hush, Ivy."

Verity frowned and sat down in a quilted chair. Ivy's room had been decorated with surprisingly good taste. The former madam had adjusted with perfect ease to the life of a genteel lady. Queen Victoria would have approved of Ivy's selections in finery.

"I take it I was mistaken," noted Ivy.

"Quite mistaken." Verity curled her legs up on the chair, resting her chin on her knees. "He doesn't want me anymore."

"Honey, I find that hard to believe."

"I don't know what I'm doing wrong. I took off all my clothes, and he didn't notice. Maybe it's because I'm too fat now. I thought I was too skinny before—"

"You were," agreed Ivy. "Right now, you're a sight any man would give his left arm for. Trust me, Garrett Knox wants you."

"No. He doesn't." Verity drew a long breath. "He says he can't feel. He says he's 'dead.' I don't know why. I've asked, and he says it's nothing. He swears it's not Caleb's resemblance to Ethan. I tend to believe him. No, I think he's stopped loving me."

Verity's eyes puddled with tears, and Ivy rose to comfort her. "There, there. Honey, you got to look at this more clearly."

"How?" Verity sniffed and dried her eyes. "You understand men, Ivy. What do I do to make him want me again?"

"The thing I've learned about men is just this: They've all got a little boy inside them. A little boy who set himself up in the world, and now depends on whatever he's learned to get by.

"Young Ethan, he learned that if he was as respectable as he could get, people might not notice the shame of his birth. No wonder he's so stiff. Adrian learned if he was wild and reckless and threw himself hard at things, no one would notice how scared he was. Jefferson learned nobody was going to give him nothing if he didn't take it for himself."

Verity listened to Ivy in astonishment. "That's true. And Westley tried to be so good and noble, all to make up for his father's sadness, to prove to his father there was something to be happy about." Verity paused, remembering how Cabot Talmadge had smiled when he looked at his son's face. "I guess it worked."

"It works for all of them," said Ivy, her voice low and sad. "For a little while. But deep down, Ethan thinks he'll never be right. Adrian was still scared. Jefferson finally had to let someone help him to get where he wanted to be. And poor Westley, he couldn't make his papa happy, because he didn't cause the sorrow in the first place."

Verity endured a wave of pain on her friends' behalf. "And still they try, still they try."

"They do," said Ivy. "You've got a good eye. Now you tell me, what about Garrett Knox?"

"I don't know. I don't understand him at all."

"Don't you? Think harder. Look at him. What do you see?"

Verity closed her eyes. She saw Garrett, and she remembered every moment beside him. "Garrett is strong."

"Why?"

"Because no one else was."

"And that meant?"

Verity squeezed her thoughts into cohesiveness. "It meant he had to be strong where others were weak. His mother died, and left Adrian a baby. His father fell apart. Garrett had to be strong."

"What happened?"

Verity's face paled. "They all died."

Tears glistened on Ivy's face, mirrored on Verity's. "Yes," agreed Ivy quietly. "They all died."

"Not only his family," said Verity. "But so many men in his command. Westley, Peter McCaffrey, Sam. Robert and Jared are missing . . . but that happened long ago. Why now?"

Ivy sighed. "That, I don't know. Something happened, something that brought it home to him. Find out what that was, and you'll open up his wound, Honey. Because he's still got a wound, mark my words. It's pussing and festering and spreading all over him. He can't lance it himself. That's up to you."

Verity considered this in silence for a long while. Her heart expanded in pity, in remorse for her anger. "I threw wine at him," she admitted. "I lost my temper."

"Probably did no harm, Honey. He thinks he can't feel. Hell, he don't want to feel. He's afraid of feeling."

"Garrett isn't afraid. He's never afraid."

"He's afraid now. He don't want to see. There's something he don't want to see. You get too close, you're inside him. If he lets you in, he's afraid you'll see it, too. Maybe make him see. And he don't want to see."

"What could be that horrible, Ivy? Garrett has already been through so much."

"I have no idea," said Ivy. A shudder twisted through her. "It must be something fairly black, all right. Maybe just a crystal moment. A moment when everything became clear. And that everything meant the end of the world to Garrett Knox."

Verity returned to her room to think about what Ivy told her. Yes, Garrett was hiding something. It tore her heart to think of him in distress, alone. *I have enough love for both of us.* She got up and crept quietly to his door. She listened a while. Silence. No light from his room.

Verity dimmed her lantern, opened the door and tiptoed in. Garrett was asleep. She saw him in the faint light of the half-moon. But he wasn't sleeping soundly. His head tossed from side to side, and his lips moved.

Verity set her lantern at his bedside. She stood watching him, not daring to wake him, not able to leave.

"Adrian—No. Get back." Garrett's voice sounded far away. Desperate. "Adrian . . ." Such pain. Verity's heart quailed. Tears filled her eyes. She knew he was watching his brother die.

Garrett's motion stilled, but then his face contorted. "Jared is up there. God, I can't shoot. They're firing. Have to fire. My boys, cover . . . reload. Fire. Bayonets. Jesus, not again."

Verity trembled. Garrett's chest rose and fell with sharp, ragged breaths. "Put him with the gut wounds." Verity heard Garrett's disgust. "Goddamn it, we can't leave them. Have to go back. Can't go back. The woods are burning, we can't go back."

His breaths grew shorter, rasping. "It's suicide. I can't lead my men across that field. We'll be slaughtered like pigs . . . orders. I'll lead them. Verity . . . Verity . . . I'll never see you again. I can't see you again. Not now, not after this . . . my son, what do I do for my son?"

Verity couldn't stand it anymore. Garrett's desperation seeped into her soul. His misery tore at her heart. His torment overwhelmed her. *What do I say to you?* she wondered. *What can I say to ease your pain?*

Garrett fell deathly silent. His lips mouthed, *No,* and his head turned to the side as if he didn't want to see. Couldn't bear to see. "No. God, no. No." His words grew louder. His head tossed, and he groaned in his sleep.

"Garrett!" Verity grabbed his shoulder. She shook him, tears streaming down her face. Whatever he saw, it was too horrible ... she couldn't leave him to face it alone. "Garrett, wake up. Please, wake up." She shook him again.

"No!" Garrett bolted upright in bed, his eyes wide, his breath coming as short, ragged gasps. He stared into the night, not seeing Verity. Tears glistened on his strong face. Verity wrapped her arm around his shoulder, she entwined her fingers in his hair, gently patting him.

"Wake up, Garrett. It's all right. You're home now."

Garrett forced his eyes to look her way, as if struggling from one plane of existence to another. "Verity?"

"I'm here."

Garrett stared blankly. Then he looked around the room. Verity turned up her lantern. Garrett drew a quick breath, then another, deeper. "I'm sorry. Did I wake you?" He was trying to sound calm, but his voice quavered.

"No. I came to see you, that's all. You were dreaming."

Garrett slumped forward, he rubbed his hands across his eyes. "It's over now. I'm sorry for waking you. Go back to bed, Verity. I'm all right. Just a dream."

"A nightmare, I'd say. And I'm not going back to bed. You need me."

"No, I need sleep."

"Sleep? So you can toss and turn and cry out all night? I thought it was the fever. But you're still dreaming, Garrett. You're still suffering."

"Just let me sleep. Please, go back to bed, Verity. I'm all right."

Verity almost complied. He didn't want to talk. He didn't want to share his pain with her. Maybe later, when the dreams got too bad, when he couldn't stand it anymore, then maybe he would share it with a bottle. But not her.

Ivy had neglected to mention one other thing common to men: They insist on handling things themselves, resisting any help.

"What were you dreaming?"

"I don't remember. It was nothing."

"Like hell." Verity seated herself at Garrett's side. She curled her legs under her body and gazed up into his face. "Tell me."

"There's nothing to tell." His voice sounded raw, strained.

"You mentioned Adrian, and Jared. You talked about orders. Thank God, you mentioned me. And you said something about burning woods. I didn't understand that."

Apparently, Garrett did. He grimaced. "Verity, please don't . . . it doesn't matter now."

"If it didn't matter, you wouldn't dream of it over and over."

"It's just a dream."

"What woods?"

"The Wilderness!" Garrett's voice exploded, burst from him with such force that Verity started. Garrett caught his breath. He shook his head to regain control over himself. "God, don't do this. It was just a dream."

Verity fought her own emotion. "The Wilderness? The battle in Virginia, before Cold Harbor?" Verity paused. "Were the woods burning?"

"The woods were burning," repeated Garrett. Now he sounded shallow, toneless. Speaking by rote.

"The lint from the muskets spread all through the trees, caught fire in the leaves. Started fires all over. We fought, we fell back. The rebels fought and fell back, too. We couldn't see ten feet in front of us. Men fell, and kept falling. And the fires grew. We tried to pull the wounded out of there, but there wasn't time. Not enough time to get all the men. We had to pick the ones most likely to survive. The others . . ."

Verity closed her eyes. For a wild moment, she wanted to tell him to stop. She didn't want to know. She couldn't know. But instead, she took his hand and kissed it. "You promised me once you'd never tell me fairy tales about this war. I never asked you to. What happened?"

Garrett met her eyes. A sea of emotion raged beneath the calm of his gray eyes. "We were moving back through the woods. Hancock's men. The best damned corps in the Union army. Scattered, lost. Burning. All of us. The man I carried died. I let him down to pick up another."

Garrett stopped. He closed his eyes. He swallowed hard. Verity waited. She held his hand in her lap.

"Another officer came by, started telling me where we were moving to. But he never finished. He saw a boy lying just beyond us. Shot all to hell. But not dead. Verity, he wasn't dead. Gut wound. Leg off. Face smashed. But a man knows his own brother."

"No." Verity caught her breath, wanting to block out the scene Garrett revealed, but she couldn't. Not without leaving him there alone to face it without her.

"The officer tried to pick up his brother. The boy couldn't be moved. He screamed at the slightest touch. He begged his brother to end it, to finish him before the fires reached him. And they were coming. We could barely see through the smoke. Men were screaming, eaten up alive by the flames. Dying in agony.

"The officer put the boy back on the ground. Then he just stood there, looking down at that writhing body, listening stone-faced to the pleas. And I stood there, too. Watching. I couldn't move. The officer stood for the longest time. Then he knelt down, kissed his brother's bloody forehead, and put a bullet in the boy's head."

Verity closed her eyes. Her tears dripped to her hand, to Garrett's. "The poor man."

"I knew what he would do next. I knew. But when he put his revolver to his own head, I didn't stop him. I just watched while he put his gun to his temple and blew his head off."

"Garrett . . ." Verity didn't know what to say. She kissed his wet hand. She cried when he had no tears.

"After that, I just went on. I did what they told me. They said, 'Lead a regiment up that slope,' and I did. Men fell all around, cut down like wheat in a field. They told us to take Cold Harbor. Cold Harbor, where Bobby Lee sat entrenched like a prince. The rebs mowed us down. They said, 'Keep going,' so I kept going. The only damned thing I saw was that officer holding his brother."

Verity's voice choked on a sob as she tried to speak. "It's over now."

"It will never end. I wake, and I hear artillery. I hear screams. I see boys in gray buckle over when they're shot. I see their dead faces."

"Should we stop fighting? It can't be worth this pain anymore."

Garrett didn't answer at once. A long weary sigh tore from deep inside him. "We have to win."

"Why?"

"Because I saw another man die. A man of color. He escaped from Tennessee just a few months before The Wilderness battle, then joined a regiment, like Jefferson—. He got shot at Spotsylvania. Where we fought all night, standing on corpses.

"This black man was in the Second Corps, part of the regiment Hancock gave me to lead. He fell, but before he died, he grabbed my hand. He said, 'Thank you.' Can you imagine? He said, 'I'd rather die as a man than live as a slave.' That's all, and then he died."

"Maybe there's another way." Verity was crying. She couldn't let Garrett go back. And she knew he meant to go back.

"There is no other way. And no men have ever fought with as much courage and honor as the rebels. There isn't a commander alive who loves his men like Robert E. Lee. And still I say, there is no other way."

"The war will go on without you, Garrett Knox. Let it end without you."

"It will never end."

"It has to."

"It will never end." Garrett closed his eyes and bowed his dark head. Verity's heart felt swollen with love, with pity. She touched his black hair, ran her hands along his shoulder.

"You are home now. Please, while you're home, let me comfort you. Please, let me hold you."

Garrett looked into her face. "You know what I want from you."

"I know."

"You know I can't give you anything else."

"All I want is you." Verity touched his face, ran her hand along his jawline. Very gently, she leaned forward and kissed his mouth.

Verity moved her mouth back and forth across Garrett's. She touched his strong face, her fingers playing over the rough stubble. Her tongue flicked out and ran along his lips.

Verity felt his kiss intensify, felt the heat of his body soar. She throbbed mercilessly, the relentless ache demanding full attention. It had been so long since she held him, since his body quenched the desire in hers.

Her lips played eagerly, tasting him. She squirmed closer, her fingers clenched in his hair. He answered her kiss, demanding nothing. Verity's hands explored him, following the line of his muscles, down his arms, over to his chest.

Verity drew back, her eyes wide and bright, her breath swift and unsteady. "Does your injury still hurt?"

"Not just now."

Garrett was smiling. The past had released its hold over him. Verity wasn't sure why, but she knew it was true.

"I was afraid you didn't want me because I'm fat." Verity adjusted her robe. "Maybe I should leave this on."

"Not a chance." Garrett tugged the robe off her shoulders,

letting it fall behind her. "This, too," he added as he untied her nightdress.

"I've changed," she warned him. Ivy said men would like her new shape. But maybe Garrett liked thin women.

Garrett caught the folds of her nightdress and pulled the garment over her head. He tossed it aside, but his eyes never left her body. "You have changed." His voice sounded thick and husky. "In fact . . ." Garrett leaned over and turned up the lantern, casting it full on her bare body. Verity winced.

"I've gained some weight."

"I see."

Verity noticed the sudden tenting of Garrett's covers. Her eyes widened and her lips curved in a delighted smile. "You're not displeased, I see."

Her confidence returned with lightning force. She adjusted her position, rising up on her knees before him. Her round breasts jutted forward, her head tipped back, and she caught her lower lip between sharp teeth.

"What do you think?"

A low, rumbling groan sounded deep in Garrett's throat. "I think it's been too long."

"It's been way too long. Kiss me."

Garrett caught her head in his hands, and he kissed her hungrily, as a man starved. His hands slid from her face, seeking. A soft breath escaped her lips when he caressed her new shape, circling the peak with a gentle touch.

"This is too beautiful," he murmured. Garrett bent to take one firm bud in his mouth. He savored her fullness. He teased the peak, torturing her with desire as it hardened eagerly against his tongue.

Verity's body released its long store of pent up need. Everywhere he touched drove her closer to orgasm. Her need wasn't youthful anymore. She now harbored a woman's need, too long denied. Garrett slid his hand over her stomach, over her soft thatch of hair, between her legs.

Verity rose up higher on her knees, giving him easier access. His fingers delved, discovered. "You have missed me."

"Yes." Her long neck tipped back as he played mercilessly with the tiny bud, then slid along her moistened entrance. Verity felt a wild desperation. She wanted him. Now. She tore the covers away, she wrapped her trembling hand around his turgid staff, squeezing gently, kneading, massaging him until his hips undulated with her skill.

"Woman, it's been too long. I can't take this without . . . Verity . . ."

She didn't listen, she didn't comprehend. Verity kissed his neck, her breath coming in warm gasps as she licked and bit him. She should lie back, let him take her. Instead, she scrambled onto his lap, still holding his length in her hand. She moved her hips until she felt him hard and hot against her sex.

Garrett caught her firm bottom, held her over his staff. "You're eager."

"Garrett . . ."

Garrett chuckled, then lay back, his hands folded behind his head. "Woman, I am yours. Do your pleasure."

Verity felt a wild tide of pure lust. She poised herself over him, moving and squirming until the blunt tip met her open flesh. She sank down over him, and his staff parted her satin folds, deeper. She'd never been more ready, but her body felt tight. She stopped.

"It's been a long time," he reminded her. "Take it slow."

Verity eased slowly over him and her skin softened as if it recognized his presence. Garrett's jaw clenched as she took his length deep inside her.

Verity braced herself on his chest. She lifted off him, sank down again. He didn't move. He just smiled up at her, watching her. His eyes focused on her breasts, he reached up and cupped them in his hands. His thumbs teased the tips, back and forth. Squeezing gently, pulling.

Verity bit her lip, then she cried out. She moved against him, and he joined her rhythm, thrusting upward, reveling in the perfect friction of flesh against flesh. She closed her eyes, head tipped back as she pleasured herself in abandon.

"That's what I want," he told her, his voice a ragged groan. "You take what you want, girl. All that you want."

"Garrett . . ." She whimpered his name. "I've missed you so." He drove hard into her, and she squealed with delight.

"I've missed you, too."

As Verity moved with growing abandon, her body had a will of its own, twisting around him, seizing pleasure. She felt his eruption, she saw his face contort with his splendid release, she felt the hot force of him inside her. They were together again, close—one thing. Her body quivered, hovering . . . then burst in fiery fragments, spreading down her legs to her toes, shaking her until she collapsed against his chest.

She lay still, listening to his heart, feeling the wild twitches of her pulse as it formed around him, still engorged inside her. She felt his pulse, too. Their breathing slackened, she kissed his chest, his jaw.

"Better now?" she asked.

Garrett smiled. "Better now."

"We'll start building down there, beyond the stables."

Garrett stood on the back lawn, his arms folded over his chest as he surveyed his land. Verity peeked up at him.

"Building what?"

"A home for the wounded men, of course. We've only got room for a few in the estate house, and it's not suitable for incapacitated men, anyway. Ethan, however, can stay in the downstairs bedroom for now."

"Ethan refuses to be moved," Verity reminded him.

"Does he? Well, he's not apt to take orders from Watkins. I, on the other hand, outrank him."

Verity smiled in wonder at the change in Garrett's mood. Maybe he felt he could affect the world again. But Ethan Hallowell might not be the easiest place to start. "I hope you can convince him. He's very stubborn."

"Runs in the family."

"Maybe, but Ethan seems dead set on dying. It's funny, because he just keeps getting better. Oh, he looks awful, like a Viking after too many raids, but he's as healthy as any man ever was."

"He's not Viking," decided Garrett. "He's English. And that's worse. Anglo-Saxon blood is generally stubborn. Jared is like that. I like to think of myself as more German."

"Germans just keep everything to themselves, I expect."

Garrett smiled. "And what of the Celts, my dear? As Sam said, you carry their blood quite strongly. They fling themselves into life, without thought of the consequences, burdened by overly active imaginations. Didn't the earliest inhabitants of Scotland paint their bodies, and race naked into battle? That sounds like you, all right."

"Enough with the slurs on my sanity. When do we start building?" Garrett's idea encouraged Verity, not least because he might take it upon himself to do the building, rather than return to battle. Maybe that would be enough.

"We've got lumber, plenty of woods. I'll put the stable hands on it, too. We'll start immediately." Garrett rubbed his chin thoughtfully. "One story. They don't need stairs. Room for privacy, for bathing. Damn, I wish I could reach Jared. He's a very passable architect, when he's not swirling some pretty belle across a ballroom. And when he's not leading men into battle . . ."

Verity took Garrett's arm. "Then you think he's still alive?"

"Until I learn otherwise, conclusively . . . fool that I am, I'll believe he's still alive."

"You're not a fool, Garrett Knox. You're a man. And you're free to want, and to hurt, and yes, to be disappointed, and to fail sometimes. But if anyone can make a difference in this world, it's you."

Chapter Sixteen

Despite protests from Mildred concerning propriety, and from Candace concerning his health, Garrett started work on the veteran's home immediately. He marked out a suitable space for a deep foundation and arranged for large amounts of lumber. By early August, a sturdy foundation was in place, and every stable hand was hard at work erecting beams and the shell of Garrett's design.

Verity sat beneath the giant oak tree, while Caleb played on the lawn. Her gaze drifted to Garrett as he worked on the home. He was hammering nails, lifting heavy boards, issuing orders and making corrections.

He worked with a band of cloth tied around his brow, wearing an old shirt with the sleeves ripped off. His muscles grew even stronger than they had been. The damaged flesh of his chest had healed with the activity, and the scar faded in the sun.

He was happy. He didn't dwell on the war's progress. It had seemed to reach a stalemate in Petersburg, anyway. The rebels dug in. Grant kept them in siege. Letters from Jefferson revealed a long tedium of waiting and skirmishes, but no significant change.

Caleb squirmed around on the back lawn, stuffing bits of clover into his mouth that Verity hurriedly removed. He was six months old, and determined to attain mobility.

"You are not a horse, dear." Verity retrieved a pink and white blossom from his mouth.

Caleb loved horses. From his earliest awareness, he felt great glee at the sight of the tall animals in his father's pasture. Whenever he cried, Verity took him to the fields, where he burbled happily, contended in the presence of serene strength.

Verity felt happy, too. She felt married. Garrett made love to her every night. He still didn't share every thought, but he seemed contended with his new task. Verity wondered if he considered heading back to war. He didn't mention it.

Candace returned from her weekly visit to Nurse Abigail's boarding house and joined Verity in the shade. She carried a wad of mail, which Verity immediately seized.

"How is Ethan? Is there anything for me?"

"Captain Hallowell is his usual solemn self. There's a stack of letters from his Bess beside his bed, but he won't read them. He won't let me read them to him, either. He's a little suspicious about how she found his whereabouts, however."

"You didn't tell him anything, did you?"

"No. I said a determined girl can find out anything."

"Very good."

"There's a letter from Petersburg. I believe it's Jefferson's handwriting."

Verity found the letter and tore it opened. She read a few lines, gasped, and let out a piercing cry of joy.

"What is it?" asked Candace. "Good news, I hope?"

"Very good. Watch Caleb for me!" Verity didn't wait to explain. She whipped the letter in the air, let out a 'Whoop!' and darted from the house. She raced down to the veterans' home, shouting all the way.

"Garrett, Garrett! Wait 'til you hear!"

"Watkins." Garrett set his hammer aside and dried his forehead with a cloth. "Report."

"A letter from Jefferson."

"How is he?"

"He's fine." Verity paused to catch her breath. "John's fine, too. But Garrett, they've seen Jared!"

Garrett didn't move. He didn't breathe. "Seen him?" He barely whispered.

"Talked to him! Jefferson says the two lines, North and South, almost touch each other in places. After the Crater battle, somehow Jared and Jefferson met. I guess John recognized him from our night at the rebel ball in Fredericksburg. You remember, when—''

Garrett smiled. ''When you spent a night dancing. Yes, I remember, your little mustache and all. Go on.''

''Anyway, they spoke quite a bit. Jefferson says he didn't tell Jared about our marriage, as he wasn't sure how to explain that you married Watkins. He thought you might want to surprise him. He says Jared has news that might surprise you, too. But he's all right. He's been made a colonel, and he's issued a challenge through Jefferson for you to get out of your bed and equal him—''

Verity stopped cold. ''Of course, he didn't mean it that way. I think you're fine as a major.''

Garrett laughed. ''Upping my rank doesn't hold great appeal for me. A colonel, is he? The rebels often pick their own officers. Quite an honor.''

Garrett stared south across the fields of Fox Run. ''I taught him to ride here, in this pasture, when he was four years old.'' He stopped and closed his eyes. ''So you made it through the war this far, after all.''

''He's all right.'' Verity scanned the letter again. ''I wonder what news Jared has? Do you suppose he's married, too?''

''That would seem unlikely. Jared has too many women to settle for one.''

''Maybe he found his spy.''

''Maybe, but she'd have to be quite a woman to hold his attention for long.''

''He seemed bored to me,'' remembered Verity. ''A spy wouldn't be boring.''

''That's true.'' Garrett drew a deep, long breath. ''The last time I saw him, he promised we'd meet one day, on the battlefield. He swore he'd lower his saber in salute. It may be that time will come, after all.''

Verity's face paled. ''You won't be on a battlefield.'' Her tone was a warning, but he didn't respond. Her heart beat slow and cold.

''The veterans' home still requires my attention.'' He paused. ''I want Ethan Hallowell safe and secure here at Fox Run. It may be time to pay another visit to our erstwhile Captain Hallowell.''

Good. Garrett was thinking of the men in his care now, the

veterans. That might be enough to keep him from actual war. "Maybe we should just bring a club, whack him over the head, and drag him out of there."

"Or Bess. A woman can work wonders."

"Hmm. Bess. I'm afraid letters aren't accomplishing much. Ethan would never let her see him."

Garrett grinned. "Where there's a will, there's a way, my dear. You should know that better than anyone."

Nurse Abigail saw Verity Knox and her large, brawny husband leaving their coach. She groaned and slapped her apron. "Not her, not them, together." Nurse Abigail spotted her husband. "Old man, it may be time we move on out of here."

"What? And leave this house?" The old man heard the bell ring and took a quick slug of whiskey from a bottle. "Not *her* again?"

"Yes. *Her*. And that husband of hers. Looks like he could move a mountain with one shove."

"Bet he 'moves' her something pretty," added Nurse Abigail's leathery husband as he wiped spittle from his chin.

"Git . . . the . . . door!" Nurse Abigail shot a forbidding glare her husband's way, then removed herself from any possible view.

Nurse Abigail's dirty husband opened the door. Verity eyed him in distaste. "Didn't expect you fine folks today."

"We don't come when expected," said Verity. Garrett maintained a steely silence, which unnerved Nurse Abigail's thin-boned husband in a satisfactory fashion. "I trust the gentlemen in your care are doing well."

"As well as peaches on the bough."

Verity looked at the scrawny man, then at Garrett. Garrett sighed and shook his head.

"We'll see Captain Hallowell now," Verity told the man. "Excuse us, please."

The man leapt at the opportunity to depart. "He's disgusting," noted Verity as they entered the boarding house. "I should have ordered Nurse Abigail to wash him, too."

Garrett laughed. *"There's* a frightening mental image."

Verity and Garrett entered the room, and an older veteran greeted him. "You may not remember me, Major Knox, but you led a charge back at Bull Run—"

"Anderson, isn't it?" said Garrett. "You fought with the old Third Maryland infantry, didn't you? You're from up near Annapolis."

The soldier beamed proudly. "That's right. Ain't you a wonder for remembering that far back?"

"Not so," replied Garrett. "The old Third made a name for itself that will never be forgotten."

Anderson leaned back on his pillow. "Oh, Major. Them seems like long days passing, now. You know, I got shot up at Gettysburg. First day. When our beautiful General Reynolds got killed. We held off the rebs, though, didn't we? Kept 'em from the high ground. Me and my boys. You know, the whole lot of us got shot up that day. Damnedest thing. Every man in my company died. 'Cept me. 'Cept for me."

Garrett clasped Anderson's shoulder. The man was missing an arm; shot in the back, he would never walk again. "You do those men honor by your life, my friend. A man with your attributes has much to contribute beyond this room."

"I'd like to know what."

"What, exactly, remains to be seen," said Garrett. "But I'm here to see you get the opportunity to find out."

Anderson didn't speak further, but his eyes were bright with unshed tears. No longer tears of grief, but of hope. Verity went to Ethan's cot. He set his jaw resolutely. "How are you feeling, Ethan?"

"As well as can be expected." He might as well have said, "Near death," but he looked fit and healthy, despite his gloomy expression.

A man spoke from the hallway, and Ethan's face drained of blood. "I am looking for Ethan Hallowell. I was led to believe he inhabits these premises."

Ethan's eyes opened wide, and his mouth dropped. "God, no."

Verity took his hand. "Ethan, what's the matter?"

Ethan had no time to answer. Nurse Abigail called from the hall. "Got another visitor for Hallowell. A real gentleman," she added as contrast to Verity's belligerent 'associates.'

Garrett and Verity turned as a formally dressed man entered the room. Verity looked at Garrett, who shrugged. "Ethan, who is that?"

Ethan didn't answer. He looked like a small boy.

"This way, Sir," directed Nurse Abigail. She pointed toward
Ethan, bowed deferentially to the visitor, then hurried away.

The man had slightly graying temples and a trimmed mustache.
He looked respectable, like the gentlemen Verity remembered in
Boston. Boston—oh, no!

He saw Ethan and stopped, his face contorted. Not with emotion,
but with disgust. Something in his expression said he had fully
expected Ethan to end this way. "Ethan. It has taken much effort
to locate you. I would have expected you to maintain yourself
with more dignity, whatever the unfortunate circumstances in
which you've found yourself."

"Sir, it was my intention to spare you—"

"Spare me?" His father gazed upward, a studied gesture, meant
to inflict shame. "Have you considered the disgrace of a man in
your condition? The shame?"

Garrett twitched, and he made a fist. "Shame?" he asked, his
voice a low, rumbling growl.

"Perhaps your guests might return another time."

Ethan seemed reluctant to send Verity and Garrett away now.
"Sir, allow me to introduce Major Garrett Knox, and his wife,
the former Verity Talmadge." Ethan sighed heavily. "Verity and
Garrett, this is my father, Calvin Pierce Hallowell."

"We're . . . pleased to make your acquaintance, Mr. Hallowell,"
said Verity. Garrett maintained an icy silence. Calvin Hallowell
studied them with renewed interest.

"Talmadge? Any relation to the Beacon Hill Talmadges?"

"That is my family, yes." said Verity. "Robert Talmadge is my
brother." Verity felt uncomfortable, considering Ethan's paternity.
Apparently, though, his father valued the connection to an old and
respectable family more than he loathed his wife's infidelity.

"I sympathize with the tragic loss of your brother, Mrs. 'Knox,'
is it?"

"Knox," said Garrett.

Calvin Hallowell scrutinized Garrett. "Then your family must
be suitable, to be united with a Talmadge daughter."

"Not at all," said Garrett. "Actually, my great-grandfather was
a cutthroat Brit who nabbed a Philadelphia street urchin against
her will. My grandfather married a peasant girl who lived in a
hovel not a mile from our farm. At least, we assume he married

her . . . and my father carried on the illustrious tradition by making off with an Amish woman.''

Calvin Hallowell grimaced in disgust. Verity winced. ''Actually, Garrett was Robert's best friend,'' she offered weakly. ''They met at school in Switzerland.''

''Where I was sent to keep me out of jail,'' added Garrett. Verity and Ethan gaped, both speechless.

''I got sent back for the same reason.'' Garrett folded his arms over his chest. For a reason Verity didn't understand, Garrett's voice betrayed a slight Southern drawl.

''Little Verity here hadn't much choice *but* to marry me, if you take my meaning. Had a 'little visitor' on the way.''

''Garrett!'' Verity's cheeks flushed pink, but Calvin Hallowell was suitably horrified.

''Ethan, you will be transported to Boston at once. I have arranged accommodations at a secluded establishment in western Massachusetts. The expense is high, of course, and only sons of the finest families are allowed admittance. The care is adequate. More importantly, the establishment favors discretion. You can spend the remainder of your life there.''

''I prefer to remain here,'' said Ethan.

Calvin Hallowell's face hardened. When angry, he seemed even more forbidding.

''There is no chance that you will do otherwise than I have directed. Your sister's husband has attained a position in the government. I won't allow rumors of your incapacity to damage his prospects.''

Ethan closed his eyes. ''Father, I will not go to Boston.''

''I have already arranged a suitable quantity of morphine. With the good will of the boarding house matron, it will be administered now. Then you will be transported to the establishment I mentioned. The morphine will be continued, in measured doses, to ensure your cooperation.''

''No . . .'' Tears flooded Verity's cheeks. ''You can't do that.''

Calvin Hallowell turned to her. ''I can do whatever I think prudent.''

''Prudent? You should have married Aunt P! You're two of a kind.''

Verity's outburst had no impact on Calvin Hallowell. He assessed her without concern, and she shrank back in fear. Such a cold man. She didn't know how to fight him, how to win.

Garrett just listened, his jaw set slightly to one side. He addressed Ethan, ignoring his father. "Captain Hallowell. You know I've requested your presence at Fox Run. I have need of your services during the building of the veterans' home. Your sense of order would be useful. However, I understand your reluctance to leave this place of your own choosing. Your 'father' has offered an alternative, limiting the nature of your choices. Your word, I think, has some value still."

Garrett was offering a solution, offering his own strength on Ethan's behalf. Verity held her breath. If he had no will to live, Ethan might cave in to Hallowell's demands. She wanted to influence his decision, but the ultimate choice lay in Ethan's hands. All time held for his answer.

"I will go to Fox Run."

Verity breathed a muted sigh of relief. Garrett smiled. "We've brought the coach, Ethan," said Garrett. "Your room is ready."

"My son will return with me to Boston." Calvin Hallowell glared at Garrett, unrelenting. "I can enlist the aid of local authorities in this matter, if necessary. Several prominent senators are known to me."

"In the biblical sense?" spouted Garrett. "Or is it just their wives?"

Calvin Hallowell was flabbergasted. And furious. "You, Sir, are a barbarian."

"So I've been told. The thing about barbarians is, they rarely lose. You recall the Fall of Rome?"

Calvin Hallowell forced his attention away from Garrett, attempting to ignore a man he clearly thought not worthy of mention. He noticed the pocket watch clutched in Ethan's hand. He took it, and examined the engraving.

Verity met Ethan's gaze. She knew what Calvin Hallowell read: *Cabot Talmadge.* Beneath it, engraved later: *Westley Talmadge.*

"How did you come by this?"

"Westley Talmadge was Ethan's captain at Antietam," put in Verity. "I gave it to Ethan before Gettysburg. He'd lost his."

Calvin Hallowell passed the fob to Verity. "He no longer has need of a watch."

Ethan's eyes glimmered with tears, and he looked away. Garrett glanced at Ethan. "Your son . . . Forgive me, but he very closely resembles a young man I knew. Westley Talmadge. Cabot Talmadge's son. Curious, isn't it?"

Calvin Hallowell paled. He turned to Ethan as if he might strangle him where he lay. "You dared reveal your disgrace to this, this—"

"I guessed," put in Garrett. "This boy is no disgrace to you, Hallowell. He has more honor and courage beneath that dirty, louse-filled beard than you do in the entirety of your family history, this boy who dared take a bullet meant for me.

"No, you're not taking him anywhere. By God, you're not filling his body with morphine while his soul bleeds. He's coming with me, and he will return to being a man. He will be a free man. Because in all my life, I've never seen anyone held in such bitter slavery as this boy you dare call your 'son.' "

Calvin Hallowell started to object, but Garrett didn't give him the chance. "I don't give a damn who Ethan's father was. Whatever happened between his parents, you kept him as your son. He deserved better. He deserved to be respected for what he is, and not having to please a son of a bitch like you."

"This has gone far enough." Calvin Hallowell wasn't backing down. Neither was Garrett.

"Damned sure."

Garrett met Ethan's eyes. "Ethan, it is you who decides. You know that."

Ethan stared at Garrett. He looked to his 'father.' His ultimate respectability hung in the balance. And his life. "Yes."

Garrett didn't hesitate. "Dare you take this boy from my care, Hallowell? If you try, I'll see the circumstances of his birth revealed like lightning over Boston. I have the resources, I promise you. Robert Talmadge shared with me the contents of his uncle's will— naming Ethan as his legitimate heir, produced by a union between Cabot Talmadge and your wife, Madeleine."

Calvin Hallowell didn't relent at once. His teeth ground together, his nostrils flared.

"Tell them I died, Father," said Ethan wearily. "You would have preferred that, I think. I would have preferred it, too."

Calvin cast a disparaging look Ethan's way. His dark eyes flashed hatred. "You're worse than dead, boy. And you know it. Lie there and rot. God be praised I won't have to be bothered with you again. Maybe you're just where you belong now—wallowing in filth, the product of a shameful union. My wife's precious bastard, who wears Cabot Talmadge's face. Ha! Let it torment her beyond the grave. I will think no more of you."

Calvin turned away, giving no thought to Ethan's stricken face or the blue eyes wet with tears. Calvin Hallowell passed Verity and Garrett without a glance. He never looked back. Garrett Knox balled his large hand into a fist and Verity grabbed his arm, pulling it back before he could swing at the departing Bostonian. . . .

"Well, Captain, it looks like you're coming with us, after all." Garrett seated himself on the edge of Ethan's tiny cot. He patted the boy's shoulder fondly. "I'm sorry to put you through that. Couldn't control myself, I'm afraid. Battle instinct."

Ethan smiled faintly. "I've never seen my father back down. Never once. I tried to please him, for so many years . . ." Ethan's voice cracked.

Verity took his hand. "He should have tried to win *your* favor, Ethan."

Ethan met her eyes. "Ivy told me she sees Westley beside me. I can't see him, but I felt him near. He told me not to let anyone decide my fate but myself."

Garrett sighed. "Ivy . . . Well, Westley was right."

"When you suggested he might 'know' those prominent senators, in the biblical sense . . ." Ethan shook his head, but he was smiling.

"That might have been a little strong," agreed Garrett. He didn't sound sorry.

"Just what does 'in the biblical sense' mean, anyway?" asked Verity suspiciously.

"It means in bed, intimately," said Garrett. "Ask no further questions, my sweet. I shudder to damage your delicate nature with life's ugly little truths."

"I've never seen you like that, Garrett," said Verity, content to let the matter of 'biblical sense' pass. "You were quite . . . something." Verity paused, and Ethan nodded. "I didn't know Damian Knox was a 'cutthroat,' though. In fact, Mildred says he was quite a hero. And a lord in England."

"He was," Garrett admitted with a laugh. "And the street urchin turned out to be a nobleman's daughter. Ah, life's little quirks!"

"Did your grandfather really marry a poor girl?"

"She was poor, yes. And she lived a mile away, in a tiny,

rundown hut, as I indicated. I neglected to mention, however, that once married she became the favored hostess of all Maryland.''

"Well, scoundrel or not, I thank you, Major. I'm not particularly fond of morphine." Ethan spoke evenly, without emotion, but Verity saw the pain in his face. She placed Westley's watch in his palm.

"This belongs to you, Ethan. Maybe I've been around Ivy too long, too, but I could swear Westley wanted me to defend you. Thank God for Garrett. I don't think I could have stood up to Calvin Hallowell alone."

"It would be harder to slam him against the wall than Nurse Abigail," agreed Ethan.

Garrett eyed Verity. "You didn't."

"She did. Picked her up by the collar and shoved her against the wall. Threatened to kill her, too. Trust me, Major, you were quite civilized compared to your wife."

Garrett took Verity's hand and kissed it. "About that, there has never been any doubt."

Ethan came to Fox Run, but his somber mood didn't alter much. Everyone treated him delicately. Mildred brought a wheelchair from Washington for Ethan's use, but he hadn't tried it yet. He just lay in the downstairs bed, unwashed, unmoved by anything. Candace slipped Bess's letters into his bedstand drawer, but Ethan ignored them.

No one dared prod Ethan into bathing, though Ivy did her best to delouse him. Verity brought him books, which he didn't read.

Garrett went to Ethan's room, hoping to inspire his interest in life. The curtains were tied back, revealing the long, green pastures beyond the white fence, but Ethan just stared at the ceiling.

Garrett took a seat at his bedside. "If you've got some time, Captain, I'd like you to look over these designs. I'm not much for drawing, and since you've got an exceptionally ordered mind . . .''

Ethan glanced at Garrett's building plans without much interest. "I have no education in architecture, Major."

"I know," said Garrett. "I just thought . . . well, you remind me of my cousin. Jared had quite a talent for design, though his work tended to be rather flowery. Southern. I thought, with your clear Yankee brain, you might come up with something that would work for these men."

"I remember your cousin," said Ethan. "He seemed confident and incredibly sure of himself. As if all the world was his for the taking. I can't think we have much in common."

Not at the moment. "You're both English, in soul as well as in blood. I'm sure, if you put your mind to it—"

"Sir, if you don't mind . . . I'm a little tired."

Garrett wanted to question the source of Ethan's weariness. He barely moved. But he didn't have the heart to challenge the boy's downcast spirits.

"Any luck?" asked Verity when Garrett emerged from Ethan's room.

Garrett shook his head. "He's becoming a rather depressing young man. I have no idea how to bring him out of it."

"Maybe it's beyond our abilities. We've done what we could. He's safe, he's well-tended. But we can't make him want to live again. The best we can do is believe it's possible."

"That's a hell of a lot more than he'd get from the elegant Mr. Hallowell."

"We spared him that. It was satisfying to thwart that devil's intentions, anyway. I think he wanted to bring Ethan to Boston just to torment him, maybe in revenge for his wife's love affair with Uncle Cabot. I can't believe he'd really care about his wife, though. It doesn't make much sense."

"No," agreed Garrett. "It doesn't. But such thinking is common to those who seek to dominate and control others. They punish those who disobey them. Ethan's very existence forced Hallowell to look at evidence that he couldn't control everything. He was, indeed, a devil. I wonder if every ill, every war, wasn't at the beginning caused by an autocrat."

Their conversation was interrupted by visitors. Horsemen, outside. "Who's that?" asked Verity, peeking out the window. Garrett looked out, his brow lifted.

"What the hell?"

Verity saw a small man on a powerful, restive horse. "Who's he?"

Garrett sighed. "Major General Phil Sheridan." He headed for the door.

Verity's pulse moved slow and cold as dread welled up inside her. "Oh, God. Please, no."

Garrett was already outside, greeting Sheridan and his staff. "Have the General's horses stabled," he told a servant. "What brings you here, Sir?"

"We need you, Garrett Knox." Phil Sheridan didn't waste time. Verity stood glaring at him from the front porch. "On August the seventh, I accepted General Grant's orders, taking forces into the Shenandoah Valley. I want commanders who men will follow. I want you."

Garrett started to speak, but Sheridan interrupted him. "Hell, Major, I know you've done your duty. Done it, and then some. You signed up for two years, then two more. Your term is done. You've got every right to stay right here, and you've done enough to fill the pride of all Maryland. I'm asking you to come back because I need you. Grant's taken over. If anyone can stack up against old Marse Robert, it's Sam Grant."

Verity listened in horror. This man could talk. Garrett started to speak again, but Phil Sheridan wasn't finished.

"I know they've been tossing you back and forth between cavalry and infantry. Well, I've seen enough damned fool charges to know what a good officer can do. The rebs are entrenched at Petersburg. We've got to harry them, cut them off. End this Goddamned war for good. Incidentally, I've had you promoted to the rank of colonel."

Phil Sheridan noticed Verity. "Now, it looks to me like you've got reason to stay right where you are."

Garrett smiled. "I've got reason."

Phil Sheridan tipped his cap to Verity and bowed. She frowned and her eyes narrowed. "Morning, Ma'am."

"Good morning, Sir," she said icily. "Garrett isn't going anywhere." She marched down from the front stairs and faced the general. Sheridan's staff members watched her doubtfully.

"Verity, allowed me to introduce Major General—"

"I know who he is. And you can't leave. You've got too much to do here." Verity placed her hands on her hips. "See here, General. You may think the war is all in the fighting. It's not. There's something afterward, and for a lot of men that something is damned ugly. We're building a home for veterans, for afterward. That matters, too."

If her language surprised the men, none dared speak up. Phil Sheridan smiled. "A noble venture, and one I admire, Mrs. Knox." He glanced at Garrett. "You finally met your match, eh, Garrett?"

Garrett smiled, too. A faint blush touched his dark face.

Verity looked up at him in surprise. "Never mind that. Now, it's good of you to visit, but you can't have Garrett."

"Verity—"

"No—"

"It's time."

"No, it's not!" Verity's voice shook. "You can't leave."

"I'm sorry, Mrs. Knox. It was brazen of me to contact your husband this way, in person. Puts the pressure on. Which is why I did it, to be honest. I need him."

"So do I!" Verity whirled to face Garrett. "Don't you dare leave me! Don't you dare!!" She couldn't stand it. He *was* leaving. She saw it in his eyes. "I'll never forgive you if you go, Garrett Knox. Please . . ."

Phil Sheridan bowed his head. "I must have your answer, Garrett. I can't even wait the night here. I just came in from Washington. Headed south before nightfall. I want you with me. Take some time, talk to your wife. We'll rest here, eat a little. And then we have to go."

Garrett nodded. "Give us an hour." He turned to a waiting servant. "Ready my horse."

Verity's face paled. Her hands clenched. Tears blurred her vision. Without a word, she spun around and darted back into the house.

Garrett found Verity in their bedroom, sobbing on the bed. "Verity . . ." He touched her shoulder. She slapped his hand.

"Don't touch me."

"You must understand—I have to go."

Verity looked around, up at him. Her face was blotchy from crying, wet with tears. "I don't understand any such thing. I understand that you're sneaking away."

"Hardly sneaking."

"How can you go back, after everything you went through?"

"I have to."

"He's made you a colonel. That's bribery." Verity sat up in bed. "I should report him."

"Congratulations accepted."

Verity rose slowly, barely inches away. "You can't leave me. You'll miss me too much."

"Verity, my angel, I must go. God knows, I'll miss you, too. We'll write—"

"Write? And if you're shot again, I'll wear black, and live on memories. How wonderful! Well, you can forget it, Colonel Knox."

She jammed her fist into his chest, then shoved him backward. Not expecting violence from his wife, Garrett stumbled back against the closed door. Verity reached around him and locked it.

"You're not leaving."

"How do you intend to stop me? Just out of curiosity."

Verity's nostrils flared with her sharp, angry breaths. "Goddamn you, I'll make you forget anything but this room!"

With sudden violence, she tore open his shirt. Buttons flew everywhere, clattering across the floor, bouncing under the bed. Garrett's eyes widened in surprise, but he didn't try to stop her. Verity ripped his shirt away. She kissed him feverishly.

Garrett returned her kiss, but her mouth left his, hungrily devouring the flesh of his neck. Her trembling fingers tugged at his trousers.

She sank to her knees in front of him and slid her hand beneath his open trousers, beneath his drawers. Garrett watched her, spellbound, as she drew his member forth. His eyes closed when her fingers tightened around his thick length.

"You'll never leave me," she whispered raggedly. Her lips just brushed the hard, blunt tip of his staff. Her tongue flicked out to caress him, to tease him.

Garrett groaned from low and deep in his throat. Bright sun flooded in their windows, casting light of varying hues on her red and brown hair. He saw her pink tongue lash out at him, her lips enveloping him. Her eyes never left his.

He felt her warm, wet mouth around his manhood. She was teasing him. Not quite fully taking him, licking him. Garrett trembled. He could see the swell of her breasts above her bodice. Her hair, tied behind her head, fell in a thick bunch over one shoulder. Tendrils escaped to tease her forehead, to tease his flesh.

Garrett's hands were shaking as he cupped her beautiful head, holding her close, feeling the movements as she swirled her tongue around his aching tip. He wanted to force a conclusion to her sweet torment, yet he wanted it to last forever.

His head tipped back, the thick cords of his neck straining as he fought to prolong the pleasure. Every muscle in his body was pulled taut, quaking for release. She took him deeper as her tongue caressed, urged. Her hand closed tight around his base, softly touching the sensitive sac beneath.

Garrett's knees quaked as she increased her pressure, the urgency of her greedy caress. She took him hungrily. He couldn't tear his eyes from the sight. That soft, wide mouth wrapped around him, those blazing eyes, daring him to defy her now. He couldn't.

"Verity . . . I can't stop." His voice was a harsh groan. She sucked harder. He wanted to catch her shoulders, to put her on her back, to fill her. But he couldn't move. Her eyes glowed with impending victory. Every muscle in his body quivered, he groaned, his fingers clenched in her hair.

"God, woman, you own me." Her hand moved with her mouth in agonizingly sweet friction. He couldn't stand it much longer, she knew. Her tongue lashed the tip again, teasing. She brushed her lips back and forth, then took him again, all of him. She took him with greedy pleasure, milking his climax as a harsh cry tore from his throat.

The magic stilled. But Verity didn't let him stop. She released her grasp, rose to her feet and took his mouth in a passionate kiss. She kissed his face, pressing close. He felt her demanding heartbeat.

In one motion, Garrett lifted her into his arms and carried her to the bed. He should be spent. Her harem skill had driven him into oblivion. Yet here he was, again, wanting her, ready to fill her.

They didn't speak. He didn't bother to undress her. He just pushed her bodice aside to kiss her breast, even as he kicked his boots off, his loose trousers. Even as he spread her satin thighs and entered her yielding body. He drove into her, and she cried out in hoarse, ragged pleasure.

Her hips moved with his, their bodies quaking seeking pleasure, giving pleasure. Final pleasure. They filled each other's need, and he gave her all that he had. Garrett felt her around him, alive and volatile, furiously loving him, desperate to keep him.

"For this moment, we are joined forever," he murmured into her hair. "Forever." Garrett's body spilled into hers, and she received him with twisting, searing joy. They met together there, on planes of bliss, held together, then faded back into their bed, into Maryland. Home.

And he was leaving.

"Stay with me."

Garrett kissed her forehead. "I'll be with you always."

Verity squirmed away from him and sat up. "Truly?"

Garrett winced. She had taken him literally. "In spirit."

Verity's small face hardened, her full lips tightening into a little ball of fury. "So you've seduced me, and now you're leaving, just like that?"

Garrett tried not to smile, but he did, anyway. "Seduced you?" He paused, as if searching his memory for accurate facts. "Seduced *you?* Who slammed who against the wall?"

Verity wasn't interested in facts. "You've had your way with me. Now you're leaving. Perhaps if you left a few bills by my bedstand . . ."

Garrett laughed. He seized her hand. "You'd be worth more than a few." She tried to slap him. Tears stung her eyes, glistening on her cheeks. Garrett caught that hand, and kissed it, too.

"Ever violent, Sweet Love."

Verity twisted away from him. She adjusted her dress. "Leave, then. Go back to the damned war. Back to hell, for all I care. I suppose you think I'll be here when you get back."

"That is my hope."

Verity's shoulders slumped. "Please don't go."

Garrett drew her into his arms. She didn't resist. "Verity, I have to go. It's something I can't explain. But I've known it all along. Since the moment I woke up. And, no, I didn't tell you. Mainly because I feared this moment. I feared saying good-bye, looking at you, and knowing I'd have to live on the memory of your face for God knows how long."

"Memory can't compare with what we've just done."

"God knows."

"You can't leave."

"The war is ending, Verity. Maybe not tomorrow, but it's ending. Phil Sheridan is an honest man. He sees an ending. He thinks I can help bring about that day. I have to do my part."

"What if you come back not loving me again? What if you don't come back at all?"

"I loved you, Little Angel. I just hurt like hell. And I needed you, but I didn't know it. I didn't think anything could help me, but you did. I won't make the mistake of keeping my heart from you again. And as for the other, I'll do my damnedest to come back, I promise you."

"I'm very mad at you." Her voice was small.

"I know."

"I don't know if I can forgive you for leaving me." Verity sniffled and leaned against him.

"Please try." Garrett kissed her forehead again. "Now look at me—I want to remember your face."

Verity looked at him and sighed. "You're so handsome, you know."

"Thank you." Garrett smiled. "Now, kiss me, whether you can forgive me or not. Fortunately, thanks to your earlier ministrations, I require little else."

Verity kissed him. "I'll always love you."

"That's what I wanted to hear."

They looked into each other's eyes. They had parted before. They both knew the pain to come. "I hate waiting."

"We have to face our worst fears, my love. I'm afraid that I can't make any difference, afraid my strength will give out and someone will fall who wouldn't have fallen otherwise. You, my Watkins, are terrified you can't change the winds of fate. Well, Angel, you can't. They'll just blow on over you. But there's something you've got to remember. You're a part of that wind. You don't have to fight it. It was blowing your way all along."

Garrett kissed her again, silencing her tears. He caught her face in his hands, running the pad of his thumb across her soft cheek. "Good-bye, Mrs. Knox. If those winds blow true, the next time we meet, the war will be over. Good-bye."

Tears streamed over her cheeks. "Colonel Knox, good-bye."

A thick, black cloud swept inward from the Potomac as Garrett swung into the saddle and turned his horse from Fox Run. Rain began, falling in a farmer's mist. Garrett rode at Phil Sheridan's side. Sheridan's men were already talking, discussing battle plans, strategy.

But Garrett slowed his mount once, and looked back. He saw his beautiful home in the rain, he felt the woman inside. *God, let her wait, let her still love me when I come home. Because I will come home. I will come home.*

Chapter Seventeen

Verity couldn't leave her room, couldn't speak to anyone. She cried until her throat seemed to bleed. Someone knocked. Verity didn't answer. Candace peeked in the door.

"Can I come in?"

"No."

Candace came in, anyway. She sat beside Verity and patted her shoulder. "Do you know what I would give to see your brother, just for a moment? I know it's hard, Verity. But you've been together. You'll be together again. You must believe in that, in the way the purest Christians believe in God."

Verity burst into tears and sobbed. "I can't stand it, Candace. I'm not like you. I hate waiting."

"No more than I do. But I love Robert enough to endure it."

"What if you have to wait forever?" Verity didn't mean to be brutal, but her nerves were raw. Candace didn't flinch.

"Then I will wait forever."

"Captain Hallowell, there's someone I'd like you to meet."

Verity stood in the door of Ethan's room. He looked over at her dismally, his hands folded on his breast.

"I'm not really up for company, Watkins."

"This isn't company. It's your new nurse."

"I don't require a nurse."

"Yes, you do." Ethan started to object, but Verity marched into his room. "It may not have occurred to you, Captain, but tending you can be tiring. I've got Caleb, and Ivy's overseeing the work on the veterans' home. Not that she knows what she's doing, but still . . . and Candace is an unmarried woman. There are some things she can't do."

Ethan blanched, more pained than ever. "I didn't mean to inconvenience you. Forgive me. I should return to Nurse Abigail's establishment."

"Nurse Abigail has deserted her post," said Verity. "We've hired someone from Armory Square Hospital to oversee the establishment, but it's not working very well. We have to bring those men here."

"I see."

"The new nurse is the only way. She'll be invaluable to us."

Ethan sighed. "Very well."

"Then you'll meet her?"

"If I must."

Verity called, and a woman entered. Ethan eyed her without pleasure. *An ugly woman,* he thought. *Not mean looking like Nurse Abigail. But ugly. Brown hair, pulled severely back. Oiled down and slicked. Disgusting.*

Ethan's gaze went up and down the nurse's figure. Not just overweight, but bulging in peculiar places beneath her dark gray dress. Large, hanging breasts, protruding hips. And her cheeks, bulging like those of a greedy chipmunk with too many acorns. A chipmunk wearing round spectacles.

"Where in God's name did you find her?"

"Ethan!" Verity glanced nervously at the nurse, who frowned. "This is Miss Maybelle. She's kind enough to donate her services to our wounded—"

Miss, thought Ethan. *No, this woman wouldn't be married. Except maybe to a blind man.* He wondered if her disposition was equally unattractive. Miss Maybelle had a strange expression on her chubby face. It straightened and she waddled across the room to his bedside.

"Captain Hallowell, is it? Rather long. May I call you 'Ethan?' "

"No."

"Ethan it is."

No. Her disposition was equally horrid. Ethan frowned and glanced at Verity, who was easing back toward his door. Exiting.

"Miss Maybelle—"

"I prefer Belle."

"Miss Maybelle. I appreciate your generous nature. But I require no tending."

"Feed yourself, can you?"

"Well, I can't make my own meals, if that's what you mean," snapped Ethan. Verity left the room, but Ethan's attention remained fixed on Miss Maybelle.

"It's obvious you don't bathe." Belle paused. "Mrs. Knox!"

Ethan struggled to sit up, to silence her. "For heaven's sake, woman, lower your voice. One doesn't bellow at the top of one's lungs for the lady of the house."

Belle ignored his protests, and Verity appeared at the door. She looked a little sheepish. Ethan could see why. If he'd stuck a wounded man with this harridan, he'd be a little pale, too.

"You called, Miss Maybelle?"

"She prefers Belle," Ethan put in sarcastically.

"I called. I want three hot bathing tubs readied. One for delousing, one for scrubbing, and one for soaking."

"You don't look *that* dirty," said Ethan.

Again, Belle ignored Ethan. Verity nodded, and darted away.

"I hope that water isn't for my benefit," said Ethan. "Because if it is, it's wasted."

"Obviously you haven't glanced in a mirror recently," said Belle. Ethan didn't answer. He hadn't looked in a mirror in over a year.

"I don't need a bath."

A loud, derisive snort cut him off. "I hope there's a scrub brush strong enough."

"Madam, I will not bathe." Ethan set his jaw. Belle set hers, too. An impasse.

Two stable hands brought the tubs while Belle supervised. She called the other women to assist. Mildred took one look at Ethan, then at the tub. "Dear God ... I can't be a part of this." She darted away.

"What an idiot!" remarked Belle. "The rest of you ladies, prepare. I want that first vat filled for delousing. Double dose."

Ivy stirred the steaming water, filled pitchers. Verity stacked soap, and Candace readied towels. Caleb wiggled delightedly around on the floor, then pulled himself up on the edge of the tub and splashed. Belle stood with her hands on her protruding hips, tapping a small foot impatiently. Ethan lay glowering.

"You look like a coven of witches. And I'm the sacrifice."

They ignored him. Belle surveyed the work. "Ready. Miss Webster, you'll have to leave, being unmarried. Take the baby, too. We don't want him splashed by louse water."

Candace looked a little disappointed. "Very well." She picked up Caleb. "We'll go for a walk out by the pastures, shall we?"

"It is time," said Belle. She turned toward Ethan. He clenched his fists.

"I told you. I'm not touching that water."

"You will bathe."

"Why, if I prefer myself this way?"

"Because you stink," said Belle. Ethan winced.

"You *could* use a bath," said Verity carefully.

"And a haircut," added Belle. She held up shears and a razor. "You, sir, are disgusting."

"I will not bathe."

Belle straightened and glared. "Ladies, if you will excuse us for the period of five minutes . . ."

Verity and Ivy scurried away. Belle waited until they were gone. Then she seated herself at Ethan's side. "Why not?"

Ethan's jaw tightened. "I am not in the habit of explaining myself."

"Have you washed since your injury?"

"No."

"Why not?"

Ethan didn't answer.

"Have you changed your clothes, even once?" asked Belle.

"I believe I was dressed in this hospital wear in Washington. I don't really remember."

"That was over a year ago," Belle reminded him.

"It was."

"This is foul beyond words." Belle studied his face. Ethan didn't look at her. "You haven't seen yourself, have you?"

Ethan glanced her way. "I've been told I resemble a dirty Viking."

"A legless Viking. You haven't looked at your legs, have you?"

Ethan paled beneath his filthy beard. His lips tightened. "As you say, Madam, there's nothing to look at."

"There is. There's the point where you were cut. There's the flesh wrapped around and sewn together."

Ethan shook his head. His throat tightened. Belle didn't stop. "It's probably a blunt end. Your wound didn't fester, which is fortunate. It's probably quite clean, like the tip of a finger."

"Stop." His voice sounded raw, strained.

"Well, Ethan, it's time you looked at yourself. Because it is yourself now. Maybe you had beautiful legs. You probably did, because you're a handsome man. But they're gone. What you've got left is something else. But I doubt it's as ugly as you think."

Belle rose. "Mrs. Knox. Miss . . . Ivy!"

"Jesus," muttered Ethan. "What a voice!" A muffled, fuzzy voice that sounded . . . Southern.

"You're not some rebel agent come to torment our side, are you?"

"Where I was born is of no concern."

"Like hell."

Verity and Ivy returned. Belle tested the bath water. "He's ready."

"I'm not."

"Either you help us, or I'll call the farmhands. They'll strip you and shove you in. I'd rather not do that."

Ethan knew she would. She was just that evil. Verity and Ivy exchanged pained glances, but they didn't argue. Ethan felt deserted. Why, when Verity had no qualms about slamming Nurse Abigail against the wall, did she let this dreadful Maybelle walk all over him?

"How do you suggest I get from this bed to that tub?" asked Ethan.

"You'll try. And we'll help. You can do more than you think," said Belle. "But first you have to undress."

"Certainly not."

"Now."

Ivy stepped forward. "Listen, Little Prince. I've seen enough men without clothes to make it just another sunset. You ain't got nothing I ain't seen before."

"I won't look," promised Verity earnestly.

"And I," said Belle, "couldn't care less about your naked body, I promise you. I, too, have seen male flesh without clothes.

I've seen enough amputated limbs to make them as common as a whole leg. Now take off your clothes.''

Ethan hesitated. Belle started unbuttoning his shirt. He swatted her hand as if it were a bug. She wore white gloves. Infuriatingly perfect white gloves. Ethan removed his own shirt.

''Whoa!'' said Ivy. ''You've been lying there, doing nothing, and you still look this good? That's youth for you.''

Ethan had more trouble with his trousers. Belle tried to help, but he refused. Better the prostitute.

Ivy unfastened Ethan's loose pants. ''Now, don't you be thinking of it, Captain. I done seen male 'secrets' before. Ain't no man who's all that different from the next.''

Ivy tugged off his trousers as Ethan closed his eyes. Ivy whistled. ''Then again, I ain't seen nothing that pretty in a good *long* while.''

Ethan sputtered in acute embarrassment, but Belle laughed. The two women helped him into the wheelchair, then lowered him into the tub.

''Scrub!'' commanded Belle. Verity turned around and Ethan longed to disappear. He sat miserably in a cramped wooden tub while Ivy deloused him and scrubbed him vigorously with a floor brush. Belle soaped his back with a sponge.

''What do I do?'' asked Verity.

''Rinse!'' Belle drew back, holding her sponge aloft as Verity dumped water over Ethan's head. ''Into the next tub.''

Verity turned around again as they transported Ethan into the clean water. At least she allowed him a measure of dignity. Unlike the evil harridan, Miss Maybelle. ''Scrub again!''

Ethan felt more visible in this water. He held a cloth over his genitals, but Verity saw his severed legs. ''Oh,'' she said in surprise. ''It's really quite neat, isn't it? I wonder if he can be fitted with wooden legs?''

Ethan cringed. Everyone had seen his legs but him. And he never would. He kept his vision focused outward.

''It's been done,'' said Ivy as she lathered Ethan's head.

Verity shook her head. ''You look like a suffering puppy.''

Ethan peeked up through the soap suds to glare at her.

''Now we cut his hair,'' announced Belle. ''And that horrid beard must go.''

Ivy produced shears and hacked away until Ethan's hair fitted neatly to the back of his neck. She left it rather long in the front, over his eyebrows.

Verity studied him intently, without shame. Ethan had never felt so exposed. "You have a flair, Ivy."

Ivy stood back to survey her handiwork. "There's nothing like a sensual, young, hard-bodied male to stir the senses." Ethan cringed, but Ivy sighed. "Ain't you a sight, Little Prince? Now, for the beard."

That disappeared, too, but Ethan was reluctant to relinquish his mustache. "My mustache remains."

"Why?" asked Verity.

"Because he'd be baby-faced without it," suggested Belle. "Too pretty."

Ethan frowned. "It stays."

"As you wish, Captain," said Ivy. "But it gets a trim."

Verity circled around the tub, studying every angle, advising if Ivy missed a spot. Ethan wondered if these women had any sense of privacy.

"You look like the young officer I met at Stoneman's Switch." Her voice trailed. "But different, still . . . you've changed, Ethan Hallowell."

Ethan's jaw clenched. "That much, I knew."

"You're not a boy anymore."

Ethan endured yet another wave of embarrassment. He hated the fact that he blushed so easily. He made certain the cloth covered his genitals completely, and cleared his throat.

For a reason that had never been clear, he'd always felt the size of his personal parts was excessive and unbefitting a gentleman. It was just like Ivy to point it out amongst a group of ladies. Well, one lady and one harridan. But still. . . .

"You look exactly like Uncle Cabot," said Verity. "I think you're even handsomer than Westley was."

Ethan glanced up at her.

"Who's Westley?" asked Belle as she gave Ethan a final scrub.

"My brother," said Ethan. He looked irritably over his shoulder at the toiling nurse. "I am illegitimate. A bastard. The foul seed of illicit lovers. No doubt it will offend you to tend such a man."

Belle looked truly surprised. She glanced at Verity, who sighed and shrugged. "Truly?"

"It's true," said Ethan. "As everyone else has learned my shame, you might as well know. So you can find other employment," he added as a broad—untaken—hint.

"Your real father must have been handsome," said Belle. "And arrogant. Now hold still while we move you to the last tub."

"Why? If you scrub me any more, I'll be bleeding more than when the rebels shot me," Ethan grumbled as Ivy and Belle moved him again, this time into the longer tub.

"You're going to soak." Belle nodded to Verity and Ivy. "You have done your part, ladies. I want him to soak for at least a half hour. I'll call you when he's ready to be moved, if I can't do it myself. Thank you."

Verity touched Ethan's head. "It's good to see you looking like your old self, Cousin."

"It's about time," added Ivy. She patted Belle's arm fondly. "Little Miss, you've done wonders. God bless you."

'Little Miss.' Why would anyone choose that term for his tormentor? Ethan thought. The other women left. "You could depart also, Madam," he informed Belle.

"My duty is here." Belle hesitated. "What do you think of your legs?" Ethan kept his eyes upward. He hadn't looked down once during the procedure.

"Look at them," said Belle.

"There's no need."

"Well, if you don't mind the fact they're purple—"

Ethan looked down. Not purple. Cream and pink, like the rest of his body. They ended, as Belle said, like fingers without fingernails. Blunt and solid. Not as muscular as he remembered, but not weak, either.

"This is what you are now," said Belle quietly. "You'll find you can get around well once you start trying. Maybe you'll even make use of wooden legs. You can certainly use this chair. As I understand it, Colonel Knox expected you to help with his veterans' home."

"Doing what?" asked Ethan grumpily. "Swatting flies?"

"Get yourself up, and find out. Of course, you could just lie here and do nothing. Let others support you. But I'd think you might want to do something for the ones who have done so much for you."

Ethan didn't answer. He didn't want to burden Verity, nor take anything from Garrett that he couldn't pay back. Maybe he had waited a bit long to offer what minimal assistance he could.

* * *

"What's this?" Belle was cleaning Ethan's room. Unnecessarily, he thought. Candace kept it spotless. He looked around to see what she was doing. She was fumbling around in his bedstand, rifling through Bess Hartman's unopened letters.

"Unhand those, Madam!" Ethan snatched the letters from her little hand. "Dear God, the impudence!"

"Written by the same hand," noted Belle. "A woman's hand, eh? Mrs. Knox tells me you've got a sweetheart."

"That, Madam, is none of your concern."

"Don't treat the girl with much respect, do you?" Belle's chubby cheeks allowed for a frown. " 'Course, Mrs. Knox tells me the girl was a rebel. That probably explains why you're so lax with her heart."

Ethan's eyes blazed with fury. He couldn't think of anything harsh and cutting enough to say. Maybelle probably wouldn't be offended, anyway. She'd just go on, insulting him, prying where she didn't belong. . . .

"I suppose you just used her, then cast her aside," Belle continued. "Ditched her like a worn out plow."

"Madam!" Ethan struggled to sit up. He wanted to reach for her, to squeeze her neck through her high, starched collar. "You will, from this point onward, mind your own affairs and remove yourself from mine!"

"Ha," said Belle. "Your affairs *are* mine. That's the nature of my employment. So, why'd you abandon her, anyway?"

Belle continued cleaning, fussing with his pillows, arranging flower vases to more pleasing positions.

"I did not 'abandon' her," said Ethan icily. "I found it necessary to end our engagement."

"It's the same thing."

"Not at all." Ethan paused. "No woman deserves to be stuck with a man in my situation. Bess is a beautiful, sweet-tempered girl. She would feel the need to stay at my side, to tend me."

"It seems you didn't give her that choice."

"How could I bear to see her face, her perfect face, looking at me now?" Ethan's voice softened, his eyes closed. "How could I see her, knowing what might have been between us, remembering what was, so briefly?"

"So you've left her with memories," said Belle softly. A wave of sympathy crossed her bulging face.

"I left her with the chance to find something better with another man."

Belle took Bess's letters from Ethan's hand. "Didn't even bother to read these," she observed in disgust. "Why, if you care so much as you claim?"

Ethan didn't answer.

"You don't care," decided Belle. "If she's sick, if she's in trouble . . ."

Ethan glanced at the letters. "I'm sure it's just sympathy, what she feels she must say."

"Let's see." Belle sat down and tore open a letter. Ethan gasped. "Don't you dare, woman!"

Belle ignored him and read a little way down the letter. "She claims to love you. Heaven knows why. She confesses that she felt relief when she learned of your injury, because you weren't dead, and you wouldn't be able to go back to war. Silly girl."

Ethan swallowed hard. He fought tears. *Stop loving me, damn you.*

Belle ripped open another of Bess's letters. "In this one, she wants to know if you harbor any fond feelings for her." Belle hesitated. "I could write back and tell her you don't."

"You'll do no such thing."

Belle moved to the next envelope. "She tells you here that two of her brothers were killed, in the space of one week. At Spotsylvania. Two widows now. The younger one took ill soon after and died herself, leaving a six-month-old baby."

Ethan's eyes filled with tears. He couldn't speak, not even to tell Belle to stop reading and reporting on Bess Hartman's life.

"Yep. She still loves you. She hopes with time you'll understand how much she needs to be with you. That love overcomes all odds."

"That is enough," said Ethan.

"Girl didn't have much to do but write, I'd say," commented Belle. "Here, let's see what she said in the last. Fairly recent, a month ago."

Belle read Bess's last letter slowly, while Ethan waited. "Hmm," said Belle as she read the last page. Ethan fidgeted, wondering. "Well, well," said Belle.

"What?" he burst out in annoyance.

"She's letting you have your way."

Ethan's face fell, but then he steeled his expression. "That's for the best."

"She's letting you go, to live your life as you please. She's promising to get on with hers, too. Says she won't be writing again. But if you ever want, she makes sure you've got her mailing particulars."

Ethan drew a long, tight breath. "Well, then. It's over. She's all right. She's forgetting me."

"Forgotten you, I'd say," remarked Belle. "This was written more than a month ago."

Ethan didn't comment. Well, he'd given her no reason to keep hoping. There was no reason to hope. He didn't want her to pine for him. He wanted her to be free. If, deep in his heart, he would never be free, well, it didn't matter now.

Bess's farewell changed something in Ethan Hallowell. He took to his chair and maneuvered himself around the estate house. He adapted the chair, with the large wheels in the front for better mobility. He ordered Belle around, instructing her to move objects in his way.

"Is there anything else? Maybe you'd like the staircase moved a little to the left?" Belle threw up her hands. "I'm taking a break, Mrs. Knox. If he gets on your nerves—and he will—you have leave to toss him out the door. Without his chair."

Verity laughed, but Ethan glowered. "The woman is a gargantuan fat spider," he said loudly as Belle stomped up the stairs to her bedroom. "Nurse Abigail was an angel of mercy by comparison."

"Ethan. How rude!" Verity repressed a smile. Caleb came tottering by, already walking at ten months. It was late in November, cool and beautiful in Maryland. "Let's go outside, shall we? I want to see how the advice you gave the workmen is working."

"The roof has probably caved in," said Ethan, but he wheeled himself out after her.

"It looks good," said Verity. She sat in an iron-laced lawn chair as Caleb toddled toward the pasture. Verity got up, retrieved him, and gestured to a butterfly, which he pursued instead.

"Have you heard from the major? Sorry, the colonel?" asked Ethan.

"Not since they drove the rebels out of the Shenandoah Valley in

October," said Verity. "He sounded better than last year, though." Verity looked over at Ethan and smiled. "At least, he doesn't seem to think Caleb is your son anymore."

Ethan's mouth dropped, and his eyes widened into blue pools of shock. "My son?" he whispered.

"He was a bit suspicious because of finding us naked that morning by the Rappahannock. It was very silly of him, I know, but since neither one of us remember what happened—"

"I remember," groaned Ethan. "God, I never dreamed. After all, when a woman has a man like the major—colonel, I mean— Why on earth would you want me?"

"There are many reasons to want you, Ethan. At least one, according to Ivy." Verity chuckled at his shocked expression. "But you're right. I loved Garrett. He should have known better. What do you mean, you remember? Everything?"

"Yes," said Ethan. He looked pained again. "I remembered later that day."

"Why in hell didn't you say anything?"

"I didn't realize the situation caused conflict between you. You married, after all."

"Garrett accepted Caleb, whether he was your son or his own."

"Garrett Knox is a good man." Ethan's eyes watered with unshed tears. "And Caleb is a fortunate child."

"What did you remember?"

"I hesitate to say."

"Ethan," warned Verity. "Out with it. Garrett might not dwell on Caleb's paternity, but I wouldn't mind being able to assure him. What happened that night?"

Ethan drew a long, miserable breath. "Nothing 'happened.' We talked."

"About what?"

"Personal matters." Ethan sounded evasive. Verity clenched her teeth.

"What matters?"

"I confessed to you certain things concerning my relationship with Bess. You gave advice, having to do with your relationship with Garrett Knox."

Verity closed her eyes. "You were a virgin, unlike most men who visit prostitutes for sexual experience. You wondered if you were doing it right. So I told you, graphically, what Garrett did to me."

Ethan's face went from white to bright red. "God, Watkins, would you please just forget—again—that conversation?"

"I had forgotten, until you reminded me. Well, well. What a relief!"

The winter passed long, but steadily. Garrett sent weekly letters to Verity, and she responded to every one. She reported that Ethan and 'Miss Maybelle' were continuing an ever intensifying banter, but that Ethan had proved to be an adept carpenter. He'd done good work on the inner spaces of the veterans' home—once again issuing orders that were ignored.

The war progressed steadily, too. In March, Sheridan's cavalry finished Jubal Early's Confederates and cleared the Shenandoah Valley. By April, Garrett's men were back with the Army of the Potomac, around the sieged city of Petersburg.

Lee broke free. In desperation, he tried to head south. Frustrated by Grant's army, he moved west again. West toward Appomattox.

Garrett felt the war's end. Tired, he carried Verity's picture over his heart. He left his tent, took a deep breath of the Virginia spring air, then went to where the officers' horses were tethered.

"Well, now, old fellow, it looks like we'll see the end of this, after all."

The bay horse touched his soft nose to Garrett's shoulder and gave a firm push. Garrett fished a dry apple out of his pocket and fed the animal. "Not much, I'm afraid. The rebs have cleaned everything out."

The horse returned to his meager feed while Garrett idly stroked the long neck. Under Sheridan's command, the Union cavalry had defeated George Pickett at Five Forks. A few days later, the cavalry blocked Lee as he tried to escape south, stilling the rebel hope of uniting with Joe Johnston's army.

Lee was retreating westward now, and the Union raced to cut him off, to surround him. The Army of Northern Virginia was finally weakening.

"Colonel, we've got the word to move," called a young major.

"Thank you, Rogerson," said Garrett. "Saddle up."

Phil Sheridan rode up, his face bright, smiling. Victory swarmed in the air. "Ready, Colonel?" he asked pleasantly. Happily.

"I am."

"Good news," continued Sheridan. "General Grant took Lee's

rear guard yesterday, in battle at Sayler's Creek. Damned fierce fighting. I've heard our esteemed general has begun corresponding with General Lee on the matter of surrender.''

Garrett just stared. His heart thudded, and his limbs felt light. ''Indeed.'' Now he was smiling, too.

''I thought you'd enjoy hearing that.'' Sheridan paused, his smile faded. ''I'm afraid it's not all good news, though. I received a message meant for you last night. From the Twentieth Massachusetts. It seems two men from your old company are down. Don't know if you remember them . . . damn fine story, though.''

Garrett waited. No, the war hadn't ended yet. ''What happened?''

''The Twentieth was in the thick of things at Sayler's Creek. Rebs putting up a fight, as always. Small group of our boys got cut off. Ragged sergeant held the rebs off 'til his boys ran out of ammunition. They fought with bayonets. But you know a lot of those boys discarded bayonets, thinking them no damned use. This sergeant, he ended up fighting with a guitar, if you can believe it. Slamming rebs with it like a club.''

''A guitar,'' said Garrett. ''John.''

''Brave fellow, he was,'' said Sheridan. ''Held them off, all right. But he was blinded in the process. Canister blast. Won't ever see again.''

Garrett took a long, weary breath. *Blind.*

''Hell of a story,'' Sheridan went on. ''Colored fellow went back for him, carried him out of there. Got shot up, too.''

''Jefferson . . . does he live?''

''Not sure,'' said Sheridan. ''We'll be riding past the first surgeon's tents, if you want to stop in. Don't take too long, though. Your orders are to wind up beyond our circle. We'll be closing in around Appomattox Station, cutting off Lee's retreat if we can. And we can. I want you up ahead, out a ways to pick up any rebs who've made it there before Lee.''

''Yes, Sir,'' said Garrett. He didn't feel happy now. It had gone on too damned long. *Not Jefferson. God, the world needs Jefferson Davis. One man who can't be beaten, who's already won. Let him live.*

Garrett couldn't imagine telling Verity. No. It couldn't happen. If anyone could beat death, it was Jefferson.

* * *

Jefferson knelt beside John, his musket over his shoulder. Garrett saw him. He stared a long while, and then he laughed. "Davis, it takes more than one army to set you back, doesn't it?"

Jefferson looked up, and he smiled faintly, but he looked tired. "Good to see you, Colonel. You've heard about John, I take it."

"Heard about both of you. Sheridan tells me you're quite a hero. Putting you up for the medal of honor, I'm told."

Jefferson's eyes brightened somewhat, but he restrained his pride. Garrett knelt beside John and took his hand. "Sergeant, they say you put up a hell of a fight."

John's head was wrapped in a bandage. Blood stained his ragged face. "Colonel, you're doing well, too, as I hear it. Made something of our damned cavalry, after all."

"We're paying the rebs back for their laughter, all right," said Garrett. "They won't be calling us fat shop clerks on ponies anymore."

"Good to hear it," said John. His low voice sounded empty. Garrett squeezed his hand.

"This will be done in a few days. Then we'll head back to Maryland. I want you men to come with me. Stay with us until you decide what you want to do with peacetime."

"Don't want to put nobody out," said John obstinately.

"That's right," agreed Jefferson. "We don't need charity."

"And you won't get it," said Garrett. "I've got enough work to do for both of you. Verity tells me that Ethan Hallowell has made himself quite a carpenter. He adopted his wheelchair to make it more mobile."

"The Captain had best be better at carpentry than giving orders," decided John. A smile curved his angular face. "It will be good to see him again. So to speak. Him, and young Watkins."

Garrett patted his shoulder. "Then come to Fox Run. We're all going to need some time. Some time to let this all unwind. Find out what we are, after war."

"Thank you, Colonel," said Jefferson. "We'll be there."

* * *

Lee was surrounded. The great Army of Northern Virginia had dwindled to less than thirty thousand men. Thirty thousand men who would stand by their beloved general until the bitter end.

"Looks to be over, don't it, Colonel?" noted an elderly lieutenant. Garrett's cavalrymen arranged on a hill crest, looking back toward Appomattox. A giant crush of Federal infantry waited to move against the tattered rebels.

"The end draws nigh," sighed Garrett.

"Sir!" Major Rogerson charged up the hill, panting in unison with his weary mount. "Sir, there's a group of them up yonder. Faced off with our infantry, and by God, them rebs whipped our boys but good. Damn, they don't give up easily. Major Thompkins is leading our foot soldiers, and he's in a fury, I'll tell you. Personally, I'd say it's because he's such a damned fool. Sending his boys up against them rebs, as if we'd already won the day. Well, sure enough, the rebs knocked Thompkins' boys back, moved on, and kept on fighting . . ."

Garrett listened to Rogerson's rushed speech, shook his head, then drew a breath. Rogerson didn't bother to breathe.

"Major Thompkins is now, and always has been, an idiot," said Garrett. "Seems to think killing rebels is sport. No respect. Well, it serves him right."

"Says he's going to blast away every last one of them. If he catches them, that is," said Rogerson.

Garrett rose in his saddle and turned to his men. "Gentlemen, for the last time, I ask you to ride with me. One final mission. God willing, let it be one of peace."

Garrett saw Major Thompkins readying his infantry. His face looked redder than normal below his black beard. "Major, this will be a cavalry operation," said Garrett without preamble. "Report to your commander."

Thompkins' face flushed darker than normal. "Colonel Knox, we are now in the process of surrounding those damned rebels. This is my charge."

"Major," said Garrett with emphasis. "Report to your command." Garrett looked toward the small rebel band, forming in a circle where the high crest of the pasture met the forest behind. So few men, yet they'd held off an infantry attack nearly ten times the numbers.

"Rebels to the end," sighed Garrett, not without admiration. He ignored Thompkins and turned to his own men. "Gentlemen, we ride in. Hold your fire. Not one carbine goes off unless ordered. Is that understood?"

No one objected, but Thompkins threw down his saber. "Damn it, Colonel, you've got to finish those grey backed bastards. Send them into hell where they belong. Goddamned gentlemen," he sneered.

Garrett assumed Major Thompkins resented Southern gentility because it so obviously eluded him. "A gentleman has as much value as any other man," said Garrett. "All men deserve the same consideration. That, Major, is why we've fought these godforsaken years of bloody war."

Garrett gave the major no further consideration. "Forward, in a wedge. Prepare to spread out, surround the enemy."

Garrett urged his bay horse into a gallop, and led his soldiers up the slope. The wind whipped his face, through his open jacket. His saber clattered against the saddle. *One last charge,* he thought. *A charge into freedom.*

The rebels were waiting. Ready, as always. A ragged group of men, gray and butternut, stood poised. One horse. Long limbed, thin. Black. Garrett sank his weight back into his saddle. His horse stopped as his cavalrymen skidded to less certain halts around him.

Garrett looked down the black hole barrel of the rebel commander's Colt revolver. Garrett leapt from his horse. A slow smile grew on his face. Then he drew his saber and lowered it in salute.

The slow smile was returned. Jared Knox drew his own saber and bowed.

"So it's over. God, I thought it would never end." Jared sat in Garrett's tent, leaning against his worn saddle. He looked tired, a little thin, like every rebel Garrett had seen, but defeat hadn't broken him.

The rebels took surrender with as much dignity as they had seized the war's great victories. Appomattox Court House was calm. Rebels and Yankees mingled together, discussing old battles.

"More coffee, Cousin?" asked Garrett. He poured himself a half-portion, but Jared shook his head.

"Thank you, no. I find, having been without, that it's hard to take in large doses."

Their eyes met, blue and gray. "It's over." They said it at the same time.

Garrett thought Jared had changed. He didn't look older, but his smile wasn't as quick. Jared Knox had suffered. He had found himself wanting something, for the first time in his life, that didn't come easily. Something he had to fight to hold. "So, little Cousin, when do I meet your wife?"

Jared had married, after all. A Yankee girl, in the middle of war. Garrett hadn't the nerve to ask if she was his spy.

"Pippa is in Richmond with my mother and sisters," said Jared. "Maybe, now that the war is over . . ." He didn't finish his thought, just closed his blue eyes and sighed.

Jared looked over at Garrett. "And you, Cousin? God, I never thought I'd see you married. Rob Talmadge's little sister. Elegant Boston aristocrat. Maybe a barmaid, but a lady? No, it's beyond me. It should be interesting to meet her."

Garrett chuckled at Jared's interpretation of Verity. "Actually, you've met."

Jared sat up, searching his memory. "Have we? What, in England? That's where I met Rob. I don't remember a girl, though."

"Not in England." Garrett drank the last of his coffee, then folded his arms over his chest. "Virginia."

"I don't think so."

"If you're searching your mind for an elegant Boston aristocrat, you'll never pick her out. No, think of something else entirely. A particularly dirty face, free-floating impertinent remarks that hit too close to the truth. And a damned good shooting eye."

Jared stared. "What?"

"Do you recall enticing a group of my men to desert their posts for the night, my friend? Luring them over into Fredericksburg with the promise of a night's dancing?"

"Ah, of course," said Jared. "An enjoyable evening. Yes, I remember. Old burly sergeant. Stiff-backed officer. Young Watkins—"

"Watkins." Garrett paused. "My wife."

A doubtful smile crossed Jared's lips. As if this might be a side of Garrett he'd never suspected, and couldn't believe. "Watkins?"

"Watkins."

"No."

Garrett nodded.

"You didn't marry Watkins."

"I married Watkins."

Jared shook his head, doubting his own senses. "But, Rob Talmadge's sister—"

"One and the same." Garrett drew out his picture of Verity and their son. He passed it to Jared.

Jared examined the picture, he looked at Garrett. "This woman is incredibly beautiful. Watkins was small and scrawny. With a mustache."

Garrett laughed. "I suppose that was the day I knew I loved her. Not just wanted her, you understand. Not just intrigued by her. But loved her. It was that mustache."

"This is something I never quite expected to hear, Garrett. That you fell in love with a soldier because of his—her—mustache. Maybe because of her lovely bosom, even her smile. No. One of us is crazy. I think it's you."

Jared looked at the picture again. "She's holding a baby."

"Caleb Robert Knox. My son."

"I see. Yes, he looks just like you. Little cleft in the chin and all."

Garrett snatched the picture from Jared's hand and examined it. For the first time, he saw the resemblance. Caleb did look like him. "Sure enough."

"Does it surprise you?"

"No. I just never noticed . . ."

Jared yawned. "Watkins," he murmured sleepily. "You married Watkins. I'll be damned."

Jared Knox fell asleep where he was sitting. Garrett eased him onto his side, but Jared didn't wake. He covered him with a light blanket, then watched his cousin sleep.

"So we didn't shoot each other, after all, you and I," Garrett said quietly. "North and South. Brothers-in-arms."

Garrett left the tent. He watched the sun set, his arms folded across his chest. Tomorrow, he would ride home to her. He would hold her again. Watkins. Verity. His wife.

"Excuse me, Sir."

Garrett turned. A young woman peered up at him. Loose amber hair fell in disarray around her small, anxious face. She led a heavy-boned horse, meant for a plow, no lady. But this lady wore trousers, high-top riding boots, and a long, gray cape over all.

Nothing, not dirt nor men's clothing nor wild hair, could disguise her beauty.

"Can you tell me where I might find Colonel Knox?"

Garrett smiled. "I am Colonel Knox."

"No, you're not! You can't be." The girl clasped her hand to her forehead. "I mean, you're not the right one. Oh, dear."

Pippa, looking for Jared. Garrett didn't have to ask. Jared's spy. And his wife.

Chapter Eighteen

"It's over. General Lee has surrendered at Appomattox. Garrett is coming home." Candace held up Garrett's short telegram. She was trembling, tears on her cheeks.

Verity just stared. She barely breathed. She closed her eyes, then leapt from her chair, raced to their bedroom and sobbed.

Five days after Lee surrendered to Grant at Appomattox, Abraham Lincoln was assassinated. The day following, he died of his wounds. The country that had soared on victory crashed into despair. Rain fell like soft tears, shed for a man whose heart bled for two lands.

Verity stood on the front stairs, her hand on a fluted pillar. Waiting. He would be home soon. He would never leave again. Through the mist, she saw horses. A coach. Caleb saw them, too. He clapped his hands as the horses approached.

Garrett rode beside the coach. He saw Verity, and his heart held its beat. She was waiting. Her letters hadn't only been meant to gird a lonely soldier at war. She'd meant every word. She still loved him.

Garrett urged his tired horse forward, into a canter. Verity came down the stairs to meet him. Caleb followed. She stopped. She couldn't move. Tears glistened in her eyes as he dismounted. Broad shoulders, filling a worn, blue uniform. A saber at his side.

Caleb wasn't frozen with emotion. He toddled forth, heading straight for Garrett's massive horse. With surprising speed, he aimed at his target. Garrett looked down at the little boy. Caleb looked up politely.

A small chubby hand reached out to pat the horse's knee. Pat, pat. The horse glanced down in surprise, then at Garrett.

"Nice hoss," said the little boy. "Me ride?"

Garrett swooped down and picked up his son. Tears flooded his gray eyes, but the little boy didn't notice. He looked hopefully between the dark man and the tall horse.

"This is Thor," said Garrett. "I'd imagine he'll welcome someone your size for a change." Garrett placed Caleb on his saddle, holding him in place with his large hand. Caleb had a surprisingly steady seat, though his legs barely reached the top of the stirrup leathers.

"Hoss!" said Caleb.

Verity watched them, unable to move. Garrett was looking at her, emotion reined in. He was smiling. "Garrett!" She burst forward and swung into his arms. Garrett caught her with one hand, holding Caleb with the other.

"Mrs. Knox, I have returned. In order, of course, to assure myself of the nature of your forgiveness."

Verity looked up at him. "You must work very hard at earning that, Colonel. In time, perhaps . . ."

Laughing, Garrett kissed her while his horse grazed. Caleb rocked back and forth, hoping for movement.

"Let me take the little fellow for a walk, Colonel," suggested a stable hand. "Had him riding the plow horses, but he's ready for something finer."

Garrett nodded and passed the reins to the groom. "Thank you."

The groom grinned. "Good to have you back, Sir. Tell you, anything's better than taking orders from Miss Ivy. Damn, but she's a hard one."

The groom led Thor and Caleb toward the stable, and Garrett took Verity in his arms. Holding her. "I've missed you, Woman. It's been a very long war."

Verity rested her head against his wide chest. "Never leave again."

"I never will."

Verity kissed his chest. She looked up into his handsome, strong face. "I love you so."

"And I, you, my love."

Verity glanced toward the coach. It stopped. The door opened. "A few of your old friends," said Garrett.

Jefferson jumped down, then helped John to the ground. John wore an eye patch, his other eye buttoned shut; but he was alive.

Jefferson saw Verity. "Watkins!"

She left Garrett's arms, hugged Jefferson, then John. "I'm so happy you're here. I have your rooms ready."

"Have you room for one more?" another voice asked from inside the coach. A familiar voice.

Verity's heart stopped. She was aware that Garrett watched her, smiling. A tall man bent low to step down from the coach. Verity couldn't breathe. Her lips parted.

He stood there, smiling amidst tears. Tall and thin, with reddish brown hair swept back from his forehead. A trembling gasp escaped Verity's lips. She moved into his arms, wrapped her arms around his neck. She cried so hard, tight sobs racking her chest.

"Robert."

Robert Talmadge hugged her, then he lifted her off her feet despite his obviously weakened state. "Little sister. You have grown."

Verity moved back to look at him. "You look thin. You must eat, Robert. There's a pig ready for roasting. Ivy's been growing all kinds of vegetables. Dear Heaven, Robert—you're alive!" She burst into tears again, and he kissed her forehead.

Verity turned to Garrett. "How did you find him?"

"He found me," said Garrett. "A trainload of prisoners came up from Georgia. I met him in Washington. And I couldn't believe it. I had to make a hurried request for your hand, I might add."

"Which I granted willingly," said Robert with a grin. "As you already have a son, it seemed wise." Robert kissed Verity again. "You married the best man I know, Little One. You can't know how happy it makes me to find you well. Tonight, I will hear how you spent this damned war. Everything that happened since Antietam. Lord knows, I've missed so much."

Verity peeked over at Garrett. "You didn't tell him?"

Garrett shook his head. "I thought . . . another time."

"That's probably pretty sound," decided Verity. Let Robert

heal and relax before learning his sister fought in two of the Civil War's bloodiest battles.

"What happened to you, Robert?" asked Verity.

Robert glanced at Garrett. "I was imprisoned at Andersonville in Georgia. The rest we can discuss later, my dear. But the truth is, I have no sure answer." Robert looked around, searching for someone.

"Candace is out in the back," said Verity gently. "She's doing something at the veterans' home, I think. Shall we go?"

"Point me in the right direction, little sister. I've spent three years wondering if I'd lost her to another man."

"Not a chance," said Verity. "Now, follow me."

Verity led them all toward the veterans' new home. Garrett patted her shoulder when he saw the finished building. "Very good," he said. "What the hell—?"

"Oh, dear," muttered Verity. Robert just stood, open-mouthed, staring.

Candace was perched up on the roof. "You men are utter and hopeless fools," she announced from her position. "As I tried to tell you—and no one would listen, because no one pays any attention to my advice—there is in fact a hole in this roof. Here."

She smacked a hammer on the offending opening. "Pass me up a board, and I'll seal it for now. This rain isn't stopping."

"Miss Webster, you come down from there, at once!" Ivy stood on the front porch of the home, her hands on her hips. "Right now. You let one of the men do it."

"Those idiots were afraid of the damp," said Candace as she spit a nail from her lips and slammed it into the roof. "One more . . ." She hammered again. "Done!"

Robert was trembling. Verity touched his arm, easing him forward. Robert walked down toward the home. He stopped, looking up at his fiancée. Spotting him, Ivy clasped her hand to her heart. "Lord be praised."

"Hello, Ivy," said Robert, his eyes fixed on Candace.

"Miss Webster, we got another one," called Ivy.

"Saints," said Candace. "Get the delousing vat ready. Scrub brush. Tell Belle to leave Ethan be, and come help us."

She started to swing herself down. Robert stepped forward and held out his hand. "Thank you, Ma'am, but I'm in no need of delousing. I bathed quite thoroughly this morning. A man needs to be presentable when he goes courting.''

When Candace saw him she fell, head first, from the roof. Robert caught her and sank to his knees. Kissing her. She caught his hair in her hands and kissed him back. ''What took you so very long?''

Robert didn't answer. He kissed her, rocking her little body against his. ''Later, my love. Later.''

Verity watched their reunion, soft tears flowing across her cheeks. Garrett took her hand. ''I've got some things to share with you, too, my sweet. Actually, one thing.''

Verity blushed, but she knew. ''Jefferson, John, Ivy will help you get situated. Ethan's in there, ordering his nurse around. Fortunately for you, he's still living up at the estate house. I didn't think the men could stand an officer amongst them.''

''Still bossy, is he?'' asked Jefferson with a grin.

''He's a bit persnickity.'' Verity sighed.

''Ethan, once and future tormentor of the enlisted,'' said Jefferson. ''God help us.''

''Aye,'' said John.

''Where's your guitar, John?'' asked Verity.

''Gone,'' he said wistfully. ''Gone now.''

''Maybe you can make use of this.'' Ethan Hallowell appeared on the porch, Belle in reluctant tow. He held up a perfect, neat guitar. ''I'm not sure I've got the strings right. Belle, take this to the sergeant.''

''Whew!'' said Jefferson. ''That's a beauty. Where'd you get it, Captain?''

Belle placed the guitar in John's hands. Those ragged hands clenched around the instrument. A smile formed on his mysterious lips.

''He made it himself,'' said Belle. ''Badgering me for exact pieces of wood, for string. *'No, Madam, this will not do. Please listen this time, and get it right . . .'* You have no idea what I went through for this pretty guitar to get made.''

John tried the strings. ''Officers don't know nothing,'' he observed at the unpleasant twang. ''But there ain't a better man to follow than you, Captain. I thank you.''

Robert lifted Candace from the ground, and he stood blithely holding her as she gazed lovingly into his face. ''We need privacy to discuss our future, my beloved,'' he said. ''If you're willing—''

''In the house,'' said Candace.

Ethan sat in his chair, his eyes on Robert, a young and hopeful expression on his face. Robert turned to him. "Captain Hallowell . . ." Robert's voice faded. "Ethan. Garrett has told me of your sacrifice, and of what you were put through on my behalf. Let my return clear you beyond question."

"Who did it, Sir?" put in John. "I'll be damned if I picked up anything, though Old Sam said he had an idea or two. Got himself killed afore telling, though."

Robert hesitated. "During the battle of Antietam, I followed a man calling himself Delaney to a meeting place he ordained. For the purpose of 'confessing,' or so he told me. He was waiting, true. But when I approached, five rebels jumped me, knocked me out, and hauled me into captivity."

Verity seized Garrett's hand. "Delaney intended to 'confess' to you, too! You don't think—?"

"Rob and I have discussed the matter," said Garrett. "We both think he intended to implicate Ethan. For the purposes of another. Who that other was, neither of us can guess."

"Westley didn't know."

"But someone thought he did," said Garrett. "I believe that was why you were followed."

"Maybe we'll never know," sighed Robert. "But it's over now. Goddamn him for killing Westley, though. That's something that I'll never forgive."

Robert turned to Ethan again. "I'd like to talk to you about my cousin. And my uncle, if you've got time, Ethan. Later, perhaps. There are a few things they'd want you to know."

"Thank you, sir," said Ethan. "I would appreciate that."

"You'll 'appreciate' a bath first," put in Belle. "You've been struggling in the heat with that guitar too long."

"Madam—"

"Now!"

Belle seized Ethan's wheelchair and shoved him up the road toward the house. Robert glanced at Garrett, who shrugged. "A lazy afternoon, spent in the company of our loved ones. Come, my darling," he said to Candace. "You're getting a bit heavy. Shall we away?"

"We shall."

Garrett watched them go, then looked at Verity. "Very romantic," she sighed. "To be carried up to one's room—"

"As you wish," said Garrett. He picked her up, tossed her over his shoulder, and marched the long path to his house.

Garrett carried Verity, over his shoulder, all the way upstairs. "This isn't exactly what I had in mind, Garrett."

"What about this?" Garrett kicked open their bedroom door, dropped her to her feet, then tilted her back in his arms. She caught her breath at the desire flaring in his dark gray eyes.

"This," she whispered, "is better." His lips descended over hers, his tongue outlined her lips, tasted her sweetness.

His large hand found her full breast, teasing her nipple through her muslin bodice. "Have you missed me, love? How much?"

"Garrett, I've missed you."

He bent her back farther, running his lips over the swell of her breast.

"Damn women's clothing," said Garrett. "It takes too long to get you out of it." He picked her up again, then set her on the edge of her writing desk. "Allow me." Garrett pulled off her slippers, then her stockings, her lacy, cotton drawers.

Verity waited, trembling with anticipation. She felt damp, warm . . . congested with need. She helped him from his uniform jacket, and his shirt, baring the hard, masculine chest. Garrett radiated power, controlled power, power he would use to send her into the sweetest oblivion.

She ached for him. Need overwhelmed her. Verity ran her hands along the thick muscles from his neck to his shoulder, down his massive arms, to his wrists, to his fingers. "You're so beautiful. Like a Roman statue, Garrett Knox. What a gladiator you would have made!"

"A barbarian," he corrected.

"King of barbarians," she murmured. "And I, a woman taken in conquest. Yours."

"Who conquered who, I wonder?"

With skilled fingers, Garrett unfastened the fat buttons of Verity's tailored bodice, then untied her corset, pushing it aside to reveal her full breasts. Breasts squeezed upward and together by her opened bodice.

"My God, Watkins, how I've missed you." Garrett cupped her breasts in his large hands, draped in a sensual cloud of her chestnut hair. "Beautiful woman."

Verity clutched his shoulders. Garrett reached down and freed himself from his trousers. His engorged manhood sprang forth, poised to enter her. Thick, aroused. A fevered shiver ran through Verity's body at the sight. She squirmed forward on the desk, striving to reach him.

Garrett slid his hand up her thigh, inward, brushing across the soft curls between her legs. Verity felt his finger against her sensitized flesh, teasing, exploring. Her head tipped back as she reveled in the tightening spirals of sensation.

"Do you want me now, Mrs. Knox?" His low, husky voice was a caress to her ears.

"I want you so. If you stop, I will die."

"Stop? Oh, love, I have only begun." Garrett knelt in front of her, parting her thighs, kissing her flesh. Verity peered down at him in surprise. He smiled up at her, his face flushed with desire, his eyes black slate.

Verity clutched his hair as his kiss moved up along her thigh. His lips touched her woman's mound. His hands cupped her hips firmly, wedging her closer as his tongue darted out to taste her sweetness.

"Garrett," she breathed. "Should you—?"

"Um," he murmured. "I should. I've been dreaming of this for seven months. And it will take a long while before I get my fill."

He teased the tiny bud at the apex of her thighs, flicked hot lashes across, around, until Verity's breath came as harsh moans and cries of pleasure. Garrett slowed his teasing touch until she squirmed, then sampled her again. Over and over.

Verity forgot where she was. She wrapped her legs around his shoulders and leaned back. Her body quaked and trembled. Each time she neared the sweet pinnacle of rapture, he slowed, retreating. Then again, building.

"This is madness," she moaned. "End this, please. I can't bear it anymore."

"No, love, I want to sample your sweetness from another angle."

He rose, his bared manhood throbbing, pulsing with furious lust. Verity encased his hips between her legs, drawing him closer, urging him to complete her desire.

He plunged inward, lifting her from the desk, holding her against him as he thrust deeply inside her. She wrapped around him, tightening unbearably around his staff, writhing against him. He drove within her, bringing them both to the edge of climax, then withdrew.

Verity gasped in ragged frustration, but Garrett smiled and set her to the floor, then turned her around, gently placing her hands on the desktop. "Hold on, Angel."

Garrett pushed her skirt and petticoats up. He maneuvered his thick staff against her, sliding its length along the sweet crevice as she trembled in anticipation.

He cupped her hips in his hands, bending her forward as he entered her welcoming woman's sheath once again. From this angle, his length touched places she'd never felt before, deep and whole and excruciatingly blissful.

Verity tipped her head back, and he leaned forward to kiss her as he thrust deeper inside her. He reached around to caress her tender breasts, teasing, drawing her whole body toward orgasm. He withdrew, thrust again, harder, lifting her onto her toes with his power.

Her thick mass of hair bounced around her head. Jars and bottles rattled on the desk as he moved within her. He clutched her shoulders, holding her against him as he took her, and took still more. Verity was flying on thick wings of desire, propelled by Garrett's lust, driven higher onto sweet clouds of rapture.

On and on, his soul itself poured into hers until they became one thing. Garrett withdrew, picked her up without a word and carried her to their bed. He tossed aside the quilt and lay down beside her. A small, satisfied smile curved Verity's lips.

"That's something I didn't tell Ethan about," she said. "Oh, well. Maybe he'll figure this out on his own. My instruction only went so far, I suppose."

Garrett's eyes widened. "Instruction? Hallowell?"

Verity gazed lazily up at him. "The mysteries of my night by the Rappahannock have been cleared. I spent it telling Ethan of the ways to please a woman. I learned from the best, after all. You."

"I'm flattered. I think."

"Don't tell Ethan, though," said Verity. "He's suffered enough embarrassment."

* * *

Ethan Hallowell sat in his bedroom, having finally lost patience and ordered Maybelle to leave him in peace. Unfortunately, his room was located beneath Verity and Garrett's. There was no mistaking the slight swing of his hanging lamp and the distant thuds of furniture upstairs.

Ethan considered moving to another spot for the duration. And from what Verity had told him on the banks of the Rappahannock, it could be long. But no, should he take up temporary residence in Garrett's study, he'd be beneath Candace's room. Something told him the condition of those lamps would be much the same.

Damn, what's wrong with me? Why do I keep having these thoughts? How can half a man be so . . . hard?

Ethan cursed loudly. Belle appeared at his door at once. "You called?" she asked.

"No, I did not." Ethan felt even more irritable than usual. "Were you lurking out there?"

He felt certain he heard a man's groan of pure pleasure. His face colored. Apparently, Belle noticed it, too. "Having a time of it, aren't they?" she observed nonchalantly. Ethan's color deepened.

"Dear God, woman, would you kindly remember decency?"

"It's a bit difficult to keep 'decency' in mind with the rafters shaking this way. Let me tell you, the east wing is just as bad. Why, with Major Talmadge and Miss Webster apart this long, I expect this whole mansion to be shaking well after dark."

Ethan fought to retain his composure. "You, Madam, talk too much."

"Getting to you, is it?" Belle grinned.

Ethan longed to sink into the floor and disappear. He prayed fervently that Belle wouldn't notice the telltale placement of his folded hands. Nothing seemed adequate to hide the bulge beneath his trousers.

A small, pink tongue dampened curved lips. Pretty, bowed lips squeezed between a chipmunk's cheeks. Ethan tried not to look.

God, if Miss Maybelle looks good to me, I'm really gone.

Maybelle set to work making his bed while he watched. Ethan cleared his throat.

"You know, Maybelle, if you lost a little weight, you might be attractive." He looked at her more closely. Fat cheeks. Decidedly fat cheeks. But her nose . . . "You have a very pretty nose."

Ethan tried to see her eyes. He didn't think he'd ever noticed the color of her eyes. How old was she? Not as old as he'd thought at first. Her size and manner made her seem old, but there was something youthful about her that defied understanding.

"I was just wondering—how old are you, Miss Maybelle?"

"Now, *there's* a gentlemanly question." When Ethan didn't retract it, Belle frowned. "None of your business."

Belle fidgeted under his sudden scrutiny. She pushed her spectacles higher on her nose. Ethan fought a mad impulse to tear them from her face and kiss her.

That's it. I've broken under the strain.

"Yes, Maybelle, if you weren't quite so fat—"

"And if you weren't so short, you might be not be bad yourself," cut in Belle. Ethan's brow rose.

"Chipmunk cheeks."

"Dwarf."

Ethan's brow rose higher. "You, Madam, are disgusting. I attempt to compliment you, graciously . . ."

Belle was ready with a suitable retort. She leaned over to fluff his pillows. Ethan caught her round face in his hand, pulled her close, and kissed her.

For one instant, she kissed him back. She clutched his hair, her breath quickened, her pulse raced beneath his touch. Her lips parted to receive his seeking tongue, then snapped closed as she lurched away from him.

"I am not a harlot for your pleasure, Sir!"

The utter ludicrousness of the situation astounded Ethan beyond words. There she stood, hands on her sagging hips, indignant at his misbegotten advance. An infuriated, greedy chipmunk.

Harlot, indeed. Greased hair, piled against her scalp. Spectacles off to one side. She adjusted them with a 'humph' noise. Ethan still couldn't speak. He had kissed her. Even now, his body burned with forbidden desire. Forbidden, because he forbade it. A man in his condition couldn't make love, however much his youthful organ demanded it.

Certainly not with Miss Maybelle.

"I have lost my mind."

"You can say that again."

"Madam, in the future, you will restrain yourself."

"Restrain *myself*? Restrain myself! You'll keep your lustful paws off my body, do you hear?"

"My pleasure."

"You're getting no 'pleasure' from me!"

Belle marched to the door, opened it, then looked back. A slight smile teased on her lips. "You know, though . . . for someone as stiff and respectable as you, you're an awfully good kisser."

Ethan's eyes widened in astonishment, but Belle winked and left. He sat, horrified and confused, alone. Listening in envy and embarrassment to the renewed activity on the floor above.

Chapter Nineteen

"Dinner is served." Ivy rang a loud bell and called at the top of her lungs up the staircase. Mildred darted from the living room to hush her.

"For heaven's sake, Ivy. The poor things are napping."

"Napping, hell! Those young folk have better things to do than nap," said Ivy.

Verity glanced up at Garrett, who grinned and shook his head. "Our home is a madhouse, Woman."

Verity couldn't argue. The front door bell sounded, a servant greeted Dan Wallingford just as Candace and Robert joined them on the staircase.

"Dan!" called Mildred. She scurried to her son's side and presented her cheek for a dutiful kiss. "Why, you're just in time for dinner, Dear Heart. How lucky!"

"Mother," said Dan. "Thought I'd visit for a while, see how things are coming along at Fox Run."

"How is Washington since the assassination, Dan?" asked Garrett as he descended the stairs with Verity's arm entwined with his.

"Damned confusing, Garrett," said Dan. Suddenly he noticed Robert Talmadge. Verity saw the expected shock on his face, but she discerned less pleasure.

"Rob? It can't be!" Dan stepped forward and held out his hand. "God, it is. What a miracle!"

"No miracle, Dan," said Rob. "Just the good will of a few rebel soldiers."

"What do you mean?" asked Verity.

"I'll tell you at dinner. I'm famished just now."

Belle and Ethan appeared for dinner. Verity noticed they avoided looking at each other, but Belle seemed unusually happy. Dan spotted Ethan and eyed him without pleasure.

"Hallowell. You've made a surprising recovery. Can't have been easy."

Ethan faced Dan Wallingford with an equal lack of affection. "No. It wasn't easy, Major."

"Dinner, Gentlemen," interrupted Ivy nervously. "Ladies . . ."

Garrett's dining room was filled to capacity. Caleb sat in his highchair, delighting in the company. Jefferson and John arrived for dinner, dressed in civilian clothing Verity had provided. Jefferson had left the gallant soldier behind, seizing the country gentleman role with equal vigor. He looked tall, lean, and handsome. Verity began to wonder when he would marry.

John looked much the same in civilian clothes as in uniform. Scruffy and ragged. He set Ethan's guitar by a tea tray and let Jefferson guide him into his seat. "Smells fine," he announced. "Roast pork, turtle soup, by God." He sniffed the air. "Biscuits with butter, young asparagus. Fine."

Dan eyed them both distastefully. "Doesn't your new building have a dining hall?"

"Wallingford," said John. His jaw clenched.

"Well, well," said Dan as he drank his wine. "The old Twentieth Mass back together again. Except for young Watkins, that is. Any of you men know what became of the lad?"

No one answered, though Robert looked confused. "Watkins? I don't remember a Watkins."

"No, he came after you left," said Wallingford. "None of you hear from the boy, eh?"

Verity wondered why he cared. He spoke casually, but he pressed the matter.

"No, sir," said Jefferson. "Not a one of us hear from the 'boy' at all."

* * *

Ethan's dislike of Dan Wallingford intensified as the meal was served. He didn't like the way Wallingford spoke to the men, and he especially resented the dark glances he cast Verity's way. Ethan wondered, too, why Wallingford cared about Watkins. It struck him as suspicious, but he couldn't keep his thoughts focused on the matter.

Garrett and Verity gazed into each other's eyes, exchanging smiles of secret memory. Robert held Candace's hand under the table. They both glowed. Naturally. If he'd spent the afternoon doing what they'd been doing, he'd glow, too.

Ethan remained tense and agitated. He snatched a fork from Belle's hand.

"That was mine. Use your own."

"You use *your* own," she replied meaningfully. Ethan blushed furiously. She dared suggest, in front of all Garrett's guests, that he apply his hand to himself. The woman was evil.

Belle glanced pertinently at his lap, and Ethan's face soaked with color. So she expected him to relieve his lust with his own hand, did she? Disgusting woman. True, he'd considered it. But she kept bursting in, so he never could be sure of privacy. If she caught him like that. . . .

"Ethan?"

Ethan looked up. Verity was waiting for an answer to a question he hadn't heard. "Forgive me . . . What?"

"I was asking if you liked the meal. That's all. You're not eating much."

"Got his mind on other things," said Belle to Ethan's acute discomfort.

Ethan seized a goblet of wine and drank. "I'm not hungry."

Sensing Ethan's mood, Verity turned her attention to·Robert. "Tell us what happened with the rebels, Robert."

"Yes, do," agreed Wallingford. "It's a real mystery."

"They had me, all right. And apparently they had orders to kill me. The thing about rebels is, they don't like taking orders much. Got to have a good reason. And these orders apparently came from someone in blue."

"No!" gasped Mildred. "A Confederate trick, I'm sure."

"I wonder what that Delaney really wanted," mused Candace. "He doesn't seem to have been particularly attached to a Confederate victory. He seems to have been using them, too."

"That's true," agreed Robert. "Since Lincoln's assassination, I've wondered—"

"What?" asked Dan. "You can't think there's a connection."

"Why not?" Garrett considered the matter, drumming his thick fingers on the tabletop. "There are some Northerners who wanted to control the nature of our victory, for their own ends. Lincoln promised peace, and reconciliation. A South rebuilt stronger and better, not weak and at the mercy of our mercenaries."

"That's right," said Robert. "Politics is an ugly business."

"Did the rebels who captured you know who betrayed you, Robert?" asked Verity.

"No, I don't think so."

"Why didn't they kill you?" asked Ethan.

"Because I wasn't what they were led to believe," said Robert. He smiled faintly. "Abolitionist, yes. Murdering Yankee, no."

Candace patted his hand. "They saw you were a gentleman."

"They had me, and they couldn't let me go. Couldn't bring themselves to kill me. So they sent me to Andersonville prison, with the strict instructions to keep my identity secret."

"At least you were safe," said Verity.

"I was lucky. I saw more men die in prison than ever fell on the field. Malnourished, prone to disease. But I never caught anything I couldn't get over."

"What are your plans now, Rob?" asked Wallingford. "Heading back to Boston soon, I'd imagine."

"We're leaving tomorrow night."

"So soon?" asked Verity. "You just arrived."

"We'll be back to visit, little sister. But the Websters are waiting in Boston. They insist we marry there. And we don't want to wait."

"I wanted you with me, Verity," added Candace. "But you've been there when it mattered."

"If you're leaving tomorrow night, then we must have a party first. A barbeque, like the rebels do. We'll play croquet, maybe arrange a shooting match . . ."

"And we know who'll win, don't we?" said Robert with a

laugh. "I don't know if you're aware, Garrett, my old friend, but your wife can outshoot the best of us."

"Shoot?" asked Dan in surprise. "I find that hard to believe."

"I have to admit that I taught her myself," said Robert. "Dressed her up in my old clothes, took her out shooting targets with my friends. What was it we called you? Vernon . . . ? No, Verrill. That was it. Verrill."

Verity blanched. "That was long ago, Robert. I wouldn't know what to do with a musket today."

No one pursued the matter, but Dan watched her with a strange expression throughout the remainder of dinner.

Ethan drank his wine, then reached for the decanter, refilling his goblet to the brim. Garrett and Verity exchanged a doubtful glance. By dessert, he appeared quite bleary.

"I," he announced, "will now retire to my room."

Ethan backed his chair into the tea tray, spun around and headed through the door. Belle shook her head when a loud crash sounded from the front hall. "There goes your Florentine vase, Colonel. I thought I'd moved it far enough . . ."

Ethan backed back into the dining room. "If you don't mind, Ivy, I'll take some of your finest to my quarters. Thank you." He seized a bottle from a side table and left again, while the others watched in astonishment.

"Garrett, you have to talk to him," said Verity. "We can't let him drown his good senses in spirits."

"It's a bad road to start down," Garrett agreed. "I'm not sure it's any of my business, but still . . ."

Garrett left the dinner table, and the others retired to the living room. Verity felt free and happy. Jefferson and John were there. Ethan was peculiar, but thriving. Caleb yawned.

"Past his bedtime, I'd say," noted Dan.

"It is, at that," agreed Verity. "Come on, little one. Mama will carry you upstairs and put you in your little bed. If you're very lucky, I'll sing you a lullaby."

As Verity took the baby upstairs Garrett knocked on Ethan's door. He heard a muffled, 'Oh, hell,' followed by, 'Come in.'

Garrett entered Ethan's room, and found him sitting in the dark with a bottle. "Mind if I turn up the lamp?"

Ethan startled. "Colonel! It's you. I thought it would be the Chipmunk from Hell again."

"No." Garrett seated himself on a chair facing Ethan. He nodded at the bottle. "Falling into that rather heavily, aren't you, Captain?"

"It's medicinal," said Ethan, slurring slightly.

"I see."

"It serves its purpose."

"If its 'purpose' is to drown your troubles, I think you're going to be disappointed, Hallowell. And damned sick in the morning."

Ethan looked at the bottle, then at Garrett. "It's not my troubles that need drowning. It's that Chipmunk." He leaned toward Garrett, over the arm of his wheelchair, and lowered his voice conspiratorially.

"You know women, Colonel. Tell me, if you didn't have that luscious Watkins, would you find Miss Maybelle . . . attractive?"

Garrett didn't know what to say. His eyes wandered to one side.

"No, I didn't think so," concluded Ethan. "No man in his right mind would."

"I take it one man has considered her charms, at least."

Ethan let out a long, drawn out sigh. "It can be damned frustrating to be a man. I just can't control it, Sir. If I had to lust for someone, in my heart, secretly, it should be your wife."

Garrett's brow rose, but Ethan didn't notice.

"I don't know if you've noticed, Major, but your Watkins has changed." Ethan maneuvered his arms in the shape of an hourglass. Garrett decided not to remind Ethan of his new rank—the war, after all, was over—unless Ethan went too much farther with this line of conversation.

"I had noticed," said Garrett.

"Men lust," said Ethan. "It's normal to lust. If I have to lust for someone, why not Watkins? Or Miss Webster? She's a pretty woman. Maybe not as beauteous as your wife, but—"

"Go on, Hallowell." Garrett's deep voice was a warning, but Ethan paid no attention.

"But no—I can't keep my eyes off *her*. Miss Maybelle. The most grotesque, abominably mannered woman ever to set a chubby foot on Maryland soil."

"Does this have something to do with your attachment to that bottle?"

Ethan nodded vigorously. "I learned, a while ago, that imbibing spirits has a calming influence on certain male functions. At least on mine."

"Male functions?"

"The implement of lust," said Ethan in a pained tone.

"Erections. I see," said Garrett. Garrett looked doubtful. Liquor never effected him that way.

Ethan nodded again.

"Do you mean to tell me that when you drink, you can't—?" Garrett stopped and laughed, a booming sound. Ethan cringed in embarrassment. Garrett rose from his seat. "I suppose that settles the matter of Caleb's paternity."

Ethan's blue eyes widened in horror. "Sir, you can't think—"

"Men in love are rarely reasonable," said Garrett. "As you've proven quite admirably yourself tonight." Garrett rose and seized Ethan's bottle. "I'm afraid you'll have to do without this tonight, Captain. Handle things on your own."

"Dear God."

Garrett laughed when Ethan misunderstood his phrasing. "Or call Miss Maybelle in here to do it for you. I have a feeling she's got a soft spot for you. But if you've got something as rich as desire, you might as well see it through."

A sharp cry cut them off. "What was that?" asked Ethan.

"Verity—"

Garrett raced from Ethan's room, meeting the others in the hall. Verity lay at the bottom of the staircase, holding her ankle and grimacing in pain. Garrett knelt beside her. "Verity, what happened?"

"I fell."

"That much, I can see."

"Something tripped me."

"Tripped you?" cut in Dan Wallingford. "That hardly seems likely. Those are treacherous stairs, Mrs. Knox. Garrett's grandmother died falling down them, as I recall. She was old, but still—"

"I caught myself halfway down," Verity told them. "Otherwise, I would surely have broken my neck. But something tripped me, Garrett. It felt like a wire, at the top of the stairs."

"I'll check," offered Dan. He bounded up the stairs. "Nothing here."

"Look at my leg." Verity pulled up her skirt, revealing a slender gash just above her ankle, on the front of her leg.

"It looks like a wire cut, all right," said Robert.

Dan checked the wound. "Could be." He looked around the hall at the others. "Who would want to cause injury to Garrett's wife? Davis, you weren't with the rest of us. Where were you during the span of time when Verity took her son to bed?"

Verity struggled into a sitting position. "Jefferson didn't trip me."

"Here we go again," said John.

"I'm sorry, Verity. But you barely know this man," argued Dan. "He was in your husband's regiment, years ago. Hell, who knows what he's doing here?"

Garrett's jaw clenched. "He came because I invited him. That's enough, Dan."

"Maybe, Garrett. But I think I'll stay around for a few days, keep, an eye on things. This veterans' home you've started, it opens a whole wide range of troubles. Oh, I know your intentions were good. But you can't always rely on your idealistic notions of brotherhood. One of these men assembled here very likely tried to injure your wife."

"Oh! For Christ's sake," spouted Verity. "For what possible reason?"

"I think that's obvious," said Dan, his voice calm and even. "These men have been long at war. I must speak frankly. You don't know what battle does to a man. He learns to take what he wants, plunder at will. Rape isn't unheard of."

"You think someone meant to trip me so he could rape me? In the front hall of my husband's home?"

"Lust can turn into anger. Anger, into violence," said Dan.

Mildred gasped, clutched her chest, but she nodded vigorously. "My Dan is right. Dear hearts, you don't know the dangers in which you've placed us bringing these men to our home. It was one thing to tend them in Washington, but at our own estate—"

Garrett helped Verity to her feet. "Something tells me there's something more to this 'accident' than raging lust. Lust may drive a man to a bottle, but whoever tripped Verity didn't plan to stick around long enough to do anything else."

Ethan blushed at the mention of lust, and Belle chuckled.

"I suggest we all head off to bed," said Ivy. "You take your wife upstairs, and we'll think on it tomorrow."

"A good idea, Ivy," said Dan. "You men, disperse. I intend

to keep a close eye on the goings on down there. If any of you is up to no good, I'll be on you like a duck on a June bug.''

Ethan lay in his dark, warm room, trying to concentrate on a proper erotic image. Naked, faceless women filtered through his mind. No, that didn't work. He needed a face. He tried to conjure Verity's. She had a lovely, sensual face, with her hair falling over her shoulders.

Maybe caught on an island somewhere, unable to reach Garrett Knox, desperate for fulfillment. Only Ethan nearby. Ethan imagined the scene; the beautiful, lush body stripped bare before him. Parted, full lips, beckoning.

This vision might work. His body responded. His hand slid down across his flat stomach.

He bent down to kiss her. Because the man in his fantasy had legs. Powerful, long legs. But wait—what was that on her pretty cheek? Dirt. And in her hand? A musket. *Watkins.* Looking up at him as if he'd just overstepped his bounds by a long reach.

Ethan's fantasy faded. He frowned.

Candace just looked at him cooly and smiled without interest. Ivy laughed and called him, *Little Prince.*

Then, for a brief, agonizing instant, Ethan Hallowell saw Bess Hartman. She was happy, unbuttoning her bodice, reaching for him.

Standing on tiptoes to kiss him. Ethan's heart twisted in pain. He remembered it in a flash; her slender body, naked. Her shy smile as he lowered himself above her. How it felt to slide his full length into her moist opening . . . *Am I hurting you, love? I like this, Beauregard Keats. Don't you dare stop.* Bess's throaty response would echo in his memory forever.

Ethan fought the image, but his cursed body responded. For love, there was no respite. But for lust, there had to be. He just couldn't stand it anymore.

The women he fantasized about were too familiar. His friends. The thought of Bess hurt too much. Ethan tried to imagine a total stranger. Maybe a black-haired witch bent on seducing him.

The black-haired witch swirled around him, touched him. She knelt in front of him—because the drunken Verrill Watkins had shared the information from Ivy's brothel in vivid detail. The witch caressed his burning erection.

The vision succeeded admirably. Ethan felt his own rapid pulse, he slid his hand beneath his nightshirt and touched himself. Awkwardly, at first. His mind fixed on his image. The witch kissed him. He could almost feel her little pink tongue on his staff, and his own hand tightened.

He repressed a tight groan as he stroked himself. He reveled in wanton bliss. Until the witch slowed her pace and looked up at him. "God, not Miss Maybelle!" Ethan snatched his hand from his unsatisfied member.

"No," he said aloud. "I refuse. I will not."

His erection burned unabated. Miss Maybelle's face still taunted him, chubby cheeks and all. She wanted him. In his dream. And in reality.

Ethan could bear no more. It was true. He'd seen that expression on her chipmunk face before; he remembered how she wet her lips, glanced at him, and smiled. A sigh, a touch. She desired him, too.

He couldn't stop himself. His hand returned to its fevered ministrations. In a moment, it would be over. He would spend himself. Sleep. Forget. Ethan closed his eyes, blood pounded in his ears. His hand jerked, faster and faster. Soon. . . .

The door popped open and Belle marched in, carrying a lantern. Ethan nearly fell from the bed. "Woman, don't you ever knock?" He sounded breathless, hoarse.

Belle held up the lantern and studied him intently. "You're not fevered, are you?" She went to his bedside and touched his forehead.

"Stop that at once." Ethan shoved her hand away.

"You're breathing hard, pulse rapid." Belle's eyes wandered over his sheets. A large, firm bulge indicated itself beyond question.

Ethan saw her knowing expression. He wanted to die, right there, and escape this evil woman forever. "Good night, Madam." His voice shook.

"You're looking a little . . . tense," said Belle. "Roll over and I'll massage your back."

"You're not laying one hand to my flesh, woman."

"Hush now, and roll over."

Ethan did so, if only to hide his arousal from her devilish, prying eyes. Belle sat down on the side of his bed. He expected her weight to make a pit in his mattress, but actually, it sank very little.

She started to pull up his nightshirt.

"Stop that."

"It won't do much good to rub your back through cotton." Belle doused the lantern. "There. Is that better? You won't have to worry about me stealing a look at your pretty secrets in the dark."

Ethan wanted to object. He intended to. But the moment Belle's hands touched his skin, he was lost. She kneaded the tight cords of his neck, his shoulders, down to the small of his back. Over his taut buttocks. . . .

"Watch where you're touching, woman," he commanded in a muffled voice. Ethan hadn't realized he was biting his pillow.

Belle didn't listen. Her hands moved as if mesmerized, slowly, down his thigh, even to the blunt severed end before Ethan realized where she was touching.

"No. Don't touch me there."

"Is there somewhere you'd prefer?"

Ethan nearly choked on the pillow. She didn't wait for an answer. Her hands slid up, between his thighs, just grazing the tight sac. . . .

"God . . . behave yourself." He was shaking. His voice quavered, so ragged and husky he didn't recognize the sound.

"If you'd roll over, this would be easier." As she spoke, she slid her hand under him, cupping the fiery steel length that burned into the mattress.

A low, rumbling, agonized groan ripped from Ethan's dry throat. Those fingers closed around him, sweeter than his own could ever be. She guided him over onto his back. He couldn't resist. Ethan closed his eyes tight, though he couldn't see in the dark, anyway.

Her hand wrapped around him, kneading, massaging. She didn't speak, but he heard her swift, raspy breaths. A young woman's breaths. Her hand moved faster, she squeezed tighter. He felt ready to explode.

It had to be a dream. He'd deluded himself. It couldn't be real. But it felt too good to let it end.

Her palm grazed his aching tip, sliding up and down. He sensed her yearning as she imagined him inside her. This was too much. Two years of pent up frustration erupted, and his lust overflowed, spilling over her hand, everywhere. He groaned, bit his lip, groaned again.

The tortuous, heavenly waves subsided. He lay quivering in his bed, half ashamed, half in a daze of pleasure. Very slowly, Ethan's senses returned. Maybelle. What had he done? Would she expect something of him now? He had nothing to give.

Maybe he could perform as a man in bed. He felt certain now that he could. But what about as a husband? What good could he be to any woman?

"Belle," he whispered. "Forgive me."

"Why?" She sounded her usual, blunt self. Unaffected by their passion. "Seemed to me like you enjoyed yourself."

Ethan tried to compose himself. "I lost control of myself. It won't happen again."

"That would be a shame. Because I enjoyed myself, too. Oh, don't be thinking I want anything else from you. To tell you the truth, I'd gotten a little antsy spending so much time with you. You know, you've gotten rather muscular working down at the home. You look almost edible."

Ethan laughed despite himself. Edible. How like Maybelle to consider him food!

"At least, I'm not fattening," he noted cheerfully.

"No," said Maybelle. She sounded serious now. "You are beautiful."

Before he could speak, she kissed his forehead. Ethan suspected she was crying, but he couldn't see her face. She kissed him again, then scurried away without another word.

Verity forgot the trauma of her fall as she immersed herself in preparations for Robert's farewell party. "If only we'd had time to plan!" she mourned when Ivy entered the house with a giant basket of vegetables.

"Don't you be worrying, Little Miss," said Ivy. "The Colonel and your brother have a firepit going. Jefferson put a fine boar on the spit early this morning. It'll be a fine party, preparations or no."

"Candace is packing her trunk, weeping and laughing at the same time. She contained herself for so long, she's just a mass of emotion now." Verity set a stack of plates aside and sighed happily. "Everything's finally all right, Ivy. For all of us. Even Ethan . . . He doesn't know it, maybe. Oh, to finally be happy!"

Ivy watched Verity. She smiled, but her expression betrayed concern. "I wonder . . ."

"What could go wrong now?"

Ivy shook her head. "I'm just thinking of your fall last night, Honey. It didn't sit right."

"True. I'm quite bruised. Fortunately, Garrett was very good about tending me." Verity's voice trailed, she smiled in memory. He had certainly distracted her from her aches and pains, anyway.

"You take care, Little Miss. I don't know why, but I think you'd best stay close to your husband. Something's in the wind, and for once, it's blowing against you. Someone wants something, badly, desperately. And that wanting runs up against you."

Verity didn't want to hear this, but she knew Ivy's premonitions weren't to be taken lightly. "I'll be careful, Ivy. But we'll all be together today, outside. What could happen there?"

Caleb toddled around behind Garrett like a small shadow. They walked in the same way; sure, firm footsteps, a long stride, hands folded behind their backs. Verity watched them together from the rear door. Garrett poked at the pork on the spit. Caleb found a stick and poked, too.

Verity's eyes watered with sudden tears. Garrett patted his son's head, then picked him up. "I love you so," she whispered. Ivy's warning came back, haunting her. "I can't lose you. I won't be separated from you again."

Candace appeared behind her, dragging a pack of croquet equipment. "Let's set up, Verity," she suggested brightly. "But I warn you, I've been practicing."

"Not enough to beat me, Miss Webster."

"We'll see," replied Candace. "Where's Belle? She knows how to play. Even Mildred said she'd join us."

The ladies set up a croquet course, arguing over advantage, bickering over who went first. "We'll let Mildred go first," decided Belle, clearing considering the older woman a weak link.

"Very well," agreed Verity. "But you're last, Belle, since you're youngest."

Ethan overheard Verity's words. Youngest? Verity herself was only twenty-two. He rolled himself down the smooth pathway, securing his chair in the shade of an aged willow to watch the game.

A narrow, but swift, stream ran through Garrett's property, cutting behind the new veterans' home, bisecting the pastures as it raced toward the Potomac. The firepit was set up near the bank.

Men from the veterans' home circled the cooking meat, each offering advice as to how it would be best prepared.

Ethan saw Anderson from Nurse Abigail's boarding house. He, too, utilized a chair. His single arm waved enthusiastically at the meat. Ethan remembered the man had once been a cook. Apparently, he was taking over now.

Ivy marched from the veterans' home with her basket of vegetables. "You men know nothing about stew," she informed them. "You, Helmut Anderson, may fancy yourself a chef, but the placement of this cauldron is all wrong."

Helmut? thought Ethan. The man was older, probably near fifty. It occurred to Ethan that Ivy might have found a suitable companion. Helmut adjusted the cauldron according to Ivy's specifications.

Candace aimed a clever shot through a wicket, seizing the lead with decidedly unladylike glee. "Match that, Mrs. Knox. You never will."

Verity just smiled, that Watkins smile, and knocked Candace's ball out of place. As she did so, her own shot went wild. Belle stepped up, aimed, and took the lead from both. Mildred was too far back to challenge anyone, still trying to get her ball through the first wicket.

Candace noticed Belle's new position and called to Verity. "Three ball dead, Belle. Watch her, Verity. She's crafty."

Belle gazed at them innocently. "I wouldn't think of seizing unfair advantage," she assured them. Ethan sighed and shook his head.

Ethan couldn't take his eyes from Belle's peculiar form. Her body sagged in the strangest places, yet she moved with surprising agility, with devilish intent, as she seized unscrupulous advantage over her opponents. Like a rebel.

"Am I disturbing you, Ethan?"

Ethan startled, surprised to see Robert Talmadge standing beside him. A knowing smile curved Robert's aristocratic mouth above his noble goatee. Ethan wondered if everyone could read his illicit thoughts.

Robert found a lawn chair and seated himself beside Ethan. "I wanted to tell you about my uncle, if you're interested."

Ethan didn't meet Robert's eyes, but he nodded.

"I was with Uncle Cabot shortly before his death. It was a long illness, but he concealed it from everyone until the very end. As I understand it, your mother died a few years previously.''

"She died when I was sixteen," said Ethan quietly. "Her death was unexpected."

"Cabot spoke of her to me. He told me how they first met, and how you came to be born."

Ethan's jaw clenched, and Robert patted his shoulder. "Cabot's marriage wasn't a particularly happy one. He had courted Prudence's older sister, who by all accounts was a delightful girl. But she died soon after their engagement. For reasons that must have involved immense, shared grief, Cabot turned to courting Prudence. He never loved her. It was impossible to love her. Even Westley didn't love her."

"So Verity tells me," said Ethan. "She says she named the woman 'Aunt P' to irritate her."

"Actually, that was my doing," Robert admitted with a grin. "How they managed to conceive Westley, I don't know. Must have involved large quantities of alcohol. But thank God, Westley took after his father. Cabot fell in love with your mother innocently, I believe. After friendship, shared laughter.

"But a time came when they recognized that their friendship had gone beyond the accepted boundaries. Apparently, they tried to end it. Instead, as often happens when passion is suppressed, it erupted between them and they became lovers."

"A common story among illicit lovers," decided Ethan.

"Maybe, but the ending wasn't typical. They decided to elope together. I remember Cabot saying that the poet Shelley had done it, after all. Your sisters were grown, but they intended to take Westley and flee to Europe."

Ethan looked over at Robert in astonishment. He imagined what it would have been like to be raised by the free-spirited, charming Shelley rather than the coldblooded Calvin Hallowell. "What stopped them?"

"They made one mistake. Being inherently honorable, they told their spouses of their intentions. Madeleine was pregnant with you by then. For some reason, they thought their love would be understood, and forgiven."

"They overlooked Calvin Hallowell's pride," guessed Ethan.

"They did, indeed. Calvin and Aunt P joined forces. By law, you were his son. Prudence had no affection for her own son, but she used him now. To keep their children, Cabot and Madeleine had to give up each other.''

"And they did," finished Ethan. He looked down to hide his tears.

"I believe they intended to find each other again, once you both had grown. But by the time Westley reached adulthood, Madeleine had died. Cabot had no connection with you, but you were all he had left of her. For this reason, he named you in his will and secured it with me.

"I showed it to Garrett and Major Wallingford. To make certain it was legal. Dan assured me it was. Maybe I had a premonition I wouldn't be around much longer. But I knew Garrett would look after you."

"Westley didn't know?"

"No. Cabot wanted to tell him. But he wanted you to know each other first. When he learned you had joined the army, he saw to it that you were placed in Westley's company, in my regiment. He instructed me to watch you, to keep you safe at all costs. I failed."

Ethan smiled, but tears glistened in his eyes. "This wound, my legs . . . it was my choice. I could have protected myself. But if I had—"

"Garrett Knox would be dead. My sister's son would be fatherless. Your action did you great honor. Your father would be proud."

"Thank you, Major. To know I come from two people who loved each other is some comfort. Yet, by my existence I kept them apart. Had it not been for me, they could have gone to Europe together."

"Maybe," agreed Robert. "But something tells me Calvin Hallowell would have found another way. Maybe it was worth it to have found love at all. I hold it that way. I think Cabot did, too."

Ethan thought of Bess. Was it enough to remember? To be parted forever, and remember? "Love, however brief, must sustain us through the long years of loneliness."

Robert smiled as he rose from his seat. "Don't condemn yourself to loneliness just yet, Ethan. Something tells me your prospects have a longer duration."

Ethan didn't ask what Robert meant. Robert glanced toward Maybelle, and his smile deepened. Ethan endured an onslaught of embarrassment.

"Garrett is setting up the targets for a shooting match," Robert noted. "Would you care to join us? As I recall, you were an accurate shot."

"I may join you, in a while." ·

Robert rejoined Garrett, and the other men gathered their muskets for the shooting contest. Dan Wallingford was with them, and Ethan's enthusiasm for the sport waned. He saw Jefferson placing green melons on fence posts.

"What in God's name are you doing with my melons, Jefferson Davis?" Ivy stomped over to inspect, but Jefferson guided her aside. Ethan saw Verity look up from her croquet match and eye the shooting range enviously. Belle again seized the opportunity to cheat.

Ethan watched as Belle's sagging hips sagged further still, to halfway down her thigh. Candace pointed, and Belle shoved her fat back into place. Ethan stared in astonishment. Even for Miss Maybelle, this was peculiar beyond comprehension.

Verity dropped her mallet and headed for the shooting range. Ethan heard Robert laughing. He saw Jefferson take the first shot.

"Curse you, Jefferson Davis. Look what you've done to my melon!"

"Stand back, Ivy, Robert is taking his shot," advised Verity. "Heaven knows where that bullet will wind up."

"Guns aren't toys," chastised Ivy with surprising vehemence. "They're for killing. You all would be best to set it aside and play checkers."

"Now *there's* a dangerous sport, if ever there was one," put in Garrett. He slid his arm around Verity's waist and she kissed his cheek.

Ethan looked back at Maybelle, who continued a fierce competition with Candace. Her left breast had become dislodged by her exertion. She shoved that into place, too. Ethan stared.

Very slowly, the truth began to dawn on him. His heart chilled, quickened, then chilled again. It couldn't be. . . .

"Miss Maybelle. A moment, if you please."

Belle huffed. "You just bide your time, Master. I'm hedging in on victory here."

"Now."

Belle cast aside her mallet. "A postponement only," she told Candace.

"Ha! Surrender," said Candace. "Victory is mine." She waved her mallet in the air, then went to watch the shooting contest.

Ethan heard the popping of muskets, a loud yelp of joy from Verity, murmurs of astonishment from the veterans. He couldn't look away from Maybelle as she labored across the lawn.

"What is it?" she asked impatiently.

"I'd like to talk to you. Alone."

"We're alone."

"Inside," said Ethan. He wheeled himself back into the estate house, to his room, where they would be assured of privacy. He closed the door behind them, then turned to face her. He stared until Belle squirmed in agitation beneath his gaze.

"Have a seat."

Belle sat on the edge of his bed. Ethan wheeled himself in front of her, closing off any escape. Belle chewed her lip. Her bulging cheeks moved in an odd way. Ethan didn't speak. He reached around her head and loosed her hair. Rather than falling in a dank heap, it bounced as if joyful to be released from its constraints, then formed wispy curls around her chubby face.

Ethan swallowed, but still he didn't speak. He calmly unbuttoned her bodice and withdrew a soft pillow. Then another. He pulled up her skirt, fished beneath her petticoat, and found three other pads of varying size. She looked up toward the ceiling, biting her lip hard.

Ethan's hands shook as he removed her spectacles. Brown eyes. Beautiful brown eyes that wouldn't meet his. The cheeks remained. Ethan touched the bulge. "If you please."

She opened her mouth and hurriedly removed two wadded up pieces of cloth. Her breaths came in little, nervous gasps. Ethan couldn't breathe at all.

"You said you'd forgotten me. That you would get on with your life."

Tears dripped down her now smooth cheeks. "I did."

"Bess—"

"Beauregard."

Ethan tried to speak, but his voice broke. She was so beautiful, her lower lip quivering, her face wet with tears. Finally, she looked at him. Those brown eyes were so wide, shimmering with tears.

"I didn't exactly forget you, though."

Ethan closed his eyes. He couldn't bear to see her. "This was a mistake." He paused, in agony. "Verity's mistake."

"She sent me your letter as she promised you. Along with one of her own. And bits of another letter, with the instructions to burn it immediately. Which I did, naturally, after reading it ... you thought you were going to die. You said we would be one thing throughout time."

"It would be easier if I had died."

Bess rolled her eyes and puffed an impatient breath. Ethan began to realize that 'Miss Maybelle' wasn't an entirely feigned character. "Easier for you, maybe. Do you think I wanted to spend my life mourning you? You can't walk, Ethan, but you're alive."

"If you can call this living."

"You were plenty alive last night."

Despite his best intentions, Ethan's face flushed to a deep, hot red. "I can't imagine what possessed you to do that."

"Lust."

Ethan drew a tight breath to clear his senses. "I can't be a husband to you. I'm a bastard. You can't marry a bastard."

"Actually, that's how you're known in my household now. *'That Yankee bastard.'* So it really doesn't make much difference."

"I can't believe your family approved of this mad venture north."

"I didn't ask. Ethan, I adore you. If you don't want to marry me, then I'll be your mistress. But I'm not leaving you, no matter what you say."

"Bessie, it can't ever be the way it was. How can I look at you, and not think of what might have been?"

Bess sank to her knees in front of him, her hands on his severed legs. Tears flooded her cheeks, but her brown eyes blazed. "You lost your legs, not yourself. They were beautiful legs. I loved your legs. But they weren't you. *You* are in that ridiculous stiff back, in your indignant expressions, in your bossy manner. In the way your heart shows in your eyes ...

"I love *you,* Beauregard Keats. If you were dead, I would still love you. But you're not dead. You're healthy and handsome. I think you're handsomer now than you were."

Ethan was crying, too. "I can't dance with you again."

"You weren't that good a dancer, Ethan. Too stiff. We'll find better ways of dancing together. Alone. Ivy has made several interesting suggestions—"

"Ivy? You've consulted a prostitute? Dear God, Bess!" Ethan

paused, wondering what Ivy had come up with. He forced the thought away. "I suppose they all know what's going on."

"They've been very supportive. It was Colonel Knox who suggested I pay you a late visit last night, actually. Verity, especially, has a gift for disguise."

"Naturally. Watkins." Unable to resist, Ethan touched Bess's soft hair. "And the spectacles?"

"Those are mine. I'm a bit nearsighted. We all have our cross to bear."

"If you're up for a trade—" Ethan smiled. He couldn't stop himself as his heart overflowed. "I love you, Bessie." He nearly choked on the words. His throat felt dry. It hurt. He had held it back for so long. "But I don't know if I can be a man to you. Maybe in bed. But otherwise—"

"I'll be around, Ethan. You will see yourself as I do, and know there is no other man for me."

Someone was calling outside. Bess kissed Ethan's legs and looked up at him. "I think it's time to eat. We can talk again, more thoroughly, tonight."

Ethan nodded. He didn't want to disappoint her. But the image of the man he had been, juxtaposed with what he was now— Ethan felt powerless. And a powerless man couldn't be a husband. Not the kind of husband he wanted to be to Bess Hartman. A girl this wonderful deserved a whole man. This, Ethan believed, he would never be again.

Chapter Twenty

"I said, eat!" commanded Ivy. No one listened. Bess and Ethan emerged from the estate house, but all eyes were fixed on the shooting contest.

Garrett watched Verity take her shot. He saw Watkins. A slight smile, steady hand, fire. The melon shattered.

"Holy Jesus, there she goes again!" cried Helmut Anderson. "Lordy, we could have used her in the old Third."

Most of the men had bowed out of the contest, not wanting to be humiliated by a young woman. Robert fought to the bitter end, but Verity bested him. Only Garrett and Jefferson remained to challenge her.

"Set our firing line back again," ordered Jefferson. "Too easy from here."

"You're an arrogant devil, Jefferson Davis," said Verity. John nodded.

"President, you're riding for a fall. Watkins here's going to set you in the dirt." John stopped and bit his lip hard. Robert eyed him suspiciously, but John fell into a coughing fit and nervously requested a drink of water from Ivy.

Robert looked between his sister and Garrett. "Watkins. Where have I heard that name before?"

"It's a joke, Robert. They're teasing me," said Verity hurriedly. Robert drew a deep breath.

"God, I hope so."

Candace leaned toward Verity. "I'll tell him the whole story once we get to Boston. When things are very quiet, maybe after brandy."

Jefferson blasted another melon at the farther distance, then handed his musket to Garrett. "Take your shot, Colonel. Beat that, if you can."

Garrett didn't boast like Jefferson and Verity. He aimed without long study of the target, his hand rock-steady, then fired and shattered the melon. He smiled slightly, then tossed the musket to Verity, who dropped it.

"What'd you do that for?" she asked in surprise.

"Always be ready for anything, son."

Verity seized the musket. "I'll show you, 'ready.' Stand back and give me space to shoot." Verity fired.

"Ivy, set us up another melon," ordered Jefferson.

Ivy groaned. "He who busts the melon, replaces the melon. You'll all be eating boiled cabbage for dessert come August."

"This could go on past dark," noted Candace. "I'm hungry. And Robert and I have a train to catch. If you three would take a break—"

"A good idea," agreed Verity. "I need sustenance to continue."

They sat outside, in the shade of the giant oak tree, eating, laughing. Bess sat with Ethan, accepted as his woman by all but Ethan himself. A soft breeze blew from the Potomac.

Garrett sat crosslegged on the ground beside Verity's chair. He watched her eating, talking. And he loved her. Caleb sat on his lap, eating his food, throwing it in varying places.

I am a contented man, Garrett thought. His son leaned against him, yawning. "Time for another nap, young man," said Garrett. "Food seems to do him in every time." Verity started to rise to take the baby, but Garrett caught her arm.

"Let me," said Candace. "I won't be seeing him for a while." She took Caleb inside, but Verity eyed Garrett doubtfully.

"You haven't been listening to Ivy, have you?"

"No," he replied slowly. "I just want to keep you in sight." Verity settled back into her chair and Garrett took her hand.

This was the way he envisioned Fox Run. This was the life he wanted.

Ivy was speaking with Helmut Anderson. They were arguing about food, but they sat close together. Robert was talking to Jefferson about the Freedman's Association, and John was strumming Ethan's guitar. Bess and Ethan sat quietly, together.

Mildred was fussing over Dan's waistcoat, offering him more food. He declined in obvious impatience.

The shadows lengthened eastward from the winding Potomac. A seagull flew overhead and called. The breeze stilled, and evening descended. Jefferson lay on his back, asleep. Candace led Robert in a mock dance across the lawn, lest he be rusty for their wedding.

Watching Verity's face, Garrett saw her contentment, her deep happiness. "You've created a haven here, my love," he said quietly. "A place for healing, for a future to be formed. Look around you. These men have been drawn out of darkness because of you. I have been drawn from night, because of you."

"When I walked into the Union campsite at Stoneman's Switch, I was looking for you, Garrett Knox. I think I was looking for a reason to live."

Garrett took her hand and kissed it. "I had the distinct impression you were looking for a target."

"That, too."

Jefferson heard them and sat up. "Target? Ah, yes. It's time we got back to proving me the best of us all. Unless you two are ready to surrender for the sake of an early night."

"Surrender, indeed. On your feet, Mr. Davis. Garrett and I are ready."

"Are we? Davis's suggestion of an 'early night' sounded good to me."

"Garrett!"

Garrett laughed and rose to his feet. "On the other hand, I don't think we'll live it down if Davis takes the victory."

The moon was rising, the sun long gone, but the shooting contest showed no signs of reaching a conclusion. They had taken a short while to say good-bye to Candace and Robert, but no one seemed ready for the party to end, guests of honor present or not.

"Damn it all, I can't see the melon," complained Jefferson.

"Neither can I," said Verity. "Ivy, we need lights."

Ivy sighed heavily. "You men go fetch some lanterns from the home, will you? And bring enough oil to see us through until morning."

Bess settled herself on Ethan's lap, resting her head against his shoulder. John played his guitar. The men emerged carrying lanterns.

"Set them up by the target," advised Dan Wallingford. "Our esteemed sharpshooters need all the light they can get."

An eerie glow haloed the melon. Jefferson blasted it into rubble, then set up another. "Your turn, Missy. Beat that."

Verity retrieved the musket and aimed at the new melon. She fired.

"What happens when you three run out of melons?" mourned Ivy as Verity went to replace the results of her perfect shot.

Jefferson pondered the matter. His eyes lit. "Tomatoes!" Ivy groaned.

Garrett watched Verity. Out of the darkness, into the eerie lamplight. Reaching to place the melon on the hitching post. He heard the shot just as he saw her fall. A cloud of smoke. . . . a scream. . . .

"Verity!"

She lay in a crumpled pile by the target. Everyone was shouting, gathering around, ghosts in the lamplight. Garrett picked her up, but he saw no wound.

"Dear God, Dear God," murmured Ivy. "Is she—?"

Garrett was shaking too much to accurately feel for a pulse. There was no need. Verity stirred, opened her eyes. "What happened?" she asked. Garrett couldn't answer, he just held her close, against him.

Everyone was silent. Stunned. Garrett's hand was covered with blood. Ivy held a lamp closer. Garrett saw a bright oozing flow of blood from the side of Verity's head. Soaking through her hair, down to her dress.

"You've been shot, love."

Verity reached up and touched her hair. "Jefferson, you should have waited—"

"Sweet Jesus, I didn't shoot you, Watkins!"

Bess ran into the veteran's home for a bandage and ointment, then shoved her way through the crowded group to wrap Verity's injury. "It doesn't look bad. But it was close. The merest speck to the left . . ."

Dan Wallingford moved into the light. "Davis, you've got some explaining to do."

"Whoever shot me missed," said Verity. She paused. "So it couldn't have been Jefferson."

Jefferson nodded. "Damned sure."

Dan wasn't convinced. "This has gone far enough. I want everyone assembled in the estate house, at once."

Silently, the guests filed into Garrett's home. Garrett carried Verity upstairs and put her in bed. "You'd better go downstairs, Garrett. Cooler heads are needed, I think."

Cooler heads. Garrett's mind twisted around memory. But memory of what? And what significance?

"I'm not leaving you alone."

Mildred appeared at Verity's door, holding Caleb. "The little fellow woke up with all the noise," she told them. "I thought he might need his mother. Don't worry, Dear Heart. I'll stay with her."

Garrett hesitated. Mildred hadn't shot Verity. She'd been in the house. He remembered seeing her silhouette in the window just before Verity took her shot. It wasn't easy to imagine Mildred with a musket, but Garrett wasn't ruling anyone out.

Verity's life depended on his ability to find out who did this, and why. "Very well, Mildred. Stay with her. Don't leave this room, for any reason, until I get back."

"What on earth is going on?" asked Mildred when Garrett left. Caleb cuddled next to Verity and fell back to sleep. "What is all this commotion?"

"It's nothing for you to worry about, Mother." Dan Wallingford entered Verity's bedroom. "Garrett asked me to speak with Verity, while he questions the men downstairs. Apparently, he's got a good idea who did the shooting."

"Shooting? What shooting?" asked Mildred.

"Someone tried to kill me," said Verity. She felt nervous. Why?

"Mother, if you wouldn't mind. I need to speak to Verity alone."

Mildred said, "Of course," just as Verity said, "I don't think that's necessary." Mildred didn't listen.

"What do you want, Dan?" she asked. Her heart was racing. She didn't know why.

Dan didn't answer. He waited for his mother to close the door. Then, in a flash of lightning speed, he grabbed Verity. Her scream caught in her throat. Violently, he gagged her, then hauled her from the bed. Caleb whimpered. Dan drew a knife.

Verity nearly swooned with terror. Dan held the knife against the sleeping baby's throat. "One word, Mrs. Knox. Do you understand?"

She nodded. Dan dragged her to the door and opened it stealthily. Raised voices from downstairs. He had to act fast. Verity knew what had happened now. Dan had hidden in the hall, waiting for Garrett to leave. He had told his mother to check on her, knowing only Mildred would leave him alone in her room.

And now . . . what? Dan had his escape planned. He yanked her down the staircase, then into the kitchen. Through the narrow door used only by servants. Out into the night. Dan's elegant, city curricle was waiting out front, as if ordered. Verity remembered that he intended to depart for Washington tonight.

She fought now, resisting as best she could. But Dan shoved her onto the seat beside him, drew the whip and lashed at the surprised hackney. Verity looked over her shoulder. Fox Run in the dark, lights inside. Home. If Dan had his way, she would never see it again.

Garrett looked at the men waiting in the living room—his men, some of them. The others, wounded in battle, men without homes. Only Verity gave them a reason to live. With sudden conviction, Garrett knew no one there had shot his wife.

"Where's Dan?" His voice rang with dark suspicion.

"He was here a minute ago," said Jefferson, suspicious, too.

"Adrian." John spoke up, his low, rumbling voice a pronouncement of doom.

Jefferson looked doubtfully at John. "Who?"

"Adrian Knox?" guessed Ethan.

John nodded. "I'm thinking that's the reason. We've been barking up the wrong tree, and that's a fact."

"John," warned Garrett. "Speak plainer."

"If possible," added Ethan.

"Somebody thought Major Talmadge knew too much. He thought young Westley did, too. But he was wrong. They didn't know. Only one person caught on to the truth. And that was your brother, Sir.''

''Adrian was killed at Fredericksburg,'' Garrett reminded him. ''Leading a charge at Marye's Heights.''

''Yep. A charge into certain death. And who sent him, Sir? Who?''

Garrett's heart stopped. ''Major Dan Wallingford.'' Garrett paused, his face paled. ''But why kill Verity? For what reason?''

John had an answer. ''He don't want Verity, sir. He came here looking for Watkins.''

''Jesus. Why?'' Garrett was trembling. ''But Dave Delaney was looking for Verity Talmadge.''

''Twofold,'' explained John. ''First, if Wallingford thought Westley knew his secret, then maybe the boy lived to say something to his wife. I expect Wallingford didn't wait to find out. But your wife, she goes 'undercover,' as it were, as our Watkins. Wallingford, being a fool, don't know nothing.

''Then, lo and behold! Verity Talmadge shows up unexpected at Gettysburg. Supposedly been nursing. Wallingford thinks he's free and clear. She don't suspect a thing. Westley didn't tell her.''

''That doesn't explain why Wallingford would be looking for Watkins, John,'' said Jefferson.

''No. It don't. I don't got the slightest notion why he'd want the boy. But he did. He asked me about the 'lad' more than once, he did.''

''Asked me, too,'' agreed Jefferson. ''Didn't tell him, though.''

''He mentioned Watkins to me, also,'' said Ethan. ''It's highly suspicious.''

''Why?'' Garrett didn't have time to ponder. ''Where is he? Wallingford!''

''Don't worry about my Dan,'' said Mildred as she came into the living room. ''He's all right. He's looking after Verity.''

''God, no!'' Garrett ran from the room, bounded up the staircase. Caleb was crying, alone. ''Ivy, take care of Caleb—send for my horse!''

The wounded men assembled in the hallway, faces drawn with fear, with helplessness. ''Men, I need you. He's taken her. My guess is he knows we're on to him. He won't kill her, not when he can use her as a shield. But that won't last long.''

Mildred burst into uncontrollable tears. She guessed what had transpired, but she couldn't face it. ''No, no. I must go to Kentucky at once. I'll stay with my daughter, yes . . ." She said no more, ran to her room and closed the door.

The men stared blankly. "What do you expect from us, Colonel?" asked John. He sounded defeated. More ever than in war.

"I expect you to help me save her life."

"I'm in, Colonel," said Jefferson. He already had his musket. Ethan closed his eyes. "I'm not sure what good I'll be," he began. His gaze lifted, and met Garrett's. "Whatever you need, Sir."

"I need you, Hallowell. You, Davis . . . And John." A plan was forming, taking shape. "To save his damned hide, Wallingford's got to get out of the country. Fast. He'll need money. That's his only choice. Davis, you get a cart ready, and you fill the end of it with gold. You'll find the gold in the safe behind Damian Knox's portrait. Seven, twenty-one, twenty-nine is the combination."

"What are you doing, Colonel?" asked Jefferson.

"I'm riding out after him. It won't take much to catch him, if he took his curricle. Wait for me. I'll be back. Ethan, I want a plan from you. And you don't have much time, so let it be a good one."

"Your husband approaches, Mrs. Knox."

Verity heard galloping hoofbeats closing in behind them. *Garrett.* She closed her eyes. Dan pulled the hackney to the roadside, stopping just passed the short bridge that crossed Fox Run creek.

Garrett drew up near the coach, but Dan lifted his lamp and drew his revolver. "No farther, Colonel." He used the title sarcastically. Verity suspected his envy of Garrett ran deep.

"Let her go, Dan. You won't get away now."

"Not if I'm fool enough to let her go," agreed Dan. "But I'm no fool. You know what I need. I need enough money to get me out of this godforsaken country and onto a British ship. You've got enough gold in that mansion to set up your own country. I want it."

"I thought you might," said Garrett.

"Not so fast." Dan smiled beneath his handlebar mustache. "As I said, I'm no fool. Come alone, Garrett. Try anything, and your lady dies." As emphasis, he drew his knife and held it at her throat.

Verity didn't flinch. She met Garrett's eyes, strong and steadily. Garrett turned his horse and galloped away. Dan sat back in the curricle and drew out a cigar, smoking nervously. He untied her gag. "You won't be needing this, will you, pretty lady?" His gaze ran over her, deliberately.

"You won't get away with this. Garrett won't let you."

"He'll hand over every bar, every nugget, I promise you. While I hold a knife to your throat, he's got no choice. And he'll have no choice but to let me ride away, with you at my side. What's to stop him from coming after me once I let you go?"

"His word!"

"Words are tools of manipulation. You're talking to a lawyer, remember? Not a fool."

"One and the same," muttered Verity. But Dan's argument had a certain logic. "Why did you do this? I'm no threat to you. I'm not even sure what it is you did, though I assume you were behind Robert's disappearance and Westley's murder."

"I got lucky on both counts. Didn't figure those damned rebels would keep your stalwart brother alive. But it didn't matter in the end. I've been after you for some time. Funny, I had Delaney all set to kill you once before. For entirely different reasons than today."

"Why?"

"I assumed your dying husband knew more than he did."

"If so, I would have accused you at once. I would certainly have used that information to clear Ethan's name at Gettysburg."

"I realized that," agreed Dan. "Two close calls. Seeing you, then your brother. Heart in my throat, then."

"You strung a wire across the stairs to trip me. You shot me in the dark tonight. Why have you been trying to kill me?"

"Not you, Mrs. Knox. Verrill Watkins."

Verity's fear eased into confusion. "Watkins? Why?"

"You don't remember a thing about it, I'm bound," said Dan. "But you'd learn. You'd see a photograph in *"Harper's Weekly,"* in the newspaper. It might trigger your memory."

"Of what?"

"Alfred Spears." Seeing Verity's incomprehension, Dan laughed. "A spy, Mrs. Knox. Mr. Spears ran a much deeper organization. But the ones who would profit are a group of highly esteemed Northern businessmen. I know who holds the real power in this land. The ones who hold the money. I've seen them get away with murder, literally. Buying justice. I decided to take some for myself. I can't join in the plunder of the South now, thanks to you. But Garrett Knox will provide for my fortune abroad.''

''Why were you dealing with the rebels? Why work toward their victory, if you wanted to plunder them?''

''Winning, now there's an abstract term,'' mused Dan. ''What is victory, Mrs. Knox? We wanted a situation we could control. Freedom? Hell, there's no such thing.''

''Apparently the concept eluded you, anyway.''

''My associates were men of cooler heads. Men of reason. We wanted control. That meant Lincoln had to go. So our boys in blue had to flounder, look bad in the press. Turn public opinion sour. Then put in a new man. Set up a peace to our advantage, wrangle it with the Southern politicians.''

''What about slavery?''

''You can't imagine that matters to men of reason? It was so easy. A few careless orders can turn a battle. Unfortunately, your highbrow brother began to notice. I had to turn the tide fast.''

''So you turned it toward Ethan Hallowell.''

''He seemed a likely prospect. Had a hell of lot to gain from Westley's death, and Robert's. When the time came, he could even profit from yours.''

''I don't understand what possible threat I could be to your loathsome plans.''

''You saw me with Spears. The day you came to wrangle a horse from me.''

Verity struggled with her memory. The day she followed Garrett on Averell's raid. He'd forbidden her to go. She'd sought out Dan for permission. ''Do you mean the other man in your coach?''

Dan nodded. ''That's right.''

''But I didn't see him. Not clearly. What's more, I've seen Spears since, at Ivy's brothel, without making any connection to you. I doubt a picture in the paper would inspire any such ideas.''

For a moment, Dan glared in bitter irony.

''You did it all for nothing,'' guessed Verity. ''I never would have associated you with Spears.''

''I couldn't take that chance. The son of a bitch was going to implicate me. I arranged a private meeting, promising to pay for his silence. He paid for his treachery instead.''

''You killed him.''

''He's silent now,'' said Dan with a chuckle. ''Never trust to another what you can do yourself. The damned ironic thing is, the only one who guessed the truth was Adrian. Reckless, wild Adrian. Never used his head when he could get there faster on courage. But he was the only one who figured it out.''

"Adrian was like a brother to you. How could you?''

"That made it easier to predict what he'd do. I knew he'd lead that charge if I ordered. Even though he knew I was working both sides of the war for my own gain. Brave, stupid Adrian. Walked right into the rebel fire. I didn't have to do a damned thing. Rebs did it for me.''

Dan leaned back in his seat, idly smoking his cigar. Verity looked at him as if for the first time. Some women might consider him handsome, she supposed. Hollow cheeks wavy light brown hair, full chin. A debonair mustache.

Verity closed her eyes. She heard the breeze in the leaves, the swift water of Fox Run beneath the bridge. She heard woodland creatures whistling. A deer moved through the trees.

"How do you justify this?'' Verity truly wanted to know. There must be a reason.

"Justify? You're just like your brother. Idealists. Just like Garrett. He lives by his own code, maybe, but he's as bound to honor as any man alive.''

Dan caught Verity's chin in his hand. "That's how I know he'll do anything to protect you, little lady. He'd die before letting harm come to your precious flesh. And if I have my say, that's just what he will do.''

Dawn was breaking. The first light penetrated through black and gray trees when Verity heard a cart approaching. "Look your last, pretty lady,'' advised Dan casually. "I don't intend to let this get very far.''

Dan shoved the gag in Verity's mouth again. "I wouldn't want you warning your husband of my intentions. Might change his plans, make him reckless.''

Garrett drove a farm cart, meant for hauling hay, for delivering feed. There was still a pile of hay at one corner. The gold glinted in the back.

"Stop right there, Colonel,'' ordered Dan. He held his knife against Verity's neck. "Get down, and move aside.''

Garrett obeyed. But Dan wasn't satisfied. "You've got a revolver, Garrett. Get rid of it."

Garrett drew his revolver and threw it a distance away. Verity noted that he threw it behind him, well away from Dan's reach.

Dan shoved Verity in front of him. "I'll take your cart from here."

"Let her go."

Dan smirked at Garrett. "That wouldn't be wise, now would it?" He approached the cart. His eyes widened when he saw the gold bars.

"Let her go, Dan."

"Not a chance. Your pretty wife is coming with me."

"Think again, Major." Both Dan and Verity turned in astonishment as John emerged from the woods. He held a musket aimed straight at Dan's heart. "I'd be letting the lady go, if I was you."

"I warned you, Garrett." Dan edged the knife closer to Verity's throat, drawing a thin line of blood. "Do you think I'm a fool? That idiot is blind."

"Maybe I am, and maybe I ain't," said John. "Maybe I've just been putting on a show, so that I'd catch you redhanded. Maybe I just feel like sending you to hell, you black heart."

"Not unless you want your little Watkins to go along for the ride. Drop the musket, fool."

"That word comes often from your lips, Dan," said Garrett in a low voice. " 'Fool.' I wonder why. Could it be the label you fear on your own name? You told me Washington needed 'cooler heads,' didn't you? I'd say those 'cooler heads' played you for the damnedest fool this world has ever seen."

Dan ground his teeth together, his jaw clenched. "Order your lackey to drop the musket, Garrett. Or she dies."

"As he says, John," said Garrett.

John tossed the musket to the earth.

"Now, I'll be taking the gold and the woman."

"I don't think so." Ethan Hallowell rose like a phoenix from the pile of hay and aimed his revolver at Dan's head. Dan jerked in shock. At the same moment, Garrett leapt toward him and knocked him away from Verity.

"Behind the cart, Watkins," ordered Ethan. He pointed his gun, but he couldn't shoot without risking Garrett.

Wallingford fought like a madman. But Garrett was stronger, larger. He hurled Dan backward. But Dan still had his knife. He slashed at Garrett's shoulder, cutting deep. Verity watched in horror as Garrett's face contorted in an agonized grimace. He stumbled to his knees. Verity yanked off her gag.

"Ethan, shoot him!"

"I can't. They're too close!"

Garrett was between Dan and Ethan's gun. Dan swung his knife, then thrust toward Garrett to kill. Garrett rolled aside and leapt to his feet. He slammed his hard fist into Dan's gut.

Verity wanted to help. Ethan was poised to shoot, his arm steadied on the rim of the cart. But the action happened too fast for a clear shot. Verity knew she couldn't help Garrett Knox now. She had to trust in the men with whom her life was woven.

Silent and dark, moving like a panther, Jefferson Davis emerged from the shadow of the bridge. Verity held her breath as he crept into position. Garrett caught Dan's wrist, and they struggled for the knife.

Jefferson aimed his musket. "Major—you are in my sights. And I don't miss."

Dan dropped the knife and shoved Garrett back, intending to bolt for the freedom he had so bitterly scorned moments ago.

"Unless you prefer death," called Ethan calmly, "I advise you to stop where you are. Because, Major, I don't miss, either."

Verity's chest rose and fell in short gasps of wonder and joy. John fumbled in the dirt for his own musket, picked it up, and aimed with surprising accuracy at the lawyer.

"You'd be damned surprised what a man can hear. Now I'd like it to be a clean shot, nothing messy. Afraid I can't guarantee something better than a gut wound, though."

Dan stopped and turned, his face sickly white. Garrett didn't bother to pick up his own revolver. He held out his hand for Verity, she scrambled around the cart and into his arms.

"You've got a choice, Dan," said Garrett. "Life or death. Most of the men we fought with didn't have a choice. Blue or gray. I'm giving it to you now. There's not a marksman here who can miss if I give the order."

Dan hesitated. For a brief instant, Verity thought he would choose death, make a break for it and run. But a greedy man is a cowardly man, too. *Maybe,* she thought, *because his greed came from a sense of his own weakness. He needed power and money to secure his own value.*

"You're good at word manipulation, Major Wallingford," said

Verity. "I expect you're a good lawyer. Maybe you can talk your sentence down to something short of hanging. But I wouldn't count on your fat Northern businessmen for support. You're on your own now."

Dan threw up his hands. "Goddamn you all. I surrender."

Garrett nodded to Jefferson. "Take him, bind him. I'll trust you and John to deliver him to the authorities."

"Will do, Colonel," said Jefferson cheerfully. Ethan tossed him a rope, and he went to secure Dan's hands.

"Don't expect we'll have much trouble now," added John. He used his musket like a staff, feeling the road as he made his way to the others.

Verity looked around at her friends. Jefferson, John, Ethan. Her heart constricted with love. "Thank you, all of you. John, how did you aim so perfectly? Can you really hear that well?"

John nodded, his head tilted back at a proud angle. "Sent Wallingford into a spin, didn't it? The President led me through the trees last night. We kept a close watch—and listen—on you, lest Wallingford try anything disrespectful. As long as he kept his hands to himself, we stuck to Plan One."

"Plan One?" asked Verity.

"Plan One of seven," added Jefferson with a grin as he secured Dan's hands. "Put Hallowell to thinking, and you come up with more than you bargained for."

"Plan One seems to have been reliable," said Verity.

"Thank God," said Ethan. "Plan Seven had me throwing myself out of the cart at Wallingford. I didn't feel entirely sure about that one."

Garrett laughed, a hearty, booming sound that told Verity his wound wasn't as serious as she feared. He held her close, protected. "I thank you, too, men. If not for your help, I might have lost something more precious than all the gold in the world."

Dan Wallingford listened to their conversation, sneering with disgust and wonder evident on his face. Verity eyed him intently. "What's the matter, Wallingford?" She didn't let him answer. "I think I know. You never expected the Union army to win the war, did you?"

Garrett glanced at her, but Wallingford nodded. "I watched our blue heroes flounder from the first battles on. We never had a commander who could touch Lee."

"Then you misunderstand the nature of our victory." Verity

gestured at her friends. "These men couldn't be defeated. Not because they were stronger or better. But because they each used his own particular strength and gave all he had to bend dark fate into triumph."

Verity looked at her friends and her eyes puddled with tears of pure emotion. John stood straight despite his unseeing eyes. Jefferson knew he could take on the world and win. And Ethan Hallowell had finally proved to himself that he didn't have to be 'right.' He was worthy just the way he was.

A worthy man could take a wife. A lucky man had one waiting.

"The war is really over now, isn't it?" whispered Verity. "For all of us."

Garrett touched her cheek. "It's really over. Freedom is won. Now, comes the real beginning."

"What about you, Garrett? We have to get you to a surgeon."

"That's not necessary," he assured her. "It's not deep. Bloody, but not deep."

Garrett eyed the dried blood on Verity's cheek, the dark stain on her bodice. His own shirt was saturated with red blood. They stood together, ready to cross back over a bridge that would lead them home. At the end of one long, dark road into light. At the beginning of a brighter dawn.

Despite his weariness and the pain in his shoulder, despite everything that had ravaged them since the war's beginning, Garrett Knox smiled and took Verity's hand in his.

"Battered, but not broken. Yankees to the end."

Epilogue

October, 1865
Fox Run, Maryland

A mist rolled in from the Potomac River, guided across the pastures by autumn's unseen fingers. Garrett's herd moved in organized groups, seeking clover amidst bluegrass. In a smaller paddock, a long-limbed black stallion stood watch over select mares, a noble king beginning a new dynasty.

Jared Knox leaned against the fence, watching the horse that had carried him through four years of warfare. "I want the first good filly he sires, Cousin. And no holding out. You can keep the colts, but Virginia has need of new stock, too."

Garrett hesitated, clenching his jaw as he considered surrendering a prime filly. "You drive a hard bargain."

"In lieu of stud fee," added Jared with a grin.

"Stud fee, indeed. Who gave you that magnificent animal, anyway?"

Ivy overheard their argument as she walked up the path from the veterans' home to the rear lawn. Three young women sat in the shade of the ancient oak, sipping lemonade, fanning themselves as they played cards.

"Three little ones on the way," sighed Ivy. "There'll be hell to pay come next summer."

"Only if they take after their fathers," said Verity. She examined her hand of cards thoughtfully, then smacked two down on the table. "Hit me for two."

"What ladylike game is this?" asked Ivy. "Whist, perhaps?"

"Poker."

Ivy shook her head, pulled off her apron and sat down opposite Verity. "Deal me in."

"Oh, bloody hell." Pippa Knox slapped her cards down on the table, her little face tightened with displeasure. "I fold." She took a drink of lemonade like a hit of whiskey.

Verity eyed Bess. "And you, Mrs. Hallowell?"

"I expect you're bluffing," said Bess in a calm, Southern drawl. She stole a furtive glance at Verity's cards. Verity cupped them against her breast, her eyes narrowed combatively.

"I'll see your bet, and raise," decided Bess.

Ethan heard his wife's bold gamble. "That's my little rebel." He wheeled himself from the estate house, Caleb seated on his lap.

"Pony, please," said Caleb. He eyed the stables.

Jared had brought a fat, gray pony from Virginia, a gift for Garrett's son. Named Traveller after Robert E. Lee's favorite mount, the little animal had seen more activity in two days than in all its previous years.

"Your papa is arguing with Uncle Jared at the moment, dear," said Verity.

"Ethan, we must get a pony for our baby," decided Bess as Pippa dealt her another card.

"Our baby isn't even born yet," Ethan reminded her.

"Rebels start riding young," said Pippa. "Jared bought another little pony with Traveller, and our baby isn't due until January. A nice chubby brown and white mare. We haven't named her yet, though. She was called 'Belle,' but that didn't seem right somehow."

"Call her Chipmunk," suggested Ethan with a grin. "It has the same meaning."

Bess looked at him reproachfully, then returned to her stealthy scrutiny of Verity's cards. "I'm holding," said Verity.

Bess chewed her lip, wanting to up the ante, wanting to call. "Damnnation! I fold." Bess waited expectantly. "Well?"

Verity revealed her hand. Bess screamed in dismay just as Jared and Garrett returned from the pasture. "Nothing! Not even a lousy pair!"

"Well, what did you decide?" asked Verity as she scooped up ear bobs, necklaces, and other offerings from Pippa and Bess.

Garrett frowned slightly. "He gets the filly of his choice. Without advice from me as to which is the best," he added pertinently.

"As if I'd need your advice to pick the best," scoffed Jared. "You've got my horse for one year, Garrett. You'd better make good use of him." Jared stood beside Pippa's chair, idly running his fingers through her mass of golden brown hair. "I've got a line of my own to start."

Pippa patted her stomach. "You've got a good start already," she said with twinkling eyes.

Verity smiled. She had felt an instant kinship with Jared's Yankee wife. Pippa had a way of looking innocent while making devilishly suggestive comments that brought an expression of complete adoration and curious vulnerability to Jared's sweet face. Every time.

Ivy took the deck of cards and shuffled. She noticed an envelope on the table bearing Jefferson's flowing script. "How are things with our wandering minstrels?"

"Quite surprising, really," said Verity. "They've reached Minnesota as planned, and Jefferson says their music is well-received. But there was some trouble with our cavalry and the Sioux which Jefferson and John involved themselves in—on the side of the Sioux chieftain."

"Davis feels our spirit of freedom hasn't been sufficiently granted to our Indian brothers," added Garrett. "Apparently, he lent his advice, and his musket, in an effort to settle that dispute."

"In gratitude for his service, a Sioux chieftain gave Jefferson his daughter's hand," continued Verity.

Pippa's eyes widened. "Jefferson is married? How lovely! Does he sound happy?" When Jefferson Davis had lived with Pippa and her father in Maine, he had been like a brother to her.

"He sounded a little bewildered," replied Verity. "But he waxed on at length about his wife's silken black hair, high cheekbones, and her sculpted features. Apparently her eyes are *'as black as the deepest night lit with a single bright star.'"*

"So he's found someone whose appearance he considers almost equal to his own?" guessed Pippa with a smile. "Poor woman."

"I doubt she knows what she's in for," agreed Garrett. He lanced down at Verity. "I know exactly how she feels."

Garrett stood behind Verity, his broad hands on her shoulders, massaging gently. She felt him like a part of her. Always. She felt his happiness, his contentment. She felt his desire in every lance.

Her second pregnancy brought no discomfort, no nausea. Ivy claimed her peaceful mental state explained her condition. According to Bess, it was because Verity carried a girl this time. Garrett said both were true.

"I have other news of interest," said Jared. "My sister fell headlong in love with the Yankee officer who took up residence in our house during the Richmond occupation. They have since moved to Boston, where they've been enjoying the good company of Rob Talmadge and his wife."

"Did the officer's family accept his rebel wife?" asked Ethan.

"Admirably," replied Jared.

Verity guessed the source of Ethan's inquiry. Ethan and Bess married a week after Dan Wallingford's arrest. With the money he inherited from Cabot Talmadge, Ethan purchased a large portion of land from Garrett. An ordered construction was now underway.

Though Bess notified her family about her wedding, no Hartman had responded. It was Bess's only sorrow. But Ethan mattered more.

"Did you ever contact the Hartmans in Fredericksburg, Jared?" asked Verity, once again ready to launch into action on her friends' behalf.

Bess looked up expectantly, but Ethan sighed without much hope.

Jared hesitated, and Verity wished she hadn't asked. "I spoke with Bessie's brother, Tom, about her marriage." Jared paused. "He wasn't entirely encouraging on the matter of reconciliation, or accepting a Yankee brother-in-law."

"Oh, well," sighed Bess.

"In Tom's mind, an arrogant Yank made off with his little sister for the sole purpose of humiliating him."

"Is that what he said?" asked Bess indignantly.

"I believe his exact words were, *'If that Yankee bastard comes within twenty miles of Virginia, I'll blow him to Kingdom Come.'*"

"I guess that lets out Southern travel," said Ethan.

"It might have," agreed Jared. "Except I told Tom that a part

of you had been sent on ahead of the rest. The result of which i
my esteemed cousin's life.''

"I can't believe Tom Hartman had much sympathy for m
condition.''

"He didn't. My words were overheard by another, howeven
And when Bobby Lee says a man has done his duty, whether blu
or gray, men take notice.'' Jared stopped and bowed toward Ethan
"Captain Hallowell, by the good will of Marse Robert himsel
you may travel in Virginia in honor.''

Ethan's mouth dropped. Bess's face lit with such joy that sh
could barely contain herself. She jumped from her seat and kisse
Ethan's face, laughing while Caleb peered doubtfully up from hi
spot on Ethan's lap.

"Why is it,'' mused Garrett, "that a kind word from Rober
E. Lee means so much more than a five page letter of congratula
tions from U. S. Grant?''

Verity felt a strange, cool thrill. "Isn't that the nature of ou
war? Isn't that what we really won, for both sides? All men hav
value. Each according to his own merit. For that reason, Genera
Lee will always be a hero. In the North as well as in Virginia.''

"Rivers to one shore,'' added Pippa softly, her eyes on he
husband's face. Jared smiled at her, slow and sensual, then ben
to kiss the top of her head.

Only Caleb remained restless. "Pony, please,'' he reminded hi
father.

"Another ride, son?'' asked Garrett. The little boy nodded. "I
my cousin will assist, another ride it will be.''

"A delight,'' said Jared.

Jared took the little boy from Ethan's lap and placed him o
his shoulders. Garrett retrieved the pony from the stables an
readied a bareback pad. "Mount up!''

Jared put Caleb astride, then seized the lead rope. "Ready
Sir?'' Jared asked.

Caleb bobbed delightedly, and the pony started off. Garre
walked beside his son, hand ready to support, but not touching.

"Five card stud,'' announced Ivy, shuffling the deck like
cardsharp. "Who's in?''

Ethan joined the ladies' poker game, but he kept his card
carefully from his wife's sight. Pippa hurriedly skimmed a sma
manual on cardplaying tactics while Ivy dealt the next hand.

Verity watched Garrett accompanying their son around the pac

ock. She saw Caleb's chubby hand gesturing toward the open
elds beyond the veterans' home. Jared looked back, and Garrett
odded.

They headed off, passing a group of former soldiers harvesting
neat garden. Helmut Anderson gave Traveller an apple as they
de by.

The mist from the Potomac faded, and the autumn sun burned
arm and strong. Jared was running now, leading the pony at
creasingly higher speeds as Caleb laughed. *Garrett looks young
day,* Verity thought. Racing beside his son. She heard him laugh-
g, too.

Verity closed her eyes and saw him, tall and strong, broad
ouldered, and handsome as he came out into the rain to meet
r at Stoneman's Switch. She saw him laughing when she returned
om her adventure in Fredericksburg.

She remembered their first night together at Ivy's brothel. The
eckers game. His kiss that brought her heart to passionate life.
hancellorsville, Gettysburg. . . .

Had any woman been as alive as she had been, felt the sweet
ssion of life in its darkest hour?

*Garrett Knox, I love you. I will die loving you. When my spirit
es, it will be at your side.*

"Raise or fold, Mrs. Knox . . ."

Verity turned back to play. "Raise, Ivy Yankees never fold."

Dear Reader,

I hope you enjoyed A BRIGHTER DAWN. Being a Maine Yankee myself, I always felt the South got the lion's share of romanticism. I set out to investigate what kind of people the Northerners really were. I found men like Joshua Chamberlain, the young professor from Bowdoin College in Maine. Chamberlain was as noble and honorable as Robert E. Lee, with a poetic sensitivity combined with military genius, and boundless courage. I found Robert Gould Shaw, who led the Fifty-Fourth Massachusetts to glory. I found my own great-great grandfather, Abner Woodward, who went to war at the age of 42, and died at City Point Virginia.

These men weren't motivated by political posturing or economics. They were motivated by a belief in humanity. When I wrote this book, I wanted to honor what they were, and how much I value what they stood for.

If you enjoyed A BRIGHTER DAWN, I hope you'll look for my next Pinnacle release, A PATRIOT'S HEART, coming in the winter of '98. My novella, Lily, is featured in the upcoming SCOTTISH MAGIC anthology from Kensington Books.

I'd love to hear from readers. You can reach me at: RR1 Box 7, Harpswell, ME 04079. E-mail is welcome at: stobie@ime.net, or visit my home page at http://www.ime.net~stobie

Stobie Piel